The House with the Wraparound Porch

~ A novel by ~

MARY PAT HYLAND

Also by Mary Pat Hyland:

The Maeve Kenny Series:

The Cyber Miracles - *Book One*, 2008

A Sudden Gift of Fate - *Book Two*, 2009

A Wisdom of Owls - *Book Three*, 2011

3/17, 2010

The Terminal Diner, 2011

This book is a work of fiction. The names, characters and plot are the creation of the author and should not be considered real. Although inspired by real life experiences, the characters in the novel do not exist and any resemblance to persons living or dead is purely coincidental.

First Edition ~ July 2013

Printed in the United States of America

Set in Georgia Typeface

Cover photos and design by Mary Pat Hyland

Author's websites: marypathyland.com & www.facebook.com/marypathyland

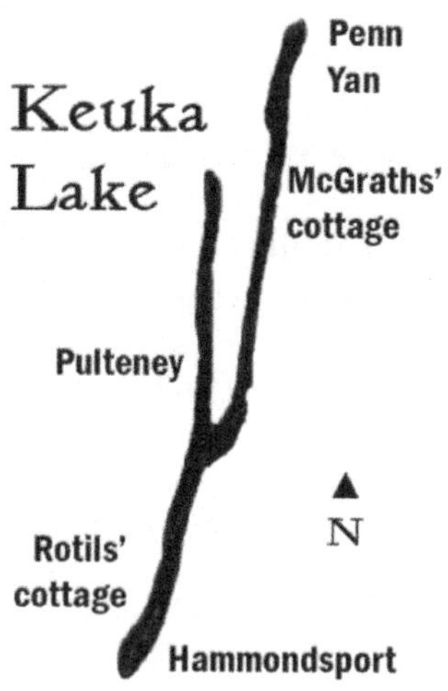

For the sisters of the lake,
Anne, Sheila, Katy & Judy
Katharine & Esther
& the sisters of the North Side,
Jo & Bea

~*~

With special thanks to my editors: Betsy Herrington, David Craig & Jordan Nicholson; proofreaders: Anne Woodard, Sheila Forsyth, Kate Graham & Sharon Hyland; Spanish language proofreader: Lori McIlwaine Hammond; beta readers: Cheryl Owen, Rich Harrington & Mollie McNair; Liz Lynch & the MINs for their support; to Scott Roberts for his perfect turn of phrase, and a Lough Méar *sláinte* to my favorite Finger Lakes winemakers, Joe & Melissa Carroll.

~*~

With gratitude to the owners of the century-old house that inspired the novel, **John Creamer & Stephanie Olsen**, for their loving restoration and care of the home of my fondest memories.

Family Tree

~ First Generation ~

O'Donoghues: Dan & Virginia (O'Malley), children Jimmy & Anne (husband Will Foley, daughter Bridget)

> **Relatives:** Virginia's brother & wife, Charles & Esther O'Malley, son John

McGraths: Martin & Rose, children Mame & Mike

> **Relatives:** Martin's sister, Bertha McGrath Smith

~ Second Generation ~

O'Donoghues: siblings Patrick & Frances

O'Malleys: Bill & June

McNamaras: Dick & Marie, son Joe

> **Relatives:** Bill McNamara & ex-wife Kitty

McGraths: Gerry & Joan

~ Third Generation ~

McNamaras: sisters Clare, Noreen, Maggie, Terrie, Eileen & Molly

McGraths: children Martin, Michael, James & Kate

~ Fourth Generation ~

Pomeroys: twin sons Philip & Gerard

Colemans: children Dorothy, Francis, Esperanza, Thèrése & Kateri

Levins: Sarah & Sol, daughter Mara

Prologue

On Christmas Eve 2005, a red hatchback with Ohio plates slipped through a quaint Finger Lakes village and climbed a gently rising boulevard toward the rural edge of town. It passed rows of stately houses crafted in a grander era of architecture, when ornament was testament to a builder's skill.

The thirty-something blonde driving the car slowed as she read house numbers aloud, and then hit the brakes when she saw an address matching the paper slip in her hand. She backed the car up and pulled into the driveway behind two cars sheltered under a broad porte-cochère. From her large shoulder bag she pulled out a reporter's spiral notebook and opened to the list of names her mother gave her and memorized them.

She stepped out of the car and the magnificence of the Queen Anne-style house caught her breath. Its beautifully turned wraparound porch spoke of a time when conversations lingered outdoors on a summer's eve. Balsam wreaths with gold ornaments and garnet-colored ribbons hung from the tall windows. On this dreary December afternoon, the amber glow of lamps within beckoned cheerfully behind lace-curtained windows.

A group of middle-aged women engaged in animated conversation within the dining room. She wondered which one of them held the key to her past. Something drew her eyes up to the carved angel frieze in the gable over the porch steps. Was this a good omen—a sign she'd be welcomed? The woman pushed her curly hair back from her face, took a breath from the depths of her being, and knocked on the front door. There was movement inside and voices neared the entrance as she fingered a Y-shaped silver pendant hanging from her neck. Anticipation blushed her face while she waited—*an eternity!*—for the door to open.

"May I help you?"

"I don't know if you can. I was looking for a woman who lived at this address at one time...."

Their conversation was brief, and then the door slammed in her face.

Chapter 1

When Jimmy O'Donoghue came to, he felt the midday sun searing his face, dampness clinging to the back of his shirt and pain thrumming his brow, just above the left eye. The stale burn of gin caught the back of his throat and Jimmy coughed, rolled onto his back and opened his eyes, squinting immediately from the razor-sharp sunlight. He recoiled and lifted his eyelids once again, slowly scanning the wall of curved oak in front of him and thinking, *where in God's name am I?*

A cool northerly breeze brushed past his cheek soft as feather down, carrying the scent of rainbow trout pulled fresh from the lake. As he became aware of a gentle rocking motion beneath him and sounds of water lapping close by, he realized, *I'm on a boat. But why? How?*

He drew his arms in; they felt wobbly, as if stricken with palsy. Jimmy used what strength he could muster to push his exhausted body upward and looked beyond the rowboat's wooden shell where straight ahead, about half a mile away, was the cottage-lined shoreline. He shifted his weight on his arms and turned his head to the left. Another shoreline was a similar distance away. Jimmy clambered onto the hardwood seat and rubbed his eyes, then looked in both directions again. *What am I doing in the middle of Keuka Lake?*

He ran his fingers through his thick black hair to scratch his scalp and felt the waxy residue of pomade. While his sapphire blue eyes scanned the horizon his memory suddenly flashed a disturbing scene from the previous night. A wave of nausea overwhelmed him and he gripped the empty oarlocks to steady himself.

It was the last Friday of June 1920 when Jimmy, Skip Mortensen and Ralph Kaminski launched this rowboat from Indian Pines Park at the northern tip of the lake in Penn Yan, New York. Their plan was to row down the West Side for a rendezvous with some Keuka College girls. The young men recently turned eighteen, and with his newfound cockiness Ralph persuaded a cluster of coeds at the drugstore fountain that they were sophomores at Cornell. It was somewhat believable since all three were tall with shoulders broadened by hours of fielding baseballs for the Penn Yan Academy Orange and Blue.

Olivia, the liveliest of the girls, had dared them to attend a party at her West Lake Road cottage that night around nine o'clock. Ralph feigned disinterest despite the allure of her dimpled smile, saying they'd stop by if they had nothing else to do. As soon as the girls left though, the three deliberated on how to get to the party. Skip offered his father's boat for their expedition.

A tickle in the back of Jimmy's throat triggered a dry hacking cough and his thoughts turned to the present need to drink water—his thirst was desperate. He wouldn't sip the water surrounding him; if it wasn't filtered it could make him sick. Instead he plunged his hand into the cool lake, cupping water to splash on his face. The moment he saw his hand underwater it chilled him. He yanked his hand back and rubbed his arms. Ripples from where he disturbed the water echoed across the lake.

His memory flashed an image of Skip rowing the boat ashore at Indian Pines to pick them up. Skip brought a bottle of his father's bathtub gin, and once he secured the boat, the boys took turns swigging the potent liquor on the shore to give themselves enough courage to approach the girls. Not much later the gin slackened Jimmy's tongue and fuzzed his thoughts. Ralph glugged half the bottle and the effects hit him harder. He sloshed words around his mouth and had difficulty steadying himself upright. Skip laughed at the two "amateurs."

"Ralph, what a baby you are. A college man has to be able to hold his gin."

"Thtop inthulting me!"

Jimmy chuckled, although he was also feeling no pain.

"C'mon, you two. Let's get a wiggle on and show up before the night is over," Skip said as he turned the rowboat around and shoved it into the lake.

Skip plopped Ralph onto the bow-end seat and Jimmy made room for himself by propping his drunken buddy upright. Skip sat across from them by the stern and stroked the oars through the water, pushing away from the shore. The night was moonless yet quicksilver glimmers danced across the water surface, reflections from cottages aglow near the shore. The intrepid trio heard Dixieland brass playing songs from New Orleans in the distance, their sassy ragtime wails luring them like Sirens to the waiting coeds. Unlike Odysseus, Skip steered unfettered toward the sound.

"I'd like more of that gin, thailor."

"I think you've had enough Ralphie boy," Jimmy said, laughing as he rolled his eyes toward Skip.

"No I haven't," Ralph whined. "I can handle it—could drink any college guy under the table right now. Heck, I'm thtronger than Jack Dempthey."

Skip snorted. "You're no Dempsey, Ralphie; you're a crazy palooka from Keuka."

"Are you mocking me? Thtop it!" Ralph swung his fist toward Skip.

"Gee whiz, settle down, Ralph," Jimmy said, pulling his friend back onto the seat. "So which one of the girls are you claiming?"

Ralph closed his eyes and grinned. "Eenie meenie minee...m'Olivia. How 'bout you, Jimmy boy?"

"Hmm. Have to say, I'm crazy for that doll Clara."

"The one with those smoky Pola Negri eyes?" Skip asked.

"That's the one," Jimmy sighed, picturing his lips on her neck.

"I have my sights set on that hot tomato Anna," Skip said. "Mmmmm. That blonde hair, saucy smile and those curves...holy Christmas, she's a regular Mae West!"

Ralph lunged suddenly toward Skip. "Gimme thome more of that coffin varnith." His forward thrust wobbled the boat.

"Pipe down! You can't have more gin. You didn't say please, Ralph." Skip laughed as he leaned away from his drunken friend. Ralph lunged again hard toward the bottle next to the oarsman's feet, both hands grabbing at Skip, who reflexively pulled the oar forward, knocking Ralph overboard with a big splash.

"Jeepers creepers, Ralph!" Skip yelled. "Why'd you make me do that?"

"Give him the oar to hang onto so we can pull him into the boat," Jimmy yelled.

Skip lifted the oar out of its well and dipped it in the water. Ralph grabbed it successfully, but seemed to have trouble hanging on.

"He's too plastered to swim," Skip said. "Dammit! I'll have to go in and get him. Here, take the oar, Jimmy." Skip's toss off occurred too fast. The oar plopped into the lake.

"Attaboy, Jimmy. That sure helped a lot. Jeepers creepers! Don't just stand there, get the other one!"

His bellowing unnerved Jimmy and he unhooked the oar as quickly as he could and held it out to Ralph. Skip unbuttoned his shirt and took it off, then slid off his slacks and shoes. "Ralph, grab the oar. You owe me for this, you sonofabitch!"

Skip dived into the lake and the spray of his wake soaked Jimmy. It was difficult to see the flailing shapes in the water. There was a lot of splashing as Skip tried to grab Ralph's waist so he could hoist him toward the boat. Jimmy, still holding on to his end of the oar, stood up so he could see them better.

"Leave me alone!" Ralph yelled at Skip. "I'm thtrong ath Dempthey."

"Pipe down and just hang on, Ralph. I'm trying to help."

Ralph brought his arm back to reach farther up the oar and elbowed Skip hard between his nose and mouth, knocking him backward and unconscious. Ralph turned to grab Skip before he sank, and their combined weight made the oar tip downward, ripping the other end out of Jimmy's hand and smacking him above the left eye so hard that he stumbled into the lake.

Jimmy recalled the numbing pain as he dropped deadweight through the pine-black water. He could only open one eye and swam toward what he thought was the surface. Because he'd tumbled into the water he became disoriented and was actually heading for the bottom of the lake. A strand of seaweed choked his ankle and he struggled to kick it free. That crazy gin fogged his brain making it difficult to sort out how to get out of this mess. The odd thing was he remained calm despite the dire situation. It occurred to him that he might be drowning and maybe it wasn't going to be that awful. *Why struggle if I'm supposed to die?*

The memory of that bleak moment set Jimmy's teeth chattering uncontrollably despite the sun's warmth on his back. Obviously he didn't drown, but how had he gotten back in the boat? He couldn't make his brain recall the specifics. Did he get a concussion when the oar smacked his head? The only memories he could muster of that moment were shadowy and vague.

His chills waned as the persistent heat drew sweat from his brow. He'd kill for a tall glass of cool water! Jimmy dipped his hand in the lake again, and when he saw his hand moving below the transparent surface, his mind flashed an image of the glow he saw above him when he was drowning. He figured that a boat had pulled up and someone was holding a lantern over the water so they could find him. He swam a bit toward the light and then heard a woman's voice yell clearly: "Breathe, Jimmy O'Donoghue!" He did take a deep breath—underwater! But how was that possible?

That's all he could remember. Somehow he got back into this oar-less boat that was now adrift. Were his friends safe on the opposite shore by the college, or had something worse occurred? His teeth chattered an involuntary S.O.S.

"HELP! HELP ME! SOMEONE, PLEASE! HELLLLLP!" Jimmy yelled, his weakened voice barely reaching the far shores.

No one responded to his cries. No boat approached from any direction. Jimmy knew he didn't have the strength to swim to either shore, and the last thing he wanted to do was get back into the lake. He turned himself over in the rowboat, away from the blistering heat, drew Skip's discarded shirt around his sunburned face and closed his eyes, praying that he would be delivered somehow from this dreadful fate.

Next thing he knew, there were voices above him.

"Is he dead?"

"Look, there's a gin bottle next to him. I wonder whose clothes those are."

"Do you think he's a bootlegger? Looks kinda young for that."

He felt a hand nudge his back. "Hey there, can you hear me?"

Jimmy nodded and turned around slowly. It was dusk now and he felt the strong northerly breeze on his face. He didn't recognize the three men staring at him who'd waded into the lake to secure the drifting rowboat.

"What's your name, son?"

His throat was too dry to speak at first. He swallowed hard. "Jimmy," he answered, coughing. "Jimmy O'Donoghue. Where am I? Who are you?"

"The name's John Olsen. Don't you know you're in Hammondsport?"

His words focused Jimmy's attention immediately. "Hammondsport! I can't be! Are you saying I drifted down the entire lake?"

"Last night's wind storm must've pushed you against the lake current. Why do you ask—you a Penn Yan boy?"

"Yes. I am."

"Who are you running gin for, son?" John asked, pointing at the empty bottle under the stern seat. Jimmy focused his thoughts enough to wonder if the man was a police officer. Was he going to arrest him?

"No. That was Skip's. Where are my friends? Where are Skip and Ralph?" He sat up suddenly to look around the beach. Pain throbbed across his forehead. He cried out and lay back down, wincing.

John looked at his friends.

"It was just you in the boat. What happened to the oars?"

Just like that, vivid memories of the horror from the previous night hit his mind like gale-churned waves pounding the shore. Jimmy gripped the side of the boat.

"Stand back, looks like he's gonna upchuck," one of the other men said.

"We have to find them! Skip! Ralph! They're back there, still in the lake. We have to rescue them." His teeth chattered as his shoulders shook involuntarily.

"Back where?"

"Near Keuka College. They need help! Let's go!" Jimmy's agitation alarmed John and he gestured to the others to grab his arms.

"Let's get you out of this boat first, son," John said, making his voice as calm as he could, "and then we can go and find your friends."

John called his wife who watched the dramatic scene from inside their cottage. "Verna, bring us a blanket! Hurry!" The men lifted Jimmy out onto the shore and sat him down in an Adirondack chair on the shale stone beach. The smooth stones, still hot from the sun baking them all day, warmed Jimmy's bare feet. It felt good to him.

Verna ran back and draped a wool Hudson's Bay camp blanket that reeked of cedar around Jimmy and handed him a glass of water. He clutched it with both hands and glugged the glass dry.

John left to call the Hammondsport police. When he returned, he waved over his wife and friends.

"They said the bodies of two young men were found in the lake near the college this afternoon. His story must be true. Officer Curtiss is coming over right now to talk with him."

"Poor child," Verna said. "He may go into shock when he hears what happened."

"Well they say no good can come from bathtub gin. Here's proof. This accident will scar that young man for life."

Verna held her fingers to her mouth as she shook her head. "And the dead boys' mothers, ruined."

Chapter 2

Mame McGrath was used to people staring at her unruly bobbed hair. Unlike a starlet's soft and glamorous Marcel waves, Mame's fiery hair rippled across her forehead like nubby Persian lamb fur. Just like her hair, her attitude couldn't be tamed, either. It amused her to see people recoil from the unsolicited opinions on women in modern society with which she peppered every discussion. Confident and fearless, this twenty-two-year-old woman had already stirred many conversations about her in Elmira, New York. That day when her family packed the car to move to their new home in Penn Yan, she pretended she couldn't hear the nattering of her neighbors.

"No man will ever marry that girl," the wife said to her husband. "Why would any sensible young woman spurn a betrothal from a successful banker like Eugene Roach for college? Did you know she was down in New York City marching around like a fool with those suffragettes?"

"Maybe she's avoiding marriage because of what she's witnessed from Mr. McGrath," the husband said. "I hear the old man likes to go on a toot now and then. You can tell when he's been in his gin because he starts yelling at the wife. "

"Hmph! That Rose McGrath is a saint!"

Mame shook her auburn tresses and raised her chin assuming an air that she was impervious to their gossip. She hated how everyone knew her private business in this town. Part of her wanted to scream to her neighbors that the reason she rejected Eugene's proposal after initially accepting it was that she realized she wasn't in love with him. Simple as that! Then again, part of her took delight in the fact that her curious decision made her mysterious to these dull people.

She was restless for a change of scenery and was more than happy to be leaving her nosy-neighbor past and heading with her parents and younger brother, Mike, to a new place for a fresh start. A recent normal school graduate with a degree in elementary education, Mame had already lined up an interview with the local school district. She hoped to challenge young minds to think openly about the roles of men and women in society. (Of course she wasn't a fool, though, and had no intention of mentioning that during her interview.)

They pulled into the asphalt concrete driveway of their new home on the afternoon of July third, just before the moving truck arrived. Bereft of breeze, the day was swathed in a sweltering humidity that made the laborious task of unpacking their belongings exhausting.

When Mame paused to wipe her brow as she yanked an overstuffed jute suitcase from the trunk, she noticed a shirtless young man rocking in a porch chair across the street. Modest girls might have looked away, but Mame let her eyes linger over his muscular physique and coal-black hair. He was movie star handsome—with a profile like John Barrymore—and she felt the urge to wave a flirty hello to him, but his expression hinted his attention was worlds away.

Mame wondered if his family was wealthy, because the Queen Anne-style house he lived in looked double the size of theirs. She studied the finely crafted details of his home. Three Shaker-style wooden rockers sat next to him on the exquisitely-turned wraparound porch. The chairs had been painted deep sage green to match the double-hung window sashes. Decorative carved grape leaf modillions propped up an angel face frieze gazing down at six porch steps. The house itself was painted light ochre and the trim was a warm ivory. It had a steep roof with a front-facing gable with two leaded-glass windows splitting light into the attic. Cutaway bay windows jutted from the left and right sides of the asymmetrical house. Paired Doric columns supported the high-ceilinged porch over the railing of square balusters. Behind lace curtain-covered windows stood an older woman who watched the McGraths lug all their belongings up the driveway and onto their porch.

Mame's father, a portly man with a florid face and walrus mustache, unlocked the front door of their new home and, with a twinkle in his eye, lifted his wife Rose up and carried her across the threshold, despite her faint protests. Mame elbowed Mike.

"Bet they sneak upstairs later for a little hot jazz!"

Mike was perpetually embarrassed by his sister's bold tongue.

"You'd better watch your mouth. The only man you'll be able to land is that crazy goof across the street."

"Who says I need a man in my life anyway? I'll be able to take care of myself just fine." She glanced back at the young man rocking on the porch and noticed he had a shock of white hair just above his left eye.

"Did you hear about him?" Mike whispered, looking over her shoulder across the street. "Father heard he got all ginned up and drowned his two best friends over some Keuka College vamps."

Mame squinted so she could see his face better. The young man appeared to be looking nowhere in particular.

"I love a man with a past; can't stand a fella who's a rube."

"You think he's the bee's knees, Sis? Hah! You'll probably end up marrying him."

Mame put her hands on her hips and smiled. "Maybe I will."

***

Her interview the next week for the third grade teaching position was before a panel of men from the school board. The recommendations they'd received from her college advisor and the school in Geneseo where she practice taught last semester spoke highly of Mame. She answered each question to their satisfaction. It was no surprise, because she spent hours preparing soliloquys in her mind on education philosophy and the proper approach to teaching. Surely the job was hers to refuse, she thought. Their final question, however, blindsided her.

"There's one more thing, Miss McGrath. Do you have a fiancé or a serious boyfriend?"

Her face slipped from confidence to a frown. *How dare they ask something so personal*, she thought. Mame started to open her mouth to make a wisecrack, but then she heard her father's voice reminding the family how he took a pay cut to get the new job in Penn Yan. They would need the extra income from her teaching post to keep the household solvent.

"No." Her reply was drawn out like a multi-syllable word despite its one consonant, one vowel.

The superintendent narrowed his eyes as he looked up from her résumé. "Well, you don't look like the gold-digger type, anyway." (She bit her lip hard. *Don't say anything, just smile,* she thought.) "Not that it's a bad thing. You do know that if you get married, you'll have to relinquish your job."

The response flew out of her mouth, with perhaps more anger than she'd intended. "*Why*?"

They looked at each other and chuckled. "Well, because your husband will support you, of course. Besides, there might be a young man out there who needs to provide for his family. You wouldn't want to deny him that right, would you Miss McGrath?"

Well then why bother interviewing me at all, she screamed inside her head. Her face did not reflect her inner turbulence. Martin McGrath called his only daughter Sarah Bernhardt for good reason. Mame smiled like a veteran stage actress who'd just relinquished a leading role to a pushy ingénue. She answered through gritted teeth. "Of course not, I understand completely."

The men nodded at each other.

"As you know, Miss McGrath, we have to fill this position quickly because Miss Andersen left town abruptly in late June. After reviewing your application and references we see that you'd make a fine candidate. We'd like to offer you the position."

Mame practically floated home from the interview, buoyed by happiness. As she walked up the bluestone sidewalk, she saw the woman who lived across the street struggling to get a box out of her car trunk. The young man remained seated in the rocking chair—still shirtless—seemingly oblivious to his mother's cries for assistance. Mame ran across the street.

"Need some help?"

"Oh, yes, thank you. I didn't think they'd put all these canning jars in one big box."

"I can carry this myself. Go ahead and open the door."

The box was unwieldy, but Mame was used to tilling their garden back in Elmira and had strong arms. She struggled a bit climbing the stairs to the wraparound porch and wondered why the young man didn't jump up to assist. He didn't even flinch; it was as if she wasn't even there.

Mame tilted the box sideways to get it through the front door and carried it into the kitchen where her neighbor pointed toward the table.

"Thank you, young lady. Didn't you just move in across the street? I believe we haven't met yet. I'm Virginia O'Donoghue."

She was a tall, beautiful woman with a pale ivory face, salmon-tinged high cheekbones and deep-set bright blue eyes with corners that crinkled deeply when she smiled. Her neck and hands were long and graceful, imparting upon her figure a swan-like elegance.

"It's nice to meet you; I'm Mame McGrath," she replied as she extended her hand.

"And it's lovely to meet you, Mame. I should have waited until Mr. O'Donoghue got home from work and let him carry in the jars, but he might be late. I want to can these cherries I picked today as soon as possible."

"What about...?" Mame said, pointing out the lace curtain-covered window as they walked toward the front door.

"Oh, you mean my son? Well, since the accident he...." Tears welled in her eyes instantly and she patted her chest as if she were trying to push down her rising emotion.

"What's his name?"

"Jimmy."

"Doesn't he talk?"

"No, not since the funerals. You *do* know his story, don't you? Everyone in the village does by now."

When she walked out the front door for home, Mame thought about Jimmy's odd behavior, as if he was completely detached from this world. She loved nothing better than a good challenge and decided that before the summer was over, she'd get Jimmy O'Donoghue to speak again. As she started down the steps, she looked over her shoulder at the young man rocking on the porch and smiled. His eyes didn't follow her. They seemed to be fixed on something in the distant tree line.

"I saw you over there flirting with your future husband," Mike teased as she walked in the front door. She punched his arm and strode into the kitchen where her father and mother were eating lunch.

"They hired me!" she said brightly with her arms open wide like an actress waiting for applause. Her mother smiled, but then glanced quickly at her husband to see what his reaction was. Martin McGrath never looked up. He folded the newspaper he was reading in half, slurped his soup and then said, "Good for you, Mame. That will tide you over until you meet the right fella and get married."

She curled her hands into fists and jammed them onto her hips. "Why do I need to get married to justify my existence? I'm a school teacher now and I'll be a damn fine one until I decide to retire."

Martin swatted the newspaper on the tabletop and stood up.

"Young woman, I will *not* tolerate cussing in this house! Apologize to your mother right now! I pity the poor man who takes you on as his wife." He shoved back his chair, scrape-squeaking it across the floor, grabbed his hat off the rack, tapped it onto his crown and strode out the front door to head back to work at the grocery.

Mame folded her arms and stared out the kitchen window as she wept silently. She turned to her mother who sat with her head in her hands while leaning forward, resting her elbows on the table.

"Mother, I'm sorry. It's just that...do you really think that...why should a woman have to...?"

Rose McGrath pulled from her sleeve a handkerchief her mother embroidered for her wedding day and daubed her eyes. "I'm afraid it's a man's world, Mame. We have to accept it." Mame noted that her mother's wrinkled face belied her true age, and the curly gray wisps straying from her loose bun hairdo added to the illusion.

"Hogwash! We just won the right to vote. Women need to band together and fight for more rights! Why should I be told that I have secured a teaching position until I get married, because I should depend on my husband to take care of me after that? Why did I go to college? If I love my profession, I should be able to keep it, no matter if I'm married or not."

Rose sighed.

"If you weren't married, mother, just think of all the things you could do in this world. You could be an actress, an aviatrix or one day, hopefully soon, president of the United States."

"That will *never* happen."

"Why not?"

"As I said, it's a man's world." Rose stood up, cleared the table and turned on the faucet to rinse the dishes.

Mame ran upstairs to her room and laid on the bed looking out at the back yard. After a while her mother went outside to take laundry off the line. Her brother sat under a tree reading a book, oblivious to his mother's labor. There was no reason for him to stop what he was doing and help her. This was his mother's role. It was an upsetting tableau to Mame. She did not want to be marginalized because of her sex. She wanted to make a difference in this world and prove her worth as an individual—not just a woman.

Her thoughts turned to poor Jimmy O'Donoghue across the street. He'd make a fine project for her. If she could get him to behave normally again, she'd be just like that Annie Sullivan who tamed the famous blind wild child Helen Keller. Perhaps one day people would seek out her teaching methods. She'd gain renown and travel the world meeting fascinating people and proving to all that indeed, women *are* important in this world.

Chapter 3

Her opportunity to begin the "Jimmy O'Donoghue Project" arrived soon afterward. One day Mame looked out the bathroom window and saw Virginia standing under the porte-cochère attached to her house, struggling with another box stuck in the trunk of the car. Mame double-stepped downstairs, opened the front door and called to her neighbor.

"Need a hand, Virginia?"

"I wouldn't refuse it."

Although Mrs. O'Donoghue was not used to young women addressing her by her first name (there was something forward and improper about it) for some reason it didn't bother her when Mame did it.

Mame carried in the package as Virginia waited at the opened front door for her. This box was lighter than the last one, thankfully, so she was able to carry it easily up the steps. Mame smiled at Jimmy as she passed him, and thought that for a second, his eyes seemed to focus on her presence.

"Canning more cherries?" Mame asked as she set the box down on the kitchen table.

"No, blueberries. The first crop is in and they're beautiful this year. Thank you, Mame."

"Glad I could help." As she stepped out onto the porch to leave, Virginia asked her to wait. She wanted to give her a jar of the cherries she canned last week. Mame stood next to Jimmy and watched him rock back and forth with the precise rhythm of a pendulum on a grandfather clock. It felt odd to ignore him as if he were a porch decoration.

"Hello, Jimmy O'Donoghue!" she said loudly, as if he were deaf.

Jimmy's eyes fluttered, but he never turned toward her and just kept rocking.

"Here you go, Mame. Please tell your mother I'd like her to come over for tea one of these days. I know you're still settling in to your new home."

"She'd like that, Virginia. Oh, did I tell you. I got a job teaching third grade at the elementary school."

"You did? Wonderful!" Virginia said, reaching out to hug her. The warm gesture from someone she barely knew startled Mame, especially since her own family made little fuss about her new job. She didn't realize until that moment how much she needed such an affirmation.

Mame crossed the street to her home as a pair of eyes followed her steps, and then drifted back to the sky.

***

In the following days Mame thought up any excuse she could to stop by and chat with Virginia, using spare moments to try to connect with distant Jimmy. It was the words of her father after a particularly delicious lunch that inspired her next attempt. "My dearest mother was right," Martin said to his wife, "the way to a man's heart *is* through his stomach. Thank you, Rose, for serving me that delightful repast." He kissed his wife goodbye, donned his hat and headed off to work.

Mame wasn't much of a cook, but how difficult could it be? She knew men liked desserts, so she baked her mother's signature recipe called Dream Bars to bring over to the O'Donoghue's.

As she carried a plateful up the front steps, Mame took one and placed it on the arm of the rocker next to Jimmy's hand and then rang the doorbell. He waited until she was inside talking with his mother before he stuffed it hungrily into his mouth. Mame's inexperience in the kitchen meant that she didn't notice the batch was made without enough liquid and they baked too dry. As soon as Jimmy started eating it, the coconut and pecans caught in the back of his throat.

It took a few seconds for Virginia and Mame to realize why he was coughing. They ran onto the porch and saw his hands grabbing at his throat. Virginia pounded his back hoping to dislodge whatever was making him choke. Mame covered her mouth with her hands, realizing in horror that her cooking was about to kill him. She thought Jimmy was starting to turn blue before Virginia gave him a good whack on the back. Mame screamed.

"*BREATHE*, Jimmy O'Donoghue!"

He coughed out the stuck cookie bits and gasped as air rushed back into his lungs. Jimmy turned toward Mame and stared at her, aghast. That voice...he'd heard it before. It was from *that* night, in the lake, when he was drowning. Jimmy's eyes widened as he looked squarely at Mame's face for the first time. Who was she? What did she want from him?

She wondered why he was looking at her with such utter terror in his eyes. "It's OK now. Don't be afraid. You're going to be fine," she said calmly.

Jimmy spun his head and glared at his mother who was standing behind him, tears tracing the length of her face. He bolted upright, ran down the porch steps, and paused to wag a finger at Mame.

"Who *are* you? Leave me alone!" He fled screaming up the elm-canopied sidewalk to the hill's crest.

"My word!" Virginia exclaimed, hand over her heart. "That's the first thing he's spoken in weeks. You *are* a miracle worker, just like that Helen Keller's teacher!"

Mame appreciated the reference to Annie Sullivan, but for some strange reason, she wondered why Jimmy's reaction hurt her feelings. She wasn't exactly beating away suitors and that Elmira banker who fell in love with her was a fluke, she decided. Mame McGrath was just too much woman for the average man to handle. Now this—a disturbed young man's rejection—humbled her further. Maybe her mother was right after all. Why bother trying to make a difference in a world whose balance tipped toward men?

***

The McGraths were invited to a gathering of relatives in Corning the following weekend and Mame looked forward to the distraction of some lively fun. She couldn't stop herself from glancing toward the O'Donoghue's porch as her father backed the car out of their driveway, though. Jimmy wasn't there. She sighed as she imagined he was probably still running away from her.

Aunt Bertha, Martin McGrath's sister, was a stylish, sturdy woman with thick chestnut hair coiled upon her head in Gibson Girl fashion. Her heavy-lidded blue eyes sparkled attentively during conversations, narrowing only when she'd unfurl a burly laugh that shook everything within proximity. She owned a sprawling Greek revival home on Southside Hill in Corning that had a presence much like her own, both sophisticated and imposing. There she entertained guests such as senators, judges and executives. Although she was a widow, Bertha McGrath Smith's opulent lifestyle was a nod to her prowess at running her husband's railroad freight empire after he died from the Spanish flu in the fall of 1918.

She'd traveled the world with him and shared mesmerizing tales from exotic locales such as Cairo and Bombay. Mame sat close to her aunt during these storytelling sessions, savoring each enticing morsel of detail that dropped from her lips. Her aunt had a knack for being so descriptive that it felt as if you could smell jasmine on an evening breeze across the Mughal gardens by the Taj Mahal or inhale the exotic perfume blend of cardamom and ginger off the spice barrels in a Marrakech souk. It was obvious to slightly jealous Rose that her daughter would have preferred growing up in Aunt Bertha's household. It was something that Mame couldn't help: her aunt was simply fascinating. Mame was torn—she felt bad paying her own mother little attention when Aunt Bertha was around, yet when she was in her presence it lifted her spirits immensely from everyday ennui. She hoped that some of Aunt Bertha's worldliness and savoir faire would rub off on herself.

That Saturday afternoon, Mame and Aunt Bertha left the others seeking shade on the porch and strolled down by the Chemung River. A swallowtail lilted through a drift of tiger lilies as they paused near the river's edge.

"Have you heard from Mr. Roach since you ravaged his heart?"

Mame noticed a slight smile on her aunt's face. "No. And I hope I never see him again."

"You won't. I hear he's taken a post with a bank in Chicago."

Chicago, she thought. *Well, that's that.* Mame's shoulders drooped as she sighed deeply. She realized there was no going back on her decision. Had it been the right one?

"Well, good for him, I suppose," Mame said, raising her chin and setting her sights toward the opposite bank. "In the meantime, I'm getting ready to start teaching in September. And, by the way, have I told you yet about my experiment?"

The sudden blush on her niece's face intrigued Aunt Bertha. "Do tell," she purred and took Mame's arm as she told her aunt all about the curious young man across the street and how she planned to help him communicate normally again by summer's end.

"Oh, what a horrible experience for young Jimmy. I'm glad you didn't kill him with your baking."

"At least I got him to speak again...well, scream again. Next I'm going to try to engage him in conversation. It might take a while because I think he's still afraid of me."

"What does your mother think of your project?"

"I haven't told her. Of course I haven't told father, either. He thinks my teaching job is a hobby until I get married and raise a dozen or so of kids of my own. Do you regret never having children?"

Aunt Bertha winced, then patted Mame's arm.

"Well, I never had a say in the matter, dear. After your late uncle and I were married, a high fever incapacitated me. My appendix inflamed and I didn't know it. The infection spread and my ovaries became gangrenous and had to be removed, rendering me sterile."

This was the first Mame heard of her aunt's private malaise. She'd assumed that maybe she was an advocate of Margaret Sanger and had practiced birth control because she wanted a career instead of a family. All these years Mame suspected that her aunt was a supporter of free love, a true bohemian. Instead, she realized that she'd become who she was through circumstances out of her control. She'd had no idea that her aunt lived with this sorrow silently all of these years.

Mame decided she wouldn't the let circumstances of her own life dictate her path. She was going to set her own course for success, societal "rules" be damned. If she met a man along the way who fit into her plans, fine. However, she wasn't pinning her life to that hope or dream.

These visits with her aunt reconnected Mame to who she thought she was and could be. Unlike her mother, her aunt could discuss confidently everything going on in the world at the time. With Mame she shared thought-provoking conversations about history, economics, the arts and literature. Mame had never once enjoyed an in-depth conversation like that with her mother. The scope of Rose McGrath's horizon was far narrower.

Late Sunday afternoon they returned to Penn Yan and when Martin McGrath turned into their driveway, Mame noticed Jimmy was back rocking in his porch chair, this time wearing a shirt with sleeves rolled up. She helped carry their luggage into the house, and then pretended she'd forgotten something in the car.

Mame opened the back door, felt the car seat, then turned toward Jimmy and waved at him casually. He was looking right at her, and his stare made her heart beat fast. As she turned away she thought she saw him raise his hand ever so slightly. A wide grin broke out on her face that he couldn't see. Miracle worker—indeed!

Virginia called Rose on Tuesday morning and invited her and Mame over for tea. Rose was delighted by the invitation. She hadn't been to tea in years.

"Do you suppose that odd son of hers will be there with us? What will we say to him?"

"Don't worry, mother. Jimmy stays on the porch in his rocking chair most of the time. I doubt he'll join us."

"Good. That boy frightens me."

Mame wanted to say, *No, you shouldn't fear him.* The poor young man had been through quite a traumatic experience. She was sure that before the boating accident, Jimmy was as amiable as his mother. However, her mother had exhibited a great sense of judging people's character in the past. Was she picking up something obvious about Jimmy that Mame was missing?

Since it was her first invitation to tea with Virginia, Rose decided to wear white lace gloves and a summery cloche hat to match her dress. This was a rare elegant occasion and she wanted to dress in a manner of respect toward the hostess. Mame wore a new cornflower cotton dress she bought in Corning. Aunt Bertha said it brought out the blue of her eyes. Her mother thought the hemline was too flirtatious and feared her strong-willed daughter might get caught up with that flapper crowd.

Jimmy rocked in his chair, staring ahead as they climbed the front porch steps. He wore linen trousers and a starched white shirt with a polka dot bow tie (looking quite handsome, Mame thought). She said hello to him but there was not the slightest hint of a response. That bothered Mame, and she wondered if the brief progress he'd made was lost. At least he was dressed up. That was a change.

Mike and his friends Tommy Boyle and Willy Franklin paused from a game of catch in the front yard just in time to witness Jimmy turn and stare at Mame as she walked through the front door of his house.

"Hey McGrath! Looks like that creep across the street is goofy for your sister."

"Shaddup, Boyle!"

"Didn't you see the way he was eyeing her."

"I doubt it. Jimmy has been flaky for some time."

"True. He'd have to be on dope to take a liking to Mame."

Mike pushed Tommy Boyle with his thick, splayed hands. “Don’t talk about her like that.” Mike’s steel-blue eyes glowered at Tommy as he folded his beefy arms across his chest, almost taunting his buddy to say one more insult about his sister so he could unfurl the rage that simmered constantly just below his surface. (Rose thought her son’s demeanor was too rough; he was not unlike like her father—a horse tamer from Addison.)

“Hey, McGrath. Is it true your sister doesn’t like men? I hear she turned down a big diamond from some banker.”

“Pipe down, Willy. Yeah, she refused his proposal, but it was because I saw him necking with some deb in the park after-hours and warned her. He broke her heart, the bum!”

“Whatever you say, Mikey boy!”

Mike snarled back, but he was thinking hard about what they said. Sure he’d teased his sister about marrying Jimmy, but what if the guy really *was* interested in her. Jimmy could be dangerous. He’d have to keep an eye on that fella.

Chapter 4

"Would you like a tour?" Virginia asked as she held open the screen door, ornamented with fancy fretwork spandrels, and beckoned her guests inside. Rose had hoped they'd be given this opportunity. She was curious to see if the inner décor matched the outer grandeur of the O'Donoghues's home. As Rose entered the reception hall, she got an answer immediately upon seeing the magnificent red oak two-landing staircase before her climb to its second floor balcony. The stairs had a wide handrail with carved decorative beads on its side and turned balusters below. At the foot of the steps were newel posts decorated with hand-carved grapes and leaves.

The walls of the reception hall were painted a pale salmon hue and finished with red oak crown molding lending the room an aristocratic air. Straight in front of her, by the closet under the stairs, was an elegant mahogany side table with a fretted trestle base. A tapestry runner lay across it topped with a Tiffany wisteria shade table lamp and a small collection of leather-bound classical poetry volumes held upright by cast-iron peacock bookends. Across the room was a cabriole leg davenport sofa covered with sage-colored flocked velvet and twin brass floor lamps with tasseled silk shades on either side. Lace curtains hung over the north-facing front windows on the wall behind the sofa.

Sheet music for popular jazz songs of the day lined the front of the upright piano at the back of the parlor on the left. The bright room included a love seat that matched the davenport and a pink damask-covered chaise longue. Virginia pointed at a set of embossed ivory tiles on a small table in the room. "I'm simply mad about mahjong. Have you played it yet?" Rose and Mame shook their heads. "We'll have to play a round some afternoon. Now over here is our den," Virginia said as they headed into the room to the left of the stairs. Embedded in the hardwood floor they crossed was a cast iron register grate molded in an elegant quatrefoil design.

The den was painted a warm white which helped brighten the east facing room during the afternoon. Next to a cozy window seat plumped with floral cushions was a Windsor rocker with a basketful of wool yarn sitting on the floor next to its rail. Outside the window "snowballs" of hydrangeas bloomed. Rose smiled when she glanced at the wall behind the rocker and saw Charles Bosseron Chamber's popular print of a blond cherubic Jesus called "The Light of the World." (The same print hung in her bedroom at home.) A few bookcases were scattered around the room and a queen-sized bed lined the back wall.

"When we have company they stay in this room. Shall we go see the upstairs?" Her guests nodded and climbed the steep stairs after her, Rose noting the parquet landing under an ornate and gilded oval mirror.

"Dan and I have the first room on the left," she said. They walked in the deep bedroom whose cutaway bay windows faced the street and west, shaded by the neighbor's tall Norway spruce trees. To their right was a walnut dresser with pedestal mirror. A linen cloth draped on the dresser top was set with a carved ebony tray holding a perfume atomizer, rouge pot, powder puff, and an ivory comb and brush set. In a small dish alongside were an amethyst and marcasite ring and matching drop earrings. A smaller tray to the left held an assortment of gold cufflinks and a mustache comb.

An ornately carved mahogany headboard framed their bed that was covered with an embroidered peach satin spread with matching pillows and bolsters. The opulence of the bed linens wrested Rose's jaw open as she whispered, "My word!" Virginia showed them the other three bedrooms that were not as grandiose. Mame noted that Jimmy's simply furnished south facing room was painted as dark as his current demeanor. His sister Anne's former bedroom faced the north and light coming through its cutaway bay windows gave the room a far sunnier disposition. A smaller bedroom next to Anne's was being used by Virginia as a sewing room, and next to the east facing window stood her cast iron treadle-powered sewing machine.

At the end of the hall was a narrow bathroom housing a toilet, a sink with a mirrored cabinet above it and a cast iron slipper bathtub with gilded claw feet. "I sewed these curtains with Battenburg lace my brother Charles brought home from his travels in Europe," Virginia said as she held the scalloped edges out for Rose and Mame to inspect.

"How beautiful." Mame admired any woman who could work such art with her hands. Virginia led them back into the hallway where a black cherry wood dresser stood. Bath towels were stored in its drawers among bars of Gilbert lavender soap, their scent stirring in the air as the women walked past.

As they headed downstairs, Rose noted the mother-of-pearl inlaid button light switch for the alabaster globe ceiling light that hung over the stairwell. Every detail in this house was exquisite. Although the McGraths' house was fine enough, it was obvious that the builder spared no expense for craftsmanship here.

They returned to the dining room where Virginia set out a Dresden floral bone china tea set on the Battenburg lace cloth covering the oak draw leaf table. The sunny room had cutaway bay windows facing west, and Rose commented that it was a cheery spot for afternoon tea as Virginia motioned to the mother and daughter to have a seat. She pushed the kitchen swing door open and carried the teapot inside to pour boiling water inside it.

"Is it just the two of you here?" Rose called to her as her eyes drifted across a stack of dinner plates on the walnut buffet sideboard, carved elegantly with acanthus leaves. Leaning against the opposite wall stood a curved front, black cherry china cabinet with cabriole legs. The glass shelves glinted with Irish crystal.

"For many weeks out of the year, yes it's just my son and I. My husband Dan is a traveling salesman for the Gilbert Soap Company," Virginia said as she carried the full teapot out and set it on the serving tray. "Our daughter Anne is married and lives in Rochester. I have one brother, Charles

O'Malley and his wife Esther. They have four children and live in the village in our parents' old home. His son John is married and lives a few blocks away. They have a five-year-old son, Bill. Our father was a doctor in the village. He and mother have both passed on. Is it just the four of you?"

Virginia noted a touch of sadness in Rose's eyes as she nodded. *Perhaps she'd lost a child at birth? Maybe that surly-looking husband of hers didn't want more. Or worse, was he having an affair?* When those dark thoughts raced through her mind, Virginia tried to be a good Catholic woman and wipe them away, but she allowed herself to note that there may be something amiss in that family.

"Mame, you must be looking forward to teaching at the school."

"Oh yes, Virginia!"

Rose touched her daughter's hand and raised her eyebrow.

"I mean, Mrs. O'Donoghue," Mame corrected through clenched teeth. She knew that propriety toward your elders was important to her mother, but Mame had made a different kind of connection with Virginia. It almost felt like they were peers. Funny, Virginia and her mother were probably close in age, but her mother's conservative perspectives made her feel like another generation away.

"Oh, don't worry, Mame. This is not such a formal household. You may call me Virginia. And I hope I may call you Rose, Mrs. McGrath."

Rose was tickled by Virginia's amiable gesture. She wished she had her neighbor's refinement.

"You may." They all laughed. Formalities had been "boxed up" and set aside. Now they could all relax and get to know each other.

"I've never been to Elmira, Rose. Do you prefer its bustling city life to the Village of Penn Yan?"

"Actually, Virginia, I find the pace of Penn Yan to be more suited to our family."

"I enjoy visiting Corning," Mame said brightly. Rose frowned.

"What she means is that she enjoys being under the spell of that live wire, Aunt Bertha, there," Rose said in a joking tone, though her jealousy was obvious.

Mame shook her head. "I'm not under her spell."

"Why then did you heed her advice instead of mine about Mr. Roach?"

"Mr. Roach?" Virginia asked slyly as she poured tea.

"She's talking about Eugene Roach—my former fiancé."

"I didn't know you were engaged previously. What happened?"

"She wanted a career instead of marriage," Rose said, then stirred cream into her tea. "There is nothing wrong with that young gentleman. He is good looking, wealthy, rising in the banking world...."

"And is probably lollygagging with all the loose women of Chicago," Mame interrupted, tossing her hair with an exaggerated flick of her hand.

Virginia sighed and looked Rose in the eyes. "Dear Mame, if there's one thing you must learn about this world is that men run it. Even wives in the most stable marriages have to cast their eyes aside now and again and ignore their husbands' transgressions. The guilty men will more than make up for it by providing a good home...and the occasional piece of expensive jewelry." Virginia's hand reached up and twirled the pearl lavaliere at the end of her necklace. Rose relaxed back in her chair and winked at her new friend. Maybe she and Virginia had more in common than she'd thought. (She often wondered where her husband disappeared to Wednesday nights when he went for his "constitutional" walk through the village. She knew the route could be walked quicker than the two hours he was gone.)

Mame rubbed her thumb against the empty ring finger of her left hand. She could almost still feel the weight of the showy two-carat Tiffany diamond that Eugene had given her. The other women would have looked at it as the ticket to freedom, but to her it felt like a sinking weight.

"I have no regrets. I want a man who will be true to me and treat me as an equal. He doesn't have to provide me with a big house or fancy jewels." Rose and Virginia sniggered and Mame crossed her arms as she continued. "I'd like someone who enjoys poetry, philosophy, debating politics and would even help me with the housework." By now Rose and Virginia couldn't restrain themselves and tipped backwards in their chairs belly laughing. "I believe truly that there's a man somewhere out there like that," Mame said loudly to drown out their laughter.

The front screen door swung open and heavy footsteps approached the dining room. A hand grabbed the chair next to Mame's and Jimmy thudded into it. Rose gasped, fearing the sullen young man would commit some violence against her daughter.

The look on Virginia's face was more of amazement. Jimmy had not taken a step to engage with fellow humans since the funerals of his young friends. She was stunned by his outburst that day toward Mame, and now it occurred to her that he might be attracted to his neighbor, despite his protest.

Mame blushed but retained her composure and looked right into his spooky eyes.

"Hello, Jimmy O'Donoghue. How are you today?"

His eyes fluttered. Inside, Jimmy was thinking, *My God, this is the voice I heard that night. But I can't tell her that; she'll think I'm crazy*. Jimmy stared back at Mame. He loved how the sunlight shimmered off the surface of her tea, illuminating Mame's pretty blue eyes.

"May I have...?"

Virginia caught her breath. She couldn't believe her son was speaking. They'd been living in that house in silence for weeks now and until his outburst, she'd almost forgotten what his voice sounded like.

"Yes, let me get you a cup." Virginia went over to the sideboard and pulled a tea setting out. Rose and Mame watched as she filled his teacup. He gestured toward the cream pitcher in front of Mame. She handed it to him, and in the transfer, felt his fingertips brush hers. The warmth of his touch flushed Mame's face immediately and she wished the other two women hadn't witnessed the intimate moment.

Jimmy stirred his tea and sipped it as the women restarted the conversation as if there'd been no interruption. Virginia was so confused. Part of her was trying to focus on getting to know her neighbors, the other part wanted to hug her son and talk with him. She was afraid that if she fussed over him, he'd go silent again.

"I forgot the cake!" Virginia bustled off to the kitchen. As they waited in awkward silence, Rose looked around the room at the fine furnishings and tallied their value in her mind. Either Mr. O'Donoghue is a skilled salesman or he married well, she thought. She wondered what would ever become of the poor young man across the table from her. Now that she could see his face close up, Rose noted he was a handsome young man, despite the shock of premature white hair over his left eye.

Mame couldn't think of a single thing in the world at the moment except for the fact that the subject of her summer project had now been lured like a lion in the wild to sit down next to her peacefully. Her heart beat rapidly as she scrambled to recall what her education professor said about encouraging good behavior in students. What could she do to keep Jimmy's progress on track?

"That's an elegant shirt you're wearing, Jimmy," Mame said as Virginia set the cut crystal stand holding a Lady Baltimore cake on the center of the table.

Jimmy rested his tea cup into its saucer and reached his hand toward the cake.

"Mind your manners, Jimmy," Virginia hissed under her breath. "Rose, would you like a slice?"

Jimmy stared at Virginia as she cut pieces of the fancy cake for her guests. When the serving knife pulled the first delicate segment away, the orange scent of the filling—dried fruit soaked in Grand Marnier—filled the room. Jimmy's eyes widened and he leaned toward the dessert, anticipating the deliciousness of the soft cake with meringue icing. As soon as his mother handed him his serving, he dug at the cake with his fork and shoved big chunks of it into his mouth. Mame's eyebrows rose as she witnessed his Neanderthal-like behavior. This project was going to be more complicated than she'd guessed. Soon, he was holding his empty plate out toward his mother.

"Want...another!"

Virginia was now both annoyed and embarrassed by his behavior. She hoped her guests would forgive his rudeness and not tell everyone in the village.

"Now Jimmy, what's that word people say when they would like something?" Mame asked, not looking his way.

"Pluh...," he said, nodding toward the plate. Now Virginia was staring at Mame. This young woman held the secret of getting through to him somehow. Why her and not the doctors at the sanatorium in Rochester? Virginia smiled at the divine providence that had made Mame reject Eugene Roach's proposal so she could be here at this moment to bring her son Jimmy back to life.

When they finished eating their cake, Rose took her neighbor's hand.

"Thank you, Virginia, for a lovely afternoon. We must be going. Mr. McGrath will be expecting his supper soon."

"Rose, I'm so glad you and Mame could join me...us," she corrected, smiling at Jimmy, who'd resumed his distant stare after finishing his cake and tea. "You'll have to come over again soon."

"I'd like that."

Mame rose from her chair and as the two mothers were chatting she thought she heard Jimmy whisper, "Pretty dressssss."

After dinner that evening, Mame and her mother washed the dishes while her father smoked a cigar in the sitting room and Mike read the newspaper. Mame thought it was ridiculous that the men in the family never had to do any of the housework. They were partners in creating the messes; why shouldn't they be partners in the cleanup?

As she tried to formulate in her mind a snappy question to put toward the men in the other room, Rose was thinking about how elegant Virginia was and how they shared the burden of complicated marriages. For Rose, it was string of miscarriages followed by the birth of Mame that disappointed her spouse. Thank God they finally had a son. Would Martin have left her if they hadn't?

She also thought about the way that young man across the street stared at her daughter. Rose noticed how deeply Mame blushed when her fingers touched his. It pained her to think of her daughter getting involved with this damaged young man. Yes, his mother Virginia is lovely and Rose believed they would become good friends over time. But that Jimmy...once you experience something so dark, how could you recover fully to live a normal life?

"I think that Jimmy fancies you," Rose said as she handed her daughter a pot to dry. Mame's heart raced when she heard the words, but her face showed no emotion.

"Why would you think that?"

"He sat next to you, didn't he?"

"That was the only open seat at the table, Mother. I don't think that meant anything."

"He never took his eyes off you after he finished eating his cake."

"Really?" Her daughter's red face confirmed Rose's fears.

"I don't want you hanging around him when Virginia isn't there. You don't know how he might snap again and...."

"He never snapped, Mother. It was an accident. They'd been drinking gin. One of them fell overboard, the second dived in to save him, and as they struggled, he was knocked in."

"Did he tell you that version?" Rose wondered if this strange boy spoke normally to her daughter when the others weren't around.

"Of course not. Mike's friends told him, he told me."

"A likely story." Rose raised her eyebrow at Mame.

"I'm telling you the truth!" Mame's cheeks turned raspberry pink. What was her mother insinuating? She hoped it wouldn't interfere with her "project" and keep her away from Jimmy after that minor breakthrough.

"Virginia is lovely. The son must have inherited his taste for gin from the father. Be careful, Mame. That's all I'm saying."

Chapter 5

Dan O'Donoghue arrived home from his Southern sales trip on a sunny Saturday morning in late July. The flair with which he dressed that day distracted from the insignificance of his stature. He wore a lightweight linen suit with a Panama hat pushed firmly over his thick charcoal gray hair restrained with pomade. His trimmed pencil mustache gave him the air of Douglas Fairbanks as he carried two suitcases out of his gleaming crimson Stutz Bearcat with whitewall tires. The heels of his black and white Oxfords clicked up the porch steps.

When he passed his son sitting mute in the rocker he could tell that little had changed with Jimmy. That was the last thing he needed to worry about now. Sales on the road were down and he doubted he'd meet this quarter's goal.

"Hello, son," he said, standing right next to Jimmy. There was no response. "I said *hello*, James!"

Jimmy turned slightly, as if a distant train's whistle caught his attention. There was no emotion discernible on his face, no flicker of recognition toward his father.

"Hey!" he said, setting down his suitcases and grabbing his son's arm. "Look at me when I talk to you!" Jimmy's head was turned completely toward his father now, but his eyes were someplace else.

"You can't do this to me! I need you here to take care of your mother. I won't always be around. You have to get over this tragedy and move on with your life, son. Do you hear me? DO YOU HEAR ME?"

Mame heard a commotion across the street and stepped onto the front porch. A man (that she guessed was Mr. O'Donoghue from the suitcases) was yelling at Jimmy, shaking him. She couldn't remain quiet as she watched him rough up his son.

"Stop it! Don't treat him like that!" she yelled.

Dan dropped his hands to his side and squinted across the street at her.

"Mind your own business, young lady. This doesn't concern you."

Mame strode purposefully across the street and stopped at the end of the sidewalk that led to the O'Donoghue's front porch.

"He needs to be treated gently. The trauma of the accident has...."

"Who do you think *you* are, Miss? Dr. Freud?"

"I'm a graduate of the Geneseo normal school."

"Nothing I detest more than a brazen woman."

Mame pushed her hands down on her hips hard. "He'll never respond if you treat him that way."

"Stop being impertinent, young lady."

"But...I know what I'm talking about. I'm a teacher and I think I can help him."

Virginia O'Donoghue peeked through the lace curtains. What was her husband Dan barking about now?

"How long have you been teaching?" Dan asked Mame. She laced her fingers in front of her and looked away, up the street where Jimmy had run that day after he yelled at her.

"I'll be teaching third grade here in September."

Dan O'Donoghue snorted. "Oh! So you're an expert on such matters although you've never taught a day in your life? My son's not a child. He's a grown man and should be out earning his keep. You know nothing about our situation. I forbid you to have any further contact with my son. Good day!"

"But...!" His angry tone frightened her and she took a few steps backward and then turned around and ran across the street to her home. Jimmy's eyes followed her—a gesture not unnoticed by his father.

"You stay away from that girl, Jimmy! You hear? I don't want any trouble starting between you two. Didn't like her sassiness. How *dare* she speak to me that way! A woman like that doesn't know her place, and that's in the home."

Jimmy turned his head and stared right at his father.

"No."

Dan's anger flared like a bottle rocket and the back of his hand flew across his son's face. The slap was so loud that Mame heard it across the street. She stopped on the front steps and turned just as Virginia rushed out the front door to protect her son from the wrath of her husband. His hand was still out as he twirled around and smacked her in the face. Virginia screamed.

Mame ran toward them, but Dan ran down the porch steps, fingers cocked like a pistol at her as he yelled "You never saw a thing! If you say you did, there's more where that came from." He charged at her like rabid dog with spittle flying from its mouth. The unbridled rage in his eyes terrified Mame. She covered her mouth as she ran back into her house. The last thing she wanted to do was spur more violence toward Jimmy and Virginia.

Her mother was right, it *is* a man's world, Mame thought. She'd never met Mr. O'Donoghue, but after that display, she had no desire to know him better. *Poor Jimmy and Virginia,* she thought.

***

Dan O'Donoghue stayed but two weeks at home before he hit the road again. Mame figured he was the sort of traveling salesman who knew a "farmer's daughter" in every town he visited. Now she understood Virginia's reference about the jewelry. He was a brutal cur of a husband, but because he also had a strong sense of guilt, he was eager to dispense trinkets that he thought would fade her memories of his transgressions.

As soon as her husband was back on the road, Virginia called Rose McGrath and invited her over to tea again. Mame was miffed that the invitation had not been extended to her. Virginia's husband must have banished her from their household forever.

While the two women gossiped over cups of Earl Grey that afternoon, Mame scraped at the dirt with a cultivator in the flower beds out front, lopped off spent rose blossoms and cut a bouquet of brown-eyed susans. When she'd pause to wipe her brow, she'd glance over at the porch and notice Jimmy watching her. She'd blush and then turn away, trying to act nonchalant. That would last about five minutes before she'd look up at him again. Their eyes would lock briefly and she'd feel a warm rush through her body. The sensation unnerved her, and she moved on to the gardens at the back of the house to step out of his line of view.

A line of carmine red gladiolas by the rear of the house flaunted their frilly blossoms like a line of can-can dancers. Mame cut two stalks to add to her bouquet. There were some lingering tiger lilies that she also snipped and arranged with the vivid flowers. A few sprigs of early white asters would soften the bright colors. She walked back to where the flowers bloomed in front of the house and noticed out of the corner of her eye that Jimmy was not on the porch. He'd probably gone inside for tea and cake with their mothers, she thought.

Something made her turn around, and when she did, Jimmy was standing right in front of her. Mame was so startled that she opened her mouth to scream, but stopped when he held out a pink hollyhock stalk he'd picked from the far side of her house. She caught her breath and smiled.

"For me?" she asked. Jimmy nodded. Mame added the cheery blooms to the bouquet in her left hand.

"They're beautiful. Thank you, Jimmy." She looked at his cheek where a faded maroon bruise from his father's hand remained. Mame touched his face gently. He winced. "I'm so sorry he did this, Jimmy. You didn't deserve it."

He glanced down at his shoes for a few seconds, and when he looked back up at her, he clasped his hand onto hers, still caressing his cheek.

"If you ever want to talk about the night of the drownings, Jimmy, I will listen. It's my firm opinion that you did nothing wrong. What was meant to happen, did. It was God's will, just an awful accident." He released her hand and she hugged the flowers he gave her to her chest.

"You were there," he said slowly. "Why?"

Her heart started to pound at the sound of his voice. She'd never heard him speak in a normal tone like this.

"I was *there*?" she asked gently, afraid to upset him or scare him away. "But Jimmy, we weren't even living in Penn Yan then. How could I have been there?"

He turned away and closed his eyes for a few moments, as if he were replaying the scene in his mind.

"You called to me. You told me to breathe. It was *your* voice!"

"But that's completely im...."

Her denial agitated him and he pointed at her.

"YOU were there!" The intensity in his eyes reminded Mame of his father. It unnerved her, but she tried to remain calm.

Two pairs of eyes watched through the lace curtain across the street.

"What on earth is he saying to her?" Virginia asked.

"They look like they're having a real conversation," Rose answered.

"I don't know what it is, but your daughter has some way to get through to my son. It would be a miracle if he returned to the way he used to be. Oh, that awful day. I remember when the sirens repeated three slow blasts, indicating there was a drowning, all morning after the accident. I was waiting for news about my missing son and feared I'd get a call that they'd found his body. When we got the call from Hammondsport that he was alive, I was thrilled. But when Dan and I drove down there to pick him up, it was as if Jimmy died, too. All I want is my son back to normal."

"Well, I trust Mame's teaching instinct. If she can bring the Jimmy you knew back, even I'll be impressed."

"You don't suppose he likes her?" Virginia pulled back from the curtain to watch her friend's reaction.

"I know my daughter, and if Jimmy does like her, it's obvious her feelings for him are the same."

"Wouldn't that be something," Virginia said as they walked back over to the table, her fingers fiddling with the triple strands of her pearl necklace. "Oh, did I tell you that Dan brought these back from New York for me. They're real."

Rose's eyes widened. "Lovely. They must have cost a fortune."

"Oh, he paid a high price all right," she said with a wink as she sipped her tea.

"They remind me of a choker Mr. McGrath gave me that he said was in appreciation for the birth of our son, Michael, and the fact that his family name would carry on. It took me three miscarriages after the birth of Mame before I 'earned them'," Rose said. She stared at the reflection of her weary face in the amber steeped tea. Virginia reached across the table and took her hand.

"You did well, Rose. Your children are beautiful."

***

Over the last two weeks of summer, Mame continued to find small tasks in the garden whenever Jimmy was on the porch. Sometimes she'd be out there for close to an hour before he'd cross the street, but he'd visit her daily. Their conversations were brief, simple exchanges but each time she'd try to coax a little bit more information about the accident out of him. Mame would replay the scene, jogging his memory each time. She thought talking about that night would help him heal, but she was also curious why he thought she was there. It was such an odd thing. So far they'd covered the entire scenario up until he was knocked into the water.

"Jimmy, tell me if I'm correct. At first you were in the boat watching Skip try to keep Ralph afloat, and then they flipped up an oar that knocked you into the water. You tried swimming to the surface, but you'd gotten all turned around and it was the bottom of the lake, and then...."

"I took a breath."

"Now Jimmy. Think harder. You're not a fish. It's impossible to take a breath under water."

"No!" he said as he gripped her arm tightly. "I took a breath...a deep one."

"But it's impossible. You must have been in shock and thought you did."

"No! And *you* were there. You told me to breathe. I know it was *you*; I recognize your voice."

"What did I say?"

"*Breathe, Jimmy O'Donoghue*!"

The words flashed Mame's memory back immediately to that day Jimmy ran away from her, yelling up the street. It made sense now. This was why he was so upset after he was choking. What an odd turn of events, she thought. It was as if a foreshadowing of her had been implanted in his life before they met because she was to become important to him. God's mysterious ways, indeed! Just as she was about to respond to her rushing thoughts, he embraced her.

"Thank you," he whispered in her ears as his arms held her tightly.

This gesture was so inappropriate, so forward, so out in the open, yet Mame did not shrink away, but followed the instinct to hug him back as tightly as he held her. She felt his heart beating rapidly, just like her own. They parted enough to look at each other's face and Mame was surprised to see him smiling at her, with aware and twinkling eyes that until that moment had seemed only lifeless.

Virginia happened to peek out the front window at that moment and witnessed the exchange. "Come! Look at this, Rose," she called to her neighbor who'd been in the kitchen with her canning peaches.

"What is it?" Rose asked as she wiped her hands on a kitchen towel. She was embarrassed to see her daughter and Jimmy's public display. "My word!"

"I never thought I'd see him smile again." Virginia's voice cracked with emotion. "Penn Yan was smart to hire your daughter. If she can achieve this with Jimmy, imagine what she'll achieve with her students."

"How wonderful!" Rose had to admit that she was proud of what her daughter accomplished. "Wait until your husband comes back. He'll be quite surprised."

"Oh, he won't be coming back," she said in a solemn tone as her hand released the curtain and she walked back to the kitchen. "Please don't tell anyone. He left a note on the dresser before he left for Poughkeepsie that he was abandoning us for his *whore*. That's my word, obviously. There will be no shame of a divorce. If I agree to pretend we're still happily married, he'll send me a stipend every month."

Rose was shocked. This agreement was appallingly racy in her opinion. Yet, at the same time, part of her cheered secretly for Virginia that she'd somehow managed to turn her husband's sordid affairs around to serve her advantage. She'd never have to worry about finances or endure the shame of being labeled a divorcée. If Mr. O'Donoghue kept his promise, she could live the life of a lady of leisure in this grand house with a wraparound porch. Now that Jimmy had regained his lucidity, things should improve immensely for her.

Rose shifted her thoughts to the other issue at hand: what was developing between her friend's son and Mame?

Chapter 6

Jimmy's moods raced from placid to agitated when the school year began because Mame was gone so much of the day. In just a short period of time, she'd become his critical link to understanding what he'd experienced that awful night in June. He'd pace on the porch until she was due home and as soon as he spotted her bouncy auburn hair coming up the street, he'd run down to greet her. Often she'd be exhausted from a long day of working with restless children, but Mame was ever patient and before she'd stop home, she'd sit in the porch rocker next to his as he told her the latest bit of recovered memory. Over and over, they'd connect new pieces to the puzzle as he'd share theories of what he could have done to save his friends.

Soon it became apparent to Jimmy—after weighing every possible scenario—that there was absolutely nothing he could have done that night that would have prevented the tragedy (except not getting in the boat). That was the day he sobbed straight for twenty minutes as Mame sat still in the rocker next to him, silent yet holding his hand, knowing no words were necessary, her presence was enough.

By now all of their neighbors were aware of Mame's project and no one paid them heed during their time together on the porch. One mid-September day, Jimmy asked if she'd like to take a walk. She was delighted by the gesture and accepted the invitation eagerly.

"All of this time I've never asked a lick about you, Mame," Jimmy said, hands in his pockets as he scuffed his shoes on the sidewalk. "I'm sorry. Will you please forgive me? Tell me, why did you want to become a teacher?"

His words gave her pause. Not even Eugene had asked her that. She started explaining her philosophy of education, watching his eyes carefully to see if they'd drift off to other thoughts crossing his mind. That was the usual reaction she'd get from men—even her own father—when she tried to have an intelligent conversation with them. Jimmy's eyes remained intently on her and he nodded in agreement about the need to instill a love of reading early in life.

Mame never enjoyed such thoughtful exchanges with her few female friends either, except with Aunt Bertha. She realized that she was a bit of a loner, although it wasn't intentional. She just preferred to spend her time with individuals who would challenge her mind, not natter on about busybody nonsense. There was so much in the universe she was curious about.

Without fanfare, Mame and Jimmy became close friends. Mame found him easy to talk with, and soon their daily walks and conversations shifted to discussions of the world around them, philosophies of life and even faith.

One early fall day they went for a walk and were discussing the high school football team's prowess as they crossed the Main Street Bridge over the Keuka Outlet. Crimson maple leaves drifted underneath following the path of the old Crooked Lake Canal toward Seneca Lake, about seven and a half miles to the east.

"What were you going to study in college, Jimmy?"

"Chemistry. I wanted to be a pharmacist. It was my goal to save lives, not...." He stopped and glanced below at the leaves spinning toward a destiny out of their control. She saw his tears and fought back her own.

"You could still do that, you know," Mame said. He nodded. "Think of it as a way to honor their lives." He bit his lower lip as he stared at the sidewalk, then looked up at her. Those honest blue eyes of hers wore down his fears when he gazed into them. They sparkled like the late afternoon sun off Keuka's waters. In her eyes he saw his previous happy life filled with memories of lazy afternoons floating on the lake in an inner tube or racing to jump off the end of the dock with his sister Anne, hitting the water like exploding cannonballs. When she talked deeply about her love of education, Mame's eyes danced like laughter drifting across the lake on a warm summer's evening. They radiated the intensity of the joy she felt for life.

"I sent the college a letter to see if they would consider admitting me for next semester on account of all that happened."

"Attaboy, Jimmy!" She took his arm as they turned left onto Elm Street and chatted about how wonderful college was for her, how it had changed her life. Their engaging conversation had been so intense that they lost their bearings of where they'd walked. Their footsteps paused as they realized they were in front of the Catholic cemetery where Ralph and Skip were buried. Jimmy cast his eyes up the hill toward their graves and sighed.

"You haven't been here since the...?"

He shook his head.

"Let's go say hello, then." Mame took Jimmy's hand and they climbed the uneven slope to where his friends were buried. In a coincidence of timing, Martin McGrath passed by in a car driven by the regional manager for the grocery chain that employed him. They were heading down to Bath to visit another store's manager to discuss pricing of goods.

"Look at those young lovers heading off to no good," Martin's boss said, hissing at the couple.

Martin winced when he realized it was his daughter with that disturbed fella from across the street. It was all he could do to not stop the car, run up the hill and drag her home. He knew though that his boss was in town to review his work for a possible promotion, so he couldn't say a thing. What was more important at that moment: preventing the possible deflowering of his only daughter, or saving a promotion that would feed his family for years? That daughter of his was too strong-willed to control anyway. Let her pay her own price for her sins, he thought.

"Say, how do you like this Buick? I've been thinking of trading in my Model T," Martin said, as his daughter disappeared in the distance.

That was enough to divert his boss. He rattled on all the way to Bath about his automobile and how much he liked it. Martin pretended that he was listening, when he was actually thinking what he was going to do to that Jimmy O'Donoghue when he got home tonight. How dare he bring such shame upon their family!

Sparse grass sprouted from the upturned earth covering Ralph and Skip's graves. Mame steadied Jimmy as he paused to pray over each of his friends. A sentinel crow watched atop a Scotch pine post, ruffled by an insistent breeze carrying the grapey-sweet scent of a vineyard where Catawbas slipped their rose-suede skins. Jimmy's words swept away from him like dust swirling up an empty street. No tears came at this moment, but his grip tightened on Mame's hand as he led her over to a grassy spot beneath a sprawling beech tree. She tucked her dress around her legs to protect her modesty, but she wasn't afraid of Jimmy. She believed that beneath the darkness imprinted on him from the tragedy was a solid foundation of goodness. (Then again, after witnessing what his father was capable of doing, part of her wondered if Jimmy could also be violent. And here they were, un-chaperoned, deep in a vacant cemetery.)

Jimmy looked up the hillside of granite monuments to the tall Celtic cross marking the O'Donoghue's plot—his final destiny. It made him think about what lay ahead before he joined his friends on this slumbering slope.

"We'd promised each other once that when we were thirty, no matter where we were living at the time, we'd come back to Keuka and swim across by Bluff Point. I'd have my own pharmacy. Ralph would have been the football coach at the high school and Skip, he'd have probably been a millionaire by then. Now we won't ever get to...because I...."

She'd had enough of this self-blame.

"Stop saying 'I'! It didn't happen because of anything you did wrong, Jimmy. Did you force Ralph to drink that gin? Did you tell Skip to jump in after him? You were knocked in the water by the oar, remember? This was all part of some plan by God, a plan that none of us can understand."

"God damn it! Why did this have to happen? These cursed memories...they make me want to end my miserable life!" His booming voice echoed down the cemetery, across the road and sifted through the cattail wetlands to the end of the lake. She recoiled from his rage, fearing he'd raise a hand to her like she'd seen his father do to him. Somehow she mustered courage to rebuke his outburst of self-pity.

"Shush! Show some respect for the dead and this hallowed ground! Why are you so ungrateful?" Mame stood up and brushed the leaves off her skirt.

"Ungrateful! *Ungrateful*?"

"Your life was spared. You've been given a second chance!"

"You call this living?" Now he was standing, yelling in her face.

"What purpose would ending your life serve?" she said, her voice rising to an equal volume. "Honor their memories by making the most of your life. Live, Jimmy O'Donoghue!"

He grabbed Mame and kissed her quivering mouth hard. His wild passion frightened her and she broke his embrace, fleeing down the hill. Jimmy raced after her, catching Mame by the arm and pulled her close once more, staring into her eyes in a way no man had ever done before. She trembled as his fingers dug into her arms, locking her into his grasp.

"Well I can only live my life if I'm with you, Mame!" Jimmy was no longer the timid, unthreatening shell of a person rocking on the front porch across the street from her house. What had she unleashed? Her jaw dropped. "That's right; when I graduate from college first thing I'll do is make you my wife."

She gasped, startled completely by his words; they both frightened and thrilled her. In that moment she realized he was no longer just a project now. She realized that inside, she shared his romantic aspirations. How did this happen? So many thoughts rushed through her head. If they married she'd lose her job. What about her career? What would they live on? Would anyone in this town hire him after what occurred?

Jimmy released his grip and stood back, a bit stunned also by the words that had flown out of his mouth. Mame felt overpowered by the commanding stare of his dazzling sapphire eyes framed with impossibly long black lashes. Her knees felt like they'd buckle.

"Yes!" she blurted, and then covered her mouth with her hands, realizing what she'd said, and ran away. Jimmy grinned as let her flee toward home. He'd gotten the answer he wanted.

Chapter 7

It was July of 1935 and Jimmy and Mame O'Donoghue were getting ready to go away for the weekend to celebrate their tenth wedding anniversary. The actual anniversary date had been the previous December, but the couple postponed the trip they'd planned then because Jimmy's mother died.

Virginia succumbed to double pneumonia the same week as their anniversary. Her death was a terrible shock to the family. She had never gotten over the news that her husband died the previous year and his paramour didn't bother to contact her. He was still the father of her children, for heaven's sake, and Virginia felt wronged that she—his actual wife—was kept from his funeral, despite their estrangement. The stress of the shame it caused her compromised her health, making Virginia vulnerable to a respiratory infection she caught in the waning days of '34.

Once her estate settled in March, Jimmy's family moved from their Lake Street apartment into her house with the wraparound porch, left to them in Virginia's will. His sister Anne did not contest her mother's wishes. She had no interest in the big house and was just happy it would stay in the family. Anne said that since Jimmy was the one with the larger family, it suited him better. She and her husband Will Foley had one daughter, Bridget, and they were fortunate to have recently purchased a lovely new bungalow in Rochester.

As he'd hoped, Jimmy graduated from pharmacy school and lucked into an opportunity (with some financial backing from his parents) to become a partner in the bustling drug store near the corner of Main and Elm streets. Mame of course had to relinquish her teaching job at the public school, but was fortunate to get a job teaching second grade at the Catholic school. She was adept at finance thanks to the business advice shared by Aunt Bertha. Because she kept them on a tight budget, they did not feel deprived as most did during the Great Depression. This kept their income relatively stable during the worst economic era in American history.

Despite her efforts, they were not awash in cash that could be spent willy-nilly on an anniversary celebration. Through Jimmy's connections at work, they knew an innkeeper in Hammondsport who offered to put them up for free to celebrate ten years of married bliss. Mame's mother Rose volunteered to watch her grandchildren Patrick, who was nine years old, and Frances, aged seven, at her home across the street.

On the sweltering evening of Friday, July 5, they drove to O'Hara's Octagon Inn, just outside the village on Pleasant Valley Road. Although Jimmy was getting more relaxed with being near the water—the McGraths now owned a small cottage on the east shore of Keuka—he preferred not to be lakeside. This inn was tucked along a willow-lined creek at the base of a rolling hill. As soon as he saw the inn's rural setting he relaxed. Mame was willing to concede to his wish. Over the years of their marriage his night terrors gradually lessened and Mame wanted to do anything that would help them disappear altogether.

After their arrival, the couple had a late supper in the high-ceilinged dining room with art deco wall sconces that shimmered off the metallic periwinkle and champagne wallpaper. The softly whirring fan above them stirred faint relief from the stagnant, close air outside. They ordered the lake trout special and sparkling wine that had been bottled just down the road. For the first time in years they were able to relax and enjoy each other's company uninterrupted. The room's elegant atmosphere and extravagant furnishings made them feel as privileged as if they were dining at the Waldorf.

Jimmy still made Mame's heart skip when he looked into her eyes, though by now his hair was prematurely fully white. She thought it made him look distinguished. To her Jimmy was as handsome still as he was that first day she saw him in 1920.

He kissed her hand after the dishes were cleared from their table. How had he been so lucky to have this vivacious, intelligent and beautiful woman come into his life? As he watched the dancing candlelight from the table reflect in her eyes, he recalled the light from cottages on the lake that tragic night fifteen years ago. And because of his wife's patience with his recovery, his thoughts did not immediately go to that dark place. Instead he was able to acknowledge the connection and the passing feelings they stirred, yet refocus on this rare moment with his lovely Mame. She was not just his wife; she was his lifesaver.

"O'Hara says there's a jazz band playing at a jitney-style dance on Shethar Street. Shall we step out tonight?"

Mame nodded enthusiastically. "How swell! We haven't been to a dance in forever!"

Jimmy drove their Nash Lafayette sedan about a mile down the road to a crowded dance club near the village square. They could hear the band playing "You're the Top" as they pulled up. Mame entered with a happy bounce as she crossed the oaken floorboards. She had spent considerable hours turning Jimmy into a presentable dancer, and despite his earlier protests, he loved nothing better than to cut a rug with his spunky wife. She couldn't wait for this moment to show off his dance skills. They got a table in the back, ordered Manhattans and sipped them for but a few minutes before the band started playing "Night and Day." Jimmy swept her immediately onto the dance floor for the foxtrot. How she loved dancing in his arms! He transformed in seconds from a staid pharmacist into a suave Fred Astaire. She could tell that the other women in the room were jealous of how in sync their footsteps were.

Nothing made Mame feel more alive than dancing to music like this with her handsome husband. There wasn't a wisp of cool air to spare in the club and they both were sweating profusely. She couldn't care less—dancing overpowered her with joy. By the grin on his face, she could tell that he felt exactly the same way. He no longer resembled the shell of a man she'd met that day they moved to Penn Yan. Now Jimmy savored life with a zest few had. He knew how easily it could all slip away.

The next morning they strolled down the road into the village. It was "a good stretch of the legs on a blistering hot day," Jimmy would recall to his children many times later. Mame carried her swimsuit in a stylish beach tote with a wooden toggle button. It looked perfect with the wide-brimmed straw hat that matched her peep toe wedge-heeled shoes. She changed in the beachside locker room, dove off the dock and stroked gently through the water as Jimmy read the newspaper nearby, sitting sideways on a park bench to shift his view away from the lake. A stifling humidity rose with the sun; its oppressiveness diminished any respite from the occasional breeze. Jimmy wiped away the sweat on his forehead under his straw boater and fanned himself with the newspaper. He was so desperately hot that he considered stripping down to his underwear and diving in alongside his wife. (She'd just laugh, though he'd surely be arrested.) As he glanced over his shoulder toward the lake, Jimmy noticed ominous clouds billowing on the western horizon.

"Looks like the weather's about to turn, dear. Whaddya say we get some ice cream sundaes in the square, my treat?"

"Marvelous! Oh darn, it's already starting to rain. Let's hurry."

She re-emerged quickly from the locker room wearing the sunny dress that matched her bright eyes, even on this overcast day. The drizzle that persisted on their quick walk to the ice cream shop swelled into a downpour by the time they were standing safely under the roof of the gazebo in the village square. Jimmy and Mame sat on the railing as rain thundered on the roof above them. Another man stood on the far side of the gazebo facing Pulteney Street taking long drags from his pipe and releasing the pleasant aroma of Black Cavendish tobacco into the moist air.

Jimmy stirred the sundae so he could scoop up the vanilla ice cream, chocolate syrup and Spanish peanuts in one mouthful. "Tin Roof Sundaes, how appropriate for this weather." On cue, the rain fell even harder. They laughed.

Mame sighed as she finished her sundae. "Wish we could take this roof with us. It's going to be a soggy walk back to the inn."

"No need to worry about that," the stranger said as he turned around. "I can give you kids a lift. Which direction are you heading?"

"We're at O'Hara's Octagon Inn up the road."

The man nodded. "Ah yes, I know it well—an Italianate stucco house erected in the last century. You know, I built the new porch for the main entry. Used lumber from the surrounding hillsides."

"You don't say! Oh, the spindles and framing of the porch roof are beautiful," Mame said. "They remind me of the work on our home. The brackets holding up the porch roof are hand-carved grape leaves."

He smiled at her slyly. "Grapes you say? Hmm. Where are you from?"

"Penn Yan."

"Do you live on Main Street?"

Jimmy wasn't comfortable with the man's line of questioning. "Why do you ask?" he interrupted.

"I'm an architect as well as a builder. What you described sounds like the Queen Anne I built on that street."

"Does it have a wraparound porch?" Mame asked, clutching the empty sundae dish to her chest.

"Of course, and it's a grand one, too. Do you folks live there?"

The architect introduced himself as Albert Rotils and offered the couple a lift in his Packard Runabout parked across the street. After a breathless dash to the vehicle, they had a lively conversation about local architecture during the drive back to O'Hara's in the pouring rain. Jimmy enjoyed their enlightening conversation so much that he invited Mr. Rotils to join them for afternoon tea. Over strong Darjeeling and light, summery sandwiches, the trio waxed poetically about the home that Rotils built.

"One of my favorite parts of the interior is the L-shaped staircase," Mame said. "I love the wide landing and those posts with the carved grape bunches."

"Oh yes, I did those also. Found the inspiration for the carving on some William Morris wallpaper. Say, you should come and see my lakeside bungalow while you're in town. Think you'd appreciate my handiwork there. Doing anything tomorrow? I'll have my wife make her famous roast chicken dinner. We live about five miles outside of the village in Urbana, just down the West Lake Road. Won't take you long to drive there."

Mame looked at Jimmy and grinned. "Well, we didn't give my mother a specific time when we'd be home, so sure. We'd love to join you."

The rain hardly let up that afternoon after Mr. Rotils left, putting a damper on sightseeing plans. Jimmy suggested they catch a movie at the Park Theater. "That Gary Cooper film, *The Wedding Night*, is playing at eight. Let's go."

"Sounds like an appropriate title for our anniversary celebration," Mame said with a sly smile.

During the movie they heard insistent rain falling on the theater's roof. Sometimes its drumming was so loud it almost drowned out the conversation on the screen. Then what started out as a funny romantic film took a dark twist. Jimmy and Mame grimaced as they exited the theater. *So much for setting an amorous mood*, he thought.

"Well that was quite the spirit lifter," Jimmy quipped as opened their umbrella.

"Do you suppose the wife left him? Oh, what a sad tale," Mame said as she wrapped her arm around his and snuggled close to him under the fabric dome. She accidentally stepped into a puddle of standing water and it splashed up her leg, soaking the hem of her dress. "Jeepers creepers, hope I haven't ruined my shoe."

Cold rain muddled with the muggy air, conjuring eerie phantoms of mist that raced toward the windshield as they drove back to the inn. The wipers had difficulty keeping pace with the downpour and Jimmy gritted his teeth as he struggled to see the edge of the road. They were relieved to be back on the inn's porch and shook water off their sodden umbrella over the railing that Albert Rotils built.

"Wonder if this rain will ever end?" Jimmy said, noticing water pooling on the lawn.

The next day the sun did come out and it felt as hot to him as it had that day he was adrift in the rowboat—an uncomfortable memory. The blazing sun bore down like a blowtorch on the rain-soaked village grounds. Steam rose from the sidewalk as they arrived for the nine o'clock Mass at the Catholic church. Parishioners fanned themselves while the pastor read the Gospel account of Jesus giving a lakeside sermon.

Jimmy closed his eyes and pictured the scene as Jesus standing in that same rowboat he'd drifted in fifteen years ago, and he was talking to a crowd gathered in a vineyard down the lake road. In his own version of the gospel, he saw farmers planting rooted stock into freshly tilled soil curving down toward Keuka. Then suddenly a dark cloud drifted over the hilltop and unleashed a furious rain. The people strained to hear the words of Jesus, who seemed not to notice the torrent racing down the slopes toward him as it yanked out the freshly planted vines. Jimmy realized that as he and Mame were standing on the shore listening, they were being surrounded by rising water. When they cried out in fear, Jesus picked up a vine floating by and said "Hold on to this and climb to safety." They did as he said and made it over the hill to a field where the sun was shining.

Jimmy crackled out a snore so loud that it startled him awake. He saw the congregation turn their heads toward him and laugh. Mame blushed a deep scarlet as she shrank in her pew. On their way out of the church, the priest shook Jimmy's hand. "Hope you had a good rest, son." He winked at Mame. She rolled her eyes.

Jimmy's face displayed no reaction to the pastor's humor. "Actually, it was a bit of a nightmare. Jesus was giving his sermon from a boat out on the lake here," he said pointing down the street. "A terrible storm came up and he gave us a grapevine to hold onto."

The priest leaned toward Jimmy and whispered, "Now son, remember that even in this village of plentiful, wonderful wine, temperance is wise. Hello, Mrs. Carroll, have you and your husband gotten used to life on the new farm?" he continued, talking to the woman behind Jimmy and Mame.

"You better take a nap before we go over to the Rotils' house for dinner this afternoon," Mame said. I'll call mother and let her know that we'll be home sometime before ten o'clock."

Chapter 8

Albert Rotils and his wife Yvonne lived in a stone and wood bungalow nestled in a cove about five miles outside of the village. She greeted them at the door and led them through the house to the lakeside screened porch where Albert was reading the Sunday paper.

"Welcome, friends, have a seat. What can we get you to drink? Wine? A highball? Iced tea?"

Jimmy mopped his sweaty brow with the back of his hand and thought a Manhattan would be just the thing, but recalled the pastor's admonition.

"I'll have an iced tea. Honey, would you like a Manhattan?" Mame nodded and followed their hostess into the kitchen.

It wasn't the best day to be roasting a chicken—the kitchen was as hot as a brick oven—but the aroma was heavenly. At least where the men relaxed there was a breeze off the lake rustling pendulous willow boughs shading the porch. The women chatted about family recipes as Albert and Jimmy sat down to discuss the All Star Game that would be played at Cleveland Stadium the next day. (Albert was curious when Jimmy moved his chair around so his back was to the lake.)

"Hope Gehrig eats his Wheaties tomorrow." Albert said.

Jimmy nodded and laughed. "Good thing Lefty's pitching. I think the American League can't lose with him. Do you think the Yankees will make it to the Series?"

"Watch that Bill Dickey, I say. Not only can he catch, his batting skills keep improving. Did you hear that Browns game back in June when he had four RBIs?"

"When they slaughtered St. Louis? You bet!"

Yvonne and Mame returned with drinks for the men and then set the table in the dining room.

"Here's mud in your eye, Jimmy." Albert clicked his glass with his dinner guest, sipped his Manhattan and then sat back in his chair looking out at the lake. "That brook alongside the cottage is sure noisy today after all this rain."

"We could barely hear the movie at the Park," Jimmy said.

"I suppose it's good after the drought we've had this summer. Sometimes it can become too much of a good thing. Now the ground is saturated."

Jimmy looked up toward the sky above the brook and noted it was getting cloudy again. "Well, we'll find out soon. It looks like more is on the way."

Yvonne set out a mouth-watering meal of roast chicken, giblet gravy, buttermilk biscuits, mashed potatoes, green beans and a fruited gelatin mold. She told Jimmy to sit on the end of the table facing the lake, but he balked.

"Oh, may we switch seats," Mame interrupted, "I just adore looking out at the lake."

"Are you sure? I thought the gentleman would like to sit at the foot of the table."

"Please humor my wife, Yvonne. She's a helpless romantic and never tires of sunset-gazing." Jimmy kissed Mame as they passed each other and he whispered, "Thank you." He didn't want to have to explain his phobia of the lake to their new friends just yet.

It was such a filling meal that they decided to clear the table and wash the dishes before having coffee and dessert on the porch. It was raining softly when Yvonne brought out her signature yellow cake slathered with thick milk chocolate frosting. The rain clamored on the roof making conversation over dessert futile. Each was silently concerned by the fervor with which it churned the brook.

"What time is it, dear? I told Mother we'd be back home by ten."

"Just after nine."

Mame nodded to Jimmy. "We better get going. It will probably be foggy again on the lake road. Albert and Yvonne, thank you for a lovely meal. We'll have to reciprocate on our own wraparound porch."

"I'd love to see that house again," Albert said as they headed for the driveway. "Would like to get a look at how she's holding up. I built her twenty-two years ago. We finished just before the snow flew that fall."

"I'll have Mame call Yvonne and arrange a date. Thank you both for a delightful visit." Jimmy shook Albert's hand, and then they dashed to their car in the pouring rain.

As the Rotils waved at their departing guests, Yvonne said "How odd. Did you notice how he wouldn't even glance toward the lake?" Albert nodded.

"Wonder if he has a fear of it."

Water streamed down the short rise of the driveway, and once they turned onto West Lake Road toward Hammondsport, they noticed water cascading from private driveways across the road toward the lake. At a bend in the road near Urbana Gulch, water rushed so fast across the road that the car floated slightly toward the other lane. Mame gasped as Jimmy hit the gas and steered back into their lane, out of the temporary stream.

"Do you think we should pull over until the rain stops?" Mame asked as she looked up the road. Jimmy glanced in his rearview mirror at the water they'd just driven through and gripped the steering wheel tighter.

"No, we could get caught here. Better press on to Hammondsport." The scene made Jimmy recall his nightmare in Mass that morning. Was it coming true?

"Honey, something's in the road up ahead. Be careful!"

Headlights illuminated a good-sized tree bough that was blocking both lanes. A car was stopped on the opposite side of the road and they saw the driver get out and try to move the bough, but it was too heavy.

"I'm going to go help him. Stay put, dear," Jimmy said as he went to open the car door, then turned back and kissed his wife.

The men gestured to each other in the downpour and Mame watched as they dragged the bough into the culvert on her side of the road. Jimmy tipped his fedora at the other man and got back in their car.

"You're utterly drenched, dear. Thank God that nice man was coming along the other direction."

The rain doubled its intensity and Mame used a handkerchief from her purse to wipe fog off the windshield so Jimmy could see the road better. Up ahead cars were starting to swerve into their lane and then the car in front of them came to a sudden stop.

"Rats! Traffic's all balled up. Wonder what's going on?" Jimmy said. As cars started to move again slowly, the headlights illuminated a collapsed bit of pavement in the other lane, worn out by the water gushing down the steep rise across the road.

"At this rate we won't get to Hammondsport before midnight," Mame said quietly.

"Well, at least your mother lives across the street from us. If she needed to, she could bring the kids over there to sleep." Before he finished his words, a bright arc of lightning flashed over the lake followed immediately by a crashing boom.

"I hope Patrick and Frances aren't afraid. You don't suppose she's out anywhere with them?"

"On a rainy Sunday night like this? Pshaw! She'd have more sense than that. I'm just glad I didn't have a Manhattan or four. Could you imagine driving through this if you were zozzled?"

Mame smiled briefly as she shook her head. They edged around the detoured traffic and continued down the road. Windshield wipers were useless in the torrent and through their distorted view they saw kerosene flare smudge pots flickering ahead, where apparently the shoulder washed out completely.

"We've got to get off of this highway before it all crumbles into the lake," Jimmy said in an agitated tone. He rolled down the window to get a clearer view of the danger. The stress of the situation unsettled Mame.

"It's my fault we're caught in this mess. Why did I have that second helping of potatoes and gravy," she asked, rubbing her stomach.

"You're right. If you hadn't eaten that, we'd have missed all of this fun," Jimmy teased in a tone that she knew had no malice.

"Maybe I saved us from plummeting into that hole in the road before they got here and put out the flares. You may thank me now."

Jimmy took his right hand off the steering wheel and gave Mame a quick embrace. "We're going to get out of this just fine. Right?" She nodded, but then bit her lip.

If it had been a pleasant evening, they would have completed the five-mile trip back into Hammondsport by now and would be well up the East Side of the lake toward Penn Yan. On this horrid evening, though, in all the time since they'd left Albert and Yvonne's home, they'd made it just three miles down the lake. Then they encountered a large uprooted tree blocking the road. Several men gathered around to attempt to drag it out of the way, but it was too heavy.

"Oh dear, what are we going to do? What if the rain doesn't stop? We'll be swept into the lake!" The pitch of

Mame's voice rose as she spoke. Jimmy shared her fears, but had to pretend he didn't.

"These men will figure something out. Don't worry," he said touching her shoulder. He got out of the car just as a man from a nearby cottage walked up the road carrying a couple of crosscut saws. The men got to work on the trunk, but trying to cut through the wet wood was laborious.

Mame tapped her foot unconsciously as she waited in the car (it had been a good hour and a half by then), but she didn't want to be out there in the rain either. She glanced over her shoulder at the side of the road, illuminated by headlights. The deep culvert was nearly filled with water and soon the water would rise on the road around the car. They HAD to get out of there quickly. She heard a cheer and looked toward the men to see them rolling a hunk from the middle of the tree out of the road. Jimmy ran back to the car, his clothes wholly soaked, and was the first to drive through the "gate."

The intensity of the rain varied so every once in a while they could actually see the road ahead clearly, but there were still several obstacles they encountered that kept slowing their progress. Mame gasped when they cruised by an overturned car being attended to by other motorists who stopped to help. Jimmy thought about pulling over, too, but all he could see in his mind were the faces of his son and daughter. They had to get home safely and as soon as possible for the children.

As they neared the village of Hammondsport, West Lake Road turned into Pulteney Street. Cold Brook Creek ran beside it, along the northern edge of the village from the Hammondsport Glen to the lake's inlet below. A stone retaining wall had been built to channel the water on this path instead of the direction it took naturally years ago through the center of the village.

Several inches of rain that fell on the hilltops Sunday evening merged with runoff from Saturday's downpour. It rushed down the glen's gorge, cascaded over fifteen waterfalls, raged through the creek bed and crashed into the distillery at the foot of the glen. The force of the water uprooted a large tree nearby and tossed it over the retaining wall, wedging it against two trees at the corner of Church and Pulteney streets. Its massive trunk dammed water behind it and diverted the swollen creek into the heart of the village. When water burst through the distillery it also freed 1,200 casks of brandy (weighing a quarter of a ton each), sweeping them up into the current rushing through Hammondsport.

At this ill-timed moment after midnight Jimmy and Mame finally reached the village. Their car stalled when it encountered the flash flood racing down Pulteney Street. Jimmy struggled to restart it so he could back up the car, but water crept up the tires too quickly.

"C'mon, engine. Start, dammit!" He looked toward Mame just as a brandy barrel careened toward the car.

"Watch out, Mame! *NO*!" he screamed as the impact tore off the bumper and sent the car spinning back down the road. They clutched each other as the car slid off the pavement, away from the flood and tipped onto the passenger side.

"You all right, Mame?" Her mouth gaped from the shock and all she could do was nod.

"Hurry! We have to get out before the car fills with water." Jimmy kicked open his door, grabbed Mame's hand and fueled by a rush of adrenaline pushed her out on top of the sideways car, then pulled himself out. They'd had just enough time to steady themselves upright, when the water switched course and swerved back toward them. As they clung to each other, a dark mass of debris smashed into the car. The impact knocked them against a tree and they both reached out and grabbed onto it, pulling themselves into the crook of a wide, sturdy bough. Another brandy barrel plowed toward the car. Metal groaned as the massive barrel smashed into the car's hood. The debris chasing its wake shoved their car toward the lake.

"This is our only chance for survival, Mame. Hold tight," he said wrapping his arms around her to grab onto the trunk.

"Jimmy! Oh, Lord! Save us—for Patrick, for Frances!" Mame yelled; her cries were barely audible over the roar of the water and debris rushing through the village.

"Wonder what's gonna be left in the morning," Jimmy added as rain lashed his face.

"Let's just pray that we live to see it." Mame dug her fingernails into the tree bark to tighten her grip.

Soon the fast-rising water lapped at the soles of their shoes.

"How are you holding up, Mame?" Jimmy asked about a half hour later.

"OK, I guess," she said, her tremulous voice not matching her words. "And you?"

"Same here."

Just then a neon-bright lightning bolt stung the lake and they were shocked by the devastation it illuminated. Mame cried out when a tremendous thunderclap exploded a split-second later. Its concussion felt like an artillery gun fired next to them. Jimmy rubbed her back with his hand. With one hand free, his body shifted and he slipped down the tree a little. Mame screamed.

"Jimmy, NO!"

Hearing her voice, and surrounded by water in the darkness reminded him of that horrible night. His eyes fluttered and he wondered if he was still back in that moment of drowning and he'd just hallucinated the past fifteen years. His dark thoughts were deflected when a kitchen chair floated past and pinged his ankle. Jimmy yelped with pain, but was happy for the reminder that no, he was still alive—at least for now. He mustered the strength to climb to his previous position on the tree. Together they hung on through the night, at times reciting the rosary, at times singing Cole Porter songs, anything to keep each other alert until a hint of dawn seeped through the clouds.

What they began to see around them was unbelievable. Keuka Lake's beautiful blue water had swollen way beyond its banks, taking on a chocolate brown color as it swirled against first-floor windows of cottages down the road. A flotilla of brandy barrels bobbed in the lake. Random debris floated alongside, from grapevines to a store manikin, a dead milk cow and a baby carriage. When dawn arrived fully, they saw eight- to ten-foot-tall piles of stones and concrete rising from where the road and several houses had been. The water receded gradually around them leaving a peanut buttery muck.

"Thank you, Lord! We made it, dear." Jimmy sighed as he jumped down from the tree, his shoes sinking into the mud below. "Jump to me, Mame." He caught her and set her legs down gently. They leaned against the tree that saved them, hugged tightly and sobbed. A policeman digging through the debris up the road heard their crying and yelled out to them.

"Hey there! You two OK?"

"Yes. Our car is probably in the lake, though."

"Cars can be replaced. Stay put and let me show you the path through this mess."

Mame felt like every muscle in her legs had been stretched like a rubber band after clinging to that tree for hours. (The distress gave her a wobbly gait that lasted for a few days after the flood.) Jimmy walked alongside her, his arm supporting her lower back, as they followed the policeman on a meandering path over crossed floorboards through towers of debris.

"You kids were sure lucky to escape drowning."

His words chilled Mame and she paused to hug Jimmy, noting the tears in his eyes. He nodded at the policeman.

"Wait until you see Orchard Street. The flood dredged it down about seven feet. Looks like the Erie Canal!"

With the sun fully up they saw that charming and picturesque Hammondsport had been tumbled and ravaged like a war zone. Debris piles cast shadows over upended cars, uprooted trees and houses pushed off their foundations. Workers pushed steam shovels through the mess, releasing scoops of soggy debris into waiting dump trucks.

"I need to get back to Patrick and Frances. How are we going to get home?" Mame cried as she pulled on Jimmy's shirt.

"Ma'am, you aren't going anywhere today. We're getting reports that the West Lake Road is impassable and parts of the East Side highway are missing."

"Is your phone working? May we use it to call my mother-in-law and let her know we're OK?"

"No, but the radio is. We can call the station in Penn Yan and have them bring a message to her. In the meantime, there's a shelter being set up where you can stay until the roads are clear."

"Thank you. Let's hope that's just hours, not days."

Chapter 9

Mame rarely travelled more than five miles from her home after that terrifying night. She felt that just like her husband, she'd been given a second chance at life and didn't want to do anything that would tempt fate. That mileage was her self-imposed safety zone, a distance she determined she could walk if she had to make it home without a car.

Instead of her going anywhere to see her friends, they would come visit her for a chat on the wraparound porch. As she rocked in the chair next to her husband, she began to understand why the motion brought Jimmy such comfort years ago. Maybe it was the dappled light slipping between the tall elms to dance across the bluestone sidewalk. Maybe it was the gentle creaking of the rockers against the cedar floor. Maybe it was the serenity of their quiet street, broken occasionally by the laughter of children in distant yards.

She preferred that her children play on their own property. They'd be out front when she was in the rocking chair, they'd move to the back when she was in the kitchen and could see them from the screen door. Jimmy noted this obsessiveness, but who was he to talk? It was he who suggested finally that they get in the car for a drive to their favorite ice cream stand a couple of miles away. That was their first outing near the lake after the flood.

It was a sunny day, which helped soothe Mame's nerves. She didn't want to go anywhere in the car if it was raining. She'd developed an automobile-specific claustrophobia that kicked in whenever there were dark clouds on the horizon or even the faintest spit of rain. Her tension triggered panic attacks and she'd feel as if she couldn't breathe, her palms sweated and a sense of hyperawareness of herself took hold of her (as if her mind separated from her body). The attacks terrified her and shifted her mindset to her own mortality. She began wearing a Miraculous Medal under her clothes hoping that it would invoke the protection of the Blessed Virgin Mary to calm her fears through the attacks. Jimmy suggested that she try chewing gum when unease hit, and so she also never travelled anywhere without a pack of Chiclets.

The Flood of '35 had a profound effect on Mame. She'd lost some of her spunk, self-assurance and fearlessness. Her focus shifted to domestic issues rather than the world at large. She improved her cooking skills, much inspired by the notes Virginia left behind in her cookbook. The smells of roasts or bread baking in the oven brought her a comfort comparable to what a child feels when tucked into bed at night. Her family did not mind this newfound creativity in the kitchen. The ever-lanky Jimmy began to gain weight for the first time in his married life.

Unfortunately, the flood also carried away some of her natural good humor. Jimmy tried to keep all conversations light, despite when they'd drift toward difficult subjects. But then Mame would zero in on the negative. When she got together with friends, she'd be the first to rattle off a litany of friends who had illnesses or a death in the family. It concerned Jimmy to see this marked change in his wife, although he understood fully its source. After all, the car tipped onto her side during the flood. What if he hadn't been there with her? She'd have drowned! He, more than anyone close to her, knew precisely what that fear felt like.

With this shift in his wife's personality, Jimmy stepped forward to help more with raising their son and daughter. They were both bright children and Mame had already done a wonderful job teaching them to read, giving them access to books beyond their grade levels. He grew concerned when she mentioned she was having second thoughts about teaching this fall and perhaps she'd better contact the school to let them know in time to get a replacement. One day he sat her down and pointed out that her life was a lesson to their children. If she gave in to her fears, why would they ever try to achieve anything in their lives? He reminded her of what she'd told him after his earlier brush with death.

The example resonated with Mame's memories of his struggles and she decided to keep her job for now. However, once school resumed, they started their weekdays at daily Mass and remained afterward in the church to say a decade of the rosary. Patrick grew restless with this new ritual quickly. He could be home reading his comic books instead of sitting here, droning decades of Hail Marys. The prayers had the opposite effect on Frances, who was convinced that she was destined to become a nun like that Carmelite, Saint Thérèse of Lisieux. She hadn't told her mother about this revelation; she did mimic Thèrése by spending her days doing little things quietly to bring her closer to Jesus. Those things included remembering to put the lid on the milk bottle tightly or taking a spider found in the house outside so it could escape the swipe of her fastidious mother's broom. May became Frances's favorite month for the ritual of picking fresh flowers to place before the statue of the Blessed Virgin Mary in their den.

Jimmy was the first to note his daughter's religious fervor. She was a beautiful child with deep auburn hair that matched her mother's and a thin build that matched his. He knew one day she'd be fighting potential husbands away, but he feared that could be undone by a detour to a convent. He was grateful that she'd inherited their faith but hoped, secretly (and felt some guilt about this), that she wouldn't miss the opportunity to get married and raise a family.

***

Being the firstborn child and only son, Patrick received a lot of attention from his father who wanted him to learn as many life skills as possible early on so he'd be prepared for any emergency. During the summer Patrick turned three years old, that included letting Aunt Bertha teach him how to swim at the McGraths' cottage. She was a strong swimmer and showed much patience with her pupil. Jimmy had loved to swim, but not surprisingly after the accident, he would just sit on the dock and dangle his feet to watch the lessons. It gave him great satisfaction to watch Patrick doggie paddle successfully to his great aunt in the shallows by the dock.

Mame, who had spent much of her time working on Patrick's reading skills, grew frustrated when he became easily distracted. As soon as he was old enough, he preferred to spend the day outdoors playing rather than stuck inside with a book. Despite his indifference, each night before he fell asleep he insisted that his mother read to him from *The Boy's King Arthur*.

Patrick would place his hand on the page, preventing his mother from turning it when he wanted to savor the detailed illustrations by N.C. Wyeth.

"What's that?" he'd ask his mother, pointing at Sir Lancelot's uniform.

"Chain mail."

"Is it heavy?"

"It's made of links of metal."

"I could lift that. I'm strong."

"So you are," Mame said with a smile as she continued the story.

By the time their son Pat (as he was later called) was in high school, he'd earned the nickname Tiger, not only for his red-orange hair but for his strength and tenacity on the baseball field. One of the umpires gave him the nickname and it stuck unfortunately. He was also tall and lean at a young age—like his father, so when he ran for a steal (even when the coach wasn't signaling for him to do so), he'd dive toward it with arms fully extended, clawing toward the base. Jimmy was so proud of him that he'd try to get out of work early on game days to at least catch the last couple of innings.

Pat was scouted to play baseball by a couple of colleges. However, despite the scholarships offered his way, he chose to enlist in the U.S. Army fresh out of high school and served in the Pacific Theater toward the end of World War II. Mame wondered if it was all those hours of reading about the Knights of the Round Table that inspired him to defend his country.

Chapter 10

Frances O'Donoghue grew to be the perfect blend of her parents. From her mother she inherited a love of dance, reading and a tendency to speak her mind even though her opinion had not been sought. From her father she inherited an insatiable interest in science and deep blue eyes that gave her an authoritative air. Her older brother's instincts were sharpened to protect her—it was no bother walking her to and from school. She didn't mind his attention although she felt she could do it on her own.

Unlike Pat, Frances was a voracious reader and her mother had to encourage her to go outside for fresh air and exercise. When Frances did, she was often found reenacting a scene from one of her favorite books, James Fenimore Cooper's *The Deerslayer*. Her mother laughed when she'd wander around quoting Natty Bumppo: "'Tis nature, 'tis nature." Frances excelled in school and most years had the highest average in her class.

Mame had great hopes for her daughter's life: a fascinating career as an educator, perhaps a foray into politics or maybe she'd go into medicine, like her father. Instead of a pharmacy degree, though, Frances would be likelier to get a veterinary degree—oh, how she loved animals! Her mother dubbed her Francine of Assisi for the way she cared for injured wild animals in the neighborhood, fed the birds in the back yard and even picked up worms on the street displaced by rainstorms and resettled them among blades of grass. Frances named the chipmunk that used to show up in the far corner of the wraparound porch—"Reginald." She'd set out little treats for it daily. Patrick teased her ceaselessly about this habit, but she just ignored him and kept feeding her "pet."

Mame taught her daughter how to garden, which they did together on afternoons when Pat and Jimmy played catch in the front yard. She noted that her daughter's skills lay not so much in cultivating flowers and vegetables, but in removing all the weeds and bugs that threatened the plants. She'd dump the weeds in a pile behind the garage, noting that the birds often used them for nest building. Slugs were carted off the tomato and pepper plants and placed in a nice bit of damp ground under the back hedge that rimmed a dairy cow pasture.

When she was twelve, Frances was delighted to hear that her cousin Bill O'Malley and his wife June were expecting their first child. She couldn't wait for the arrival! Grandmother Rose taught her how to knit, and Frances began making a wardrobe for the baby. She was convinced that the child would be a girl, and with money saved from babysitting, she bought several skeins of pale pink wool yarn from the department store downtown. Frances knitted a sweater, booties, a tasseled hat, scarf and mittens. Once she finished a piece, Frances wrapped it in white paper tied with a blue grosgrain ribbon and dropped it off at Bill and June's house a couple of blocks away. June was near her delivery date now, so it took her a little bit longer to answer the door than if Bill was home. She always welcomed Frances warmly and often served her milk and peanut butter cookies.

One late October afternoon when Frances stopped by June winced during their conversation on the couch.

"Simmer down in there," she said laughingly.

"What's the baby doing?" Frances asked, her eyes widening.

"It feels as if it's kicking me."

"Hah-hah, the little rascal! Do you know what you're going to name it yet?"

"Well, if it's a boy we'll name him George after my father. I like the name Maggie if we have a girl. Ooh! There the baby goes again. Want to feel it?"

"Really?" June placed Frances's hand gently on her abdomen where the baby was kicking.

"Do you feel it?" June asked.

Frances held her breath waiting for a sign from the baby. And just like that, she felt it kick faintly. She giggled.

"Wow, this baby's strong!" Frances rested her head on June's abdomen. "The baby just kicked my ear," she laughed. "Hey you, stop kicking your mom!"

June laughed, and then winced again, groaning as she shifted in her seat.

"Ow, that must have been a big kick," Frances said, grimacing sympathetically.

"That wasn't a kick, but it can't be a contraction," June said as she held her abdomen and her eyes fluttered. "I'm not due until a few more weeks. These pains are much worse today. I started having them two days ago. I think this baby will be here sooner that we thought. I hope it waits until Bill arrives home."

Frances smiled. She couldn't wait to hold that baby. She handed June the neatly wrapped package. When she opened the gift, June held up the delicate sweater with buttons shaped like roses. "Oh, this is just adorable. Your work looks so professional." Her words made Frances grin. "With all this pink, though, what will I do if the baby is a boy?" June asked, laughing. Frances shrugged.

"Maybe he can set a new style?" She folded her arms and wondered if her instinct *was* wrong and the baby was a boy. It would be sad to see these clothes go to waste. "I know! I'll dye everything blue."

June laughed heartily and folded the sweater on the coffee table. Her smile faded as she let out a deep groan. Frances felt a pain in her abdomen, too, as if her body was acting in sympathy with her cousin's pain.

"Honey, would you be a dear and call your cousin Bill at work. The number is right next to the...," June paused and grimaced, "to the phone. I think it might be time to get me to the hospital."

Frances was eager to help at this exciting moment and dialed the telephone. As she waited for Bill to answer, she heard June groan again, this one sounding more intense. Again she felt a sympathetic pain in her own abdomen.

"Bill, this is your cousin Frances and you have to come home right now 'cause the baby is coming and June is screaming and...."

"Oh dear Lord, my water just broke!" June yelled.

"The baby? It's coming *NOW*? I'll be right there, Frances." Bill hung up before she could say anything else.

Frances ran back to June, who was gritting her teeth to fight the pain.

"Listen carefully, Frances." June continued deliberately, "I need you to boil some...water, *OWWW*!" When June yelled it terrified Frances. "Get some towels and come back here with a kitchen knife."

"A knife? But...why do you need that?"

"PLEASE, Frances. Just do as I *sayyyyy*. *OWWWoooo*!"

Frances froze for a few seconds as she tried to imagine what the knife was for, and when June cried out again she ran to the kitchen and did as she'd been told. She found a three-quart pot, filled it with water, set it on the stove and turned the burner under it on high. There was a thick pile of dish towels in a kitchen drawer that she grabbed along with the butcher knife. Her hands shook as she held them out to June. She noticed there was a wet spot on the couch and at the same time, Frances felt like she'd wet her own underpants from the fear of what was occurring. She didn't pay much attention to her own problem because June was screaming nonstop now.

"The baby's coming, Frances! Help me get ready. Get some extra...*OWWWooo*, some extra pillows from the other couch." Frances fluffed the pillows and helped June get comfortable on the couch with her legs bent, ready to deliver. Frances stayed as calm as a delivery room nurse, even though she was shaking visibly. She even had the courage to not look away and prepared herself mentally for the baby making its way out of the birth canal.

June screamed so loud it hurt Frances's ears. Again, she felt a sharp pain in her own abdomen.

"Where's Bill? Didn't you call him? He needs to be here, that *sonofabitch*!"

Frances had never heard a woman swear before and her jaw gaped.

"Something's wrong, Frances. I can feel it. Can you see the baby yet?"

Frances did not want to look "there," but when she did she saw tiny toes exiting June's birth canal. "Now I see what's been kicking you. Two tiny feet." She smiled as she thought how perfect they were.

"FEET? Oh *NO*!"

"What's the matter...?" Frances asked, confused that her cousin wasn't happy. Just then Bill raced up the front steps and blew through the front door.

"Honey! You can't have the baby here. Stop!"

"Stop, Bill? I can't stop!" June screamed at her husband. "Dammit! Something's wrong and the baby's breech. Get the doctor!"

"Frances, call the doctor!" Bill ordered. "Please! His number is by the phone."

She nodded and ran to the phone. When the doctor's receptionist answered Frances couldn't help but blurt the message. "Get the doctor here as soon as possible. The baby's coming! Its feet are already out!"

The receptionist tried to calm Frances down. "Who are you and who's having the baby?"

"It's June O'Malley! Over on Henry Street. This is her cousin, Frances O'Donoghue."

The receptionist flagged Dr. Thompson and covered the receiver of the phone. "Sounds like the O'Malley baby is coming right now and it's breeched."

"Tell Bill I'll be right there. Call an ambulance!"

Frances didn't know what to do in the midst of all the commotion and just stood by them, dumbstruck. June was screaming and Bill was trying desperately to help her. The baby's legs were out completely now, but why were they bluish? At the same moment, she felt another stab of pain in her abdomen.

"Oh Lord, this doesn't look...," Bill stopped the sentence when he realized he was speaking aloud.

"What? What's the matter?" June lifted up her head and then felt another blinding flash of pain.

"Push, dear. PUSH!"

June scrunched up her face, curled her hands into tight fists and pushed as hard as she could. It worked! The edge of the baby's abdomen was now visible.

"That's it! Good work, darling. Wish that damn doctor would hurry up and get here. Hang on now, she's almost here!"

"She?" June said as she gasped backward from the pain. *It's a girl*, Frances thought, and she immediately smiled as she pictured little baby Maggie dressed in her soft pink sweater.

"What's this child doing in here," the doctor said as he pushed open the front door and raced to June's side. "GO!" he barked at Frances. The doctor carried his bag over to the couch and knelt beside June. "Let's see. OK, she's almost out. I'm going to have to coax the head a bit. Bill come over to this side of me and hold your wife steady."

Frances stood in the kitchen crying, nervous about what was going on in the other room. She could hear the doctor speaking in a low voice to June and Bill. It seemed to be taking forever in there. Finally she heard the doctor yelling.

"Dammit, the umbilical cord is caught on her neck!"

June raised her head slightly as Bill patted her shoulders.

"Relax, darling. I'm sure all will be OK," he said as he saw the doctor take scalpel out of his bag. He nodded at Bill to keep holding on to his wife as he severed the cord and then tried to unwrap it from the baby's neck.

The room went silent as all held their breath.

"I don't feel my baby inside me anymore. Is she out?" June asked, opening her eyes and seeing tears streaming down Bill's face.

"Yes," Dr. Thompson said. That's all Frances needed to hear. She ran into the living room just as the doctor placed the lifeless baby on a towel. The moment was surreal to her. The beautiful baby was formed perfectly yet she was blue and still. Dr. Thompson sat staring at the dead child with his arms outstretched, as if he were in shock. There was blood all over his hands. It looked like a crime scene.

Frances couldn't help herself and gasped. "Oh no!"

"What's going on? Why isn't she crying? Is something wrong with my baby?" June cried out in mournful unison with the ambulance siren coming up the street. Frances couldn't take it anymore and escaped out the back door. She ran up the few blocks to home and once she arrived, noticed there was blood on her legs. To think she had the blood of that sweet baby on her made her tremble and she locked herself in the bathroom to clean it off. There was blood all over her legs. But how? She wasn't that close to the baby. Was she being tested, stricken like a saint? The bleeding wouldn't stop. Frances sat on the closed toilet seat and began to sob. Her mother heard her and rushed to the door and knocked.

"What's wrong, dear?"

Frances needed her mother now and opened the door, clinging to her as she shook from her sobbing. Mame looked down and saw the red stain on the back of her daughter's dress and gave her a hug.

"Now Frances, there is nothing to cry about. That blood means you've just become a young woman today."

"I didn't want to see it. It died...."

"What? Oh daughter, nothing died. It's perfectly natural."

That didn't seem to console Frances so Mame held her out and looked into her eyes. "Every young girl goes through this around your age. Once a month now you'll bleed as a way of preparing your body to carry a baby one day, just like Bill's wife June." Mame had no idea why those words made her daughter hysterical. Was this tied into that religious fervor of her daughter's?

"The baby...died!" Frances's lower lip trembled, her teeth chattered and her whole body began to shake.

"What baby? Oh heavens, wait...not...June's?" Mame asked, aghast. Frances nodded.

"I was there and she started getting contractions and I called Bill and the baby was breech and the doctor came but the umbilical cord was wrapped around her...," she sighed deeply, "and then June screamed, and then...."

Mame hugged her daughter, stroking Frances's wavy auburn hair that looked like her own when she was that age. "Now Frances, calm down. Breathe. It's hard to understand why God took this baby before she could live. He must have loved that baby so much that He asked the angels to bring her straight to Him." Frances snuffled into her mother's shoulder. "Hush now, my child." Mame slipped off the Miraculous Medal she always wore and draped it around her daughter's neck. "The Blessed Mother will watch over you always, Frances. Take comfort in her eternal love."

Frances, still clinging to her mother, held the medal in her hand. The serene face of Jesus's mother calmed her sniffling. Mame realized to her horror that the arrival of her daughter's first menstrual period coincided with the death of Bill and June's first child. *Oh, poor Frances,* Mame thought. *She will always link these two events.* Mame hugged Frances as long as it took to quiet her sobs—about an hour—and then cleaned her up, showed her how to fold a rag to catch her flow and put her to bed.

"I'll tell father and Pat that you've come down with a cold. OK?"

Frances nodded as she winced from another cramp.

When Jimmy came home from work, Mame called him away from Pat out to the far front porch rockers and sat for a talk about the day's events.

"Poor Bill and June, they must be racked with grief," Jimmy said, staring ahead. Mame reached over and touched his hand as a tear slid down his cheek. Upstairs, Frances could hear their voices drifting into her bedroom from below.

"I guess the baby was beautiful," Mame said. "Well, at least she was born into a family that loved and wanted her."

Her mother's words stunned Frances. How could anyone *not* want a baby? Were there actually people who would give away—or worse—abandon a child? She thought about all St. Joseph and the Blessed Virgin Mary endured before the baby Jesus came into the world. That's right, she'd forgotten, there were some people who didn't even want him alive at that moment. The pain of another menstrual cramp reminded her that now her body was preparing itself to carry a baby someday. No matter what happened, she would always protect the lives of her children. She closed her eyes and saw the doctor's bloodstained hands held out like those of Jesus on the cross. The synchronicity of these two events had a meaning, she thought. She wondered if it was a revelation from God that He had a significant mission for her.

Chapter 11

Frances's religious fervor did not abate as she advanced into high school, making Mame and Jimmy consider the real possibility that she might pursue the religious life. They'd even discussed it with their pastor, Father O'Neill. What should they do? Father suggested that they just let the Lord lead her way. What neither imagined was Frances being led to the likes of Joe McNamara.

He was three years ahead of her at Penn Yan Academy, and the brilliant Frances was a year ahead of her age group, but their paths never crossed until the graduation party at Betty Rae Miller's cottage on the West Side of Keuka Lake. Betty Rae and Frances had been best friends since first grade. Joe's buddy Eddie Barker lived in a year-round home next to the Miller's summer place. When he saw Betty Rae's mother decorating the tables outdoors and hanging up a Class of '44 banner, Eddie called Joe saying they'd have the opportunity to meet a party of girls. It wasn't an issue with either young man, actually. Since both were ineligible for the draft—Joe had a punctured eardrum and Eddie lost a kidney to disease when he was young—they were in great demand by attention-starved girls their age whose boyfriends were overseas fighting. By then, even Frances's brother Pat was somewhere in the South Pacific.

Joe arrived at Eddie's house after the party had been going on for an hour. They sat on his front porch watching the girls' lakeside revelry and deciding which of the chattering flock they'd aim for.

"I'll take the redhead," Joe said to Eddie as he lit a Lucky Strike. The two young men waited until Mrs. Miller went inside to serve her husband dinner and then strode across the lawn like movie stars in front of the press.

"Good evening, ladies," Joe purred. The girls nearly swooned as the tall young man with sun-kissed chestnut hair, deep dimples and green eyes with long sweeping lashes approached. He was dressed in khakis and a snug tennis sweater that garnered their attention immediately.

"Mind if we join the party?" Eddie asked as he sat down at the picnic table next to Betty Rae and draped his arm around her shoulder. She feigned annoyance but her blushing indicated something else.

"Eddie! You weren't invited," she protested with an elbow to his side. He mimed falling backward as if she'd delivered a mortal wound. Eddie took the ensuing laughter to mean the other girls were on his side.

"Who here wants to throw us out?" Joe asked with a smirk, scanning the crowd until his eyes locked on Frances. The girls grinned at each other, except for one. Frances stood up from the table and folded her arms in front of her.

"I do."

"Is that so, Red?" Joe asked.

"The name's Frances. Have you no manners? You weren't invited. Leave." The others laughed but Frances remained stern. Joe walked up to her and extended his hand to shake hers. She batted it away.

"Oh. I see you want to play hard to get!" He grabbed Frances, draped her over his shoulder and her sandals flew off onto the lawn. Joe carried her kicking and pounding her fists into his back as he sauntered to the end of the dock and tossed her in. The girls shrieked as they saw the splash and their friend struggling in the water. They couldn't believe he'd do such a rude thing. And Frances had never been a strong swimmer.

"That oughta cool off your hot temper," he yelled as she flailed in the water. Her dress created weight and resistance to her swimming. For a fleeting moment Frances thought of her father and panicked, splashing hard as she tried to swim to shore.

"Eddie! Your friend's a cad," Betty Rae said. "Go rescue her!"

Eddie ran toward the lake, but Joe had already removed his sweater and dived in to assist Frances.

"Leave me alone, you brute!" she screamed at Joe as he put his arm around her waist to escort her to shore.

"Relax, Red! I'm sorry. I just want to help."

"If you really want to help, then call me by my real name."

"How could I forget a beautiful name like Frances?" Joe dropped his cocky demeanor and purposefully gave her a wistful look. He saw the corners of her eyes soften slightly and knew he'd made a chink in her armor.

"C'mon, give me your hands and I'll help you stand up." She relented and struggled to her feet. Her water-weighted dress clung to her body, emphasizing each curve of her breasts and hips. *Wow*, Joe thought, *what a looker*. Frances noticed him staring at her in this vulnerable state and as soon as she was upright on the rocky bottom, she pushed him into the water and strode onto the beach.

Betty Rae ran forward with a beach towel to cover her up and they laughed as Joe dragged himself out of the lake. He walked over to the two girls and shook water off himself like a shaggy sheep dog. They cringed when he grabbed the towel from Frances to dry his hair. She crossed her arms in front of her body as if they could protect her from his stare.

"Where'd you learn your manners?" Betty Rae asked with her arms also folded tightly.

"Ask my future wife," Joe said as he tossed the towel back at Frances and pulled the tennis sweater on teasingly slow over his brawny *Tarzan*-like chest. He stuck a toothpick from the platter of hardboiled eggs between his teeth, winked and waved goodbye. Eddie followed reluctantly.

"Why'd you have to spoil all the fun, Joe?" Eddie said, trying to walk as fast as his friend.

He turned around and put his hand on Eddie's shoulder. "You've gotta leave them hungry. Did you see the look on Red when I tossed the towel back at her? She wants me. Bad."

"I wouldn't call her Red. I don't think she likes it."

"Oh, you're so wrong. She *loves* it. I can tell."

***

Mame answered the door one late June evening and was surprised to see Thelma Barker's son Eddie standing on the porch with another young man.

"Good evening, Mrs. O'Donoghue. This is my friend Joe. We were walking over to the county fairgrounds and thought we'd say hi to your daughter on the way. Is she in?"

Mame scrutinized the two young men. She couldn't recall Frances ever mentioning Eddie or this Joe fella. Had her daughter been spending time with these boys in secret? That wasn't like Frances at all. From what she'd heard, Eddie was a good kid but far from a scholar. Why would Frances have anything to do with him? She could tell that this other one was sure his looks would project provocatively across the silver screen. His cocksure stance hinted that he had no trouble attracting women of *any* age. The same would not be likely for his bumbling sidekick.

"Frances," Mame yelled toward the stairs. "A couple of boys are here to see you."

At that same moment Frances was updating her diary with the Joe McNamara incident. She'd stuck the end of the pencil in her mouth and paused after writing that Joe called her his future wife. She was envisioning her wedding dress and bouquet, and then imagined how her groom would look at her when she walked into St. Urban's on the arm of her father.

Joe was the most handsome young man she'd ever met in Penn Yan and even though she was annoyed by his rude behavior at the party, something about him fascinated her. She underlined the word *wife* and then said quietly to herself, "Did he really mean that?" Her reaction to being interrupted by visitors while she was daydreaming about their wedding annoyed her. It was probably Freddie

Brewster and George Travis, two bookish classmates of hers who'd drop by to play chess on Saturday afternoons.

"Who is it, Mother?" she called from her room.

"Thelma Barker's boy Eddie and another young man named Joe."

Frances dropped the pencil onto her diary and covered her gasp with her hands. She leaped from the bed and combed her fingers through her hair as she examined herself in the mirror. *Oh dear*, she thought, *I look an awful fright*. A reflection from the bedroom light glinted on her Miraculous Medal and she kissed it. "Thanks, Blessed Mother!"

"Offer them some iced tea and tell them to wait on the front porch. I'll be down in a few minutes."

Mame understood perfectly what her daughter was saying. This was proof that she was attracted to one of these fellas. She doubted it was that thick-witted Eddie. On the other hand, Mame knew that those bedroom eyes of Joe's would be no match for her inexperienced daughter. What should she do? Something about this young man's demeanor also reminded her of her fiancé Eugene Roach, and not in a good way. She wished Jimmy was home to put the young man's over-confidence in check.

"Have a seat," Mame said pointing toward the rockers. "She'll be down in a few minutes. Would either of you like iced tea?"

"Yes, ma'am," Eddie said eagerly.

"I would love some of your satisfying tea," Joe said, winking at Mame. *Oh dear*, she thought, *this boy's delusional if he thinks he's as suave as Valentino.* As she walked to the kitchen, Joe whispered to Eddie, "And would you add a shot of whiskey, too?"

Eddie thought that was the funniest thing he'd ever heard and nearly missed the chair when he sat down, he was laughing so hard.

Upstairs, Frances rifled through her dressers trying to find something pretty yet sophisticated that she could wear. Humidity frizzed and thickened her hair into an unruly mess. She pulled it back into a loose ponytail and tied it with a blue ribbon. The bow matched the sleeveless seersucker blouse she wore over an A-line white skirt with blue wedge open-toed sandals. Frances daubed her wrists with the tea rose perfume that Great-Aunt Bertha had given her and finished her preparations with a touch of red lipstick. *Not too bad*, she thought as she tucked the Miraculous Medal under her blouse.

Mame brought the boys a plate of fried cake doughnuts to go with their iced tea. Eddie grabbed one as soon as she waved the plate in front of him.

"How is your mother, Eddie? I haven't seen her since Mildred's card party."

"She's just fine, Mrs. O'Donoghue," he said through a mouthful. "Say, these fried cakes sure are swell."

"Glad you like them." Mame smiled as she turned to his friend. "Who are your parents, Joe? Do I know them?"

"Probably not. Dick and Marie McNamara. They're up in Rochester. I live here with Dad's sister-in-law, Aunt Kitty, over on Cherry Street."

Hmm, Mame thought that domestic arrangement was odd. His address would put him on the wrong side of the tracks, too.

"Are your parents not well and that's why you're living with her?"

"Nope, we agreed that this would be the best for everyone." Joe sipped his iced tea knowing that the pause would drive the curious Mrs. O'Donoghue crazy. "It works for Aunt Kitty, too, especially since she hasn't had a man in the house since Uncle Bill ran away with the councilman's daughter."

His odd candor distracted Mame from her initial concerns. Oh yes, she had heard those rumors. Joe's uncle got the girl pregnant—and she was barely eighteen. The story was that they fled to Scranton. Now this young man was living with his aunt who wasn't even a blood relative. What a sordid mess! It wasn't the type of information one would talk about casually, either. It was a sign this young man lacked good breeding.

Frances ran down the staircase and stepped onto the porch breathless. Her daughter looked so innocent yet beautiful at this moment that it pained Mame to know she was running toward wolves. To Joe's credit, Mame noted that he stood up immediately when Frances came onto the porch. Eddie finished his doughnut before aping his friend's good manners.

"Aren't you a vision of American beauty, Miss Red, White & Blue," Joe said with a suaveness that reminded Mame of Clark Gable's Rhett Butler in *Gone With the Wind.*

"With that bow in your hair, I feel like I've won first prize at the fair."

Mame hoped Frances didn't see the roll of her eyes at Joe's clichéd compliment. She hoped she'd taught her daughter enough about men so she could see past this suspect flattery, but by the look on Frances's face and the blush of her cheeks it was obvious that he suckered her into believing his sugary words. Her poor daughter had so much to learn.

"Who said you've won anything?" Frances zinged, though her blushing deepened at the same time. (That retort made Mame grin unabashedly.)

"Speaking of blue ribbons," Eddie added, "we're walking over to the county fair. Care to join us?"

Frances looked at her mother, hoping she'd approve. Mame didn't know what to say, but her daughter had to learn some lessons on her own, just like she did about her philandering fiancé back in Elmira.

"Yes, go ahead. But I want you home by eleven. OK?"

"Yes, Mother," Frances said as she kissed Mame's cheek.

"Be careful," Mame whispered. Frances scrunched her nose and hoped Joe and Eddie hadn't heard her.

She skipped upstairs to get her sweater, should the evening turn chilly, and then the three wandered down the hill toward the fairgrounds. Mame watched them disappear into the night. Of course she trusted her daughter, but something about that McNamara boy unsettled her. Mame sighed deeply as she opened the porch door. Yes, Joe was too smooth for a boy that age. How long would it be before this wolf tried to lure Frances to his den?

When Jimmy came home from working bingo at the Elks Club that night, he saw his wife smoking a rare cigarette in the kitchen. She jumped up and crushed it into the sink.

"Sorry to have interrupted, dear," Jimmy said in a teasing tone. "You must be here alone. Where's Frances?"

"Off at the county fair with two boys, a few years her senior."

"*Boys*? Do I know them?"

"Eddie Barker and Joe McNamara."

Jimmy raised his eyebrow. "Is Joe related to that Bill McNamara?" Mame nodded.

"He's the nephew."

Jimmy curled his hands into fists and leaned back against the kitchen counter.

"He told me he lives with his Aunt Kitty, Bill's ex-wife, up on Cherry Street, past the tracks. I told her to be back by eleven."

They glanced at the kitchen clock and saw it was a quarter past ten. Jimmy did not like the sound of this boy and he could see by his wife's nervousness that she didn't trust him either. He let a few silent Hail Marys slip heavenward and then went out on the porch to sit in his rocker. The katydids were out tonight, and as they continued their pointless conversation, he wondered if Joe did or didn't try to put the moves on his daughter.

Chapter 12

Over on Lake Street, the crowd had thinned on the fairgrounds midway but Joe convinced Frances to go for one more ride with just him, this time on the Ferris wheel. Eddie leaned against the Skee-Ball booth to watch, and devoured a hot dog as he ignored the carny taunting him to test his skills.

It never occurred to Frances that she had a fear of heights until the giant wheel climbed skyward and she could see lights from the village and the west shore of Keuka Lake in the distance. The fear manifested itself when the ride shuddered and then stopped dead with their chair swinging just below the summit.

"What just happened?" she asked Joe calmly.

"Dunno. Maybe the machine is broken and we'll be stuck up here for days."

As she leaned over to see what was going on below, their chair pitched forward. It was impossible to keep herself from screaming. Frances's unbridled, terror-filled tone affected others on the ride and they started screaming and crying in concert. She rested her hand on her neck, letting her fingers grip her Miraculous Medal tightly, a gesture Joe noted.

Wandering among the crowd below were her Uncle Mike and Aunt Susie (his wife who grew up on a farm in

Kansas). They'd been chaperoning the 4H exhibit that evening. Mike happened to glance up just as Joe put his arm around Frances. Joe's move startled her and she screamed. Mike was pretty sure it was his niece and as soon as the ride was fixed he planned to take a swing at whomever that ruffian was trying to neck with her. He wondered if he could climb the metal structure holding up the giant wheel to rescue Frances, and with the adrenaline from his building anger, Mike knew he'd have no fear of scaling it.

Joe slid his hand onto Frances's neck, turning her toward him and planted a deep kiss on her trembling lips. It calmed her all right, but had the opposite effect on her uncle.

"Hey you, get your paws off my niece Frances! Leave her the hell alone!" Aunt Susie tugged Mike's sleeve and shushed him, saying that people were watching.

Joe broke away from Frances and laughed when he saw the man more than a hundred feet below them shaking his fist. "Do you *know* that person?"

Awkward couldn't describe what she felt at that moment. Here she'd been stunned by Joe's gesture—a moment she'd dreamed of—but never imagined it would occur in the midst of a terrifying situation. And her uncle and aunt witnessed it, too. Frances was mortified. She gripped the spoke of the 100-foot wheel supporting their chair and just let her eyes glance down to Uncle Mike talking with the mechanic below. Joe was lucky that she didn't throw up on him from the combined nerves of her fear of heights and his advances. Now she was imagining her uncle telling her parents about Joe giving her the rush on a carnival ride.

Her face must have been scarlet from both embarrassment and shame (because to be honest, she rather enjoyed his kiss). The thought of it all made her woozy and she caught herself mid-twirl from a dizzy spell. Joe noticed it and was concerned that she was about to faint so he draped his arm around her neck again to keep her upright.

"Don't look down, Frances. You'll make it worse. Just close your eyes and don't worry. I'm right here to protect you."

She did as he suggested and turned her head toward him so she could snuggle close to his chest and allay her fears. When her uncle saw this he started yelling again.

"Young man, you keep your mitts to yourself or so help me God I'll...."

"She's dizzy, you idiot. I'm just trying to help her."

"Help, like you just did when you smacked her lips? What do you take me for, a fool?"

The mechanic fixed the stuck gear and restarted the Ferris wheel, jerking it forward slowly. Frances screamed and buried her head in Joe's shoulders. Mike saw this and ran over to where the ride worker was helping people out of their chairs. Eddie finished his hot dog, saw Frances's uncle standing there, utterly livid, and came over in case his friend Joe needed a hand with this guy.

"Uncle Mike!" Frances said as she ran away from the ride once she got off of the chair. "It's not what you think."

"Don't tell me what I think. I know what I saw up there. Your mother and father would be ashamed of you, Frances!"

She looked toward Aunt Susie. "Please, tell him it was nothing. I was so scared and he was just trying to...." Just as she turned to explain what happened, Mike lunged toward Joe with flailing fists. Eddie didn't want to sit back and miss the action, so he jumped on Mike's back. Joe, who was trying to fend off the punches being lobbed his way, landed his fist on Mike's jaw and sent him spinning to the ground.

A carny noticed the ruckus and ran over to stop it, but not before Mike hit Joe's nose and it started bleeding profusely. At the same moment, the three Lennon brothers—childhood friends of Pat and Frances—rounded the midway and stumbled upon the rumble in progress.

Tim Lennon was especially close to Frances, not just because they were the same age. The two were inseparable in their childhood, playing for hours in the back yard under Mame's watch. Often they pretended to run a veterinary hospital and they'd wrap the paw of Tim's cat with gauze or fill jars with insects to study. His teasing annoyed her, but it wasn't as she suspected that he thought she was silly. Tim had always carried a torch for his neighbor despite her apparent lack of romantic interest in him.

The idea that anyone was fighting over her flared his fury instantly. He put two fingers in his mouth and whistled louder than a passing train. His brothers followed the battle call and leapt into the melee. By the time the police arrived to break it up, there were several black eyes, one sprained wrist (Uncle Mike's), a bloodied nose, two upended vendor carts and a thoroughly mortified Frances. What would she tell her parents?

Jimmy was pacing the front porch in the dark when the police car pulled up at half past midnight. He waited on the steps as Officer Frank Reilly escorted Frances up the sidewalk. She couldn't even look at her father and sulked past him, through the front door and ran up the stairs to her bedroom.

"What happened, Frank?" Jimmy asked, holding back his anger toward her.

"That pair in the car started a rumble," he said, nodding toward the squad car. "I think it was something about a kiss on a Ferris wheel. Between us, Jimmy," he said with cupped hand shielding his mouth, "I'm still trying to sort it out."

The dome light in the car illuminated a young man glowering next to his brother-in-law. Jimmy snickered. "Mike's involved in this? Hah! Good for him." He waved toward the car and Mike shrugged back at him.

"Did my brother-in-law win or lose the fight?"

"Mike? I believed he bloodied the nose of your daughter's boyfriend."

Jimmy grinned. "Well thank you, Frank. I'm sorry for any trouble my daughter may have caused tonight. And I can speak for Mike—he's a good man who has never been arrested. He just loves his niece as much as I do." He glanced back at the car to get a better look at the handcuffed Joe, sitting in the car staring ahead. *Hmm,* he thought, *that kid's destined to make trouble wherever he goes.*

Mame, awakened by Frances slamming her bedroom door and the voices outside, put on a bathrobe and came downstairs. She was not as cheery as her husband. If she didn't have her bathrobe on, she would have marched across the street and given that Joe McNamara a black eye.

"Hooligan!" she said as they came back into the house. "Frances O'Donoghue, you come downstairs right this instant! Do you hear me?"

Her muffled sobbing grew louder.

"Let her be," Jimmy said. "We need to get some rest and discuss this in the morning with clearer minds."

"OK, but I never, EVER, want to see that Joe McNamara in this house again!" Mame said as she reached the top of the stairs.

Hearing her mother's anger made Frances tears fall faster, but as sleep neared her thoughts drifted to how soft Joe's lips felt on her mouth as they paused on top of the world.

***

Not long after that night, the soda fountain waitress at Jimmy's pharmacy quit. She was moving to Olympia, Washington, to be near her husband in the Army and he was stationed at Fort Lewis. They needed to fill her job as soon as possible and Jimmy suggested to Mame that Frances would be a good candidate. Plus, he could keep a close eye on her.

Frances was hired soon after and enjoyed the work (although she would have preferred to take the summer before college off). Her job was to serve customers at the six booths alongside the pharmacy's Main Street windows. It took but a few days for her to become completely familiar with the menu of ice cream sodas, milkshakes, malteds, sandwiches and burgers. Although the pay wasn't great, she earned enough tips to pay for a new dress and tickets for the movies with Betty Rae.

She was still new at the job the day that Antoinette Roma walked in surrounded by a chattering cloud of girlfriends. They sat in the far booth, Antoinette facing the front door. Frances gathered menus to bring over to the group, and as she approached, Antoinette held out her left hand. Sunlight reflecting off the storefronts across the street made something sparkle on her ring finger. Her girlfriends' voices rose in pitch and when Frances held out menus to them, Antoinette sneered.

"Oh, Toni, that's the most beautiful engagement ring I've ever seen," one of the friends said in near swoon.

Frances felt air rush out of her as her face reddened.

"Don't just stand there, Francine," Antoinette purred, "congratulate me. Timothy and I are getting married!"

Words wouldn't form in Frances's mouth. It wasn't a complete surprise to her; after all her friend Tim had been dating her for two years now. That said, she was still stunned by the news. (And she *hated* being called Francine.)

"Better shut that mouth of yours; you don't want to catch any flies with it." Antoinette laughed as her friends tittered over the surprised look on Frances's face.

Frances couldn't walk away from the booth fast enough. Her thoughts returned to one afternoon during their junior year of high school. It was a Saturday in September when Tim stopped by for a surprise visit. They sat on the porch rockers talking about their childhood "veterinary clinic" and what they'd like to do after graduation. Out of the blue, Tim started discussing how much he liked Fred Astaire.

"Don't you wish you could dance like Ginger Rogers? Imagine how much fun it would be!"

Frances didn't know what to say. For the first time in her life she pictured Tim as a leading man in her life, dressed suavely like Astaire. She'd never thought of herself as glamorous or attractive to boys in any way. None had tried to kiss her yet or even hinted at asking her out. "She's too brainy," was what her girlfriends repeated from the boys in their class. Yet, at that moment, she *could* picture the two of them as a couple and her face turned scarlet. She bit her lower lip and nodded shyly at Tim.

"Maybe we should take dance lessons together," Tim said. His face had the kindest smile as he waited for her reply, but Frances didn't know what to say. She was still stunned by the revelation that perhaps her childhood friend was now interested in her romantically. All she could do was shrug her shoulders and grin.

"Do you think you'd like to go to...?" Before he could finish his question, Jimmy walked out the front door.

"Mr. Lennon! Haven't seen you in a while, son. How's the family?"

"Everyone's great, Mr. O'Donoghue," he replied as he stood up and shook Jimmy's hand. "Thank you for asking."

"The football team is doing swell this year. I'd say much of the reason is their ace running back," Jimmy said with a wink. "Are you ready for the big homecoming game next weekend?"

Tim glanced at Frances. "Yes, I am." She smiled as it occurred to her that maybe he was here to ask her to the homecoming dance.

Mame appeared at the front door. "Dinner's ready, you two. Oh, hello there, Tim. Care to join us?"

"No ma'am. Thank you for the offer but it's my mother's birthday and we're having a special dinner for her tonight."

"Good for you. Please send her my regards. Nice to see you, Tim."

Jimmy went inside as Frances stood up and walked shyly toward the door. "Guess I have to go. Please wish your mother a happy birthday for me, Tim."

"I will be sure to do that," he said. "So, I guess I'll talk with you again in school on Monday."

"OK. See you then."

Tim walked down the porch steps and paused to look back. Frances hadn't moved. She waved and smiled warmly at him. Tim broke into a spontaneous Fred Astaire impression and danced down the sidewalk.

"Bye, Ginger!" he called out. Frances clasped her hands over her heart as she turned to go inside the house.

She arrived at school Monday wearing her favorite pink sweater and her hair styled high off her face like Ginger Rogers in her latest film. Frances was so nervous for Tim to see her. But when she saw him coming around the hallway holding Antoinette Roma's hand, the sight of the new couple shocked her. Wasn't he trying to ask her to the dance Saturday? Had she misinterpreted his signals?

As the school gossip mill churned, Frances learned by the end of the day that Antoinette intercepted Tim on his way home from the O'Donoghue's house. The plate of cookies she handed him was to wish him luck for the homecoming game, Antoinette said. Then she burst into tears and told him that her grandmother was dying. Grandma Roma's one regret, Antoinette said, was that she'd never seen her granddaughter in a formal gown. When Tim heard that, being the gentleman that he was, an invitation to be his date slipped right out of his mouth, and shortly afterward she gave him his first kiss. From that moment on, Antoinette had firm clutches on Tim Lennon (and her grandmother remained healthy as a horse).

The night of the homecoming dance, Frances cried herself to sleep. Would any boy ever like her? If only she'd had the confidence, like that fast Antoinette, to pull the invitation out of Tim that he intended to ask her. What made things worse after that night was the fact that Wagner's Photography Studio on Main Street displayed the official Homecoming Dance portraits in their storefront window. The photos showed the girls standing with their escorts behind them. In the photo of Antoinette and Tim, she'd pulled both his hands around her waist and given the camera a look of "He's all mine."

And that was why witnessing Antoinette display her engagement ring in the restaurant smarted like bee stings on bare feet. It was difficult for Frances to remain cheerful as she waited on the group of girls. Resentment, or perhaps jealousy, rose in her and she imagined throwing the ice cream sundae Antoinette ordered in her face. Of course she didn't, and endured their snickering as she cleared away the dishes when they were done.

After work she finally allowed her emotions to show. A few tears slid down her face as she walked home wondering, *when will it be my turn? When will I finally have a real boyfriend?*

That summer a rare and stubborn cold virus spread aloft on sneezes through the community. The usually healthy Jimmy succumbed. He told Mame it was probably from all the customers coughing at him as they waited in the pharmacy line. It was odd for Frances to go to work that Friday and not see her father smiling at her from the back of the store. The soda fountain was so busy though that she didn't give it too much thought. Late that afternoon as she cleared a table, Joe and Eddie came in and sat at the counter where Pete the soda jerk waited on them.

Joe turned to watch Frances greet customers at the far booth. He wolf-whistled as soon as she turned around to give Pete their order. Her face reddened with anger when she realized who was whistling. She glanced toward the counter where her father usually worked in the back for a sign of assurance, but of course he wasn't in today.

"Hah-hah! She looks like she just saw Lon Chaney," Eddie said guffawing. Frances wanted to smack his head with a menu.

"What would you two fellas like?" Pete asked.

"I'll have the young lady dipped in chocolate sauce and topped with whipped cream," Joe said pointing at

Frances. She blushed even deeper, fearing the customers overheard his fresh talk.

"Don't forget the cherry on top," Eddie whispered to Joe with a leer.

Pete waited for the crestfallen Frances to walk behind the counter before he whispered, "Don't listen to those dopes." He quietly carried a torch for Frances. *If she was only five years older*, he thought.

"Hey Joe," Eddie said when he saw the exchange, "looks like this soda jerk is hitting on your girl."

Frances focused on the fact that Eddie called her Joe's "girl," while Pete grabbed the collars of both young men. He'd fought at bantam weight when he was in the service. These two punks didn't frighten him at all.

"Out of here you two, right now, before I introduce you to my left hook. This is a respectable place. We don't allow that type of behavior in here. Scram!"

Joe and Eddie noted the anchor tattoos on Pete's beefy forearms as they slid off the stools and mumbled out the door. Frances turned so the customers couldn't see her face. She wished she could just go home and hide in bed, she was so embarrassed.

"Thank you, Pete."

"Sorry you had to hear such filth, Frances. No gentleman would ever address a lovely young lady like yourself that way." His smile, though sincere, had just a hint of smarm to it, which made the thought flitter across her mind that maybe those two boys were the least of her worries.

A week later Frances waitressed on the second shift until the soda fountain closed at seven. As she started walking home, she heard her named called when she neared the intersection of Main and Elm streets. She turned and saw Joe McNamara standing before her with a bouquet. It was a rumpled-looking bunch of orange marigolds and she suspected he'd just yanked them out of someone's garden. It didn't diminish his apologetic tone to her, however, and she accepted both with grace.

"I'm not usually like this around women," Joe said. "Something about you must bring out the animal in me." He laughed and Frances caught her breath as she saw light from the salmon-hued sunset brighten his handsome face. "Forgiven?" he asked, as he pouted and tipped his head slightly. She nodded and smiled.

"Then, doll, what do you say we go to the movies tomorrow? That Charles Boyer thriller *Gaslight* is playing."

Frances could hear her mother's voice in her mind saying how she never wanted "to see that Joe Mc-Na-ma-ra again" (the emphasis on each syllable of his surname was Mame's way of marking him as bad news). Yet Frances knew that if her mother had seen this gesture and his sincere apology, she'd have realized that she judged him too quickly. Maybe she'd have a change of heart. Thing was, despite all that had occurred, Joe captivated Frances and she didn't want to scare this rare chance at love away.

"I'll meet you there at seven-thirty," she said, not waiting for his reply and continued on toward home. Her sudden confidence surprised and thrilled her, as if she were a scarlet woman planning a tryst. This was something adults, not mere high school students, did. Then again, she knew her parents wouldn't approve. She'd have to fill her girlfriends in on this secret rendezvous and ask them to help cover it up. If her mother found out, she'd explode.

It was easier than she expected to make the date with Joe for the eight o'clock showing unbeknownst to her parents. She'd told them that her girlfriends were meeting at Diana McKie's house to drive to a dance in Dresden. They thought nothing of it when she walked down the front porch steps and headed for downtown.

Frances nearly died when she saw Joe because his hair was slicked back and he wore a long-sleeved dress shirt and tie—on a summer night! She was glad she'd decided to wear that new polka dot dress with princess seams and a sweetheart neckline. Oh what a handsome couple they must make, she thought.

The house was near capacity for the popular film that evening, so Joe led her to empty seats in the back row of the balcony. Frances noticed all the couples around them sidling close. As soon as the lights dimmed, the couples unleashed their pent-up passions. She couldn't believe it. Not a couple around them was looking at the screen.

In a move as smooth as Boyer, Joe yawned and then casually draped his arm around her shoulder. He leaned toward her and whispered how much he liked that dress and how she looked prettier than Ingrid Bergman. His breath felt like a warm breeze off the lake. Frances smiled keeping her eyes on the screen. She was afraid to turn toward him, because of those eyes of his—her mother had warned that he had dangerous bedroom eyes—and she could sense that something was about to happen.

He took her hand in his. At first their palms just rested together on the arm of the theater seat. Soon, though, his fingers caressed her hand as he pulled it to his mouth and kissed it. She thought the gesture was gentlemanly, like something a suave leading man would do in a film. Frances made the mistake of looking into his eyes at that moment, and Joe seized the opportunity to kiss her lips and then slid his mouth down the side of her neck. The slightest touch of his hair on her neck thrilled her and when she gasped, he kissed her mouth again, hard. The power of it frightened her and the sensation was almost unpleasant—she felt a little as if she was suffocating—but as he slid his hand up her thigh she was overcome by the desire to kiss him back with the same intensity. All inhibitions melted the moment his hand brushed against her breast.

When she went to bed that night, she hugged her pillow and imagined she was still locked in a passionate embrace with Joe. She giggled to herself when she realized they hadn't seen any of the film except its credits. There was still a touch of Joe's after shave on her hands and neck, and each time she turned in on her pillow it released the fragrance. Her thoughts drifted to imagining that he was lying right there next to her. The glow lasted but a few moments when she remembered that such lustful thoughts were a sin. She'd have to go to confession and tell the priest what she'd done. How embarrassing. He'd recognize her voice and know she had dirty thoughts. Maybe she could go to confession at that church in Hammondsport.

Frances started to worry that her mother might smell Joe's after shave on her. She jumped out of bed and went into the bathroom to try to wash it off, even though it was the last thing she wanted to do.

When she looked in the mirror, she saw to her horror that there was a mark on her neck where Joe had kissed her for a long time. "Oh no, did he give me a hickie?" she whispered. She'd have to put makeup on that before going down for breakfast the next morning. Dear Lord, what would happen if her parents ever saw that!

Over the rest of the summer of 1944, Joe and Frances had a standing Saturday night date at the movies. They'd sit in the same back row seats surrounded by the same necking couples. No one ever watched the screen, and thoughts of brave men facing death on foreign war fronts were as distant as the stars. The usher would come by halfway through the movie with a flashlight. Joe would slip the kid a quarter and he'd leave the young lovers alone. Frances laughed to herself about it and nicknamed the balcony The Necking Club.

Each encounter with Joe grew more passionate and on Labor Day weekend, before she left for college, he insisted that they meet downtown to go for a walk along the Keuka Outlet. They strolled down Water Street under the light of a nearly full moon and there was just the slightest chill in the night air, hinting that fall was on its way. Joe led her onto a dock across from the old ice house. The moonlight was so bright they saw fish swimming below.

"You're leaving for college now, practically a full-blown woman," he said, circling her waist from behind.

Frances detected whiskey on his breath as he kissed the back of her neck. Had he stopped at a bar beforehand or was he carrying a flask of it? Joe pushed her hair off her neck and nibbled playfully at her earlobes. She blushed at his affection. When she was around him, she no longer felt like a girl.

"I don't like the thought of you going away to college. All those football players will be trying to woo you and I won't be there to defend you. Can I trust you to be true to me?"

Frances was stunned that he would ask such a silly question. Wasn't it obvious how deeply she cared about him? "Oh of course, Joe, of course!"

His demeanor turned sullen and he released his hold. Joe walked to the end of the dock and paused as if he was considering jumping in. Just as her fear was rising from his odd behavior, he descended the dock's ladder and stepped onto a tethered rowboat.

"What are you doing, Joe? That's not your boat!"

"If they didn't want people to use it, why was it left here like this?"

"Maybe they don't have a boathouse."

He held out his hand toward her. "C'mon, Frances, get in the boat with me. Let's go for a spin on the lake." This boldness was proof that he *had* likely been drinking and it made her think of the awful incident in which her father's friends drowned. Frances wouldn't budge.

"What's the matter? Cat got your tongue?"

Frances shook her head, and then looked down at the water. "Joe, have you been drinking?" He laughed and sat down on the rowboat's seat.

"Sure! Why do you ask?"

"Well then, I don't think this is a good idea. The lake is dangerous at night."

"What are you more worried about, the lake or me?" he asked with a sly grin. "Are you a woman or a little girl?"

Frances folded her arms and looked away. "Don't be so mean, Joe. It's the truth. Bad accidents can happen on a lake at night."

Now he folded his arms and looked away. "Geesh, Frances, after all this time I guess you don't trust me. You don't really love me."

Did he just say love? Frances couldn't believe that the word which described how she'd felt for weeks had finally been spoken.

"But I do, Joe! I do lo...trust you."

"Then show me. Get in this boat with me now. We don't have to row anywhere."

Handsome and dangerous, it was a combination that attracted and repelled her at the same time. He made her nervous; he thrilled her. Should she ignore the concerns of family memories past or be spontaneous like those glamorous women in the movies. Frances was about to turn and walk home when Joe stood up and held out both arms to her.

"Please, my love. *Please.*"

She took a deep breath, climbed down the dock ladder carefully and then took Joe's strong arm as she stepped into the boat. They sat next to each other in silence as he stroked her hair. It was so bright out she could almost see the green of his eyes in the moonlight. Those eyes, those bedroom eyes—their charm tonight was more powerful than she'd ever recalled. He folded his arms around her and she melted into his embrace. Although she was caught up in the passion of the moment, she was also thinking to herself *could there be a more romantic moment than this*?

"Let's get comfortable," Joe said as he propped two seat cushions behind them so they could lie back against the stern of the boat. "Come here, doll. We can look at the moon and the stars together." She snuggled next to him and felt the beating of his heart against her.

"I'm going to miss you, Frances."

She smiled and patted his chest. "Don't worry. Cortland State isn't that far away. You can always come and visit me."

"I need to know you'll be true to me. Will you?"

"Of course," she said, kissing him lightly as her fingers intertwined with his. After a few minutes, he pulled away and his face grew so serious she was worried he had something awful to say.

"Would you prove it to me tonight?"

"What do you mean, Joe?"

He rolled onto his side toward her and then pulled her body against his. Their gentle rocking rippled the water surrounding them and echoed far across the lake.

Chapter 13

In mid-October Frances came home for her first weekend from college and Mame noticed subtle changes in her daughter. She looked pale and there was a bit of fullness about her jaw she hadn't noticed before. Had the late hours of study and college dining taken a toll? When Mame fried pork chops for dinner that night, she noticed that the smell was making Frances queasy. How odd; she'd always loved this recipe. Something was amiss with her daughter, but what was it?

"You look so tired, dear. Perhaps you're coming down with something. Why don't you skip meeting the girls for the movie tonight?"

"But I can't," Frances said, as she held her stomach. "I have to meet...," she stopped speaking when another wave of queasiness hit.

"Whom do you have to meet?" Mame asked. Her daughter looked like she was about to get sick to her stomach.

"Betty Rae and all my friends are home. I haven't seen them in a while."

"Why don't you get together with them tomorrow afternoon instead? You look quite poorly, Frances."

She couldn't tell her mother why she needed to go into town. Joe had not contacted her at college, even though she'd given him her address and residence phone number.

Had they broken up? Was he upset about her lack of experience that night in the boat? Had he already met someone else to replace her? She was a jumble of emotions.

Mame suspected that at that moment her daughter's anxiety had something to do with a boy, and she'd be willing to bet it was that McNamara fella. One of her friends from the gardening club mentioned she thought she saw the two of them walking together down Main Street a few days before she left for college. Frances thought the woman must be mistaken because her daughter was with friends that night (or so Frances told her). Had she been seeing Joe McNamara on the sly? It didn't make any sense that she'd be so agitated about not seeing her girlfriends.

She decided to test her theory and patted Frances's hand.

"Don't worry if you miss seeing Joe this time home. It's better to make a man wait and not always be available to him. You need your rest. Joe can call on you next time." Mame's experiment provided instant results. Frances's eyes watered and she bit her lower lip to restrict any hint of a cry.

"So you *have* been seeing him behind my back." Mame could have shown the true anger she felt inside, but decided it was wise to hold her tongue. The terror on Frances's face indicated she was suffering enough at the moment, knowing that her secret relationship was exposed.

Frances burst into tears. The confident college coed melted into a gangly teenager. She looked so young and vulnerable to Mame at that moment, as if she had been back in elementary school and someone had made fun of her on the playground. The deep heartache her daughter was feeling was evident. Mame drew her daughter into her arms and held the back of her head in the palm of her hand. That maternal gesture drew deeper sobs from her daughter and her shoulders began to shake.

"Mother…I'm…so sorry."

"You are forgiven daughter. Let's just forget about it. Maybe I got a bad first impression of him, that's all. Has he been a gentleman and treated you like a lady?"

Frances buried her head in her mother's shoulder and stared across the room. Mame thought that was a curious reaction and stood back from her, lifting her daughter's chin up so she could see her face.

"Hasn't he been a gentleman?" Frances cast her eyes toward her mother's feet. "Oh dear child, has he made you do something you didn't want to do?" Her daughter's eyes moistened. That was answer enough for Mame. Damn that Joe McNamara! Of all the young girls in Penn Yan, why'd he have to latch onto her only daughter? She gave Frances a hug that said farewell to her childhood and hello to her womanhood. Frances clung to her mother and sobbed.

"What is it, Frances? Was he rough to you?"

"It's just that…well I'm afraid that…it's been six weeks since…."

Mame gasped and her heartbeat skipped to an odd rhythm. Good Lord, was her daughter trying to say she's pregnant? What should she do? Would they have to send her away to that home in Rochester? Was this the end of her daughter's college education? She wondered how long it would be before Frances looked pregnant. *Oh dear Lord, what will I tell Jimmy and my mother?*

"We'll schedule an appointment with Dr. Smith. Have you told anyone yet? Have you told Joe?"

"No! You're the only one who knows." Frances hung her head and grabbed the wall as another wave of queasiness washed over her. She pictured her mother telling her father and his look of disappointment when he'd hear the news. *Imagine Pat coming home from the war and hearing this, too. He'll want to kill Joe*, she thought.

"All right then, do not share this with a soul. We'll figure it all out. What's important now is keeping you healthy for your baby. Why don't you go upstairs and get some rest. If the doctor confirms our suspicions, we'll have a talk with your father."

Mame changed her plan that night when she went to bed. In all of their marriage she'd never kept a secret from Jimmy. Why should she start now? And when Jimmy expressed concern about how pale Frances looked and he wondered if she had more than simple indigestion, Mame saw an opportunity. It wouldn't work to sugarcoat the news—she'd just tell him the truth.

"What is it, Mame? You look so worried! Is Frances sicker than I thought?"

"Jimmy," she said as she took his hand, "I suspect that she might be preg...."

He bolted upright in their bed. "Holy Mother of God don't tell me that that damn McNamara boy is to blame! Did he? Is she really?"

Mame patted his shoulder.

"Shh! Calm down, Jimmy, you'll wake the neighborhood—especially my parents across the street. We don't know anything for certain yet."

"Oh, I'll wake the whole damn neighborhood all right if I find out that bum has gotten our daughter pregnant. I'll wake the whole damn village up! *That sonofabitch*! Why did our only daughter have to get mixed up with that Cherry Street trash? She could have had her pick of good young men in the village and she settled for that misfit?"

"Guess she's her mother's daughter," Mame said, trying to add a little levity to a situation they could not control.

"Need I remind you that I was born on the right side of the tracks?"

"Need I remind *you* that the whole village thought you let your friends die?"

She'd stopped his rant cold with that uncomfortable reminder. Jimmy laid his head back on the pillow and pounded his fists next to him on the bed. They lay together in silence for several minutes. It seemed like just yesterday he was pacing on the front porch of their former apartment as his wife gave birth to Frances.

"I'm sorry for my anger, dear, but she has such a rough road ahead of her. We don't need to add to her misery. Wonder if he'll have the guts to marry her? If not, who knows if he'll stick around once his bastard is born? Will they live here in town or move away? Shucks, I'll be a grandfather by this time next year."

Mame elbowed him. “Don’t count your grandkids ’til they’re hatched, Jimmy. Remember, we aren’t sure if she’s indeed pregnant.”

The rabbit died.

Not long after, Jimmy and his brother-in-law Mike paid a visit to Joe’s Aunt Kitty. They were there waiting on the davenport when Joe came home from work at the lumber yard. He took one look at their angry faces and just knew it had something to do with that night on the outlet. Joe’s first thoughts were not of remorse. He realized that his plans to move to California had just been clipped by this girl’s predicament. (Of course it was hers alone, he thought, since she was the one who allowed it to happen.) The anger he felt toward Frances for ruining his dreams of being discovered in Hollywood twisted his face. Mike interpreted that as an insult to his niece’s honor. Jimmy was not able to run across the room fast enough to break the men apart until Mike’s thick hand busted Joe’s cheekbone. A violet shiner bloomed around Joe’s right eye as the two men left with a promise that Frances’s honor would be saved by a quiet marriage.

Mame waited to break the news to her mother until Joe’s promise of marriage had been secured.

“She’s leaving college to get married and I’ve never met this fella?” Rose asked as she set down a doily she was tatting. She lowered her head and peered over her glasses at Mame.

“Well, at least that child will be born within wedlock. Let’s not tell Father everything right now. He’ll figure it out with time.” Mame nodded and that ended their discussion.

Frances returned to Cortland on Monday to resign from the general science education program. As she packed up her belongings, Frances's roommate whispered to their friends that a rush wedding would be held the coming weekend.

On Saturday morning, Joe and Frances were married in the side chapel of St. Urban's. Betty Rae was her maid of honor, Eddie was Joe's best man. Frances wore a cotton eyelet dress in ecru with a wide-brimmed hat and chrysanthemum corsage. Joe borrowed an old double-breasted worsted wool suit of his Uncle Bill's, lent to him by Aunt Kitty. The bridal party, her parents and grandparents posed for a terse wedding portrait on the front steps of the church before heading off to brunch in the back room of the bar where Kitty worked. Jimmy and Mame paid for the couple's overnight honeymoon at a Seneca Lake inn. Upon their return, they lived with Aunt Kitty for a few months before she insisted that they find their own place.

Eight months later on a beautiful May morning in 1945, Joe and Frances welcomed Clare Marie McNamara. Frances stayed home to raise their daughter in the tiny apartment they rented on Keuka Street. Joe continued working at the lumber yard and his boss promoted him so he'd get a salary boost, knowing what his circumstances were. Mame visited daily on her way home from teaching to give her daughter advice on how to care for a newborn. By now the chattering about Joe and Frances's shotgun wedding died down and when they walked the baby in the carriage down Main Street, people stopped to fuss over her.

"Isn't she cunnin'," Mrs. Chelmsford said when Frances and her mother walked into the post office. They were there to mail off baby photos to Pat who was fighting the Japanese in the Philippines at the moment. "I see she has your beautiful auburn hair, Frances."

"She looks just like my daughter did when she was that age," Mame said. The baby grinned at the three women cooing over her, which made them fuss over her even more.

Before they walked home, Frances asked her mother if they could stop at St. Urban's to say a rosary for a special intention of hers. Mame didn't want to pry, but she wondered if her daughter's request had to do with their rocky marriage. Frances didn't talk much about Joe, which seemed so foreign to Mame. She and Jimmy were like one person with two minds. They didn't do a thing without discussing it with the other. Mornings were spent lingering over the newspaper with coffee and sharing their philosophies about matters of the world. There was nothing they liked better in the evening than to listen to the radio together. They completed each other's sentences. They could sit rocking on the porch in complete silence and be utterly content. Mame never once got the impression that her daughter's marriage was anything like theirs.

Mame lifted the baby out of her carriage when they went into the church to pray. As she held Clare, she realized that no matter what became of the union that created her, what mattered most was this precious child in her arms.

The young couple must have had something going for their relationship, because within six months of Clare's birth,

Frances was pregnant again. Although Joe was making a decent pay for the type of labor he did at the lumber yard, he had to take on a second job once they found out about the impending birth. With the war over, more men were in town to compete for the types of jobs he could do. He got a tip about a security guard vacancy at the Penn Yan Trust Company on Main Street. After working there five months, he met the head of a new insurance company who was looking for sales people. He figured Joe with his movie star looks he would probably do well "wooing" women clients.

The following July, the McNamaras welcomed their second daughter, Noreen Anne. Her middle name was a nod to Jimmy's sister Anne in Rochester. She was the spitting image of her father and had his wavy chestnut hair and green eyes with long eyelashes that made everyone remark that she looked like Elizabeth Taylor.

Pat was happy to be finally home from the war by then so he could be present when his sister had her baby. Mail from home telling him about his sister's marriage and Clare's birth got lost for several months and he'd read both just before his return to Penn Yan, giving him little time to adjust to the news. On the three long flights home he thought about the bum who'd knocked up his kid sister and his emotions fluttered from rage to sorrow that'd he won a battle for his country, yet wasn't home to prevent a huge loss for his family. What would he say to his brother-in-law whom he'd never met? He knew his sister would be able to read his face in an instant. Upon his arrival, would his presence start a family battle or would he be a peacemaker?

Pat's limp and odd appearance shocked the O'Donoghues when he returned. He explained why. One night while defending a beachhead in Luzon, he was nicked in the ankle by deflected shrapnel as he rescued two injured soldiers downed by enemy fire. They would have died if Pat hadn't risked his life for them. The shrapnel splintered his ankle and tore part of his Achilles tendon. He was never able to walk with a normal gait after that injury, dashing his dreams of playing professional baseball. The valor he showed in Luzon earned him the Silver Star Medal and a Purple Heart.

Although he looked quite handsome in his uniform, Pat was much thinner than they recalled and had a yellowish tan—like a roasted peanut, Jimmy remarked. It was so odd because he was usually the first to sunburn each summer. Pat explained it was a side effect of the Atabrine soldiers were given to ward off malaria.

The moment that he dreaded most—meeting his brother-in-law—was eased greatly by the first time he met his one-year-old niece Clare. His war-forged steely demeanor melted as soon as she handed him a Teddy bear and said "Da-da?" *Yes, I will protect you like a father*, he thought. He scooped her up and held Clare above his head. She giggled with delight and he hugged her. Oh, after those long dreadful months stuck in the mosquito-infested jungles of the Philippines ready to kill another human at a moment's notice, how joyous it was to celebrate a beautiful little life and her sister about to be born. It was he who held Clare when she met her sister Noreen. And when he saw that newborn baby smile at the two of them, it was probably the happiest moment of his life.

Chapter 14

Despite his nickname "Tiger," and his aggressiveness on sports and battle fields, Pat was a gentle soul. He was grateful to be hired as a clerk for Reynolds' Department Store soon after the war. Pat was tenacious when it came to tabulating details for orders and sales. His boss appreciated the quality of his work and gave him a raise after a few months on the job.

Pat's social shyness made it challenging to chat up ladies, despite his better-than-average looks. Other veterans would brag about their exploits on the battlefields to woo women. Not Pat. He never wore his medals in public. He rarely talked about that chapter in his life. It was his way to honor the dead who fell on both sides.

Pat preferred to blot out war memories with the mundane routine of his job. What mattered more was working hard and saving money for that one day possibly, like his fellow veterans talked about, when he'd meet the right girl and settle down. His boss sensed that's what he was doing and convinced him to move out of his parents' house and lease an apartment close to his job.

"No dame worth her salt wants to hang around a man still living with his folks," his boss warned.

Pat took those words to heart. Yes, he probably needed to start a family of his own. However, he still walked to his parents' house for dinner most nights and lingered there until they excused themselves to go to bed. On weekends he took to sleeping over in the den. Within a month, he was living back home and a For Rent sign was propped in the window of his former apartment.

His boss's warning proved prophetic. Although several women tried to win Pat's heart, once they were invited to dinner with his parents they realized they'd always be outsiders and deemed him a lost cause. It wasn't for a lack of graciousness on the part of Jimmy and Mame. It was more that the bond between mother and son was impassable because Mame had set, by her example, too high a standard of how to be the perfect wife. Pat wanted exactly what his parents had, the type of relationship that was a true merging of body and soul.

The single women in town figured he was not a serious marriage prospect. Pat's lack of a prestigious job made him even less marketable. But actually, Pat did not appear dismayed by this and seemed content living the bachelor's life (even though it was under his parents' roof). Mame was concerned that he would miss the joy of raising a family of his own and suggested a few names of eligible women to date. When he responded that he preferred to experience the joy of being a good uncle, it dawned on her that perhaps he was not interested in women at all. She never mentioned the subject again.

On Sundays, Mame cooked a big dinner for the family. The McNamaras would join them for simple feasts such as chicken fricassee or roast pork. At these meals, Pat and his brother-in-law Joe forced conversations that were inevitably short lived. They shared so little in common and to be honest, Pat brooded over the fact that Joe never served his country. (So what if he had a punctured ear drum? Was it any worse than the ankle injury he sustained, yet continued to fight in the war?) Pat was dismayed by how distant Joe acted toward his sister and suspected that his brother-in-law might be cheating on her, but he sure didn't want to bring that up. (Joe reminded him of the smooth-talking married men he met in the service who spent their free time cavorting with Filipinas.)

When Frances and Pat got together, they did a lot of reminiscing, much to Joe's annoyance. Their favorite topics were pranks they pulled on each other when they were kids and hanging out at the cottage with the Lennon boys from next door. The Lennon brothers were close in age with matching bright green eyes and dark blond hair. Frances got along best with Tim; Pat preferred hanging out with Steven. Little Frankie just whined until they'd let him join in their fun. Joe had already been introduced to the fists of all three, of course, during that melee at the county fair.

Pat always imagined that Frances would marry Tim when they were old enough. Heck, they acted like an old married couple when they were barely in their teens. They'd sit together on the wraparound porch, reading comics or the latest issue of *Scientific American*, absorbed in the stories and not speaking a word to each other. Pat heard that their close friendship ended abruptly once that flirty cheerleader Antoinette Roma caught his attention, though. They went steady junior and senior year then married soon after high school. Tim served briefly in the war, the bulk of his time spent during the occupation of Japan. A little more than nine months after his return, he and Toni—as he called his wife—started their family with the birth of twin sons.

Pat often saw his friend when he walked by the hardware store near work. Tim was a stock boy there in high school and after the war he'd worked his way up to assistant manager. Sometimes Pat and Tim met for lunch at the diner by the tracks. Their conversations were easy, unlike those with Joe, and it felt as if *they* were brothers-in-law. The friends of course shared war stories, but they preferred the topic of baseball, discussing animatedly the achievements of that new kid Jackie Robinson and veteran Ted Williams. Pat was a Yankees fan; Tim was a diehard Dodgers fan. That rivalry didn't ruin their friendship though.

One day late in the summer of 1949, Frances decided to take the girls out for a walk. She'd do this whenever she felt blue, and with Joe now working in insurance sales full time he'd be on the road a lot. It was too lonely to stay in the house all day. Her beautiful daughters always drew attention, especially from people asking if they were fraternal twins. She was hungry for conversation, even it if was simple cooing at the girls.

Pat noticed a commotion near the beauty counter of the department store where he worked and went over to investigate. He was delighted to see his sister and nieces commanding the center of attention.

"What a great surprise, Sis!"

"We were just in the neighborhood and I thought maybe I could treat you to lunch."

"Oh," he said with a slight frown, "I have plans to meet Tim Lennon at Mabel's Café." It wasn't lost on him that the mention of their friend's name lit up Frances's face. "Hey, whaddya say you and the girls join us? We'll surprise old Tim."

"I'd love to! I haven't talked with him in years."

Tim was sitting at the diner's counter when he saw the reflections of Pat and Frances coming through the door. He immediately slid off the stool to greet them. Frances was still as beautiful as he'd recalled and her daughters obviously inherited her good looks. When she neared there was an awkward moment when he went to hug her and she held back, so they patted each other's shoulders instead.

"Your girls are gorgeous. What are their names, Frannie?" She never liked that nickname but for some odd reason it was endearing when Tim called her that.

"This is Clare," Frances said gesturing to her older daughter, "and this is Noreen."

"I have twin boys and Toni's expecting our third. Sound familiar?" he said with a laugh. "When the girls get old enough, you'll have to bring them over so they can play together. I'm sure Toni would love to see you again."

Ugh, Frances thought, she had never forgiven Antoinette for breaking up the friendship she shared with Tim. Antoinette had to be the center of attention, though, and even if she had other plans she forbade Tim from even stopping by for an innocent chat on the O'Donoghue's porch.

It wasn't that Frances was interested in him romantically then, but she did savor their friendship. She hated to see that relationship disconnected from her.

Now here they were chatting together like it was fifteen years ago and no time had passed. Frances liked how attentive Tim was when she talked about her girls and how they were growing so fast. Joe always seemed to tune out Frances when she discussed their daughters, as if his mind was focused on something else. They shared few interests outside of their mutual physical attraction. She never saw Joe reading a book or newspaper. Like Tim, he had an interest in baseball. But unlike Tim, he didn't seem to be curious about much else past his own horizon.

"You know what? I still have those *Scientific American* issues we used to read on your porch, Frannie."

"Really? Why'd you hang onto them?"

"Guess I supposed the boys would enjoy reading them one day as much as we did. Maybe it will inspire them to become scientists. Speaking of, I always expected you to become a veterinarian. Remember our pet hospital behind your garage?"

"Hah! And don't forget the cemetery I dug up for the ones that didn't respond to your, ahem, 'cures'," Pat interrupted. Frances elbowed him.

"Don't knock our love of science, Tiger."

"Grrr, I hate that nickname! I wonder, will people still call me that when I'm eighty?"

"Lighten up, O'Donoghue," Tim teased. "Anyway, Frannie, what made you give your dream up?"

Pat coughed and she kicked him under the booth. Noreen wailed suddenly as if she was in pain, and every customer in the diner turned around.

"A foolish mistake, but at least I have some consolation with its outcome." She picked up Noreen and comforted her but then Clare pouted.

"May I?" Tim asked before Clare started to wail. Frances nodded and it made her heart pang to see the gentle attention that Tim paid her daughter when he lifted her onto his lap. Joe never volunteered to quiet the girls. Instead he'd yell at her to "do something" about them. Clare calmed right down in Tim's strong arms, and for the flash of a second, Frances imagined that they were a family and that Antoinette and Joe did not exist. How different would her life be then? She probably *would* be a veterinarian—Tim was the type of man who was not threatened by a working woman. He also had a strong faith. They'd often shared their concept of God during those scientific discussions on the wraparound porch.

The last time Joe was in a church was for Noreen's baptism. In contrast, Frances went regularly and had not lost her devotion to St. Thèrése. She still tried to do little acts of goodness every day. For example, on Sundays she got in the habit of taking the girls to nine o'clock Mass by herself. Joe would be home sleeping, worn out from his travels. It was just easier if she let him sleep while they were at Mass, otherwise he'd get angry if they disturbed him. That side of him frightened her. After Mass, once Joe was well rested, they'd head to her parents' house for Sunday dinner.

After their spontaneous get-together with Tim, Frances made it a point to visit her brother at work once a week. It made Pat happy because he got to see his nieces, whom he adored. It made Frances happy because they'd eventually make their way to the diner and end up having lunch with Tim. She needed a lift in her spirits. Tim didn't seem to mind, either, and Frances noted that he always dressed neatly and was a model of good manners around her.

One Saturday morning when she dropped by to visit her parents for coffee and fried cakes, Frances said hello to Pat as he came downstairs to head for work. Her brother mentioned casually how much Tim was enjoying their lunchtime get-togethers. Mame shot a glance toward Jimmy whose eyebrow was already raised toward her. After they left, Mame shook her head.

"That's got to stop."

"I agree. If Joe doesn't pay more attention to his wife, he'll lose her."

"I hope divorce won't come into this family, Jimmy. Wish we could get Joe and Frances to talk with the priest about this, before it's too late."

"Fat chance of that happening." Jimmy poured another cup of coffee. "When was the last time he darkened the aisles of St. Urban's?"

***

The next morning when Frances was at Mass, Clare had a coughing fit. Frances felt her daughter's brow. It was warm, but not feverish. Still, it concerned her and so she left right after communion to get her little one back home. She noticed a red Mercury that she'd never seen before parked across Keuka Street in front of their apartment. When she walked inside the foyer, there was Joe discussing house insurance with a beautiful blonde wearing a wool swing coat (an odd outfit for such a warm afternoon). Frances paused in the doorway and couldn't think of a word to say. She was stunned. Since when did he do business on a Sunday and at home? Frances mumbled hello then excused herself to the kitchen to feed Clare and Noreen. What was going on in the other room, she wondered, and what she should do?

When she brought the girls upstairs for a nap, she noticed Joe outside talking with his client who was sitting in her car. He closed the door for her and she reached out the window and touched his wrist in a way that upset Frances. It was a gesture of intimacy, not of agreeing on a deal to purchase house insurance. She held her stomach with one hand and the wall with the other. Was he cheating on her?

Frances could not look at him when he entered the kitchen, fearing she'd notice lipstick on his collar or the smirk of a man on the prowl.

"You're home early," he said tersely as he poured a cup of coffee.

"You're doing business on Sundays now?" She glanced at him and there it was—that damn smirk. It was the same look he made after he threw her in the lake at Betty Rae's graduation party. Frances pushed past him, picked up her purse on the counter and headed for the front door.

"I'm going out. Take care of the girls, especially Clare. I think she might have a fever."

"Hey, you can't leave them here! I have things to do!"

Frances paused halfway out the door with her hand still on the knob and turned toward him. "What have you *already* done, Joe? That's the problem. I'll see *you* when I get home!" When Frances slammed the door, her neighbor was outside weeding her flower bed. The woman stood up, pushed back her straw hat and waved. Frances avoided making eye contact with her and breezed past. She had no idea where she wanted to go, but instinctively turned left onto Chapel Street and then right onto Main Street. Her feet were taking her to her parents' home, but then she thought, maybe it wasn't a good idea. She was an adult now and had to figure out this mess by herself. Frances turned right onto Elm Street instead and stopped in front of the movie theater. There was a matinee at the Elmwood, the latest Abbott and Costello, and she thought she could use a good laugh to lift her foul mood.

The balcony was filled with restless children, which was good because that was the last place she'd wanted to sit with all the history she had there. Instead she sat in the middle of the lower level, off to the left side near the end of the row. As the newsreels rolled she noticed someone came in late and sat in the last seat of her row. She turned and saw Tim Lennon, alone, looking as surprised to see her as she was to see him.

They laughed as Tim moved two seats away from her.

"May I interest you in some popcorn, young lady? Or, care for some jujubes?" Tim extended the snacks to her and Frances chose the popcorn.

"Thank you, young man. What brings you to the movies today?"

"Toni took the boys to see their grandmother in Geneva. I'd have gone but Grandma Roma is not a fan of mine. Calls me 'you dumb Mick' to my face."

"Ow! That's mean."

"She always thought Toni should have married that clown Pete Pagliacci. She's said so several times in front of me." He shrugged. "So, where are your girls? Don't tell me Joe volunteered to watch them."

"Hah! No, I decided that *I* needed a day off since he's already put in some work today with some blonde while we were at Mass. I decided to treat myself." She turned toward the movie screen so that he couldn't see the tears welling in her eyes.

Tim grimaced at Frances's levity over a situation so awful. This wasn't a matter to be joked about. In his mind it was a crime to treat this wonderful woman with such disregard. He reached into his pocket and took out his handkerchief that Toni had embroidered with his monogram.

"Here," he said as he stretched his arm out over the seat between them. "Even though the movie's a comedy, you might need this."

Frances's lower lip trembled as she reached for the cotton square. Their fingers touched briefly and the whisper-light impact rippled deeply through both of their souls. Thoughts of "what if life had been different" crowded both of their minds at that moment. She put her head down as she daubed her eyes and tried to clear her thoughts. If she didn't welcome them, then they weren't a sin, right? Her fingers clutched the handkerchief tightly throughout the movie.

By the time the house lights came back on the handkerchief was completely dampened with her tears. Not only had she released her anger at what she saw that morning, but she also cried away the hurt she felt all those recent evenings when Joe was working at the office into the night. She had begun to feel like a widow, and in a sense she was, because Joe's involvement in their marriage seemed to have died right after Noreen's birth.

She and Tim went their separate ways as soon as they walked out of the lobby. It wasn't until she was halfway home that she realized she was still clutching his handkerchief. She stuffed it into her purse and planned to wash and iron it so she could return when she saw Tim next.

On Wednesday she took the girls into town and stopped by to visit Pat. It was no coincidence that she arrived just when he was ready to take his lunch break. They all strolled over to the diner where Tim was waiting. She smiled widely as soon as she saw him and reached into her pocket to get his handkerchief which she'd laundered and pressed.

"Hi, Frannie," Tim said. "Long time no see. What's it been, a week?" He laughed as he waved at the girls.

And at that moment she knew that she could never tell anyone about their accidental meet-up, innocent as it was. Her hand released the handkerchief and instead pulled out two rattles for the girls to play with and then she sat down in the booth.

The following Sunday when she returned from Mass, Frances was relieved to see there was no car out in front of their apartment. Joe looked odd, though; he was wearing slacks with no belt and an undershirt, as if she'd interrupted him mid-dress. Was it just her imagination, or did she smell the slightest hint of perfume on him when he lifted Noreen out of the stroller? Then she heard what sounded like the back door closing and a couple of minutes later noticed a car backing out of her neighbor's long driveway. Frances drew back the curtains to get a better look at the car because she thought the Tafts were still on vacation in Florida. To her surprise it was not their black Buick; it was that red as sin Mercury.

Frances glanced at her husband who knew he'd been caught. She didn't say a word as she calmly picked up her purse and walked out the front door again. Her neighbor was reading the Sunday paper on her porch and lowered it as she watched Frances cross the street briskly.

"You can't cry now," she said under her breath. "Not here. Wait until you get inside the theater." Part of her hoped that Antoinette was at her mother's house again so that she'd see Tim. She even sat in the same seat hoping that he'd sit down and offer her more popcorn. Tim never arrived though, so she pulled out his clean, neatly pressed handkerchief and caught a steady stream of tears that fell over the next hour.

Frances emerged from the theater with a red, puffy face. She kept her eyes focused on the sidewalk so no one would see how upset she was. Oh, she was such a bundle of conflicting emotions. How could she go home like this now?

Instead of turning up Keuka Street she continued up Elm as it turned into West Lake Road. The temperature had plummeted overnight, drawing out crimsons hues from the maple leaves. The sky was as blue as the Blessed Virgin Mary's garments she thought as she stopped to finger the Miraculous Medal around her neck. Frances needed to pray about her shaky marriage, but where? Her feet had led her to the Catholic cemetery. Maybe it was a sign? Up the hill there stood a proud old beech tree. She sat down underneath its leafy shade and hugged her knees.

From her vantage point Frances watched sunbeams filter through the leaves above her, occasionally lighting upon her cheek. Her fingers traced patterns on the bark of the magnificent tree sheltering her as she wondered what she should do about her cheating husband. Confront him? Ask Father O'Neill to counsel them? Who is this mystery woman and how long has Joe been involved with her? Should she pack up the girls when she got back and move away, never leaving a forwarding address? But what about the sacred vow of marriage she'd made? Her mind wrestled these thoughts as she lay down under the sprawling tree, still as a corpse. She started thinking that if this was your view for the rest of eternity, it wasn't too bad. Frances closed her eyes for what she expected to be just a few moments. The turmoil inside her mind had exhausted her, though, and before long she'd fallen asleep under the same tree (unbeknownst to her) where her parents professed their love so many years ago.

It was nearly dusk when Canada geese honks woke Frances. She watched their large V flying overhead while she strolled out of the cemetery gates and wondered, *Has Joe even missed me?* She pictured her return like the happy ending of a movie in which she walked into the house and saw dinner on the table, with the girls and Joe waiting there for her. He'd run breathlessly toward her and embrace her with all his might, apologizing over and over. And then, fade to happily ever after.

When she stepped onto the porch of their apartment, though, she noticed there weren't any lights on inside. She unlocked the door and saw his note right away, sitting on the table by the door.

"*Girls are at your parents. Away on business call.*"

"What business? With your *whore*?" Frances yelled as she wadded up the note and threw it across the room, pinging the mirror on the opposite wall.

She was furious. Now that he'd dropped the girls off at her parents, she'd have to explain what was going on. Of course Joe had the car, so she'd have to walk up there, too. It wasn't a situation in which she could just call her father and ask that they'd be dropped off. Mother would have served Sunday dinner by then and they'd be in the middle of it. Frances knew she'd have to come up with some good excuse for her actions. She wondered what lies Joe told them.

Her anger quickened her steps up the slowly rising hill to her parents' home. The old porch floor creaked as she stepped on it. Mame heard the noise and raced to the door.

"It's *you*! You're here! Oh, thank the Lord! We've been so worried." Mame grabbed Frances and hugged her as if she'd been gone for years.

"I had some errands to do. That's all. Joe dropped off the girls with you?"

Mame stepped back from her daughter. What was going on? It looked as if there were leaves in Frances's tousled hair. Why was she obviously lying to her?

"What type of errands does one do on a Sunday? Nothing's open."

"Oh, well...."

Car doors slammed out front and they heard quick footsteps on the porch.

"Any word from her? Oh, you're *here*!" Pat said as he walked through the door. His sister and mother stared back at him with serious faces. Frances sighed, and when Tim followed her brother into the house, the sight of her search party made her turn away and burst into tears.

"Thank God you're safe," Tim said, wanting to go and hug her, but he held back out of respect. She turned and their eyes locked briefly, making her heart flutter. Clare must have awakened from all of the commotion downstairs and cried for her mother. Frances took the opportunity to get out of an awkward moment, excused herself and ran upstairs to her old bedroom.

"Where was she?" Pat asked. Mame shrugged.

"We were just getting to that when you two arrived," she said.

"Well, looks like you don't need me around here anymore," Tim said as he patted his friend's shoulder. Pat shook his hand.

"Thanks for all your help, Tim."

"Don't mention it. I'm just glad the story had a happy ending."

"Hmm," Mame said, almost to herself, "I don't know about that."

When he met Tim for lunch at the diner on Wednesday, Pat told him that Frances had not heard a word from Joe yet. He'd made a large withdrawal from their bank account and she feared that she might not be able to pay the bills with what was left. Tim was incensed. *How dare that jerk treat Frannie so badly*, he thought. That night over dinner he told his wife that he was investing in a business idea with Pat and he'd need to withdraw some money from their bank account. She agreed to let him do it.

The next day he took an extended lunch hour, walked to the bank and then over to Frances's apartment. She was surprised to see him at her door.

"May I speak with you, Frannie? I just need a few moments of your time."

Frances looked past him and saw her neighbor out weeding her garden, hat pushed back as she watched the conversation.

"Of course, Tim. C'mon inside where there isn't an audience," she said quietly rolling her eyes toward the nosy neighbor. Frances led him to the kitchen where she was feeding the girls their lunch. "Would you like something to drink?"

He nodded and as she pulled out a bottle of pop from the refrigerator, he noticed the framed print of St. Thèrése hanging on the wall by the clock.

"You always did remind me of her," he teased, pointing at the print. Frances laughed, but felt a little uneasy having him in her house though they'd been friends forever. She folded her arms protectively in front of her. Clare ate part of her sandwich and then held it out to Tim. He laughed and pretended to take a bite out of it. That made Clare laugh and then Noreen got the giggles, too. It wasn't lost on Frances that such a moment was rare when Joe was around the girls. Joe had never mastered the skill of parenting.

"Can't stay long," he said, "I'm on my lunch break. Listen Frannie, Pat told me what was going on with Joe and, well, it's none of my business but I felt the need to help you out." He slid an unmarked envelope out of his suit jacket. "This should cover the rent for the next few months. If it runs out and you need more, just let me know."

Frances held the thick envelope in her hands for a few moments as she pondered the weight of his gesture. "Thank you, but I can't take this, Tim."

"No buts, Frannie. Consider this as a gift for the girls."

"Oh, Tim. But you must need...."

"Listen, my father-in-law has a prosperous construction business in Geneva. There's a pretty deep well there if we need help, and Toni has no shame about tapping her parents' resources when we need to."

Frances laughed through her tears. Tim held out his hands to prop up her shoulders.

"You're going to get through this, Frannie. OK?" He bent forward and kissed her forehead. She loved the fatherly gesture, but when their eyes met as he pulled away, she feared the feelings growing for him. Frances held out the envelope to say that she really couldn't take his money, but it was too late. Tim was already out the front door and waving hello to the gawking busybody.

She was grateful that Tim's money got her through that month. Then Joe returned suddenly one night with no explanation of where he'd been and life inexplicably picked up its dysfunctional rhythm again. Frances was afraid to ask about his whereabouts during his absence because he seemed to have returned to his old personality and was suddenly warm and attentive again. Had she imagined his disappearance?

Joe noticed the money from Tim in their savings account, but he figured it came from Mame and Jimmy. Frances wasn't working. Where else would she have gotten that much cash?

The first weekend in October, Frances was awakened at dawn by strange sounds downstairs. She turned and saw Joe wasn't in their bed, so she put on her bathrobe and went to investigate what was going on. He was in the living room surrounded by a stack of cardboard boxes.

"I'm going to need you to pack up your belongings."

Frances tightened the belt on her robe and folded her arms.

"Why," she asked, afraid of what his answer would be. "Are you throwing us out?"

He looked at her strangely. "Why would you think that? No, I have good news! I got a promotion at work. I'll be running the Binghamton branch. We're moving there this afternoon and Eddie Barker's coming by with a truck from his produce company at three."

"Moving? *Today*? But...you never told me!"

"Just wanted to surprise you, dear, that's all. We've got a cute little house on the East Side with a fenced-in yard. The girls will love it."

"A house? In Binghamton? But can we afford...? And my parents, what will I tell them?"

Joe grabbed her in his arms and swung her around before setting her down dizzy. "Tell them that your wonderful, handsome husband is going places. Tell them that he's on the fast path to financial success. Tell them that he thinks he has the most beautiful wife in the world."

Frances was a jumble of emotions. This was crazy. They couldn't just up and leave. She didn't know whether to be excited that they were getting their own home or sad to be leaving the comfort of Penn Yan. And this look in Joe's eyes, she hadn't seen it since their night on the rowboat. Maybe this was all he needed in his life, a sense of accomplishment and knowing he was finally in control of his destiny. He stroked her hair and then pulled back from her, his hand caressing her glowing cheek.

"Then again, maybe the packing can wait for a while," he said with a seductive smile.

Oh, those eyes of his. Lashes that long should be outlawed, she thought. His desirous gaze dazzled her like a full moon rising over the lake. How could she retain any anger toward him in this passion-charged moment? He lifted her into his arms and carried her upstairs, past their daughters both sound asleep. When Joe laid her down on their bed and kissed her like he hadn't in years, she felt it would be more than love they'd be making.

She was right.

Chapter 15

A few months later she decided that though Binghamton wasn't that far away—about two hours by car—it felt as if her mother was living on the West Coast. She chalked it up to the haywire hormones that were making her depressed and missing home. It had been an uneventful pregnancy, but she still wished her mother was right there to cheer her when she'd have an off day. Their third child was due in July of 1950, and Frances had a hunch that it was a boy. When she neared her due date, she called Mame a couple of times a day. She feared the calls were a drain on her mother, because each time Frances called, Mame sounded more tired than the last time they spoke. The day she felt her first contraction, Jimmy answered the phone.

"Mother's taking a nap. She's been doing that a lot lately."

"Is everything all right, Dad?"

"She seems OK, just much more tired than usual."

At his daughter's insistence, Jimmy took Mame to the doctor and discovered his wife was indeed ill with double pneumonia. Frances was having a deep contraction when the phone rang that morning. She was hoping it was Joe, who was off on another business trip. Instead it was her father.

"Who gets pneumonia in late June?" Frances asked in an exasperated tone. Her mother could be in the hospital for weeks. Would no one from the family be there when she gave birth in July? She doubted that Uncle Pat would come for the birth, though he'd definitely arrive with armfuls of gifts when the baby was born. (How he loved spoiling his nieces!)

Binghamton was in the midst of a heat wave, and later that afternoon Frances struggled to keep cool while dragging the Electrolux canister across the carpet. She paused when she heard Clare and Noreen fighting over a storybook, then wiped sweat off her brow with the back of her hand. The girls' high-pitched shrieks pierced her skull. Frances was about to yell at them, but then the plucked, warbly jingle of an ice cream truck silenced their storm.

"Mommy! Mommy! Can we get ice cream, pleeeease?" Clare said as she ran full tilt toward her mother. She smashed into Frances's tender abdomen so hard that the force knocked her mother to the floor. Frances grimaced as she pulled herself slowly back upright by holding onto a chair, trying to not cry out in pain.

"Clare! What have I told you about running in the house?"

"I'm sorry Mommy, but I really *need* some ice cream. Pretty please?"

Noreen tugged on Frances's maternity smock. "Mommy, can I get ice cweam, too? Pwetty pwease?"

Ow, that collision with Clare really hurt, Frances thought as she leaned on the kitchen counter. "OK, *OK*! Let me get my wallet." Frances led her girls down the front steps of their home and waited as they ran to the curb to buy soft-serve cones. A little boy in front of the line had the same chestnut hair as her husband, and Frances ached for Joe's presence. He was missing this precious moment of his daughters' wide-eyed wonder when the driver handed them towering swirls spangled with sprinkles.

She first saw the dyed blonde out of the corner of her eye and felt a slight sense of recognition. When the woman took her son's hand and turned briefly toward her, Frances saw that she was wearing a maternity dress (and was as far along in her pregnancy as she was). Something about the swing of red dress hem looked familiar, and then Frances recalled where she saw her face before. *This* was the woman who was in her apartment with Joe that Sunday! She gasped loudly and the woman looked up and made eye contact with her, then yanked her son's arm as they ran down the sidewalk.

Perhaps it was the weight of the humidity or just the shock of the moment, but Frances became woozy. She wanted to follow them and see where the woman lived, but instead felt compelled to get back inside. Frances climbed the steps slowly with one hand clutching the porch railing, the other supporting her abdomen, and by the time she'd crossed the threshold, her water broke.

"*No*! This can't be happening!" She screamed for help. Clare's and Noreen's ice cream cones melted down their hands as they stood frozen, confused by what was happening to their mother. A neighbor heard Frances yelling and called an ambulance.

When Joe got home late that night from his travels he was surprised to see his next door neighbor's wife babysitting. He rushed to the hospital but arrived moments after their newborn son died. Frances was asleep when he was allowed in the room to see her, sedated heavily after her hysterical outburst when told of their heartbreaking loss. The nurse said she'd probably be asleep for hours. The kids were being watched, there was nothing for him to do here, so he headed to an East Side pub near his home to drink away his sorrows.

Joe slowed the car when he drove past the home of his "other family." He knew he was crazy trying to keep these two worlds separate just blocks away from each other, but he genuinely cared for both of the women in his life. If he had never started an affair with Beverly Gaynor when Frances was at Cortland, he wouldn't have known about the job at the insurance company owned by her best friend's father. That job allowed him to support Frances and the girls as well as Beverly and their boy, Joey (born shortly after Clare). He had no shame that two women were expecting his children around the same time. In fact, he was quite proud that he'd been able to juggle both worlds effortlessly. He wasn't the first married man Beverly carried on with, so she was used to living discreetly. She was the first married woman he'd been involved with, though. Her AWOL Army husband was rumored to be shacking up with a Filipina in Zamboanga.

Duffy's Place was a no-frills tavern squeezed between a butcher shop and an appliance repair business on Robinson Street. It was named for a local boxer who'd gained fame after a bout in the Twenties with the future World Light Heavyweight champion, Jimmy Slattery of Buffalo. Joe lit up a Lucky Strike when he sat down in the musty room, nodding to the barmaid. She brought over his regular—a double bourbon with a glass of water on the side. He raised the bourbon to his lips, took a long sip and felt its burn spread like wildfire across his tongue and down his throat. Joe's fingers scratched his furrowed brow as the cigarette held taut between his fingers curled blue smoke into the amber light. They'd lost a son. Sure he had one to spare, but this one would have carried his full name legitimately. He felt the bourbon gnawing on his empty stomach.

Joe dragged deeply on his cigarette. Beverly would give birth any day now. He'd of course be happy about that child, but his heart ached sincerely for Frances and the sorrow she'd know in the days to come. With his twisted perspective, he knew that keeping her around lent him some class, which surely helped his business career. She'd been a great wife and the perfect homemaker.

In contrast, if you took one look at Beverly's scarlet pout and platinum pinup hairdo, you could see why she was comfortable onstage teasing burlesque club customers. He was sure drawn to her—she had curves more luscious than a Coupe de Ville. But ever since high school, he'd been trying to shake his wrong side of the tracks image. Beverly was not going to make that easy.

Sirens keened in the distance. He thought the sound was appropriate for his reflective mood. Joe's world was aflame, yet here he was trying to quench it with firewater. His thoughts turned to Clare and Noreen asleep at home, clutching the Teddy bears he won for them at the field days in May. Why was he here instead of guarding them as they slept? As he drained the glass he nodded to himself that of course he should have been paying more attention to them. It was disappointing that they hadn't been boys, but he knew Clare was as smart as a whip and Noreen would be fighting away the boys when she was old enough.

"Another, Joe?" the barmaid asked as fire trucks whizzed past the bar, sirens drowning out conversation until they passed. He nodded.

"Sounds close," he said as he paid for the drink.

"Probably someone set off fireworks again. Don't know why they can't wait for the Fourth." She pulled a cigarette out and Joe leaned forward to light it for her. She raised an eyebrow toward him and smiled slightly as she drew in her breath. He pretended to not notice; the last thing he needed was to get involved with another woman.

The door to the bar opened and draughts of acrid wood smoke rushed inside.

"Holy cow, they're going to have a tough time fighting that one," the man said as he sat down next to Joe. A couple of ambulances raced past, their piercing wails further unsettling the bar's mood.

"It's a hot night to be fighting a blaze," Joe said. "How near is it?"

"Just off Robinson—it's that little house on Louisa."

The glass of bourbon fell out of Joe's hand and shattered on the linoleum floor.

"Beverly!" he cried. Joe tossed two dollars toward the barmaid as he rushed outside to run down the few blocks to

Louisa Street. With his first view of the orange flames licking the sky, Joe just *knew* it was her home. An ambulance crew pushed a stretcher with a small, blanket-covered body away from the blaze. Joe raced breathlessly up to them.

"Wait, I think that's my son! Please! Let me see...."

The fire chief grabbed Joe's shoulder and pulled him aside. "I'm sorry. We did all we could, but...."

"No! Not my boy! Oh please, God! Tell me this didn't happen!" Joe clamped his hand over his mouth as tears flowed unabated. Funny, he hadn't shed one tear for his other son yet. Why did the loss of Joey mean so much more to him? Perhaps it was because they'd had four years together. Or was it that the boy's shabby childhood mirrored his own? Oh, this would be so hard on Beverly. But wait, he thought, where was she?

"Your son was found behind the pantry door where we're pretty sure this started. He must have been playing with matches in there. We found your wife on the floor of the kitchen, overcome by smoke."

"Oh, she's not my...." Joe caught his words as the fire chief gave him a curious look. "Where is she? Is Beverly going to be OK?"

The fire chief noted that Joe did not acknowledge the woman they'd rescued as his wife. He could smell the bourbon on his breath, too. *Perhaps if this bum had been home with his bastard instead of out at a bar, the kid wouldn't have been playing with matches*, he thought.

"She's in the ambulance. Took in an awful lot of smoke trying to rescue the boy. Think she's gone into labor."

The ambulance sped off before Joe could reach it. He sprinted back to Duffy's to get his car and followed chase to the South Side hospital. Doctors were trying frantically to treat Beverly's burns at the same time she was giving birth. Joe paced in the waiting room and winced when another nurse or doctor raced past him. By now Little Joe would be in the morgue a few floors below as his sibling was being born in the maternity ward.

It was too much trauma for Beverly's body to fight—labor induced by her extreme fright and then the severe burns she sustained trying to rescue Joey. Beverly died the moment their daughter was born.

"Congratulations, Mr. McNamara, you have a daughter," the nurse said when she came out to the waiting room. Joe put his head in his hands and sighed. "Thank God, I was so worried that…."

The nurse took his hand. "She's been moved to Intensive Care as we monitor her lungs to make sure they weren't affected by the smoke." She took a deep breath, "I have some other news. I'm so sorry, but her mother…the burns…they were so severe…."

Joe collapsed backwards into a waiting room chair as the doctors and nurses gathered around and told him what had happened. In one day he'd lost two sons and his lover. Yet, he'd gained another daughter and she needed immediate attention as did his grieving wife. What was he going to do?

The bourbon had not gone out of his system completely, and it made him believe that the best course of action was to tell his wife about his daughter. Beverly had no living relatives. She was an only child and her estranged parents died years ago. If they didn't take his daughter in, she'd end up in an orphanage. Joe couldn't let that happen. Perhaps they could help each other. Frances's body was obviously equipped at the moment to breastfeed this newborn, and maybe his daughter could help her deal with the loss of their son. The alcohol made it all seem so logical.

He kept thinking of his daughter as his last hope and when he did propose the idea to Frances, he mentioned that Hope would be a lovely name for the flaxen-haired beauty. Frances was still in shock over the death of their son, though, and couldn't grasp what her husband was really telling her. She thought it was something about an abandoned baby and in her sedative-induced haze, she could think only of the day her cousin's wife lost their daughter Maggie. Maybe this was her spirit come back to this world in another body? When Joe and the nurse brought his daughter in, Frances thought yes, she *would* help her cousins out by raising their daughter.

"Hello, little Maggie," she said taking Joe's daughter into her arms. He wanted to correct her and remind her that the baby's name was Hope, but he was just happy to see that she'd embraced the idea of taking her in.

It all happened so fast that Joe never got a chance to phone his in-laws Jimmy and Mame to let them know about the loss of their grandson. What if he pretended that it never happened, though, and made them believe that Frances gave birth to his daughter? How would they ever find out? They didn't know anyone in Binghamton. His name had been left out of the news reports, too. There was no trace. (He'd arranged for a private burial of Beverly and Joey afterward in the cemetery on Mygatt Street.)

When a finally lucid Frances got the first phone call from home and her parents went on and on about how excited they were to hear that she'd had another daughter—and how they loved the name Maggie—she couldn't bear to break their hearts by telling them the truth about her philandering husband whose lover and son died from a fire. She agreed to go through the formal adoption process with her husband with the promise that their son Michael be buried quietly under that beech tree in the cemetery back home. On her first visit home then, no one would have reason to suspect that she wasn't Maggie's mother.

Her family accepted it as truth, but more than one person from Penn Yan wondered about the blonde child with green eyes. Frances's former neighbor noted that the child resembled Tim Lennon who she saw leaving Frances's apartment. And when she counted how many months it had been since she saw him there, it added up to nine. She just *had* to share her theory with a few close friends, who in turn told *their* close friends. The rumor made its way around town eventually to the department store where Pat worked. When he overheard it, he thought about his niece's looks and thought, no, she wasn't a Lennon. Was someone else the father, though? It would truly surprise him, because his sister was a strict Catholic and appeared devoted to Joe, jerk that he was.

***

Adopting Maggie as their own daughter forged a unique bond between Joe and Frances and everyone commented that their marriage appeared stronger than ever. After the fire, Joe made a pact with himself to never neglect his children again and Frances was surprised when he began attending Mass with them once in a while. He doted on Maggie like crazy, causing a bit of jealousy from her sisters. His attention to his third daughter surprised Frances, but she was just happy they'd made it past another rough spell.

They welcomed two more daughters, Terrie three years later and then Eileen, two years after that. Life was good. Joe's sales were the best in his insurance division, earning him a couple of promotions. That afforded him the ability to buy a Rambler station wagon for the family and a red Mustang convertible for himself. They were living comfortably in their cozy home, but when they'd go back to visit Jimmy and Mame, Joe envied the spaciousness of their house and its wraparound porch. He could imagine his family resettled into a house like that where he'd read the paper in a porch rocker after work with a bourbon highball in hand. Frances would be cooking the steak dinner in the kitchen, its primal aroma enticing his appetite.

Joe didn't share his dream with Frances. He'd been looking for a bigger home on the classier West Side of Binghamton, and was hoping to surprise her one day with the keys to a new place. The real estate firm he'd contacted called him at work one afternoon in the summer of 1961. They'd found a house that was similar to the description of what he was seeking and they could arrange a tour when it was convenient. Any time was good because the owners were on vacation in California for a month. The next day, a young woman from the office—a platinum blonde reminiscent of a young Marilyn Monroe—gave him a walk-through of the two-story home with a screened porch (though not a wraparound liked he wanted).

Joe was used to getting looks from women, but this twenty-something intern definitely seemed to be coming on to him. Here he was, nearly forty with grayed temples, five daughters and yet he still had it. She was such an easy mark for his flirtations, too. As they wandered through the house their wordplay turned bawdier and bawdier. She opened the door to the master bedroom and announced in a breathy whisper, "By the way, did I mention that my doctor put me on the Pill."

Before he knew it, his hand was sliding under her dress and over her garters as he pressed her against the closet door. She was not inexperienced, to his delight (what were they teaching at college these days?), and her hands seized his buttocks and pulled him against her. Their dance of lust circled the room and they ended up splayed across the bed as tousled as the sheets on which they made love. He reached out for a final caress of her silky blonde hair and then let his hands linger once more across her full breasts.

"Are you sure you're on the Pill?" he asked as he kissed her neck and then let his lips climb up to meet hers.

She looked at him with a curious expression. Oh no, Joe thought, she doesn't think this means anything, does she? His thoughts must have been broadcasting across his face.

"You look like you've seen a ghost."

He had, and his name was Joey. She pulled away from him and he sat up to start dressing. Her hands massaged his shoulder blades as he re-knotted his tie and she leaned forward, her hair brushing his face.

"Of course I am. So, have I made a sale today?"

He kissed her cheek and winked. "Let me sleep on it."

Joe dallied with a decision named Debbie all summer, in just about every empty two-story house for sale on Binghamton's West Side. She called him one Friday in late August to say that she actually found a house like the one he'd been seeking. It was on a quiet street—a bit of a fixer-upper—but this Queen Anne beauty did indeed have a wraparound porch. When he stood out front of it and saw the green rockers just like the O'Donoghues had, it reminded him about the real purpose of this quest: finding a bigger home for his family. Then after a passionate necking session with Debbie on the davenport, he announced: "The search is over. I'll take this one."

Debbie was thrilled that she could report to her boss at least one sale for the summer. She pulled away from him immediately, buttoned her dress and redrew her lipstick in front of a tall, Venetian-style mirror.

"Wonderful! I leave tomorrow for my final fall semester. Wanda will handle the sale's paperwork and transfer of deed. Just make sure the lock is on when you close the front door. Nice meeting you, Joe."

He was stunned! He'd been played! He'd been fooled by a woman half his age into thinking this lustful arrangement could continue. All he meant to her was a bonus check. Had his skillful lovemaking not impressed her?

It surprised him how deeply this rejection hurt him. He'd *always* left the ladies wanting more. Was he losing his touch? Was she faking her cries of passion all along? His virility aged more than a decade in a second. Joe refused to accept the inevitable outcome of this silly fling and when he went home, knew he had to prove her wrong. That night he made love to Frances with more ardor than he'd expressed toward her in years. Her surprised gasps pleased him, but he wasn't satiated. Despite the fact that the outcome of that passionate evening began to show soon on his wife, he probed each pair of female eyes he encountered afterward for willing partners. He'd be damned if he'd allow himself to lose the one true skill he had.

Their daughter Molly was born on May Day 1962. Joe took that date as a symbolic warning that he *was* in imminent danger of losing his virility if he remained shackled by marriage and fatherhood. He arrived home later and later from work. The girls helped their mother take care of little Molly, but Frances was still so busy with the day-to-day chores, that she was exhausted at day's end and didn't have time to keep track of her husband. Then one torrid June night he left a farewell note stuffed with half of their savings onto the dresser. As Frances lay sleeping, he revved the Mustang, sped to a burlesque club by the tracks to pick up a Betty Page-wannabe named Brenda, and then disappeared into the night, destination: Savannah, Georgia. His paramour was ten years older than Clare.

Chapter 16

Frances hadn't slept well during the night wondering when her husband would get home. She finally fell asleep around three, but the baby woke two hours after that for her feeding. Once little Molly was fed and her diaper changed, Frances fell back asleep hard.

"Mommy, wake up," Terrie said at her bedside. "We need our lunch for school." Frances turned toward the nightstand and squinted at the alarm clock. She bolted upright when she saw it was ten minutes until school started.

"Where's your father?" Frances asked, sliding her arms into the sleeves of her bathrobe and knotting its belt.

"I dunno."

Molly was still asleep in her cradle so Frances shooed Terrie down the hallway, peeking in the older sisters' rooms to make sure they'd already left for high school. They'd both be taking Regents exams today. She hoped they'd studied hard enough last night.

"Joe?" Frances called out as she stepped off the stairs and turned for the kitchen. "You up, honey?"

"Daddy's not here," Eileen said as she ate a bowl of cereal. She'd draped a paper napkin across the Peter Pan collar of her school uniform and was sitting with perfect posture at the kitchen table. Terrie was not so neat, and had apparently eaten a cupcake for breakfast (from the telltale crumbs on her uniform).

Maggie clomped into the kitchen and gasped. Her mother was just now wrapping bologna sandwiches in wax paper and stuffing them into their lunch bags? "You've got to be kidding me! You're not ready yet?" she groaned. "We're going to be late! It's bad enough that I have to be *seen* with you two. I don't want Sister Lucretia snapping at me again."

"Meanie!" Terrie yelled and stuck out her tongue.

"Stop it!" Frances snarled. "Maggie, have you seen your father?"

"No." Maggie picked up Eileen's school bag from the floor and thrust it into her sister's arms. "Let's go!"

Frances looked out the window toward the driveway and saw Joe's Mustang was gone. She nibbled her fingernail as she tried to recall if he had mentioned anything about an early business meeting, but with the new baby and five other daughters in the house, she'd been so distracted lately. As the three youngest girls left for school, Maggie slammed the front door so hard it shook the house and woke the baby. The loudness of the sound elevated the piercing tone of Molly's fearful cries. Frances sighed and went up to comfort her.

As she held Molly, Frances hummed that old Irish song about the milkmaid that her father sang to her when she was a restless infant. She yawned as she walked slowly around the bedroom, and perhaps it was seeing that facial gesture which finally calmed Molly down. Frances rested her daughter's head on her shoulder as her own eyes fell on her bed. The blankets on Joe's side had not been disturbed.

"He hasn't been home yet?" Her voice stirred Molly and she began humming again while considering the possible reasons why he hadn't been there. She set Molly back in her cradle and lay down on the bed to think. Her lack of sleep caught up with her, and the next thing she knew, Molly was crying and the clock on the nightstand now read half past one.

There was housework and shopping and cleaning to do. Molly was hungry and probably needed a diaper change. Her first move though was pulling back the curtains to look down the driveway. Still just the Rambler there. She hated to call Joe's office, but Frances needed to know if he was there—or if she needed to call the police. The flustered secretary a Joe's office transferred the call quickly to his boss.

"Why are you calling, Frances? Didn't Joe tell you that he resigned yesterday? He said he was moving out of town. I thought of course you were...."

"He what?" The receiver slid out of her hand and bounced on the bedroom carpet. She thought their marriage had been stable for a while, especially after the birth of Molly. Had he never given up his philandering? Frances ran into the bathroom and threw up. Waves of sorrow and bad memories rose with each heave of her diaphragm. *How could he abandon us? What are we supposed to live on?* Her mind raced as she patted her face with a damp washcloth.

Molly cried and Frances steeled herself to attend to her daughter's immediate needs. She wondered whom she should call to discuss this. Her parents? Her brother? Her priest? Frances had never been a joiner of clubs or social committees. Despite the fact that they'd lived in Binghamton since 1947, she'd made no close friends and had no support network here. Her solitude magnified the pain of his rejection.

An hour later after wandering aimlessly around the house in shock, she showered then came back to her bedroom to get dressed before the girls got home. Frances glanced at the dresser top as she combed her wet hair and saw Joe's note. Her hands shook as she carried it over to the bed to read. A stack of money fell onto the chenille bedspread when she opened the card. She counted three thousand dollars, about half of what they'd spend in a year. Where did this come from? Then she read the message and the card slipped through her fingers onto the bedspread. Her thoughts raced faster than the tears down her face. She'd have to get a job, *or two*, immediately. But doing what? How would she be able to pay for Clare to go to college next year? Would she have to move back in with her parents? Could she handle the shame of all Penn Yan knowing how she'd been abandoned?

The front door opened and for a split second her hopes rose that he'd changed his mind. But then she heard Clare and Noreen discussing their exams. Frances scooped the money into the note and hid it a dresser drawer. She hadn't decided what to tell her daughters. Now was not the time—she'd have to think this through.

The sisters chatted amiably in the kitchen, and when Frances walked in, Clare stopped speaking and gave her mother an odd look.

"You OK, Mom?"

"Yes. Why do you ask?" Frances feared that it was obvious she'd been crying.

Her eldest daughter looked her up and down with the contorted face of a fashion designer examining a model about to walk the runway.

"It's just…I've never seen you…."

"Mom! Why are you wearing a Madras shirt with striped capris?" Noreen blurted before Clare finished. Frances glanced down at her wardrobe and groaned as she pressed her fists against the temples of her head. Clare raised an eyebrow toward Noreen as their mother's face reddened.

"Because I damn well feel like it!" Frances ran upstairs and slammed the door to her bedroom, waking Molly. Clare and Noreen gasped to hear their mother swear. Her muffled sobbing and the baby's cries drifted down through the ceiling.

"What's the matter with *her*?" Clare asked.

"I dunno. Was what I said mean?" Noreen nibbled her fingernails.

"You were just stating the obvious. Wonder if she had another fight with Dad."

An hour later the other sisters came through the front door bickering noisily. Maggie was mad that Terrie told everyone on the playground that her older sister liked Lou Warner. (Terrie had seen her scribble his name on the side of a notebook.) Lou's buddy asked Maggie if it was true. She was mortified. They were calling each other names when they arrived home, but quieted when they noticed Clare and Noreen sitting with solemn faces in the living room.

"Shush, you guys. You'll wake up Mom."

Maggie gave Clare an odd look. "Wake her up? Why's she asleep *now*?"

It was too late. A few moments later, Frances came downstairs—this time wearing the top that matched her capri pants. Her daughters took one look at her puffy face and knew she was upset about something.

"Mommy, are you too sick to go to my art show tonight at school?"

"*Eileen*, can't you see Mom's tired?"

Frances saw her daughter recoil from Clare's tone. She draped her arms around Eileen and kissed her head.

"What time is the show?"

"It's at seven, Mommy. In the gym."

"OK. Let's have some dinner and then we'll all go."

"All of us? But I have to study for my last exam tomorrow," Clare said, pushing her hands onto her hips.

Frances drew in a deep breath and said in a measured tone, "We're *all* going. No buts!"

Clare caught herself mid-sigh and held it in. Her mother was acting strange. Her father had not been seen since yesterday and she was, frankly, afraid to ask of his whereabouts. She directed her sisters to set the table as their mother tossed an iceberg lettuce salad and broiled grilled American cheese sandwiches for their dinner. While her daughters were in the dining room, Frances poured a double scotch on the rocks.

They sat down to the simple dinner, and after saying grace, all of the sisters started eating except Eileen.

"Mommy, aren't we going to wait for Daddy?"

Clare and Noreen glanced at each other as their mother picked up her glass, drained its scotch and clinked the ice cubes as she stared out the window.

"Daddy won't be eating with us tonight." Frances went back into the kitchen and poured another double. Noreen took advantage of her absence to whisper to her little sister that their father went away on a business trip. It was enough to quell Eileen's curiosity for the moment.

Frances ate half of her sandwich and offered the rest to Terrie, who'd been staring at it as if she was willing her mother to relinquish it. Molly woke up crying and Frances heated a bottle of formula, and then went upstairs to feed her. When she came back down holding Molly, the table was cleared and dishes washed. Usually her daughters fought over whose turn it was to take care of that chore. She was relieved to not have to listen to their bickering tonight.

"OK, let's go see Eileen's masterpiece," Frances said as she passed Molly to Clare and picked up her pocketbook.

Heat trapped all day in the hallways of St. Malachy's School had backed into the gymnasium that night. There was no relief, despite the back door being propped open with bricks to catch a breeze. A stale polyurethane odor from the floor's varnish made Frances slightly nauseous as she carried Molly inside. The art awards ceremony had already begun and Sister Lucretia was announcing the best work from each grade.

"And a blue ribbon for the best artist in first grade goes to Eileen McNamara."

Seeing Eileen's surprised reaction and grins on her sisters' faces elevated Frances's mood. Eileen skipped back to the family clutching the ribbon to her heart.

"I'm so proud of you!" Frances gave her a big sloppy hug. Noreen glanced at Clare when their mother's balance wobbled.

After the awards ceremony, the family strolled around the gym looking at the display. Frances led them backwards, starting with eighth grade, and it embarrassed Clare that her mother appeared unaware that they were the only family moving through the show counterclockwise.

"Mommy, there's my drawing. Come see," Eileen said excitedly as she took her mother's free arm and pulled her across the gym. Frances smiled when Eileen stepped in front of her artwork. Once her sisters gathered next to her mother, Eileen stepped away from the crayon drawing and said, "Ta-da!" Hung by masking tape onto the folded wooden bleachers before them was a portrait of the McNamara family. Joe and Frances stood in the center holding baby Molly and the other sisters surrounded them in descending height. Above her parents, Eileen drew a crucifix with Jesus watching over them.

"Hey, that's us," Terrie said.

Frances stared at the drawing as she realized, *no, that's not us. That's never been us.* She squinted at her daughter's depiction of Joe and replaced his face in her mind with Tim Lennon's. A fleeting slight smile formed with her thoughts. *What would our lives have been like if Antoinette hadn't hogtied him for the homecoming dance? Would* we *be married now? Would we have daughters, or sons, or both? Would he tell me that I'm beautiful and mean it?* Then one last thought got her really thinking: *Would he be trustworthy or were all men unfaithful like Joe?*

Clare saw her mother staring at the drawing and looking sadder by the second. They had to get her out of there, but Frances was riveted by the imagery of the perfect family Eileen had envisioned.

"Penguin alert!" Maggie muttered as Sister Lucretia strolled toward them, her wooden rosary beads tucked in her waistband clacking softly as she approached. Frances smoothed her bangs to distract from her bloodshot eyes, trying not to acknowledge the rising fear of this unavoidable encounter. They were trapped; the shadow of the tall, soft-jowled nun already fell across them.

"Ooh, look at how little Molly is growing," Sister Lucretia said. She stuck her face right up to the baby, whose tiny fist grasped at Frances's shoulder. "Where's your father this evening? Didn't he want to see his daughter win a prize?"

Terrie spoke up. "He's on a business trip." Frances was grateful for the unprompted explanation.

"Oh. Is that so?" Sister Lucretia said as she came around to face Frances. The intensity of her stare felt like she could read thoughts flitting across Frances's mind. "Well it's a pity he had to miss this big moment in Eileen's life." Frances felt the inner corners of her eyes moisten but clung to her tears, not wanting to give any hint to the principal that something was amiss. It didn't matter. Sister Lucretia caught a whiff of the scotch on her breath. That, and the absence of Mr. McNamara, spoke volumes to her. She drifted away toward another cowering family.

"Dammit!" Frances wasn't even aware that her thought had been vocalized. "Let's get out of here. *Now*!"

Noreen, Maggie, Terrie and Eileen nestled in the back seat of the station wagon as Clare held Molly in the front seat, diaper bag at her feet. Frances drove out of the school parking lot and headed toward Main Street. When it was apparent that they weren't heading home, Noreen asked where they were going.

"I don't know." Her solemn tone silenced the sisters. Clare noted the way her mother's hands gripped the steering wheel—like an eagle's talons on a salmon. As soon as Frances turned onto Route 26 in Endicott, Clare knew where they were heading.

"Mommy! Are we meeting Daddy at the lake?" Eileen asked with such innocence that it pained Frances.

"Maybe," Clare answered for her. "We'll just have to wait and see what the surprise is."

Eileen wove her arms in front of her. "I love surprises!"

Noreen frowned. "But, Mom. Clare and I have exams tomorrow and...." Frances's response was to press the car's accelerator so the roar of the engine drowned out Noreen's complaint. Eventually all became quiet inside the Rambler as it disappeared into the humid twilight, curving down country roads with the honey-sweet smell of blooming dame's rocket whirling through the car's open windows. Cricket conversations grew and faded within the grassy shoulders as the car whizzed past. Frances clicked the floor high beams as cars approached. The rhythm of the clicks and country-fresh air lulled Eileen to sleep, followed soon by Terrie. Even Maggie found herself nodding off as her thoughts turned to that boy she fancied.

Heat lightning flashed over the horizon and Noreen hoped that they'd get to their grandparents' house before a storm hit. When she was young Joe told her the story of Mame and Jimmy's scare in the Flood of '35, and she'd feared thunderstorms ever since. No one knew of her phobia, although Frances suspected it. As soon as the first thunder rumbled in the distance, Noreen fled into the house. This time, however, Frances didn't notice the fear rising in her daughter or even the lightning in the distance. Her thoughts were focused on a much different approaching storm.

The station wagon glided down steep Odessa Hill toward Watkins Glen, and Noreen panicked. *What if the storm hits as we're driving through and the Seneca Lake rises quickly*, she wondered. *Will we be trapped down here?* The village was at the foot of both a deep gorge and the biggest of the Finger Lakes, and its southern end was hemmed by waterfalls and wetlands. Too much water surrounded them, Noreen thought, as her aqua-claustrophobia rose. The closer they got to Watkins Glen, though, the storms appeared to be passing to the north, and the bright moon approached the zenith of the sky.

Frances stopped to get gas at a Sinclair station. A cloud of mayflies danced around a light post by the green brontosaurus statue as she went inside to buy cigarettes. The service attendant smiled at Molly asleep in Clare's arms as he squeegeed winged splatters off the windshield. Frances returned and instead of heading up the west side of the lake, turned east toward Lakeside Park on the southern shore of Seneca Lake. She stopped in the parking area, got out and lit a cigarette as she sat on the hood of the car to stare at the lake.

"What's she doing?" Noreen whispered to Clare.

"I have no idea. She hasn't smoked in ages." Clare said.

"Why are we here? We need to get to Penn Yan before a storm hits. Mom looks so angry. Did she and Daddy have a fight?"

"Something's happened. I think it's pretty bad."

Frances snuffed the cigarette into the gravel, wiped her moist eyes with the backs of her hands and opened the car door. The rustling noises stirred Molly a little, but soon she fell back asleep, her head sweaty against her sister's neck. Clare shifted her gently and glanced at her mother's face, glowing eerily from the dashboard lights. She was scowling fiercely at the highway ahead, her hands still clenched on the steering wheel. Clare wondered what her mother was thinking and what her grandparents would say when they arrived unexpectedly at their house at this hour. They had no suitcases, no change of clothes. The whole thing was so odd.

Her mother's silence unnerved Clare. Was she just angry or was she hurt by something? She wondered if their father had abandoned them, or were they meeting him there?

As they crested the Second Milo hilltop on Route 14A, the lights of Penn Yan came into view. Once in town, they continued heading straight on Brown Street instead of making a right on South Avenue toward her grandparents' house. Clare glanced at her mother and noticed her expression looked dazed.

"Uh, Mom. You just missed the turnoff to Grandma and Grandpa's."

Frances acted as if she didn't hear Clare and once the road became Liberty Street she made a left onto Water Street, following a narrow road down by the outlet. Clare turned her head slightly and caught Noreen's wide eyes. She shrugged, suggesting she was just as clueless as to why they were there. Frances parked the station wagon near the docks across from the old ice house. Without saying a word, she opened her door then reached over and took Molly from Clare's arms.

"What are we doing here, Mom?" Noreen asked out her window.

Frances ignored the question and walked briskly toward the dock.

"Is she sad or angry now? I can't tell," Clare said.

Maggie woke up and looked out her window.

"Where are we?"

"Penn Yan."

"But *where* are we?"

"What's Mommy doing with Molly?" Terrie asked.

A flicker of a dark thought made Clare's heart palpitate. *What* is *she doing?*

"You don't think she's going to throw...." Before she finished her own question, Clare jumped out of the car and raced across the gravel lot to the old dock. Noreen and Maggie followed to assist her. Their palpable fear frightened Terrie who wanted to see up close what was going on, and when she slammed her car door shut, it woke Eileen.

"Hey! Where is everyone?" she cried. Eileen stepped out of the car rubbing her eyes and wandered after them onto the long dock. A lone light bulb shone from the back of the ice house across the outlet. The half-moon played peekaboo with the clouds and heat lightning glowed like a nightlight on the eastern horizon. Frances hugged baby Molly as tightly as a mother sending a son off to war. Noreen gasped when her mother's feet neared the end of the dock.

"Maggie, what's going on?" Eileen asked groggily.

"Shhh!"

Clare tiptoed up to her mother and extended her arms. "Mom, I think Molly needs a diaper change. Give her to me and I'll take care of it."

Frances gripped Molly tighter and raised her face toward the moonlight that cast her shadow on the water. *How fitting,* she thought. *Last time I was here with Joe it was a full moon. Now both half of the moon and my marriage are missing.* As she dropped her head forward, a tear slid down her chin and into the black water.

"No, Mom!" Clare pried Molly from her mother's arms as Noreen grabbed Frances's waist and pulled her back from the edge. Clare ran off the dock cradling her baby sister and paused breathlessly on the shore. The run jostled Molly awake and she whimpered.

"Mom! What's *wrong* with you?" Noreen asked as she spun her around.

All the years of hurt she held in from her difficult marriage released at once. Frances grabbed the dock piling and bent over it, sobbing so loudly that Eileen hugged Maggie out of fear. Suddenly Frances grew calm and raised her fists at the moon.

"DAMN YOU, JOE McNAMARA!"

Frances's voice resonated not only off the silvered wood of the ice house, but across her daughters' hearts. They all recoiled from the angry outburst, except Terrie. She stepped up bravely to her mother and gave her a hug. "It's gonna be OK, Mommy." Terrie rubbed her mother's back gently. Her healing touch softened Frances's demeanor, and it was evident that the worst of her internal storm had passed.

"Let's go back to the car, Mom," Noreen said, as she took her trembling mother and led her slowly off the dock.

Frances looked at her confused daughters lined up against the Rambler. *My God, what's become of me,* she thought. *I almost....* Her thoughts triggered more tears. She covered her mouth as glanced back at the dock, at the outlet, at the literal start of her own family. She held her hand over her heart and groaned, releasing the pain of the dreadful day, and then ushered her family back into the car.

"Let's go home," Frances said.

"Home?" Clare asked, astonished by the suggestion. "At this hour? Don't you want to stay overnight at Grandma and Grandpa's house?"

"You've got to get back tonight. I don't want you and Noreen to miss your important exams tomorrow."

The sisters climbed into the car and when Frances put the key in the ignition, she turned around to look at them. Before she spoke she took a deep breath.

"Girls, your father has left us. He's moved down South. It's just us now. I'm so sorry. We'll have to take care of each other from now on. Always remember that. Promise?"

"Yes, Mommy," Eileen quavered. "And I even Keuka swear on it." She held up her hand so her thumb and forefinger made a Y shape. The other sisters followed suit, touching their fingers together across the car seat, and then Clare touched baby Molly's brow with a Y. Not another word was spoken on the long ride home. Each wondered in silence what they'd done to cause their abandonment.

Chapter 17

Frances struggled to keep self-pity from drowning her optimism, but she made about as much progress with it as you would rowing a boat in a squall. It seemed crises gathered like stray cats on the lawn every night as she slept, sneaking inside at the first crack of the front door. The furnace died, the car radiator leaked, and then the dentist said Terrie had a mouthful of cavities and needed several fillings. Immediately. On top of all that, Frances would not have been able to meet the mortgage payments if not for assistance from her parents and the part-time job at a Catholic relief agency. That financial relief helped her keep the pantry stocked, her daughters dressed stylishly enough and the regular bills paid on time.

Pat called on Wednesday evenings, and if he sensed a bit of exasperation in his sister's voice, he'd mail her a check the next day, always writing "For clay & wattles" on the note line. It was a reference to their mother's favorite poem, "The Lake Isle of Innisfree," by William Butler Yeats. Mame said its imagery was as relaxing as a summer afternoon spent rocking on the porch. His code message to his sister was that this was money not to be used for the mundane, but for little splurges that would lift the family's morale above their difficulties.

Unbeknownst to Pat, Frances stashed a few dollars from each check he sent in the false bottom of her cedar jewelry chest. She wasn't sure what she was saving it for. Then one day she got her answer when a nun dropped off brochures at the office about a retreat center on Skaneateles Lake.

It was midsummer 1966, and she was dreading the approaching Labor Day weekend anniversary of when Joe first got her pregnant. He'd been gone from their lives four years now, yet the stress caused from memories of that evening twenty-two years ago immobilized her psyche like Omaha Beach nightmares to a World War II veteran. She picked up the brochure and her eyes lingered over photos of the white mansion with its peaceful lake views, willow-shaded lawn and meditative garden paths. Just thinking about the possibility of a getaway there lowered her blood pressure.

Frances's daughters were growing up fast and she felt her control over them slipping. A publishing house in Manhattan had hired Clare as an entry-level editor and she would start work there in September. Noreen had one year left to go at SUNY Cortland. She'd probably be employed at a school district by next year. Maggie was by then a moody, sneaky sixteen-year-old who needed the steady influence of her calmer sisters. What would be better than to force the three to spend one final summer vacation together?

Frances called her mother and asked if the girls could visit the last week of August so she could go on retreat. Mame conferred with Jimmy and Pat before saying yes. (She'd need as much help minding the youngest girls as she would with Maggie.) It just so happened that the McGraths were planning a family reunion then. What better time for the girls to visit?

When she shared her idea for their week's stay in Penn Yan, Molly and Eileen squealed. Clare rolled her eyes and sighed exaggeratedly; she knew she'd be working as her sisters' surrogate mother this vacation. Translation: she'd be policing Maggie! Noreen and Terrie took the news with little reaction. Maggie pushed her chair from the dinner table and folded her arms.

"You have *got* to be kidding me! What if I already have plans?"

Frances didn't even look her in the eye as she said, "Well, as of now they are canceled. End of discussion."

She dropped the girls off on the last Saturday morning in August. They stood on the wraparound porch with slightly bewildered expressions and waved goodbye as Frances drove toward the village, then the thruway and beyond that her first week of freedom since the summer of 1944.

The absence of immediate responsibility made Frances giddy. She could go anywhere if she wanted. Flitting scenarios of what else she could do with her freedom lifted her broken spirits, as did the passing vistas of breeze-rippled wheat fields under a cyan sky.

Back at her parents' home, the girls unpacked for the week ahead. Clare and Noreen claimed their mother's former room on the grounds that the eldest had the first and best choice. Maggie and Terrie didn't argue and claimed the twin beds in the back room. Downstairs Eileen and Molly opened their suitcases on the queen bed in the den. Jimmy brought down a small spare dresser from the attic and set it up in for them.

After all of them were settled, Mame thought it would be fun to take her granddaughters to Bingo at the Elks that night, her treat. They sat at a cafeteria table in the back of the crowded hall. It was sweaty-hot and a blue haze of cigarette smoke lingered near the pressed tin ceiling. Pat disappeared soon after with his lodge friends and they hung out at the bar chatting about baseball and eating handfuls of Spanish peanuts chased with draught beers. Jimmy had Clare join him at the concession stand to help carry back the popcorn and bottles of orange pop he bought them while Mame showed the others how to play. Molly bored quickly and inked the back of her hand with the red dauber for the special paper card games.

"I'll take that," Mame said as she thought, *this is going to be a long evening*. Molly just shrugged and sipped her orange pop noisily through a straw. Next she started arranging her grandmother's plastic bingo chips into piles of red and green. When the announcer tested the microphone and its ear-splitting feedback squeal startled Molly, her hands hit the chips, scattering them onto the floor. Maggie sniggered at the mess her sister caused next to her as Clare jumped up from the other side of the table and came around to help Molly pick them up.

Mame's head throbbed and she rubbed her forehead. "Thank you, Clare," she whispered as her granddaughters cleaned up the mess.

Terrie took to the game with much fervor, keeping an eye on not only her numbers, but also those on her sisters' cards. She was annoyed that Maggie wasn't paying attention and kept nudging her. Maggie didn't even notice; she was squinting at the florid, big-boned farm wives scanning multiple bingo cards at once and imagining they were a field of Holstein dairy cows, lying on grass, chewing their cuds.

A group of young men tanned from hours of water skiing arrived and huddled at the hall entrance. Within seconds Noreen and Maggie excused themselves to the ladies room, not to return until it was time to leave. Jimmy kept an eye on them from the concession stand as the sisters flirted with the group. The others were almost evicted from the hall when Terrie yelled "Bingo!" (far too soon, some players grumbled) and Molly jumped up with her orange pop in hand, spraying it all over the nearby players' paper cards. Mame offered to buy them replacements, but the players wondered if they'd bring them more bad luck and refused.

When they got home, Mame had a rare late-night glass of scotch with Jimmy in the kitchen.

"It's going to be a long week," she said with a deep sigh. Jimmy raised his glass and clinked hers.

After Mass the next day, the girls and their grandparents were invited to a cookout at their Great-Uncle Mike McGrath's cottage. They looked forward to seeing him again, as well as Great-Aunt Susie, their son Gerry McGrath and his wife Joan, and their children, Martin, Michael, James and Kate. Uncle Pat begged off; he had plans to play golf in Canandaigua with friends.

After they arrived and greeted everyone, Molly had one priority—she couldn't wait to jump into the lake. Clare suited up immediately and chased her four-year-old sister down to the water, serving as lifeguard as Molly splashed in the shallows much of the afternoon. On the dock next to them, the Beach Boys harmonized from the transistor radio while Kate, Noreen and Maggie sunbathed, the scent of their Coppertone drifting onto shore. The McGrath brothers were becalmed in the middle of the lake, struggling to trap a breeze with their candy-striped Sunfish sail. Terrie was oblivious to all of the sensory delights around her as she read comic books under the willow tree, her imagination chasing hero avengers in shadowy metropolises. Upstairs in the cottage Eileen exhausted her grandmother and Great-Aunt Susie with her knowledge of Mahatma Gandhi's hunger strike for peace as they set out sandwiches for all to graze upon when they came back onto the screened porch. The older women found the subject too intense for a lazy summer afternoon and switched the topic to the health of some women in their bridge club.

Uncle Mike powered up the motorboat later that afternoon to take the sunbathers and sailors water skiing. Molly sat in the seat next to him, her gleeful face showered by spray flying over the windshield as they smacked wakes churned by other boats. Her life preserver was as big as she was, encasing her thoroughly with its mildewy orange fabric. By the time the sun was far west in the sky, all the cousins had succeeded at their attempts, Maggie even skiing into shore to finish her run.

The evening's cookout menu was hardly innovative, but in that lake air after spending a day immersed in Keuka's refreshing waters, it tasted as marvelous as a buffet laid before an emperor. Jimmy charred the hot dogs and hamburgers artfully on the grill. The corn on the cob had been picked from the slopes of the lake that morning, and when it was slathered with melted butter and dotted with salt crystals, a bite of the kernels burst with the flavors of summertime. The dinner included side dishes of pasty thick, bacon-dressed beans, potato salad (Aunt Bertha's recipe) and wedges of chilled, juicy watermelon. Dessert was delectable peach cobbler baked by Joan.

When it was time to clear the tables, Mame was embarrassed to notice that all of the older girls and the three brothers were conveniently missing. As the adults were distracted by dinner, Martin had snuck a couple six-packs of beer from the basement refrigerator and the group slipped out of the cottage one by one to wander up a neighboring creek to go drinking. Terrie was off somewhere with her comic books, but Eileen volunteered cheerfully to wash the dishes after they were carried into the kitchen. She shooed Mame, Susie and Joan out of the room and told them to go relax.

Jimmy shuffled the deck of cards as he started a game of Scat with Mame, Susie and Molly on the porch. Meanwhile, Mike and Gerry gathered kindling for the bonfire and Joan rounded up the inflatable rafts strewn across the beach, stashing them in the cottage basement. She dragged out more folding chairs and set them on the lawn near the fire pit. Once the logs ignited fully, the men yelled up to the others to come down and join them.

"Eileen, be a dear and grab the bag of marshmallows and skewers on the back porch," Aunt Susie called to her as she headed down to the lake.

Tall flames licked at the twilight above. Below the fiery nest, shale pebbles overheated until they exploded like popcorn, pinging the beach. Gerry took an old laundry detergent bucket and dredged it into the lake water, setting it nearby for any emergency.

"Molly, want to try a sparkler?" Uncle Mike asked.

"Don't you think she's too young?" Aunt Susie cautioned.

"Nah, I'll help her. OK, Molly? I'll light it for you." She nodded as he poked the silvery rod into the bonfire then pulled it out when gold sparks shot off it. When he cupped Molly's small hand around the end of the rod, a cloud of stinky smoke hit her face and she coughed, nearly dropping the firework.

"Hold on tight. Let's make circles in the air," Uncle Mike said as he waved her hand around like a windmill blade. Molly giggled with delight. The magic was gone too quickly; the sparks faded but the rod still glowed. "Now go drop it in that bucket." The rod hissed when it hit the water. Molly liked that sound almost as much as the fireworks.

"Another one!" Molly held out her hand to her great-great-uncle. How could he resist her delightful plea? Eileen dropped the skewers and marshmallows off to Aunt Susie, then held her hand out to her uncle, too.

"Can I try one?"

"Only if I can, too," Mame said. The three of them lit their sparklers at the same time, making a magnesium fog roll over the beach as they looped sparking circles in the air.

By the time the older kids returned from their drinking escapade, Molly had fallen asleep on her grandfather's lap from a toasted marshmallow-induced "coma." Mame and Susie were singing "Heart of My Heart" in two-part harmony as the young cousins sauntered past them to the end of the dock. They sat down and dangled their feet in the sun-warmed water beneath an orange gibbous moon.

The evening's laughter faded gradually like the once proud bonfire, now reduced to humble embers. Soon the McNamara girls were back at the house with the wraparound porch, sound asleep in their beds.

***

On Tuesday evening, two young men showed up on the O'Donoghue's front porch.

"Are Noreen and Maggie in?" one of them asked Jimmy. He recognized these kids; they were the boys his granddaughters were talking to on bingo night.

"And you are?"

"I'm Rob and he's Dave," he said. "We met them the other night. We're going to the drag races at the fairgrounds and wanted to know if they'd like to join us."

"Drag races. Hmm, OK. I'll go call them. Have a seat, boys," Jimmy said, pointing to the rockers. The first thing Jimmy did was ask Mame to come out from the kitchen and see if she recognized either of the young men. She shook her head.

"They must be summer people," Mame whispered as she noted the expensive Mustang convertible in the driveway. "What do they want with the girls?"

"They're inviting them to the drag races up the hill."

Jimmy's sigh said it all. Mame experienced a moment of déjà vu from the first night she met Joe McNamara. *Oh Lord, please don't let this be a repeat of history*, she thought. Mame wasn't concerned at all about Noreen. (But was that naïve?) If any of the McNamaras were apt to repeat the mistakes of their mother it would be Maggie.

"Should we let them go?" Jimmy asked.

"Only if they walk there, it's not that far. And only if Clare goes, too. She's got the most sense of the lot."

"Good thinking, Mame."

The two sisters were delighted by their surprise visitors. While they chatted on the porch, Mame cornered Clare and asked if she could do her a favor by chaperoning them.

Clare rolled her eyes but agreed. She could not think of a duller pastime than drag racing. The two young men were equally dull to her, though she admitted they were cute. Clare longed for what she imagined to be a more exciting life filled with fascinating men awaiting her in Manhattan.

Mame worried all evening, but it was for naught. The three girls returned from the date a few minutes before the imposed curfew of eleven. She detected no lingering odors of alcohol or cigarettes. They walked up the porch steps laughing and happy. It had been an evening that even Clare enjoyed. The five planned to get together again that week.

Despite the fact that the date appeared uneventful, memories of what occurred with Frances years ago weighed on Mame's mind that night as she struggled to fall asleep. When she awoke the next morning, a lingering question haunted her: What if she and Jimmy had refused to allow Frances to go off with Joe and Eddie that night? These six lively girls wouldn't be here probably. What would her daughter have made of her life? Would she be a veterinarian or a teacher now? Would she have married someone else?

Mame mulled the possibilities all day. She considered how the actions in one's life rippled into someone else's, whether in this generation or the next. That set her off on another train of thought: What if she'd married Eugene Roach instead of Jimmy? Would she be living in a fancy house in Chicago? Would she have been a teacher?

"Potato salad for your thoughts," Jimmy said, distracting her.

Mame laughed. "Sorry. My mind's a bit preoccupied."

"Care to talk about it?"

"Just worried about Frances. How is she ever going to be able to raise these six daughters alone?"

"Well, she does come from that strong McGrath stock, and I can attest that they never give up."

She was grateful that he made her laugh, distracting her thoughts. "Speaking of the gang, where have they scattered to?"

"Clare, Noreen and Maggie walked downtown to shop. Terrie's watching the baseball game on TV with Pat. Eileen's reading in the den and Molly...." Before he could finish his words, Molly swung open the back screen door and held out a fist of fruit-laden snowberry bush branches as a bouquet to her grandmother.

"Look what I picked for you, Grandma!"

Mame noticed leaves entwined in Molly's curls, and then saw her scratched arms, her dirt-caked knees.

"Oh, that's lovely," Mame said, thinking that her granddaughter must have harvested the bouquet from inside the shrubbery. "Let's find a vase to put them in, Molly."

As she filled a tall glass with water, Mame held the white berry globes and they reminded her of something she read in the newspaper.

"There's something rare about today, Molly. Do you know what it is?"

Molly put her finger on her right dimple as she thought. "It's quiet here?"

"No," Mame laughed, "that's not it. Tonight there's a blue moon."

"Made of bleu cheese, no doubt," Jimmy added. Molly's eyes widened.

"Ignore your silly grandfather. A blue moon is rare, the second full moon in a month."

"Can I stay up to see it?"

"If the sky is clear, I promise you'll get to see it."

The phone rang an hour later and Mame was surprised to hear her daughter's voice.

"Everything OK, dear?"

"Yes, Mother. It's so peaceful here. But I'm just feeling guilty for enjoying my solitude a little too much. How are the girls?"

"Wonderful. They're having a great time. The McGraths reunion was fun. I took them to bingo, too. Terrie won!"

"Oh, she must have been thrilled."

"Right now the younger ones are reading and Clare, Noreen and Maggie walked downtown to shop."

"Is Pat with them?"

"No." Mame sensed the fear rising in her daughter. "But don't worry; I'm sure they'll be back in time for dinner. The three went on a date the other night with two nice young men and came home before their curfew."

"You let them go off on a date?"

"Frances, it was fine. Clare chaperoned. She's twenty-one now, remember?"

"But Maggie...."

"She was well-behaved, as was Noreen. We have no reason to suspect anything bad occurred."

After they said goodbye and hung up, Mame felt Frances's worry growing inside her. Had her grand-parenting been careless this week? Had she been too trusting?

Jimmy challenged the girls to a poker tournament that night and they set up a felt-covered octagon table in the living room. He provided each girl with a Styrofoam cup filled with twenty pennies. They placed their bets carefully, treating winnings as if each penny was worth a hundred dollars. Mame helped Molly, but they had little luck and were the first to be knocked out.

Molly pouted until her grandmother brought out cones filled with peach ice cream and they sat on the porch to eat it. The combination of a day spent playing outside and the late infusion of sugar made Molly sleepy. Mame tucked her in bed early.

The poker playing lasted hours and it was down to Uncle Pat and Maggie. Her sisters stayed by, cheering her on. Jimmy and Mame got a kick out of her natural poker instincts. *Hah! Her skills must come from her father*, Mame thought. It was nearing midnight and Mame recalled the nervousness in Frances's voice. The youngest girls should be in bed, she thought. She didn't have the heart to ask them to quit, though. It was rare to see the sisters getting along so well with each other and she was happy that Maggie was having this opportunity to shine.

Pat saw a hint of worry on his mother's face and suspected she wanted the game to end. He purposefully threw away one of the cards from his full house and then wagered all of his winnings. Maggie looked at her sisters for approval to stand her ground and met his bet. The hours of playing came down to the reveal. Everyone held their breath as Pat displayed two aces and two kings. They looked for a reaction on Maggie's face, but couldn't discern if she was a winner or loser. This moment of power delighted her and she laid her cards down one at a time, all clubs, a six, seven, eight, nine and then....

"Ten! It's a flush! Hah-hah, Uncle Pat, you sucker! Hand me all your cash."

The girls cheered and Jimmy patted his son's back.

"Nice try, son. Nice try. I should have warned you from the get go that she was a ringer."

"Thanks for nothing, Pops!"

The older girls chatted in their bedrooms long after the rest of the house fell asleep. Noreen and Clare were talking excitedly about her upcoming job in Manhattan. Noreen envied Clare's exciting future. She knew that a year from now she'd probably be teaching at an elementary school in upstate New York, while Clare would be conversing with famous authors at fancy restaurants. Although she was looking forward to starting a teaching career, wiping the noses of first-graders lacked the glamor that would surely be in Clare's big city life.

Down the hall, there was a different tone. Maggie, still empowered from her glorious poker win, was bragging to Terrie about how many boys she'd kissed. She'd had the opportunity to kiss both Rob and Dave at the drag races the other night and was comparing their styles, not that Terrie had asked about it. Her older sister made it sound like kissing was effortless, but Terrie wondered how you'd keep from smashing your nose into the boy's face. She didn't feel a strong desire toward any of the boys she knew, yet Terrie thought kissing must be something good since people seem to desire it so much. In a few weeks she'd be starting high school and Terrie knew it would be difficult to follow the dating reputations of her older sisters. To be honest, she wished she could just avoid that whole aspect of life. She'd be content to spend her time reading comics and hanging out with pets instead of boys.

The giggles from the two bedrooms across the hall kept Mame awake. She wondered what the girls were talking about at this hour. The siblings' bond was something she'd never experienced being the only daughter in her family. Were the girls always like this at home?

Her thoughts returned to the enormous pressures Frances faced raising her daughters alone. The task felt insurmountable to Mame. One bad emergency could wipe out Frances's bank account and they could lose their house—oh, how the dire things she was thinking of gave her an upset stomach. She folded her pillow to prop her head hoping it would ease her discomfort, but the acid still burned inside.

Mame tiptoed downstairs to the kitchen and pulled out a box of baking soda from the cupboard. She stirred half a teaspoon into a juice glass of water and looked out the back door as she drank it. The lawn was brightened by the light of the full moon. Oh, she'd nearly forgotten—the blue moon! Then she remembered her promise to show it to Molly. She couldn't let this opportunity pass.

Molly was asleep on her side facing the door when Mame entered the den. She whispered to her granddaughter, trying to not wake up Eileen. It didn't work. They both stirred from their sleep, rubbing their eyes.

"The blue moon is out. Do you girls want to see it?"

Molly nodded through a big yawn and grabbed her grandmother's hand. Eileen walked jerkily after them, still sleep drunk. Mame unlocked the back porch door, then pushed open the screen door. Its hinges yelped for oil, waking Jimmy who was confused to hear faint conversation downstairs. When Mame released the screen door, it slammed shut, stirring the rest of the household from their sleep.

"Oops! Let's go out in the yard to have a good look at the moon," she said.

"There it is!" Molly yelled. Mame pantomimed a shushing sound, putting a finger over her mouth.

"But Grandma, it's white not blue." Eileen just wanted to be back in bed and was confused by this midnight silliness.

"It's the second full moon in the month of August, a rare occasion. Ever hear the expression once in a blue moon?"

"Yeah. This is what that means?" Eileen rubbed her eyes again and tilted her head back to get a better look.

Jimmy noticed Mame wasn't in bed, tied on his bathrobe and came downstairs. He was alarmed to see the back door open, but when he saw Mame out there with Molly and Eileen he grinned.

"Do you want the neighbors to think you're mad, dear?"

"Grandpa! Grandpa! Look at the blue moon!" Molly ran toward him then waved her arm like a windmill, encouraging him to come off the porch and see.

"Look at all that bleu cheese," Jimmy said rubbing his stomach. "Makes me hungry for a big salad."

Molly put her hands on her hips and frowned. "Grandpa, you can't eat the moon. It's too far away."

"Why I think I can reach right up and...oh, this is harder than I thought. There! A nice chunk of bleu cheese for meez." His pantomime made Molly laugh loudly. They were underneath Pat's window at that point and the conversations woke him up. He peeked out his bedroom window and called to them.

"What's going on?"

His father pointed up in the sky, but the moon was out of the visibility range for Pat, so he also put on his bathrobe and went outside, the screen door slamming again. This time the noise awakened completely the other four sisters.

"What time is it?" Maggie mumbled into her pillow.

"I dunno. I don't think it's time to get up," Terrie said. "But I hear voices downstairs."

Clare and Noreen were at the top of the staircase when Maggie and Terrie emerged from their room.

"What's happening?" Maggie asked.

"Everyone's up. Their bedrooms are empty. Hope nothing bad has happened," Clare said. The sisters descended the stairs quickly and headed toward the light coming from an empty kitchen.

"Look! They're all outside." Noreen pointed at the back yard.

"Hey you guys!" Molly yelled. "It's the blue moon."

"The *what*?" Maggie asked thinking that she was not amused.

"This is a rare thing," Eileen said. "It's the second full moon in the month of August."

Clare folded her arms and rolled her eyes at her sisters. "Our family is nuts."

"C'mon, you old sourpusses," Uncle Pat teased. "Haven't you heard the song about it?" As he launched into the first verse, Jimmy grabbed Mame's hand and swung her around into a dance hold and they swayed together across the lawn.

Noreen sighed. Oh how she would love to marry a man as kind and romantic as their grandfather. The sight made Clare wistful, too. She'd yet to meet any guy with whom she could have both an intelligent conversation and be as playful as these two lovebirds. Oh Clare had no difficulty attracting young men: she'd often been called a "looker" for her beautiful face and model-slim figure. But they had difficulty retaining her interest. Most bored her thoroughly before a first date ended.

Maggie thought her grandparents were the coolest couple on earth. Here it was after midnight and they were out in the yard dancing under a full moon. She wanted to know what that felt like.

"May I cut in," she asked her grandmother. Mame smiled.

"Be my guest, Maggie."

She'd never seen anyone slow-dance like this at school. Maggie thought having your partner hold your hand as you danced was far more romantic than draping your arms around his neck. Jimmy noticed she picked up the steps quickly and then broadened their stride to waltz her around the yard, released his hold on her back and then spun her under his extended arm. She laughed gleefully and then he dipped her for the big finish. Maggie drifted dreamily away from their moondance.

"Next?" he asked extending his arms toward the girls. Terrie stepped forward shyly and her grandfather took her hands and smiled tenderly as he positioned her to dance. "And away we go," he said. Uncle Pat ran out of verses so he just continued to hum the "Blue Moon" melody.

Mame put her arm around Molly and pointed at the snowberry bush hedge. "Look, the lightning bugs are dancing, too."

"Let's go catch some," Molly said. She grabbed Mame's hand and yanked her toward the hedge. Molly learned quickly that the art of catching lightning bugs was tricky. When they flashed their bioluminescent bellies, she ran toward them, but then she'd have to guess which direction they'd fly next to try and catch them midair. Mame noticed one on a snowberry branch, making the surrounding globed berries light up like a streetlamp.

She gestured to Molly and they tiptoed close to the bug. Molly brought her hands together around it.

"Did you catch it?"

"I dunno," Molly said as she opened her hands and the bug flashed into the sky above her.

"Nooo!" she cried like a mournful beagle.

The dance session dispersed toward the back of the yard to see what had happened. Uncle Pat heard Molly's explanation and went inside the kitchen, returning with a small glass jar that Mame was going to use for peach jam.

"Here, Molly. Catch them into here. Then you'll be able to see if you've got one and it won't escape.

"Good idea, son," Mame said.

Another lightning bug landed and Molly lowered the jar over the branch and caught it. Uncle Pat clamped his hand over the bottom and they maneuvered the jar off the branch successfully.

"She needs a lid for the jar with holes in it so the bug can breathe." Jimmy went back into the house and came back to them with a piece of metal screen that he adhered to the jar with duct tape. "Voila!"

"Hey! I caught one, too!" Eileen yelled, standing next to the quince bush.

Uncle Pat assisted the transfer of her catch to the jar, lifting the tape off just enough so she could release the cargo from her cupped hands.

"You've got night lights for your bedroom now," Noreen said to Molly.

"What are you going to name them?" Terrie asked.

Mame stroked her youngest granddaughter's humidity-curled ringlets. "You must name one Titania, for the queen of the fairies."

"Oh, I *love* Shakespeare," Clare said, brightening at the recognized reference. "My favorite is *King Lear*."

"You have good taste, Clare."

"My favorite is *Romeo and Juliet*," Noreen said trying to sound equally sophisticated.

"Of course it is, you hopeless romantic." Clare laughed teasingly, but Noreen took unintended offense. Mame sensed the rivalry bubbling up and quipped back, "Aren't we all hopeless romantics? What other family comes out in their pajamas to dance by the light of the blue moon?"

Jimmy had gone back into the kitchen and re-emerged with a small plate covered with a napkin. "I think that before we all return to bed, we need to sample a piece of the moon." He drew the napkin away from small chunks of bleu cheese and offered a piece to each of them.

"What were we saying about hopeless romantics?" Mame winked as she popped a piece in her mouth. "Mmm, the blue moon is delicious."

They ate their pieces except Molly who spit hers out instantly. "Yuck!"

"All right, off with you all to bed!" Jimmy shooed them back into the house, and after he locked the back door, stole a kiss from his waiting wife.

Chapter 18

The first fuse blew at nine that hot morning in July 1973. Jimmy and Mame's house was showing its age: the wiring was no match for the strain of granddaughters trying to use high-voltage hair dryers all at once. Jimmy didn't mind that it happened and laughed while descending the creaky stairs to the basement, a package of new fuses in hand. It was a joy to have such life buzzing through the house again. Most days it was just he and Mame reading the newspaper silently downstairs and the enthusiastic play-by-play of a baseball announcer broadcasting from Pat's radio upstairs.

He couldn't believe that his second-oldest granddaughter was now 27 years old. Mame was delighted by Noreen's request to get married in Penn Yan instead of Binghamton. Here was where her happiest childhood memories occurred. Back then each sister got a week alone with the grandparents. And Noreen spent long summer days there playing with dolls in the downstairs den or Parcheesi with Grandpa on the porch.

Mame asked Father Kane, the pastor of St. Urban's, if the wedding Mass could be held there even though her granddaughter wasn't a parishioner. He said it would be fine, and Noreen and her fiancé Gary Pomeroy met with him for premarital counseling sessions. Noreen especially wanted her reception to be lakeside, and Jimmy was able to secure the boat club for it. He was not crazy about the idea of a bunch of young kids drinking near water, so unbeknownst to her he hired a few muscle-bound dock workers to patrol the beach that night.

Mame wanted to help Frances with the wedding plans more, but she'd not been feeling right lately. Blinding migraines hit her during the mid-afternoon for no apparent reason, and she'd been waking up in the middle of the night with indigestion. Mame found that if she propped her head with two pillows, it seemed to allay the discomfort and she'd drift back to sleep. However, she'd awaken still tired for the first few hours of the day. Perhaps it was just her age showing, but she always used to be filled with pep first thing in the morning.

On this special day, she dragged herself out of bed early to make fried cakes, as much for her daughter as the bride-to-be and bridesmaids. The smell of the fresh-made doughnuts and brewing coffee lured the girls away from their beauty routines to straggle downstairs. All were here except Maggie who was driving in with her date from San Francisco as part of a cross-country trip. The sisters' loud chatter and laughter around the dining room table delighted Mame, although it did trigger a headache.

Frances saw her mother wince and asked, "Is it too early for a drink, mother?" Mame raised her head and laughed heartily.

"If you're pouring, daughter, I'll take a double Manhattan."

"That'll be two, then," Frances said with a wink.

"How's that new job going?" Mame was proud of the way her daughter rose to the challenge of becoming the family's breadwinner.

After Joe disappeared, the Binghamton Catholic relief agency assisted the family with buying clothes and food, but it also hired Frances part-time for office work. One of their donors provided scholarships for single parents to continue their education. Her boss was impressed with Frances's organizational skills and nominated her for a scholarship to the community college. Frances accepted it eagerly and excelled at the business curriculum. It was worth the extra effort and hours added to her already hectic day; the agency just promoted her to office manager. In gratitude for all they'd done for her, she also volunteered to oversee the start of their Right to Life efforts.

Mame wished her own mother was alive to see how far her granddaughter had come to celebrate this day. Frances never complained about her lot in life. She reminded herself that she was on a path chosen knowingly. All her friends told Frances that Joe McNamara was a womanizer yet she'd ignored their warnings. To Mame the great thing about Frances's achievement was that she could see her granddaughters were proud of and inspired by their mother's determination, although some never expressed it.

"How's it going, girls?" Mame asked as she brought out a fresh plate of fried cakes, some dredged in cinnamon sugar, the others in confectioner's.

"Terrie's been ready for hours," Clare said. "No surprise there. Someone better keep an eye on Molly here and make sure she doesn't walk down the aisle with fried cake sugar on her face."

Molly, a hypersensitive 11-year-old, set down the doughnut she was about to bite and folded her arms in front of her. Oh how she wanted to savor the crunch of that doughnut with hints of nutmeg and cinnamon sugar clinging to its shortening-fried crust. Clare's curtness ruined her culinary bliss. She was not grossly overweight, but she noted people had been referring to her lately as "chunky." That hurt! It was such a loathsome word. Didn't anyone think she had feelings? She was used to that being the sixth daughter. Sometimes she felt completely invisible to her family.

"Leave Molly alone, Clare. You're always picking on her. Did you ever think that your words might hurt her?" Eileen draped her arm around her younger sister. Molly loved how Eileen was always looking out for her. She was the kindest sister, in her eyes. It was as if Eileen sensed and carried the pain of all the earth. She was always pointing out the slightest of injustices to her sisters. Thanks to Eileen's observation about how difficult it was for older people to open food packaging, Molly would help her grandparents as soon as they reached for a bag of potato chips or a package of saltines.

"Eileen, you're going to have to use a lot of hairspray today to keep that frizzy mop of yours in control with this humidity," Clare said. The sisters stared at her. She was, and reminded them constantly, the alpha sister herding the rest. There was no debate. Clare had assumed that air of authority ever since that dark night on the outlet dock. It was as if the girls had two mothers. Whatever Clare said overrode what all the other sisters said, and sometimes even her mother.

Noreen rubbed her eyes as she walked into the dining room wrapped in a bathrobe and blue curlers clasped to her hair.

"Any word from Maggie yet?" she asked while filling a coffee cup.

"Who's that fella driving her here from California?" Mame asked.

"He's her editor at the weekly newspaper," Clare said. "His parents are from Rochester, so he's planning to visit them, too. Worked out to be a road trip vacation for them."

An hour later a Volkswagen Beetle decorated with daisy stickers and sporting California license plates parked in front of the O'Donoghue's home.

"Man, dig that porch," Ronnie said to Maggie. "Do your grandparents have a lot of bread?"

"Nah. I wouldn't say that—they're middle class."

Maggie sighed as she looked once again toward the porch where she spent hours playing as a child. She'd crouch behind the wraparound part when playing hide-and-seek with Terrie and Eileen. The porch rocker next to her grandfather's was where she read *Anne of Green Gables* on those hot summer afternoons of her youth, cicadas buzzing in the elms. When she turned nineteen Maggie spent the whole summer of 1969 living in this home. Frances made frequent trips up, too, because she was considering a move back to Penn Yan at the time, and probably would have if it were not for the events of one weekend in August.

Ronnie lit a joint, took a deep drag off of it and then handed it to Maggie.

"You look like you could use this."

She laughed and took the joint gratefully. As the smoked swirled in the car, so did the memories of growing up without a father around most of the time. The clash of female hormones seemed constant. But this porch was the one place where everyone mellowed out.

"Hmm, I'm not ready for this. I haven't been back in this town in five years. Would Noreen hate me if we split? I'm getting bad vibes. Coming back here's just going to bring me down."

He reached over and put his arm around her. "Yeah, I can dig that. My old man thinks I'm a nothing but a hippie freak. Wait, I am. Hah-hah!" Maggie handed him back the joint.

"My family's certifiably crazy, Ronnie. I swear Noreen's just marrying this bozo to best Clare. How freaky is that? And man that chick's so uptight; she'll probably go all Norman Bates on us at the wedding."

"Are you talking about Clare or Noreen? I'm confused." Ronnie giggled. Whenever he was high he'd get the giggles, and it struck Maggie as weird that such a big guy could have such a high-pitched laugh.

"I'm talking about *all* of them. Hey, don't bogart that! I need another fix."

Molly heard a noise and peeked through the lace curtains. She saw Ronnie's car out front and then ran gleefully over to the table and punched her oldest sister in the arm. Clare was livid and wanted to hit her sister back, but Molly yelled "Punch buggy!" and was already out the screen door and onto the porch before Clare could retaliate.

"Hey! My kid sister's coming. Get rid of that!" Maggie tried to wave the pot smoke out of the car.

Molly ran down the porch steps and Maggie opened the door, scooped her up and spun her around on the sidewalk.

"Maggie!" Molly yelled. "Hey, you have flowers on your car. That's cool!"

"This is my friend Ronnie, Molly. It's his car."

Molly had never seen a boy in real life with hair longer than hers. She was a little shy, but at the same time fascinated by the droopy mustache which made him look like that singer in Three Dog Night.

"You like those daisies?" he asked. Ronnie pulled something out of a Mexican blanket tote stashed in the car trunk (that Molly couldn't believe was in the front of the car) and handed it to her. It was a small yellow daisy sticker with a pink center.

"Flower power!" Ronnie said as he raised his hand in a fist. Molly giggled as she took the sticker and skipped back toward the front porch.

Mame held open the screen door and sighed when she saw the hot pants on Maggie, then the shoulder-length hair of her escort. She knew both would set off Frances. The mother and daughter always seemed to have a contentious relationship, but to show up like this on her sister's wedding day was just asking for trouble. Still, Mame got a kick out of

Frances's wild child Maggie. She saw a lot of her own spunk in her granddaughter and probably because of that they had a special relationship.

"Grandma!" Maggie squealed as she gave Mame a big hug. The embrace practically knocked the wind out of her. "You look as beautiful as the day I left. Missed you!"

Mame held her granddaughter out at arm's length and grinned. "I see California agrees with you."

Maggie smiled briefly, but inside wondered if her grandmother noticed the growing curve to her abdomen covered purposefully with a loose peasant blouse.

"Who's this handsome young man?" Mame asked, extending her hand.

"This is my wedding date, Grandma. He's my boss back at the newspaper."

"Nice to meet you, ma'am. I'm Ronnie Stern. My parents are from Rochester."

Maggie sniggered when he said "ma'am." Ronnie was never one for formalities.

"Oh, so you're practically a local boy then. What do your parents do?"

"My old man's a surgeon at Strong Memorial. Mom's an art professor at RIT."

Mame nodded in approval. "So tell me about your newspaper."

"*The Rap Session*?" Ronnie glanced at Maggie and saw her nod. "Hah, uh, well it's a weekly rag I publish. We review concerts, books, write political essays, offer vegetarian recipes, list meditation classes and offer sex advice. You know, the usual dope. If you want to know what's happenin' in the Haight, I'm your source," he said with his string-bean arms extended, hands pointing at himself.

Mame hoped the young man would not detect any mirth she felt at his response.

"I'm a reporter there, Grandma."

"That's wonderful, Maggie. You know your Great Aunt Bertha had a brief foray into the Fourth Estate and loved it. I know she'd be proud of you."

"Yeah, I really dig it. I cover the women's issues beat, writing about things like affordable birth control, how to prevent rape and the need to end back-alley abortions."

Frances arrived at the doorway just in time to hear Maggie's incendiary words. They hit like lightning on desert-dry tinder. Anger blazed across her mother's face and Maggie stepped back to grab Ronnie's hand. Frances caught her furious response before the words escaped her tongue.

"Glad you made it home safely, Maggie," Frances said, teeth clenched. "This must be Ronnie?"

Maggie sighed as lightly as she could, though she could still feel the slow burn of her mother's stare.

"Nice to meet you, Mrs. McNamara. It's an honor to be invited here today and an extreme pleasure to be your daughter's escort this afternoon."

All of them stared at Ronnie, bemused by his unexpected deportment.

Jimmy came up from the cellar, where he'd been puttering with some tin cans he intended to attach to Noreen and Gary's "getaway" car. Molly ran up to him and stuck the sticker in front of his face. "Flower power!" she said before running away, giggles trailing her.

As soon as Jimmy had taken one look at Maggie's escort his heart sank. The kid looked like a drug dealer. Oh, poor Frances, he thought, this is the last thing she needs to see today. It had been difficult enough for his daughter to raise the girls by herself, and that Maggie had always been a handful. Her wild streak must come from that bad McNamara blood, he thought.

The rest of the family crowded the living room to greet the travelers from California. After eyeing her sister's clothes and unruly hair (noting all she found distasteful), Clare stepped forward and hugged her Maggie. As soon as she did she smelled the lingering scent of pot in her sister's hair.

"Nice of you to be stoned for your sister's wedding, Maggie," she whispered. Maggie frowned.

"I'm perfectly fine. You could use a toke to loosen up. And by the way, if you can handle this freak show so well, why did you flee to New York City to get away from the family?" she whispered back in an acidic tone, pinching Clare's arm. If any of the sisters could put Clare in her place, it was Maggie. They got along well enough, but if Maggie sensed that her sister was full of B.S., she was never afraid to call her out on it.

Eileen hugged Maggie warmly and did the same to Ronnie, as if she'd always known him. He didn't flinch. It was almost as if she had a Haight-Ashbury vibe and he liked that.

"Peace, Ronnie," Eileen said as she stepped back and Terrie came forward, still holding the sci-fi comic book she'd been reading on the couch.

"I'm Terrie. Hi." She extended a limp hand to him and Ronnie noted she was reading one of his favorite comics.

"I like your taste. Did you read his latest one about the parallel galaxies?"

Terrie's eyes brightened and a rare toothy smile widened her face.

"Are you kidding? Of course! It blew me away."

"Yeah. Far out," Ronnie said, as they nodded in tandem.

"Hey, Terrie," Maggie said as she ignored her sister's handshake attempt and dived at her for a hug. "How are all those pets of yours?"

She grinned. Terrie loved to talk about her pets the way parents loved to go on about their children.

"I got a new tabby last week. He needs a name and now I think I have one. Maybe I'll call him Ronnie, if that's OK." She glanced sideways at her sister's wedding date for a reaction. He nodded enthusiastically.

"Groovy!"

"Someone help me find my shoes, *please*!" They turned toward the stairs from where a hysterical Noreen descended with blue curlers rolled on her head like a tiara. Maggie took a deep breath.

"You finally made it!" Noreen screamed as soon as she caught a glimpse of her sister. She blessed herself then came running at Maggie full tilt. "Oh thank God, I thought, I can't get married without Maggie here. And Gary kept saying, 'Don't worry, you always worry too much.' But I'm sorry, I *do* worry and now I don't have to. Gary's oldest brother, Brett, will be your groomsman, Maggie. He's intelligent and well-versed on politics. Brett helped run Nixon's campaign upstate until, well, of course now he's working for Ford."

Ronnie couldn't contain his giggles. Jimmy had never heard a man giggle like that and wondered if the boy was high. Frances glared at Maggie thinking, actually shouting inside her mind at her daughter, *Don't even think of making one of your snide Nixon comments*. Maggie was just stunned to see her sister showing so much enthusiasm toward her. It touched her genuinely and she hugged Noreen.

"I know you're in curlers and all right now, but geez Noreen, you look beautiful."

Clare rolled her eyes. Terrie was already re-immersed in the comic book and Molly had peeled the protective paper off the sticker Ronnie gave her and stuck it on the glass of the ornate gilded mirror at the landing of the staircase. "Flower power!" she said to herself as she snuck back into the kitchen to grab another fried cake.

"Noreen, this is my boss, uh, my friend Ronnie. Will we be sitting together at the reception?"

"Of course not, you'll be at the head table. He'll be sitting with Grandpa and Grandma. But you can dance with Ronnie all you like. It's nice to meet you, by the way. Hey, has anyone ever told you that you look like that Three Dog Night singer?"

"All the time, man. Cool."

"Have you tried on your dress yet, Maggie?"

"Uh, no," she laughed. "*Jeez Louise*, I just walked through the door."

"C'mon, we have to make sure it fits. Grandma can fix the hem or anything else that needs to be altered before the wedding. It's hanging up in Mom's old bedroom."

Maggie whispered "Help!" jokingly to Ronnie, and then followed her exuberant sister upstairs. When Noreen pulled the dress out of the garment bag, Maggie cringed. It was beyond hideous. It looked like a Pepto Bismol bomb exploded in a ruffle factory. At least she had to wear this frightening frock only once.

Noreen went into the bathroom around the corner to apply her makeup while Maggie slipped on her bridesmaid's dress. The fit was snug over her abdomen, and she feared that someone would notice the slight bump there. Maybe if she carried her bouquet low no one would notice.

"How's it look?" Noreen asked as she barged in with a mascara brush in her hand.

"I guess OK," Maggie said, clasping her hands strategically in front of her.

"Hmm, it looks a little tight there," she said, eyeing her sister's stomach.

"Hey, have you heard anything from Dad?" The question provided the exact diversion Maggie hoped it would. Noreen plopped onto the bed.

"Not a word."

"Does he even know?"

"Mom didn't want to tell him, but Clare sent him an invitation anyway. Typical Clare, right? Part of me would love it if he came and met Gary. Part of me is so angry for what he did to Mom."

"And what he did to us," Maggie added. "She'd freak out if he showed up though, don't you think?"

Noreen traced her married name with her finger on the chenille bedspread. "Probably. It's just that, you know...I love Uncle Pat, but...a father is supposed to give away...."

Maggie's heart broke for her sister. If this was her wedding day, she'd have eloped by now. But Maggie understood that to Noreen all the trappings of a traditional wedding were essential. She was so sorry that her sister's wedding ceremony would inadvertently highlight their father's absence.

"Are you going to tell Mom about the baby, Maggie?"

So much for the diversion being successful, Maggie thought as she shook her head.

"Please tell me, Sis, that the stoner downstairs is *not* the father."

Whoa, is Noreen taking nasty lessons from Clare these days? Maggie wasn't quite sure how to respond.

"No. Help me take this off, will you?"

"How far along are you?"

Maggie bit her lower lip. "I think four months."

"Well then, who *is* the father?"

"He's a graduate student in physics at Cal State. What they say about once is all it takes is true. Kevin and I met at a Grateful Dead concert. We had instant chemistry."

"And instant physics apparently," Clare quipped. She'd been outside the door and overheard their conversation. Her eyes focused on Maggie's abdomen. "What are you going to do about the baby?"

"Not sure, to be honest. I've got about five more months to figure that out."

"What's to figure out, Sis? Uh, man, you aren't thinking of something like an abortion are you?"

"It's legal in California and it's my body. I'll do what I want!"

Eileen entered the bedroom just then, catching the end of the conversation. She reached out to her older sister and hugged her gently.

"Oh please, Maggie. Don't choose an abortion. There are plenty of alternatives. You could give the child up for adoption. You could also...."

"Shut up, Eileen! I'm don't need to hear you judge me with any of Mom's Right-to-Life crap. This is my decision. Leave me *alone*!" Eileen stepped back, waiting for Maggie's anger to settle.

The others were stunned by her abrupt reply. Maggie's tone was especially harsh toward Eileen, a gentle spirit who'd never say a bad thing about anyone.

"*You'd* better shut up," Clare countered. "Mom will go ballistic if you start talking like that today. She's been through so much raising us. We owe her the decency of showing respect for her today. Stop being so selfish."

"She's not selfish, just confused," Eileen said. "You're young, Maggie, and your life is filled with so much promise.

It has to be scary to think that your life will be changed forever by this baby, no matter what you decide."

Maggie cupped her abdomen with her arms as she listened to their words. Eileen was right; having this baby would limit her life's choices. She'd been so stupid not to go on the Pill. If she had the baby, she'd probably be forced into an endless chain of dead-end jobs to earn enough money for the two of them. That's not how she envisioned her life. She was going to be a writer. People would someday read her words and be changed by them.

"When you have the baby, will you have it out there or come home to deliver it?" Eileen asked. *There she goes, continuing to plan my life for me,* Maggie thought.

"You're having a baby?" an innocent voice asked from the doorway. Maggie's heart sank when she saw Molly and Terrie standing there. "Does this mean I'll be an aunt?" Molly asked sweetly.

Terrie grabbed her sister's hand and started to pull her out of the room. "Let's go help Grandma and Mom with the table favors, Molly."

"Wait!" Maggie gestured for all of the girls to get together in the room. "I need you all to promise not to tell anyone about my news, OK? This is Noreen's wedding day and that's what's important right now. Can we make a Keuka swear on it?"

Clare rolled her eyes and folded her arms. *Oh, Maggie, you live in such a fantasy world,* she thought. *How could you ever handle the responsibility of being a parent?* Clare had a good friend in Manhattan who'd been trying to get pregnant forever. The woman was quite wealthy, but was hesitant to adopt a child, not knowing the full background of the parents. Maybe she could get Maggie to let this woman adopt her baby for a good price. That way Maggie might gain some financial stability for a while and the baby would be raised in a stable home environment. She'd have to have a chat with Maggie later in the weekend.

The other five sisters waited with their right hands aloft, thumbs out and index fingers pointing toward the sky, mimicking the shape of Keuka Lake.

"C'mon, Clare. Keuka swear!"

Ever since that frightful night with their mother on the outlet dock, the sisters used the hand signal to signify unity. It often marked a pact of silence about some deed that they knew would upset their mother. Frances had begun the habit of drinking a glass of scotch after dinner and on days when they were behaving badly, that one glass would be replaced by at least two more. They didn't think their mother was an alcoholic; she didn't do this every day. But when she did have too many drinks, she'd express all her remorse about her marriage that she normally kept in check. The outbursts especially terrified the youngest sisters. On those occasions, Clare would make the Keuka swear sign and they'd scatter around the house, making sure they didn't do anything to upset their mother. With no audience to complain to, Frances's rant would lose its steam.

Now on her sister's wedding day, the urging eyes of her sisters were too much. Clare raised her hand and they all touched their index fingers to hers.

Downstairs in the kitchen, Mame and Frances conversed about Maggie.

"So help me God if she starts a scene at the wedding and embarrasses Noreen on her special day, I'll kill her."

"Why would you think that might happen, Frances?"

"She had to make that jab at me about abortion. You were there. You heard it, Mother."

"What I heard was an opinionated daughter discussing her work. I didn't hear her weave you into the discussion." Mame was trying to smooth things over, but she actually didn't believe it would work. She knew these two were like oil and water. "Unfortunately, I think Maggie inherited her fearlessness to speak her mind from me."

Frances looked at her mother and thought, *If only you knew the truth about her, Mother. If only you knew.* "You don't agree with her, do you?"

"Of course not, Frances. Her inability to shut her mouth just reminds me of myself at that age."

They heard laughter from upstairs.

"Well, I better see how the dress fitting is going," Frances said. "You might have to get that sewing machine revved up. I think Maggie's gained some weight." Mame didn't dare express what she was wondering about her granddaughter.

Frances swung open the door to her old bedroom. "What's all this laughter about?" The view caught her breath and she smiled. She hadn't seen Maggie wearing a dress in forever. They all stood back as Frances took a good look at her hard-edged bohemian softened with frilly chiffon.

"That pink is so flattering with your blonde hair, Maggie. You look beautiful." She tilted her head as she looked at her daughter's figure and squinted. "Are you happy with the way it fits?"

"It looks perfect on her, doesn't it," Noreen said toward the others. Molly smiled at her mother and nodded.

"OK, Grandma's got some sandwiches ready in the kitchen now if any of you get hungry before the wedding. We have two hours to go before we leave for the church. Let's not be late girls, OK?"

Frances closed the door and the sisters looked at each other wide-eyed.

"Phew! I don't think she noticed anything," Clare said.

"I'm starving," Terrie added. "Let's go eat."

"That's surprising; just a little while ago you ate at least four of those fried cakes."

The other five sisters glared at Clare. Why did she have to say something so mean to Terrie on this special day for Noreen? Maggie suspected it was her pent-up jealousy slipping out that her younger sister was beating her to the altar, and Terrie just happened to get caught in her crosshairs.

"I'm starving," Maggie said as she draped her arm around Terrie. "Let's go see if Ronnie's hungry, too. By the way, I think it meant a lot that you want to name your cat after him." Squall becalmed.

Uncle Pat asked Tim Lennon if they could use his van to transport the bride and her sisters to St. Urban's. Tim offered him something better. His brother-in-law ran a limousine service in Geneva, and so he hired Mario to shuttle the girls to the church and reception. It was his wedding gift to Noreen and Gary as well as giving Frances some peace of mind.

The long black Lincoln pulled into the driveway and Mario the chauffeur left the motor running as he knocked on the front door. Jimmy called his granddaughters downstairs and they gathered on the wraparound porch.

"Wait, let me get a photo of you girls," Pat said as he arranged them on the steps around Noreen. He thought she looked like the white center of a pink daisy. Pat took a few photos from different angles with his Instamatic camera, Molly blinked unfortunately with each burst of light from the flashcube.

"OK, now let's get a couple with Mother, Father and you, Frances."

"Here, let's get you in some," Mario said as he came over and took Pat's camera.

As Mario composed the photo, Mame looked across at her old home. She remembered the first day they arrived in Penn Yan when she saw Jimmy rocking on this porch. Mame chuckled to herself when she recalled all her schemes back then for getting to know him and how he was her "project" that summer. Now here they were more than fifty years later posing with their granddaughter on her wedding day. In between there had been so many memories tied to this porch. Here was where she walked back and forth comforting her two babies on hot summer nights when

Virginia was still alive. And after the home became their own, she used to love to sit out here during thunderstorms, listening to rain tap dance on the roof and swish-splash down the gutter spouts as she rocked safe and dry. She closed her eyes briefly and heard the sound of feet running up and down those steps, first her children's and then her grandchildren's. She recalled pulling back the lace curtains just in time to see Clare being kissed for the first time. *What was that boy's name? Arnold Saddlemire was it?* He lived three houses down and they'd gotten to know each other during her summer stay when she was sixteen.

Mario interrupted her daydream. "OK, everybody say 'macaroni!'"

And in a flash, another wraparound porch memory was preserved.

***

Tim Lennon went for a walk down Liberty Street just after two o'clock that day and when he reached the front of St. Urban's, he paused to chat with his brother-in-law Mario. The limousine's passenger-side window was rolled down and Tim leaned inside to converse. They didn't notice the tall man with dark grey hair and summer suit climb the steps and enter the main vestibule of the church.

"You should see the bride, Tim. Gorgeous girl!"

"You know, maybe I will take a peek inside. No one will notice except maybe Father Kane if he looks up. Right?"

Tim was glad that he was wearing nice khaki slacks and a golf shirt in case anyone turned around. Straight down the aisle he saw Noreen and Gary standing before Father

Kane as they professed their vows. *Wow, how beautiful Noreen looks all grown up*, he thought. She reminded him exactly of Frances when they were both that age, except for her chestnut hair. He looked at the right side of the church and saw Frances sitting in profile next to her brother and parents, her hair still that beautiful auburn he used to tease her about growing up. She was stunning in a sea green chiffon dress with her Grandmother Virginia's drop pearl earrings.

Noreen said "I do" clearly and loudly—her words echoed through the church—and Tim heard a soft sniffle from the direction of the confessional to his right. He turned and his temper flared instantly. *What the hell is Joe McNamara doing here? Sure Noreen's his daughter, but he stopped being a father to any of the girls long ago.*

Tim approached.

A few of the wedding guests turned around when their agitated words to each other became louder than whispers. When Noreen and Gary turned to face the guests after Father Kane pronounced them man and wife, they saw Tim shoving Joe out the front vestibule door. She glanced at her mother who was thankfully watching them teary eyed and missed the scuffle at the back of the church. Noreen smiled back, grateful that her mother didn't see her father. He *did* care enough to be present—that was all the confirmation she wanted and needed. No, he didn't give her away, but he was dressed like a gentleman. That was the one wedding gift he could give her. Now all of her wedding day hopes were complete.

***

When they arrived at the boat club, Jimmy was not happy to find the air conditioning broken. It was stifling inside. The reception hall had a view overlooking the water and at least the deck screen doors were open to catch the faint lake breezes. Mame was out of breath after climbing the stairs and sat down by a fan as he went to get her ice water from the bar. Frances welcomed guests while Pat was off with the bridal party at the official photo shoot in nearby Indian Pines Park.

Mame felt woozy as she waited for Jimmy, blaming it on the heat and busyness of the day. Noreen was a beautiful bride, Mame thought while she replayed the ceremony in her mind. Her granddaughter had inherited the best features of both her parents: she had Frances's beautiful skin and high cheekbones and Joe's wavy chestnut hair and stature. She blushed just like Mame's mother Rose used to, also. The passing thought of Rose made Mame wistful that she wasn't here to see this day.

What adventures lay before this couple, Mame wondered. She a silent prayer for God to bless Noreen as well as all of the McNamara girls: *May they live in a world in which they will find equal opportunities to pursue the dreams they hold, and may their hearts overflow with love received from good men who will be their equal partners in life*.

When the bridal party arrived at the reception, Noreen gestured to her sisters to get the pink tulle-wrapped little boxes next to their place settings at the head table. They opened their gifts at the same moment and held out the contents—sterling silver pendants in the Y-shape of Keuka Lake hanging on delicate chains.

"I've been wearing mine all day," Noreen said as she slipped hers out from under the neckline of her wedding gown. The McNamara sisters helped each other fasten the necklace clasps and then stood back to admire them on each other.

"I just LOVE this, Noreen," Maggie said.

"It's so cool!" Molly said as she traced the lake with her finger and stopped on its East Side. "Here's where Uncle Mike's cottage is!"

"Just think of this as a symbol that we are 'Sisters of the Lake'," Noreen said. They gathered together in a tight circle, arms draped around each other, and let out a loud whoop. "Keuka swear!"

Chapter 19

Most of the wedding guests drifted out to the deck for the cocktail hour as the staff rushed around setting up more fans inside. Maggie and Ronnie leaned on the railing as she pointed out to him where important sites from her life were located on the lake.

"I don't know why you said you were getting bad vibes from this place, Maggie," Ronnie said as he grabbed them each a glass of pink Catawba wine from the waiter walking past. She recognized the brand of the wine as soon as she sipped it. This came from Garrett Wine Company and the fruity sweet taste triggered unpleasant memories.

She watched the vermillion sun setting beyond the becalmed lake and recalled a scene from her childhood in Binghamton. Frances had invited the Legion of Mary members over for a card party one Saturday afternoon in May. Maggie—by then a fully mobile toddler of three—tossed off the lilac organza dress her mother put on her, yanked the matching bow out of her sausage-curled blond hair and streaked through the dining room as she cried "Wheeeeee!" The women gasped and Clare chased after her sibling, picked up her naked body and carted her out of the room. Eyebrows were raised; teacups were set down. The party ended almost an hour earlier than Frances had expected with profuse excuses. She never forgot the shame her daughter brought upon her that day. The strain it caused kept growing over the years.

Of course, Maggie knew that she was thought of as the McNamara family's difficult child. If there was mud within 100 feet of the house, Maggie found it. She brought home stray cats. She'd pick the neighbor's prized roses and deliver a bouquet proudly to her mother. Unlike her siblings, she had sophisticated taste for a young child and preferred cold, leftover steak from the previous night's dinner to sugary breakfast flakes sodden with milk.

"This one has the heebie jeebies!" Sister Agnes, the first grade teacher at St. Augustine Academy proclaimed to Frances at parents night. "Watch her intake of sugar," the nun whispered. If only calming down her headstrong child was that easy! As soon as the school day was over, Maggie would toss off her St. Augustine's uniform, put on dungarees and a T-shirt, and then run breathlessly outdoors until called repeatedly to come home for dinner. If she didn't return when called right away, Clare was sent to fetch her across the East Side back yards, which she did mumbling under her breath. Maggie's typical hiding place was in an old Norway maple tree whose low boughs made it easy for her to climb.

In the summer Maggie was a lake girl. As soon as she was old enough to doggie paddle, her mother brought her into the water right near the dock of the McGraths' family cottage. Maggie's father Joe would be upstairs in the cottage, cigar in one hand and a beer in the other. His lack of interest in the development of his children incensed Jimmy. He knew the lake would always be part of their lives; it was better to develop a strong respect for it early in life. His son-in-law's lack of urgency in this respect was appalling, especially when it came to the uncontrollable Maggie. *What if she fell off the end of the dock when no one was around*? Jimmy noticed Maggie was drawn to the water. *Thank God Frances has the presence of mind to teach her how to swim,* he thought. As years went by, whenever the McNamara cousins came over to the cottage for a visit, Maggie would be the first to dive in and they'd have to drag her out of the lake, lips blue and teeth chattering, when it was time for supper.

It was no surprise years later, that of all her sisters, Maggie was the first to try skinny dipping. It happened during a thirteenth birthday party for her friend Eve at a cottage on the West Side. Once darkness fell, one of the boys attending the party issued the challenge that he'd kiss the first girl who'd swim naked in the lake. The girls clustered into a twittering circle near the dock. Not Maggie. She disappeared behind the boat house, came out screaming naked from around the corner, dumped her clothes on the beach and ran right off the end of the dock!

"The water's great! C'mon in, you chickens!"

The girls stared gaped mouth at her. The boys stopped what they were doing and gathered around Sam, the boy who'd issued the challenge.

"You gonna French her?" one asked Sam, poking him in the ribs.

Before he got a chance to answer, Maggie ran out of the lake, scooped up her clothes in front of her and kissed him squarely on the mouth before dashing around the corner to get dressed in the darkened boat house. The boys whooped with delight; the girls folded their arms and glared. No thanks to that display, the boys in their class would now expect far more from them than they'd ever wanted to offer at this age.

Maggie emerged, fully dressed but with sopping hair, and walked toward the girls. They turned their backs and strode toward the cottage. Sam came over with a bottle of cola and handed it to her. Maggie accepted with a smile, but watched sadly as her summer friends abandoned her. It was not the last time she'd be dismissed like that by girlfriends. Sam took her hand and they walked out to the end of the dock and sat down. Not only did he try to French kiss her (Maggie was unimpressed by his awkward attempt); Sam let the hand of the arm draped around her shoulder sweep across her budding breast. He tried to give off the cool aura of just making a gesture while he was talking. Maggie knew he did it on purpose so he could brag to the other boys. Again, she wasn't impressed.

Her grades in high school back in Binghamton were barely high enough to get accepted at the community college in town. Maggie did not lack for intelligence. She bored easily and was too interested in life and boys to settle down with her studies. In the summer of 1969, after a listless first year at the community college, her Great-Aunt Kitty got her a job working at the Garrett Wine Company tasting room in Hammondsport.

Kitty met the winery's owner during Memorial Day Weekend while she tended bar at The Tackle Box in Penn

Yan. She'd told him how difficult it was for her nephew's estranged wife to support six daughters on her measly salary. Aunt Kitty knew too well how difficult it was to be abandoned and was mortified when her nephew behaved just like her ex-husband. When she could spare them, Kitty mailed her bar tips to Frances and they'd arrive often when Frances needed money most.

Vincent Garrett, a handsome single man in his thirties and a fourth-generation winemaker, said he could find work for one of Frances's daughters. Kitty suggested Maggie. The next day Vincent called the O'Donoghue's, where Maggie was staying for the holiday weekend, and offered a summer job without even meeting her.

Jimmy and Mame said they'd be happy to let Maggie live with them. Uncle Pat volunteered to drive her. When he dropped Maggie off for her first day of work on the Monday following the Fourth of July, he wished her luck and said he'd be back at five to pick her up. She thanked him and found her way to the winery's front office, but Vincent hadn't told his secretary Melanie that she'd be starting that day.

"He's up in the Baco Noir vineyard. Walk up the hill to the right of the tasting room as far as you can go, then turn right. Can't miss him. He's got that silly Panama hat on." Maggie was dressed for working in the tasting room, not the vineyards, but what could she do? She trudged up the hill in her mini-dress with chain link belt and go-go boots. Maggie was a diehard fan of the Mary Quant look and wore her hair in a chic blonde bob with thick black eyeliner and white lipstick.

At the top of the hill she looked back toward the winery and felt almost dizzy from the height. The view of Keuka was spectacular, though. Off in the distance she heard someone singing "Blowin' In The Wind." Soon she saw a white Panama hat, beaming in the sunlight amongst the lime-green grapevines.

"Mr. Garrett?" she asked.

Vincent stopped tying up a vine and turned toward her. His eyes seemed to be making a topographical map of her body, and Maggie folded her arms in a subliminal protective gesture.

"And you are...?"

"Maggie McNamara. You offered me a job starting today in the tasting room. Remember? The secretary knew nothing about it and told me to come up here and discuss it with you."

"Ah yes. I heard about you through your Aunt Kitty, is it? She mixes a fine highball."

Maggie turned away and looked back at the view.

"Um, is there a job or isn't there?"

"I have one question for you: Do you like wine?"

She scrunched up her nose. "Um, sure. I guess."

Vincent chuckled slightly. "Do you know what Baco Noir is?"

She put her hands on her hips. This was annoying her and she just wanted to start her job. Maggie pointed at the grapes on the vine.

"OK, you're hired. Let's go down to my office and get the paperwork done." He took her arm as they walked the steep stony path. Maggie noted that he wore cologne scented with patchouli, a tooled leather wrist cuff and a brass peace sign pendant dangling from a matching chain around his neck. His embroidered jean shirt with sleeves rolled up precisely was draped with a fringed suede vest. *Boy, is he trying to be cool*, she thought as a slight grin curled her lips.

Vincent's office was in a barn behind the winery. The distressed wood exterior gave it an abandoned feel, but once he slid open the door, she saw beautiful pine paneled walls covered with watercolors of lake views from the vineyards.

"Wow, I love these paintings. Are they your work?" she asked as she examined them up close.

"Yeah. I dabble." He lit up a cigarette and stared at her. "I also paint nudes. Ever consider modeling?"

Maggie, though not a prude by any means, blushed. "No." *What an odd thing to ask someone you've just hired*, she thought. She shrugged it off figuring the guy was just quirky.

"You should consider it. You have great bone structure. That makes all the difference when you're capturing light and shadow."

His compliment made her blush again, though part of her liked it.

"Hold on a second, I have something I want you to try." Vincent opened up the refrigerator next to his desk and pulled out two bottles of wine. He took down four wineglasses (in two different shapes) from the cupboard next to the refrigerator and set them on his desk. One set was rounded, the other thin and narrow.

"I want you to show me how to taste wine. First of all, which glass would you pour this Maréchal Foch into?" He held up the bottle of red wine.

Ugh, Maggie was ill prepared for this type of test. She studied the two shapes and thought the smaller one looked like the glasses her mother served Sauternes in.

"Those," she said, pointing at the round goblets. Vincent smiled.

"Correct. Now, pour some red wine into the glass." She did as asked, barely filling the glass a third full. "OK, good. How should I taste the wine?" When she turned 18, her friends took her on a winery run and Maggie was trying to recall what the tasting room staff told them. She cleared her throat.

"Pick the glass up by the stem, not the palm of your hand against the bowl, which can warm the wine." He seemed to agree with that, so she continued. "Now swirl the wine around in the glass a bit and hold it up to the light."

"Why should I do that?" he asked.

"Swirling brings oxygen into the wine," she said, almost with the intonation of a question. "And when it hits the side of the glass, if it clings that means it has arms. And that's the sign of a good wine."

Vincent laughed. "You mean legs. Continue."

"Now you put your nose deep into the glass and inhale to catch the aroma of the wine. Then you sip a little bit, hold it on the end of your tongue and draw in your breath, to make bubbles in the wine and let the taste develop in your mouth."

"Pretty close. It's a little more like this." Vincent leaned in and kissed her, sucking lightly on her top lip. She backed away with a gasp, stunned by his action.

"Did you feel that?" he asked matter of factly, as if this was the way all wine tastings were done. *Did she ever.* Maggie nodded and noticed his eyes matched the blue of the deepest waters of the lake. She liked the way his fitted jean shirt set off his toned tan arms. A red bandana tied around his neck looked sun-faded, like something a cowboy in Montana should wear.

"Good. You just earned a raise."

That summer Maggie's work hours lasted long after the tasting room shut for the day. Vincent always had some new vintage for her to try in his office. And each time, before she left, he'd kiss her a little longer, a little deeper. She never saw him outside of work after he dropped her off at her grandparents' home. Their romance, if you could call the odd arrangement that, was definitely confined to the four walls of his office.

But then one Wednesday morning in August he asked if she'd like to assist him in a delivery to a liquor store near in the Catskills. He assured her that she'd be compensated for the long day trip. She didn't bother to tell her grandparents about it; after all it was just another day's work. Problem was, once they neared Monticello, traffic slowed to a crawl as thousands of young music fans headed to a weekend concert on a nearby farm in Bethel.

"We've got some time. Want to check out what's happening?" Vincent asked. Maggie shrugged her shoulders as they detoured off Route 17 and parked the car along the camper van-jammed shoulder. They followed the surge trekking up the country road to a big pasture where they spent the afternoon talking with strangers.

"Yeah, man, I heard a rumor that The Who will be here. I'm hopin' the Stones will show up, too. You never know. Right?" a bearded guitarist said to Vincent as he handed him the biggest joint Maggie'd ever seen. Vincent toked long and deeply on it, then grinned as he handed it toward Maggie. She wasn't quite sure what to do. She hadn't smoked anything since the time her mother discovered her with a pack of Joe's Lucky Strikes behind the garage. The humiliating grounding Frances dispensed as punishment was enough of a deterrent. Her first inhale triggered a brief coughing spell.

"No, like this," Vincent said, taking another hit. She watched carefully and tried again. It wasn't unpleasant and at first it reminded her of the mellowness that followed sipping wine. The more she smoked it and the other joints passed her way, the less she cared that they'd been there for hours and it appeared they'd probably be staying the night. A barefoot woman wearing a peasant blouse, long skirt and kerchief approached them with a plate of brownies.

"Thanks, I'm starving," Maggie said as she grabbed several.

Four days later they arrived back at the winery in a mud-caked haze, not quite remembering the long drive home. Vincent went into his office and passed out. Maggie had enough wits to call a cab and get herself home.

"WHERE have you been?" her mother demanded when she opened the door. The first thing Maggie thought was, *Oh God, what's she doing here*? Frances had come up for the weekend with Clare and Noreen to deliver Molly for a week's stay. "I've been worried sick! You've been gone for *days*! Why didn't you call your grandparents let us know you were all right?"

Her mother was the last person Maggie needed to see right now. All she wanted to do was find her bed and lie down for the next few days.

"Woodstock, with Vincent. Sorry. Gotta crash."

Maggie brushed past her mother and plodded upstairs to the back bedroom that was hers for the summer, smelling like an awful blend of rancid bacon and cow manure. Frances never recalled her daughter's hair looking so filthy. She could tell Maggie was dead tired. Tomorrow she'd ask her questions about the adventure. There was no use in attempting to try now. Frances was grateful that her parents were at the store and didn't get to see her in this awful state.

"She looks like she's still stoned," Clare muttered to Noreen as they watched from the dining room.

Maggie had a fitful sleep of weird dreams, residual sensations from her LSD trips and ears still ringing from the wailing of Jimi Hendrix's guitar. When she woke up the next afternoon, clearer memories began to form. She recalled seeing music notes float from Carlos Santana's guitar into her mind where they bloomed into lotus blossoms of knowingness. At that moment, she was hyperaware that each person around her was connected equally with each other and to the earth below them, muddy as it was. Her thoughts drifted to Saturday night. Had she really smoked a joint with Janis backstage? Or was that the brownie lady? Where had she slept those four nights? She couldn't recall.

A disturbing image of Vincent flashed in her mind, whispering that it would be OK, don't be afraid, he'd be gentle, but she didn't like what was happening. They were in the back of someone's VW microbus. The air smelled like hashish. His fingers were entwined in her hair as he laid her down and then.... She wasn't sure what happened next. Had he raped her? Then she had a memory that confused her. Ohmigod, she thought, was it just Vincent or were there others in the VW? She thought she recalled another guy's voice saying "Wow, she seems to really dig it."

She stared at the ceiling thinking vague thoughts of possibly more than one man taking advantage of her, but realized she would have been too stoned to fight them off. Trying to process the foggy memories made her sit upright suddenly. Were they actual memories or hallucinations? Maggie grabbed her arms and hugged herself as a wave of chills hit her.

"*Oh God*!" she exclaimed as softly as she could. Clare and Noreen were probably snooping around outside her bedroom door.

What if she *had* been raped and then got pregnant? Of course she wasn't on the Pill. Her mother would have a cow if she was pregnant. That imagery made her start to giggle. "Hah, Mom having a cow. In a field. At Woodstock.

Hah-hah!" Her mind refocused on the seriousness of her boss's indiscretion. That made her nauseous. She rolled over on her bed and saw the crucifix hanging on the wall by the light switch. Her grandmother had hung one in every bedroom.

"Don't judge me!" she screamed at the crucified Jesus and buried her head under the blankets. "Ah, Christ! What have I done?" she mumbled into the mattress.

There was no pregnancy, luckily, but Maggie knew she couldn't work for a man who'd taken such advantage of her. What if he started telling people around town and it got back to her grandparents? It would be unbearable to stay in this tiny town, she thought. People at Woodstock were talking about the scene in Haight-Ashbury and it sounded intriguing. Instead of telling her mother the truth about her boss's advances, she hitchhiked out to California without so much as a goodbye. She never knew what really happened at Woodstock, but she knew putting a continent between her and the awful possibilities would help.

***

"Whoa there, Maggie! Where the heck were you just now? Are you trippin'?"

"Hah, not in that sense, Ronnie. I think I'd prefer a beer to this wine if you don't mind."

"Wait right here and I'll see what potent potables they have at the bar." Ronnie planted a sweet kiss on her cheek as he passed her.

Frances strolled over with a glass of scotch and stood next to Maggie by the railing.

"Can you believe your sister is married?"

"No, I can't," Maggie said, squinting from the sun. "She looked beautiful, don't you think?"

Frances sipped her drink and nodded. "I bet you'll be a beautiful bride someday." Maggie was surprised that her mother was being so nice to her.

"Nothing against Noreen's taste but I'd have a simpler wedding, I think. Maybe just have a couple of attendants. Perhaps I'd get married outside, by a waterfall. I love nature."

"With a priest there though, right?"

"Mom, does it really matter? I mean why couldn't I and my fiancé just profess our vows directly to God? There doesn't have to be an intermediary."

Frances snorted. "Well of course it's not a marriage if you don't have a priest," she said turning to look toward the lake. She tapped the fingers of her free hand on the deck railing. Her rigidness annoyed the heck out of Maggie.

"Hmm, well you and Dad were married by a priest...." As soon as she said the words, Maggie regretted them. Frances looked down at the guests below and bit her trembling lip. Clare was right. Their mother had been through so much raising them alone. She deserved some respect. Maggie felt like an absolute jerk for what she'd done.

"Hey Mom," Maggie said, touching her mother's shoulder, "I'm sorry. I shouldn't have said that."

"You're so much like *him*." Frances finished her scotch and then turned to face her daughter. "So, since we're on the topic of weddings, is *he* going to marry you?"

"Ronnie?" Maggie laughed. "We're not even dating. He's my boss and a good friend."

"Well then let me clarify, I mean the man who got you pregnant."

Of all the moments for Ronnie to return with her beer!

"Who got you...you're pregnant? Whaa...?" Ronnie's jaw dropped. "You can't drink alcohol now, Maggie. Let me get you a soda."

This was exactly what Maggie did not want to happen at her sister's wedding.

"I shouldn't have come here. Let's go, Ronnie."

"Tell me you're going to get married, Maggie." Frances grabbed her right arm as Ronnie took Maggie's left hand. "Who's the father? Who did this to you? When is it due?"

Maggie's sisters caught wind of what was going on and gathered on the deck.

"December, I guess, but you know what, it's my body and my business, Mom. Stay out of it!"

"Of course it's my business. You're carrying my grandchild! Oh, you're your father's daughter all right! There's no escaping, Maggie. You'll have to pay the consequences of your actions."

"Well maybe there won't be any consequences!"

The sister bridesmaids froze in their steps, not sure whether it was better to get involved or stay out of the argument.

"What does that mean?" Frances asked.

"Maybe there won't be a baby!"

"Don't you *dare* abort that child! I forbid you. Please, Maggie, do not take *your* stupid mistakes out on that innocent child!"

"I repeat, this is *my* body and I'll damn well do what I please. This is the *nineteen* seventies, not the eighteen seventies, Mom!"

"Well if I had your same selfish attitude, Clare wouldn't be here today!" Frances covered her mouth when she realized what she said. The scotch had loosened her tongue too much. Maggie gasped. Clare broke away from her sisters and confronted her mother.

"*What* did you just say?"

"This is none of your business, Clare. I'm speaking with Maggie." Her daughters noticed her hand shaking as she pushed her bangs out of her eyes.

"Uh, if I just heard what I think I heard, this *is* my business? Were you saying that I was born out of wedlock?"

"Of course not. Your father and I were married."

"Oh, but you *had* to get married, right? Well now, that certainly explains a lot. Doesn't it?"

Jimmy overheard the commotion on the deck and cut through the crowd. "Ladies, there are guests listening," he whispered. "And Mother isn't feeling so well. Please don't cause her any embarrassment. Noreen and Gary deserve to have this be the best day of their lives. Don't spoil it! Stifle this argument now! You can discuss this later." It was such a rare occurrence to see Jimmy angry that the mother and daughters couldn't help but obey his wishes.

Maggie and Ronnie walked immediately back inside to the reception. Clare folded her arms and stared at her mother. Frances didn't know what to say. Luckily, the waiters opened the doors and announced the meal was about to be served.

After the guests dined on prime rib and wedding cake, it was time for the bridal couple's first dance. The leader of the band called the couple to the center of the dance floor. Noreen couldn't wait to hear the first strains of their special song. Gary took her into his arms and the band started playing Three Dog Night's "Just An Old Fashioned Love Song." The McNamara sisters looked at each other and mouthed "Huh?" They knew that wasn't *the* song. Noreen tried to stop dancing in protest but felt Gary's strong hand on the small of her back pressing her in place.

"But...Gary, it's the wrong song. You know our song is 'The First Time Ever I Saw Your Face.'"

"No one wants to hear that Roberta Flack crap. I never really liked that song." He leaned in and whispered, "C'mon, Norry," he pleaded in a low, intimate voice. She hated this nickname but didn't have the courage to tell him. "This song was playing that night we first did it. Remember? We were playing foosball in my parents' game room and this was on the stereo." He nuzzled her neck but she pulled away. This was a moment she'd imagined for months, dancing with her new husband to what she thought was one of the most romantic songs in the world. Gary just hijacked that memory and replaced it with a tune he'd groped her to.

"Well, I want them to play it next then. OK?"

Gary squeezed her hand and his mouth thinned into a taut line. "No way, I hate that dumb song." The photographer approached them with impeccably awkward timing to take some shots of their dance, so Noreen faked a smile. She wanted to kick her husband, but she didn't want to give Clare the photo op of seeing her upset by his action.

Jimmy noticed Mame's watery eyes as the newlyweds swayed on the dance floor. He took her hand and kissed it tenderly. A tear glistened down her cheek and she smiled at him and squeezed his hand weakly.

"Brings back some wonderful memories, doesn't it, dear?" Jimmy said. Mame nodded. "Imagine what would have happened if you gave up on me, Mame. This moment is a direct result of your persistence, your love, lo those many, many years ago."

"Well if my memory serves me right, it was your dashing good looks to blame, not any heroic act I committed."

Jimmy grinned and laughed to himself. He turned and faced his wife fully. "There will never be another bride on this planet more beautiful than you were on our wedding day."

Mame gasped lightly and put her hands over her heart. "Nor is there or will there ever be a man on this planet who'd be more tender to his new bride than you were on our wedding night." Jimmy kissed her cheek right where that tear fell and draped his arm around Mame. She leaned toward him and savored the moment of feeling his heartbeat and the rise and fall of his breaths. God had been so good to them. He saved them that horrible dark night in 1935 and gave them the gift of sharing this joy, of seeing their granddaughter's wedding. What a treasure. She was overcome by a sense of gratefulness and let the tears fall freely. Frances saw her mother and father snuggling as the newlyweds danced. It emphasized the fact that she was there without a husband or a date, and then her eyes started tearing up, letting loose the emotions pent up from that storm on the deck with her daughters.

Although Mame was supported by her husband's strong arm, she felt a slight wave of dizziness. She blamed it on the heat of the day which was still trapped within the crowded reception hall. Mame clung tightly to her husband and he looked down at her and thought that perhaps the time had come for them to get back home. They slipped away when no one was watching. Or so they thought.

Maggie and Ronnie were conferring in the parking lot about the earlier incident with her mother.

"Grandma, you can't leave the party now! It's just starting," Maggie said as her grandparents neared their car.

"I'm too old," Mame said as she waved her hand.

"You will *never* be old." Maggie came over to kiss her grandparents goodnight. "Love you!"

"See you back at the house?" Jimmy asked.

"Actually, Ronnie and I booked a room at an inn near Bluff Point. We have to get out of town early tomorrow to head to Ronnie's parents. I know things will be crowded at your place," Maggie said, squeezing her grandmother's hand. Mame squeezed her back.

"I love you Maggie, as much as if you were my own daughter."

"Aw, Grandma, it feels like that, doesn't it. Love you!"

Maggie and Ronnie were heading back into the reception when Jimmy caught up with them and whispered something in her ear.

***

They arrived home and Mame's breath became labored when they climbed the steps to the wraparound porch. She paused on the top step and grabbed the pillar to steady herself. The noise of children playing in the distant twilight caught her attention, and she turned back to look at her former home illuminated by the streetlight. She blinked when she saw two tree shadows on the lawn at play from the breeze. It appeared as if there were two people facing her. They were about the right shapes of her parents who'd passed on several years ago.

"I'd like to sit on the porch rocker to cool off. There's a bit of a breeze here now. Sit with me, Jimmy."

"You all right, Mame? Want a glass of water?" he asked as he led her to a chair and then unlocked the front door.

"That would be lovely."

Jimmy turned the porch light on when he returned, but Mame waved at him. "Please, it's so nice and cool sitting here in the dark with just the streetlights filtering through the elms."

"As you wish, Madame," Jimmy said and handed Mame the ice water.

They rocked gently in the chairs for a good half hour in silence. Mame recalled reading a theory once that trees can record sound, and the chills you get visiting a heavily-wooded Civil War battlefield are from the cries of terror-filled soldiers etched into the tree rings. If this were possible, Mame thought, what sounds had the wooden floorboards of this splendid wraparound porch recorded? She closed her eyes to see if she could hear them, as memories raced through her mind competing for attention. Mame heard the hard slap of Dan O'Donoghue's hand against her husband's young face. It was followed by the giggles of Pat and Frances as they stole a plate of fried cakes next to their napping father. She heard the snickers of Eddie Barker and Joe McNamara as they waited to take Frances to the fair. There was the sound of the taxi pulling up followed by heavy boots running up the steps and then Pat, fresh back from the war, hugging her with all his might. And today, new sounds were added of giggling bridesmaids as they posed for family photos. The expression on her face reflected the emotion each memory triggered. Her husband was oblivious to it all. The only sounds Jimmy heard were crickets complaining loudly about the heat and the occasional passing car groaning with effort as it climbed the hill.

"You know, I think I'll just head up to bed. It's been a long day," Mame said finally.

"Yes it has, but it's been a wonderful day." He pretended to yawn. "I think I might turn in, too." He escorted her inside and they climbed the stairs together, Jimmy just slightly behind her to make sure Mame's unsteady feet made contact firmly with each step. She started to cross the threshold to their bedroom when Jimmy stopped her.

"Allow me, Mrs. O'Donoghue," he said surprising them both by picking her up suddenly and carrying her precariously over to their bed. He set her down gently on the chenille spread, then groaned and reached his arm around to rub the pain his gallantry caused to his back. Mame laughed so hard she started to cough.

"Has my husband gone mad?" Mame said, delighted by his sudden show of affection.

Jimmy lay down next to her and folded her into his embrace.

"Ahh, my beautiful, beautiful bride. Come with me to the Casbah, and we will make beautiful music together." Mame laughed at Jimmy's terrible Charles Boyer impression, but after a long, lovely kiss, she held him tightly until falling asleep in his arms.

Car doors slamming woke Jimmy up several hours later. Frances, Pat and the girls returned from the reception and gathered in the kitchen to rehash the reception. Jimmy slipped away from sleeping Mame and went downstairs to visit with his guests.

"Hi Grandpa," Molly chirped. That one never seemed to run out of energy, Jimmy thought. Jimmy tousled her hair and opened the refrigerator to take out the extra sandwiches Mame made knowing they'd still be hungry when they got home. Terrie was already into the leftover fried cakes from the morning, he noted.

"Well, that was a grand party."

"You missed Mom dancing with Mr. Lennon," Molly said as she poured a glass of milk.

Jimmy looked at his daughter; she averted her eyes.

"What was Tim doing there?"

"I told him he could crash the party," Pat said as he popped open a beer can. "It was toward the end of the reception; Noreen and Gary had left by then. It was the band's last song."

"Oh, is that so," Jimmy said picking up a sandwich to eat. Frances was still looking away from him. Sure, he'd heard and ignored all those rumors over the years about Tim being Maggie's real father. And he could understand them because of her blonde hair that matched Tim's exactly within a family full of brunettes and redheads. He never believed those rumors. If anything, Maggie was more Joe's daughter than Tim's or even Frances's. He knew she must have heard those rumors, too, and surely they hurt her. Aw, his poor daughter, it must have done her some good to take a spin on the dance floor with Tim. They'd always been such good friends. Jimmy just filed the bit of information away and invited them all to sit down around the dining room table.

"Where are Maggie and Ronnie?" Terrie asked.

"They're spending the night at the Iroquois Inn near the Bluff," Clare said, knowing it would aggravate her mother. (She still hadn't had a chance to discuss with her the bombshell dropped earlier.) The awkward silence served to usher all through their late-night snacks quickly so they could retire to bed, and before long the house went dark.

Chapter 20

Molly awoke early the next morning in the den and rose to make herself a breakfast of juice, frosted cornflakes and a banana. It was a sunny day and so she decided to move her meal onto the front porch. Grandpa must have been still asleep, so she had no fear of sitting in his rocker. She set up a folding table, and inspired by the reception last night, took a cloth napkin she found in the dining room sideboard and laid it on top so it made a diamond shape. There were tiger lilies blooming out back and she picked a perfect blossom, stuck it in a juice glass filled with water and dressed her dining table with it.

Molly watched the busyness of nature as she ate her breakfast silently. Honeybees carried sunlight on their backs as they zipped from the hive in pursuit of dew-sweet nectar. A robin hopped past, pausing to detect worms writhing under the lawn. Squirrels spiral-chased up a tree trunk and a swallowtail butterfly danced above the spirea blossoms like a kid trying to select penny candy at a variety store.

The meal ended quickly, but the little table looked so pretty, she decided to set up a "restaurant" there and set out the remaining three folding tables. This wasn't a momentary inspiration for play. Even when she was a little girl, Molly considered the kitchen the most fascinating room of the house. She watched carefully as her mother prepared dinner and would mimic her actions when she played in the yard.

Plastic sand buckets became the pots. The driveway with some chalk circles scribbled on it served as her electric range top. Molly propped her assortment of dolls (a hand-me-down Tammy, two trolls with Day-Glo mohair ponytails and a hard-luck, one-legged Barbie) around a table she made with a sturdy cardboard top and rock piles for legs. Frances used to chuckle when she'd look out the back door and see Molly working at her pretend restaurant.

Each summer when she'd spend a week with her grandparents, her favorite part of the visit would be helping Grandma Mame make the fried cake doughnuts. First Grandma scooped cups of flour from the pull-down pantry drawer and mixed it with the other ingredients. She rolled out the dough and she'd let Molly cut the rings and place them on a wax paper-lined cookie sheet as she melted Crisco in a deep pot. When it was ready, Grandma lowered the dough rings carefully into the boiling fat and turned them when they puffed and the bottoms browned. When a doughnut had a nice uniform deep tan crust, she'd lift it out of the pot and set it on paper towels to drain away the fat. Sometimes she'd leave them as is, other times she'd dust them with sugar. The hardest part for Molly was waiting until the fried cakes were cool enough to eat. When they were, she'd carry a plate of them and a glass of milk out onto the front porch and sit in the rocker next to Grandpa Jimmy.

"This is the best taste on earth," Jimmy would say after taking a bite letting the sugar dust his chin.

"Sure is," Molly would say, rocking back and forth in unison with him as she ate.

The summer Molly turned ten Mame taught her a few more recipes. They made Aunt Bertha's potato salad and Mame emphasized that you *had* to use real mayonnaise, not that sandwich spread. Later in the week she crimped Molly's fingers over pie dough showing her how to flute the crust. "Men like pie," Mame told her. They'd spent the morning picking several pints of blueberries and then made pies using a recipe Virginia gave her years ago. It was a birthday surprise for Uncle Pat.

But that wasn't all. Molly got to make the sandwiches for lunch each day. It involved pulling the red rind off a bologna round, slathering it with horseradish mustard and topping it with a thick slice of Swiss cheese—all nestled between two slices of white bread. On her last night there she helped make meat loaf with mushroom gravy. Mame could see that her granddaughter had a natural flair for cooking and she wanted to encourage her. *Maybe this one will be a famous chef one day*, Mame thought.

There was so much Molly wanted to learn about cooking. Back home, she'd always ask to speak with her grandmother when Frances called her, to ask more questions about how to prepare this or that. Grandma Mame listened patiently and made sure that Molly understood her answers completely, often asking her to repeat what she'd said.

That morning after her sister's wedding, Molly was inspired to make scrambled eggs and bacon for the whole family at her "restaurant" on the porch. There was plenty of bacon in the refrigerator and so she decided to make it all. Who *didn't* like bacon? Molly turned on the oven and laid out the slices on the broiler pan, just like she'd seen her grandmother do. She recalled that Grandma Mame always whisked milk in with the eggs to make them scramble fluffy. Sometimes she'd add a few snipped chives from the patch that grew just outside the back door. Why not, Molly thought.

The scent of bacon spiraled through the balusters of the oaken staircase and then wafted under the noses of all asleep, gently tempting them from dreamland. Downstairs Molly had set up a buffet like the banquet table she'd seen last night. More tiger lilies were cut and put into a cut glass vase in the center of the table. She'd filled the giant soup tureen with the scrambled eggs and laid out the bacon on a large china platter. She took the rest of the fried cakes she'd helped Grandma Mame make the previous morning and placed them on a large plate. The percolator was plugged in and now the aroma of coffee was chased by the scent of bacon around the house.

"What's all of this, Mother?" Frances said when she walked into the dining room. She grabbed a piece of bacon and ate it. The slice was cooked to perfection—equally crisp. Frances lifted up the tureen cover and saw fluffy scrambled eggs. She noted that her mother had never used a soup tureen to serve them in but maybe it was just the first dish big enough she found. When she entered the kitchen she went right for the percolator and poured a cup of coffee then turned around.

"Looks delicious! You really didn't have to go to all of this trouble...*Molly*?"

Frances was surprised to see her by the toaster, buttering bread and cutting the slices into triangles. She was arranging the toast on a tray that had a jar of her grandmother's peach preserves on it, too.

"Where's Grandma, Molly?"

"Dunno. Think she's still asleep."

Frances took a deep sip of her coffee and then looked at the clock. That was odd; her mother was usually the first to rise each morning.

"So who made all of…?"

"I did. I opened a restaurant on the front porch. Would you like a table?"

Frances grinned as she tied the loose belt on her bathrobe. "Yes, I'd like one near the door, please."

"I think we can arrange that. Follow me, ma'am." Molly took a plate from the buffet and asked her mother what she'd like on it, scooping out a neat pile of eggs and crisscrossing them with two slices of bacon. She carried the plate out the front door and sat it on the table next to her grandfather's rocker. When Frances saw the juice glass bud vases on each table she was delighted.

"My, what an elegant table you set."

Molly nodded at her mother. "Hope you enjoy your meal, ma'am."

Frances loved her daughter's playful imagination. Then she tasted the eggs and was impressed. She'd half expected them to be burnt, but they were some of the lightest eggs she'd ever tasted. The toast was perfection and the bacon, as she knew, was just right.

"Care for a refill of your coffee, ma'am?"

"No, I'm all set, thank you."

"Can I interest you in the Sunday paper then?"

"Why yes, that would be kind of you."

Clare staggered downstairs next, followed by Terrie. "What's all this?" she asked Molly.

"Good morning. We have some seating on the porch if you're interested."

Terrie giggled. "Molly, is this your cooking?"

"This is my restaurant," she said proudly. "We have bacon, eggs with fresh chives, toast and Grandma's peach jam today. Care for some coffee?"

Eileen rose from her bed in the den soon after, still half asleep. She preferred to sit on the porch railing with a cup of tea and some toast as the others dined at their tables. Uncle Pat played along the best with Molly's acting. He even slipped her a five-dollar bill tip. "That's starter money for your first real restaurant," he said with a wink. The porch was humming with chatter about the wedding and reception yesterday. Molly bussed tables while her diners remarked about how they'd never had better bacon.

"Where did you learn to cook like this, Molly? Girl Scouts?" Clare asked.

Molly pointed upstairs. "Nope. Grandma."

"Speaking of which, where are Mother and Father, Frances?"

"Aren't they upstairs sleeping?"

"This late? That's not like them at all." Pat and Frances exchanged worried glances. "I'll go check on them."

His parents' bedroom door was closed and Pat wanted to respect their privacy, but something urged him to open the door a crack. Inside he saw his mother asleep in the bed alone. Where was his father? He checked the bathroom but it was empty. When he came back downstairs he realized that his father's car was missing from the driveway.

"Mother's still sleeping, but I haven't a clue where Father is." As soon as he finished his sentence Terrie pointed at her grandfather driving up the street. Jimmy smiled widely as he got out of the car and climbed the porch steps.

"Well, well, well—what have we here?" he asked scratching his head.

"It's my restaurant, Grandpa. Would you like a table?"

"Here, Dad, I'm all done. This is your seat anyway," Frances said as she stood up. "Where were you?"

"Went to the early Mass. Thought I'd come back and surprise you all with breakfast before you went to the later one. Hmm. Someone beat me to it," he said with a grin as he took his breakfast plate from Molly. "Is Mother up yet?"

"She's still in bed," Pat said.

"Is she feeling OK, Dad?" Frances asked. Jimmy nodded, but she noted a brief expression of concern on his face.

"I wonder when Maggie and Ronnie will show up," Terrie said as she cleared her table and started to carry the dishes inside the house.

"They won't be. I ran into them downtown and they said to tell you all goodbye. Something about they had to stop at Ronnie's parents before heading back to California later today."

Frances glanced down; she was both disappointed and relieved. She loved Maggie, no matter what, but the thought that she might be considering seriously having an abortion upset her terribly. She just couldn't confront her this morning and chose to push the thought of what might happen to that unborn child out of her head. They'd still have time later for a proper discussion of the subject, she hoped.

A car horn tooted and Frances looked up as Tim Lennon drove into their driveway. That brightened Frances's smile immediately, Pat noted. She folded her arms across her bathrobe as Tim got out of the car with his youngest son, Kerry, dressed in his Little League uniform. Tim and Antoinette had five boys, just one shy of pairing completely with Frances's daughters, he'd joked to her.

"How did the McNamaras survive the big wedding?" he asked with a grin, standing with hands on hips at the foot of the porch steps.

Frances blushed but tried to make light of it by feigning she was fainting. "Barely."

"Mr. Lennon, would you like a seat at my restaurant?" Molly asked. Her sincerity got to Tim, who had no intention of staying but could not resist the young girl's charm.

"We can't stay long, but I'll take a table for two," Tim said, winking at Frances. "By the way, Molly, this is my son Kerry. He's got a big game today."

"Is this really your restaurant?" Kerry asked Molly. "How come you let people wear pajamas here?"

Molly was a bit taken aback by his question, then got a mischievous look on her face as she raised her fist. "Because I have flower power. Dig?"

Eileen spit out her tea laughing. Frances raised an eyebrow at her, she didn't want Tim's son to feel uncomfortable. "*Molly*! Be nice." She ran inside the house and returned with the fried cakes.

"Here," Molly said extending the plate to their guests. "Try one. Grandpa says they're the best taste on earth." Kerry looked at his father for approval and once he got an affirmative nod, grabbed the biggest doughnut on the plate and ate it voraciously. Frances smiled as she watched him. Kerry had Antoinette's blue-black hair. Unlike his brothers who were born with stronger Italian genes, Kerry's skin was pale and his eyes matched the beautiful green of his father's, although they were hidden somewhat by his wireframe eyeglasses. Molly waited for a reaction from Kerry, but he ate silently. She put her free hand on her hips as she waited.

"Well? Do you agree?" She tapped her forward foot.

Kerry gave a look toward his father, who'd seen those begging eyes on plenty of occasions and nodded back at his son. As Kerry reached for a second helping, he looked straight into Molly's eyes.

"Nope. This is the best taste in the *universe*!"

Molly was delighted by his reaction and skipped away to get coffee for Tim and a glass of milk for Kerry.

After the porch restaurant closed, Jimmy checked on

his wife. Mame was awake but still tucked under the blankets. Her forehead was slightly warm to his touch although she had the chills. She told him that her fatigue made it difficult to muster the strength to sit up. He told her to not worry, he'd let everyone know she wouldn't be coming downstairs.

The guests packed up and by mid-afternoon they were ready to head for home: four toward Binghamton and one toward New York City after that. Clare was well ensconced in the Manhattan publishing scene by then and would catch a Greyhound to Port Authority later. Everyone went upstairs to bid farewell to Grandma Mame. She apologized profusely for not getting out of bed or kissing anyone goodbye.

"I don't want any of you to catch what I've caught." They acquiesced but each person at least took her hand before they left the room.

"Call me when you get home safely, daughter," Jimmy said before hugging Frances tightly. "You did it. I'm so proud of you. Noreen had a wonderful wedding."

Frances held onto her father with all of her strength. He'd always been so good to her, so understanding through all of her ups and downs with Joe. Her mother was so lucky to have such a strong and good man for a spouse. She wished she'd been that fortunate. Before father and daughter parted from their embrace, her thoughts drifted to Noreen and Gary flying this morning to their honeymoon in San Diego. Was she being paranoid, or did she detect the slightest hint of trouble in their marital bliss at the reception? Noreen looked livid when their wedding dance started, and though Frances liked the song, she thought there had been a different choice. She offered up a little prayer for the newlyweds, for Maggie and Ronnie to have a safe trip back to California, for her father and brother, her mother upstairs and even for herself. Frances and her daughters walked down the porch steps and got into her car.

"Let me know what the doctor says tomorrow, Dad. Love you," she said as she waved goodbye to her father.

They were too tired on the drive home to converse. Clare was still processing the news that her mother let slip about being pregnant with her when she married. They needed to talk about it, but obviously now was not the time. She wondered, *when would it be appropriate?* Terrie was thinking about how cute Ronnie was and how nice it was that he asked her to dance at the reception. It was her first slow dance, despite the fact that she was twenty now. Molly was daydreaming about running a restaurant and having Three Dog Night come to dine there. Eileen was farther away in her mind than any of her sisters—several countries away, imagining her coming Peace Corps adventure.

Chapter 21

Frances called her father to let him know she'd gotten home safely. After that she poured herself a double scotch with one ice cube, slipped off her loafers and walked barefoot across the back lawn to the webbed chaise lounge under the willow tree. She lay there with her eyes closed listening to the dusk-time birdsong among the robins, catbirds and a cardinal couple hidden in the wild rose shrub. Frances imagined she was back in her childhood at the end of their yard, crouching in the snowberry bush as a dairy cow grazed nearby.

She was exhausted, both physically and mentally. Although her parents and brother helped with the cost of the reception, her bank account was spent, too. It would have been nice if Gary's wealthy parents had offered to assist. They knew about Joe abandoning the family and the fact that she was left to raise the other daughters on her own (although Clare was already establishing herself quite well in Manhattan). Instead, Noreen tried to have a reception that would live up to the Pomeroys' standards—way beyond Frances's means. The scotch quieted her temporarily but could not allay the incoming tidal wave of self-pity.

Her thoughts drifted to that last slow dance of the evening with Tim Lennon, when most of the guests had left except her family and the wait staff. Frances revisited her previous imaginings of how different her life would be if she'd never got involved with Joe and instead, married Tim. He was a hard worker and good provider for his family, she knew that. Tim also had a deep sense of kindness and decency that Joe never had. He was a man of strong faith, unlike her wandering husband. When they ran into each other, Tim always showed the deepest respect toward her. She wondered if these what-if thoughts ever crossed his mind, too.

Frances then began to process the bombshell that Maggie dropped. This should have been a moment to relax and reminisce about Noreen's childhood and the wonderful wedding yesterday. Instead her thoughts turned to her troublemaker daughter, Maggie. Why was history repeating itself? *Oh, that McNamara blood is nothing but bad news*, she thought. She caught her thoughts and began to cry. *Oh, what type of woman have I become?* So what if Maggie didn't share her blood; after all those years raising her, she *was* her daughter as much as Clare, Noreen, Terrie, Eileen and Molly.

Forgive me God, but I'm just so worried about that unborn child, she thought. Frances did the math and figured that if the child was allowed to live, it would be born around mid-December. *Perhaps she'll arrive on December 12—the Feast of Our Lady of Guadalupe*, Frances thought. For some reason she was convinced that the unborn child was female. Frances knew that the Guadalupe apparition occurred in a land where the Aztecs had committed countless acts of human sacrifice. What better reason to pray to the Blessed Mother for a miracle to convert the darkness that had a hold on Maggie? Frances decided that tomorrow she would request a Mass to be said on that date at St. Malachy's for the special intention that this baby would be born.

***

Back in Penn Yan, Mame refused any dinner and rested upstairs in bed as a robin warbled its rain song outside her window. She was thinking about Frances and her girls—they'd grown so fast. Now that Noreen was married, what would become of the others? She hoped each of them would be as fortunate to find a partner as good as her Jimmy. That is, if they wanted to get married. Mame hoped that most of all they'd find fulfillment in their lives through careers that challenged their minds and made them the best women they could be.

It was unfortunate that Frances never got a true chance to do that, Mame thought. Why she remained married to that lothario was curious. Mame suspected it came down to Frances's faith—she believed once married, always married. If they did get divorced, it didn't seem fair that she would be punished with excommunication if she met a good man and married again. After all, she'd remained true to their vows; Joe broke them into smithereens.

A little while later Pat came home from a golf game with the Lennons. Jimmy was peeling the "flower power" sticker off the mirror by the staircase. He told his father that Mario called while they were at Tim's house and said Noreen and Gary caught their flight on time to San Diego from the airport in Rochester.

When Jimmy went to bed that night, Mame was

awake praying the rosary and he told her about Noreen and Gary.

"Well, did Maggie take the money you offered to help her out?" she asked after blessing herself with the crucifix attached to the beads.

"Yes." He pulled the covers up.

"You don't think she'll actually abort the baby, do you?"

Jimmy turned toward his wife and stroked her hair. "I don't know, dear. Can't imagine how she could do something so wrong, especially knowing how it would go against all of Frances's efforts with the anti-abortion movement."

"Well, she's not one of us, you know."

"What are you talking about?"

"She's not an O'Donoghue or a McGrath."

"Of course not, she's a McNamara."

"Exactly!"

Jimmy looked at Mame, puzzled by her comment. "What are you trying to say?"

"She's not of our blood."

"Oh, I don't believe a word of those rumors about Tim Lennon. He's a good man; he'd never cheat on his wife."

"No, it's Frances. She's not Maggie's mother."

Jimmy reached out to touch his wife's brow. She didn't feel feverish.

"Mame, dear, you're not making any sense at all."

"Maggie is Joe's daughter by a different mother."

"*What*? Hogwash! That can't be true. She didn't fake

that pregnancy. I saw my pregnant daughter with my own two eyes."

"She *was* pregnant, but they lost the baby—our grandson. At the same time, Joe's daughter was born after her brother and mother died from a house fire. The mother went into labor and delivered Maggie before she passed. Can you believe that good-for-nothing Joe? He had two women pregnant at the same time!"

Jimmy was dumbstruck by the news. It didn't seem possible. Why would his own daughter Frances keep something this important from him? Was it the shame? Had Joe threatened her in some way? He never liked that son-in-law of his. The thing that drove him nuts was that they were still legally married although Joe was shacked up down South with his exotic dancer girlfriend. It infuriated Jimmy.

"Who told you this nonsense?"

"I have it on good authority. Joe's Aunt Kitty and I had an interesting conversation after Maggie's sudden departure to the West Coast back in '69. Remember that? I told her that I suspected it had something to do with that job she got Maggie at the winery. That's when Kitty said no, it was typical McNamara behavior, and then she told me the truth."

Mame saw the anger building in Jimmy and patted his hand.

"I'm sorry I've kept this information from you, Jimmy. I promise that it was the only thing I held back all of these years. Don't you worry about Maggie or Frances or the rest of the girls now. OK? God will take care of them all. Take care of *yourself*, my love. Promise me that."

It must have been this illness of hers speaking; Mame's explanation confounded him. Jimmy looked at her beautiful face and kissed her more sweetly than he had his entire life. Her eyes sparkled and he ran his fingers through her hair once more. He hugged her, aware of how frail she felt in his arms.

"I love you more than you know, Jimmy O'Donoghue. Thank you for every second of happiness you've given me. Remember: Just breathe." She laughed, and the lilt of it sounded exactly as he'd first heard it the day she moved in across the street. He could feel the laughter reverberate off of his heart. Had he not been so tired from the busy weekend of activity, he would have stayed awake and relived some of their favorite memories. Exhaustion from the busy weekend caught up with him, though, and his voice soon went silent. Hours later, in the middle of the night, so did Mame's heart.

***

Maggie and Ronnie drove West that evening after their visit with his parents in Rochester. They stopped at a motel just outside of Toledo, Ohio, in the middle of the night. Ronnie fell asleep quickly on his bed. Maggie wished she could do the same but something was on her mind. When she was sure that Ronnie was completely asleep, she opened her purse. Maggie pulled out the envelope full of money her grandfather took from his wall safe at home Sunday morning and slipped to her when she met him for coffee. Grandpa Jimmy said he and Grandma Mame wanted her to have enough money to take care of the medical costs of having the baby. Whatever she wanted to do after that was her decision, he said. Raise the child, or put it up for adoption. Please, he begged, just let that child be born.

Her thoughts went back to the argument she'd had with her mother at the reception. To be honest, Maggie had not seriously considered having an abortion. Kevin was a nice enough guy and their baby would most certainly be cool. However, it would have been different story if a pregnancy occurred after she'd been raped by Vincent. (When her mind cleared she realized it did happen.) That would be a tougher choice. Maggie liked how empowering it felt to discuss the options with her sisters, though. Why should a woman have to give birth to a child she didn't want? Shouldn't she be allowed such basic control of her own body? Then she recalled her mother's face when after admitting that she'd been pregnant with Clare on her wedding day. Maggie wondered what her mother's life would have been like if she hadn't given it all up to have Clare. What sort of career would she have had if pregnancy hadn't defined her destiny?

For some reason, a vivid image of her grandmother came to mind at that moment. "Have the baby, *please*, Maggie," she could hear her say. Grandma Mame was so cool, far more together than her own mother. She'd had a good career as a teacher before starting a family. What a difference that made. Maggie knew her grandmother fought for women's right to vote, too. There was a special bond between them, so that's why her plea carried so much weight as Maggie wrestled with the issue. She held the cash-stuffed envelope close to her heart. This money represented her grandparents' hard work and it was given freely because of their deep love. How could she let them down? But was she ready emotionally to have a baby? It would be so difficult raising a child alone. A tear slid down Maggie's face as she stowed the envelope back in her purse. She'd have to choose wisely the right way to use this money.

***

Noreen and Gary sipped champagne on a balcony overlooking San Diego Harbor and the Pacific Ocean in the distance. Below them tourists chatted as pier lights reflected on the waves. She was exhausted from their flights and all of the weekend's busyness. He was feeling amorous, she could tell, but to be honest what she truly craved was sleep.

"It's time for bed," Gary said. "Don't keep me waiting, Norry." His breath was hot on the back of her neck as he kissed her before walking inside.

A bright crescent moon hung in the sky over the black water. It reminded Noreen of her grandmother reciting that poem about the owl and the pussycat. She imagined the peculiar couple drifting in a pea-green boat, somewhere on the horizon. Noreen closed her eyes and recalled the laughter when Grandma Mame took her to a card party once at her friend Rena Webster's house. Noreen made a fuss, demanding that Rena give her a runcible spoon for eating the mince pie for dessert. Rena looked at her as if she had three heads. She was *obviously* not a fan of Edward Lear's poetry.

Noreen loved her summer weeks at Grandma and Grandpa's. There was a bookcase in the den and Mame filled the bottom shelf with books that Pat and Frances read as children. Noreen loved the Lear books of nonsense poetry and would read them repeatedly while sitting in a rocker next to Grandpa Jimmy, her finger tracing the whimsical engraved illustrations that felt embossed on the rough-edged paper. One of her favorite memories was the August afternoon they picked fruit off the Japanese quince bush to make jam. When they finished canning it, Noreen helped Mame bake a pound cake. As it cooled, her grandmother gave Noreen a gift-wrapped box.

"This is for putting the jam on the cake," Mame said as she watched Noreen tear off the wrapping with trembling hands (she was so excited). She pulled out a silver grapefruit spoon and saw her grandmother laugh heartily at her confused expression.

"There's your runcible spoon, Noreen!"

She smiled when she thought of that spoon now tucked in the china cabinet of her new home. Grandma Mame's delightful gesture brought Lear's poetry alive to her. And when Noreen began teaching, she and Grandma Mame discussed philosophies of education and how using such examples engaged young minds. Funny, but that silly poem and spoon were probably responsible for sparking Noreen's teaching career. In turn, she passed the creative spark onto her students, and was thrilled to watch them realize how a precise selection of words can unlock the imagination.

Noreen's thoughts drifted to the wedding reception and how tired her grandmother looked, sitting there in that hot room. Argh! Why did the air conditioning have to break down on the day of her wedding? All of her life, even until recently, her grandmother looked strong and filled with vitality. Yesterday she looked shorter and frail. Noreen hoped that all was OK with her. When she wrote her thank you notes, the first one would go to Grandma Mame who'd given her a beautiful hand-painted porcelain plate that Noreen's great-grandmother McGrath brought from Ireland to America. The girl had wavy chestnut hair like Noreen and bright pink cheeks. Mame always said the plate reminded her of Noreen.

"Hey, Norry, are you coming to bed or what?" Gary asked from across the room. Noreen turned around and looked at her husband, her future. He raised an eyebrow at her and patted the pillows on the bed. Not just yet, she thought. She liked where her mind had led her to at that moment, basking in the love of her grandmother.

***

A mockingbird sitting atop the telephone pole mimicked a cardinal, an oriole and then a robin. Its pre-dawn concert wrested Molly from her dreams. Her eyes opened wide and she stared at the foot of her bed as she listened to the jangled melody. The room was dark but illuminated faintly by the glow of the streetlight. Molly turned her head toward the window to hear the bird better. Was that a Carolina wren sound the bird just made? Grandma Mame taught her how to recognize birdsongs by associating words with the notes. "Teakettle, teakettle, teakettle, tea!" the mockingbird said in its best Raleigh accent. Molly smiled. She glanced back at the foot of her bed and noticed that there seemed to be a dark figure standing there. The shadow play scared her and she drew the blanket up to her face, waited a few minutes and then peeked at the far wall again. Was it just shadows from a tree outside, or was there a ghost standing there? The eerie shape made her heart race.

Molly grabbed the pillow behind her head and covered her face for protection from whatever it was. The specter terrified her and she tried to lie there as still as possible hoping whatever it was would think she was asleep. She was not a fan of ghost or horror movies. That sort of topic always made her nervous. Her curiosity got the better of her and she lifted the pillow again to see if the weird darkness was still at the foot of her bed. It was! She screamed but nothing came out of her mouth. Was she still asleep and this was some sort of dream-fueled paralysis? She didn't know, but her thoughts suggested to her that if she thought of something pleasant, she could chase whatever it was away by her own will. Molly closed her eyes and imagined she was in her grandmother's kitchen making fried cakes. She was sifting the flour together with the sugar, baking powder, salt, cinnamon and nutmeg, and then added the milk, egg, melted butter and vanilla. When she went to stir the mix together, she felt a hand on hers guiding it around the bowl. It was Grandma Mame's.

"Good girl, now let's put the dough in the refrigerator to chill." The voice in her mind was so clear that Molly opened her eyes to see if her grandmother was in the room with her. She slowly pulled the pillow away from her face and saw that neither her grandmother nor the shadow was in the room. Ahh, she thought, I must have been dreaming all along. As Molly fluffed the pillow and propped it under her head, she thought she sniffed a trace of Emeraude, her grandmother's favorite perfume.

***

Terrie answered the phone when it rang at six a.m., a few hours later.

"Hi, Uncle Pat! What's up?" She didn't understand why he was abrupt and didn't want to make small talk with her. Terrie woke her mother, who rolled over sleep-dazed to answer the phone next to her bed, turning the alarm clock to face her. "Hello, Pat. Why are you calling so...?" Terrie knew something awful had happened when she saw her mother sit up suddenly and cover her mouth with her hand. "Oh dear, oh no, this can't possibly be...."

"What's the matter, Mom?" Terrie asked as she sat down on the edge of the bed.

"Yes, yes, Pat. I will. I'll call the girls. When do you suppose we'll have the funeral?"

Terrie gasped. "Who's dead?"

Frances reached across the bed, grabbed her daughter's hand and swallowed back her emotion before she spoke. "It's Grandma, Terrie. She didn't wake up."

Terrie ran from the room crying and Frances wanted to stop her from waking everyone up, but Pat was telling her about their father and how upset he was.

"OK, I'll probably drive up there later today. Oh, brother! I can't believe this has happened. You know, she was not herself at the wedding. The signs were all there. She was so out of breath climbing those stairs."

Terrie woke Eileen and together they woke Molly up from the most wonderful dream in which she was running a restaurant in New York City.

"Leave me alone. Why are you guys bothering me?" Molly groaned.

"Sis, get up. There's something we have to tell you."

Molly rubbed her eyes and sat up in bed just as her mother came in the room. The three of them gathered on Molly's bed.

"What's going on?" she asked, confused.

"Uncle Pat just called," Frances said with a quaver in her voice. "It's Grandma. She died last night in her sleep."

Molly looked at everyone with disbelief. "But no, she was here helping me make fried cakes a little while ago. She can't be gone."

"Huh? What are you talking about?" Terrie asked.

"We were in the kitchen and she held my hand as we stirred the batter and...." Molly pouted when she realized that as real as it felt, making doughnuts with her grandmother had just been a dream. "But Mom, is she really dead? Are you sure she isn't just sound asleep?"

Oh how Frances wanted to tell her daughter something different. She shook her head. "No, Molly. The doctor came. They tried to revive her. Grandma had been dead for a couple of hours."

"So she died in her sleep," Eileen said. "That's a nice and gentle way to go. I'm sure the Blessed Mother greeted her with open arms and led her to Jesus."

Molly remembered the dark shadow she'd seen at the foot of her bed. Was that her grandmother stopping by to say farewell before she left this world? She opened her mouth to ask her mother what she thought, but then realized that they'd all probably just think that she was crazy.

"Oh, dear, how am I going to call Noreen on her honeymoon to tell her this sad news?" Frances rubbed her forehead. "And Maggie! Who knows where she is now on her journey back to California."

"Maybe she'll call to let us know where she is," Terrie said. Eileen nodded with a hopeful expression.

Frances appreciated her daughters being so optimistic, but in her heart she felt that they wouldn't hear from Maggie until she reached California, and the funeral might be over by then. Why did she have to live so far away? At least Clare was just in New York City.

***

A few days later Maggie and Ronnie were back on the road after a brief detour to Las Vegas. He wanted to reconnect with some college friends while researching the counterculture scene made famous by Hunter S. Thompson. What could she do? He was her boss and her only transportation home.

When she decided to heed the nagging voice in her mind that was telling her to call home, Maggie asked Ronnie to pull into the next gas station with a phone booth. She called her mother's number collect but no one answered. They stopped so she could try calling again at several gas stations across the state. Each time there was no answer.

Maybe it was nothing, but something worried her about this. Her mother and sisters should have been there to answer the phone. She dug into her fringed suede purse and pulled out a pocket address book and fistful of dimes to call her grandparents' number. A woman picked up the phone but it wasn't a voice she recognized.

"Hi. Who is this?" Maggie asked.

"This is Rena Webster. May I ask who's calling?" How odd, Maggie thought. She was surprised that her grandmother's good friend answered the phone.

"Rena? Hi, it's Maggie McNamara. Is my grandmother there?"

"Oh dear!" Rena said as she dropped the receiver and raced into the kitchen to get Frances. Maggie heard all sorts of voices in the background. Was there a party going on for some reason? Sure sounded like it.

"Maggie, is that you?" She was surprised to hear her mother's voice, not her grandmother's. Why did her mother sound breathless?

"Mom! Hi! What's going on there? I've been calling you all day at home and got no answer. I was calling Grandma and Grandpa to see where you were. Everything OK?"

"Oh, Maggie. I'm so glad you called. We didn't know how to get in touch with you and, well, we're all here, but we wish you were, too. You are missed."

"Missed? Why, what's going on? Are you having a party and I wasn't invited?"

"Oh dear, there's no easy way to tell you this."

"What, Mom?"

"Grandma died. Today was her funeral. It happened last week and we tried as hard as we could to get the news to you. I called you repeatedly, but you never answered your phone and...."

"*Grandma's gone*? Nooooo!" Maggie dropped the payphone receiver and started to sob. Ronnie got out of the car and ran to her side. She hugged him as he picked up the receiver and got the information from Frances.

Ronnie led a distraught Maggie back to his car. She leaned against the hood for a few minutes, staring toward the chalky blue Sierra Nevadas rising from the Mojave Desert.

"I can't believe I missed her funeral. They couldn't have waited a few more days for me? Why not? Why would my mother do that to me? Did she think my presence didn't matter? I'm so mad...I'm never going to talk to her again!"

"C'mon, don't say that, Maggie." Ronnie steadied her shoulders and looked directly in her eyes. "What else could they do? She tried and you know there was no way for her to contact you. Besides, it's summer. You can't keep a body hanging around forever." Maggie rejected his pleading and crossed her arms across her body tightly, as if she felt a chill.

"Man, I'm so sorry," he continued, scuffing his boot across the sandy pavement. "You know, this is my fault. If I hadn't made a detour to hang out with friends in Vegas, this wouldn't have happened."

She turned her face toward him and narrowed her eyes as the corners of her mouth turned down. "No, oh no! This isn't about you. You don't know my mother. This is *her* passive-aggressive way of getting even with me for saying I might have an abortion. Of course they could have waited. This is like her way of 'aborting' me from our family. That's what she's done. She kept me from Grandma's funeral. I will *never* forgive her for that."

The fierceness of her scowl startled Ronnie. He'd never seen a vindictive look on Maggie's face. Her disposition was mostly sunny, though she often peppered conversations with sarcastic barbs. Mind you, those barbs would usually be well deserved. But this was a furious side of his friend he'd never seen before. He hoped she was just overtired from their cross-country trip.

Ronnie and Maggie didn't talk much again until they reached San Francisco. She had an important decision to make and she'd have to do it soon. When she got to her apartment, she called the phone number of Clare's friend in New York who wanted to adopt a baby. The woman was interested, but she insisted that Maggie come back East to have the baby so they could ensure that the child got the proper health care throughout the pregnancy and delivery. That was the last thing Maggie wanted to do.

There was an easier way to handle this problem. And she knew it would be the one thing that would get even with her mother for the cruelty she'd shown, making her feel so unwanted. She unclasped the Keuka Lake pendant necklace she'd worn since her sister's wedding and stuffed it into the envelope of money from her grandparents.

Chapter 22

How could it possibly be 1995, Clare wondered. She was now fifty years old and as she looked at her face in the mirror she noticed it was getting harder to keep that gray hair hidden and wrinkles from deepening at the corners of her eyes, even though she had a fantastic beauty regimen—the best money could buy.

Clare took a deep breath to calm herself (a technique from her yoga class) and recalled that once she'd been a beautiful child with ringlets of rich auburn hair, those piercing blue eyes of her grandfather Jimmy and lashes a Hollywood starlet would lust after. Until her sister's wedding, Clare Marie McNamara grew up never knowing that she had been conceived through her mother's need to prove her love to her father.

She was daddy's little girl for the first year of her life; some said he spoiled her. Joe loved to carry her in his strong arms when they were in public, enjoying the attention it elicited from women. The novelty wore off when he realized what the true day-to-day effort of raising a baby was. It was after Noreen was born, so even at an early age Clare associated Noreen with her father distancing from her.

Frances knew that Clare was a child who thrived in the spotlight and craved attention. Seventeen years later her spotlight splintered to include her five siblings, Noreen, Maggie, Terrie, Eileen and Molly. What angered her at that age was that she was forced into acting like an adult, helping to parent the others as her mother struggled to raise baby Molly after Joe left. In her mind, Clare felt she was the daughter that needed to be fussed over, not her youngest, colicky sister.

Clare's revenge for having to share parental attention was to excel in everything she did to shift the spotlight back toward her. When she was in the Girl Scouts, Clare sold the most cookies in her troop—setting a sales record it took twenty years to surpass. She always made the honor roll, had perfect attendance in seven out of eight grade school years. Just one year was spoiled by then two-year-old Eileen contracting chicken pox, infecting her four other sisters at the same time. Frances nearly lost her mind.

Uncle Pat noticed Clare's naturally keen interest in business, and when Clare visited in the summer, he'd bring her to work at the department store and let her sit at his desk. She loved stretching her arms across the wide expanse of the desktop and reading notes he'd tucked into the calendar blotter. As he tallied sales numbers, Clare flipped through the piles of merchandise catalogs. He'd make note of what items she'd point out to him—they'd often become the next season's big sellers. His one wish was that she wouldn't focus so much time on stationery supply catalogs. For some reason she was obsessed with fountain pens and composition notebooks.

English was her favorite subject in high school, so it was no surprise when she majored in literature at Harvard. Frances was relieved when she won that full scholarship, because Joe was gone by then. Clare did not want to become a teacher, despite the encouragement to do so from her grandmother. Instead she envisioned a publishing career in Manhattan. Editing would give Clare the sense of control she craved in life.

She'd been in the business for twenty-six years now, working steadily up from a copy editor fresh out of grad school to senior acquisitions editor at St. Morris Publishers. Clare was beautiful and successful. What more could she want?

Plenty!

Had she taken a third glass of Montepulciano at the outdoor Italian café that evening in May, as her boyfriend Matthew suggested, she'd have missed his subtle gesture toward the waitress that ended their twenty two-year relationship and halted the momentum of her success.

Friday was their standing dinner date night and Matthew made reservations at his friend Alessandro's bistro on Park Avenue to celebrate her birthday. It was a cozy café, marked off on the sidewalk with four giant stone jardinières spilling with clove-scented petunias, whose perfume hung in the air on that warm, late-spring evening.

She'd spent all day preparing for their date. Up early before work, she'd done the circuit of machines at her health club followed by a light jog through her TriBeCa neighborhood. After all these years she took pride in the fact that she was still a size four! Breakfast was black coffee and yogurt topped with that ginger almond granola she bought from an organic grocery in SoHo. During her lunch hour she'd stopped at a new French lingerie boutique off Fifth Avenue that her coworker Adelaide recommended. For much of their relationship Matthew spent his time undressing her, and she knew he'd appreciate the lace-trimmed salmon pink demi-bra and panties she was wearing now.

She was hoping that after their lovemaking tonight that she and Matthew could have a casual chat about the current state of their relationship. Clare sensed a palpable distance between them, and she wanted to discuss it now and before it had the chance to grow. He hated discussing their relationship at length and preferred to let it roll along at the pace it always had. They broke up twice. The first time was when she found out five years ago that he took a trip with a female coworker to Paris instead of to London with his boss, like he'd told her. What stung most about the revelation was that Clare had begged him for years to take her there. It ended up that there was some actual work done on that trip, but Clare was relieved when the woman left the firm a few months later. The second time was two years ago and she realized now that her rage over his insensitivity to her family was probably just a symptom of the peri-menopause besetting her.

Over the years she never could figure out why he insisted that they each maintain their own apartments. And marriage? Oh, she never broached the subject despite constant urging from her friends. Somehow it would seem like begging and that would be beneath her. Clare didn't need or desire a family. Perhaps she was just too sophisticated for needing a marriage license, either. After all, she was the person her friends truly envied. They were always commenting on how lucky she was to be free from the burdens of marriage and motherhood. Clare often wondered if that's why they were always scheming for her to get hitched, so her presence wouldn't be a constant reminder of how miserable they were.

After work, Clare went to a hair salon for a quick trim and styling. When she got out of the taxi near the corner of her apartment building in Midtown, she bought a sunny bouquet of gerbera daisies from the Korean grocer. She trimmed them and arranged them expertly into a cut glass vase that had belonged to her Grandmother Mame and set it on the coffee table in her modest living room. Clare closed her eyes and imagined the bouquet illuminated by candlelight later tonight, then felt Matthew's warm embrace. A huge smile burst onto her face as she wondered what his birthday gift would be. Maybe jewels to mark the milestone birthday, she thought while donning the figure-hugging teal dress she bought on their vacation to Paris (*finally*) last August. She lined her eyes expertly with the black cream she bought at the expensive makeup boutique on the Boulevard Haussmann.

Before heading off to the café, she set the timer for the coffee pot to ten a.m., their usual Saturday morning wakeup time. Clare opened up a kitchen drawer and pulled out a blue and white French linen tablecloth, draping it carefully over the cozy kitchen table. On top she placed two settings for breakfast and the box of croissants she picked up from the bakery near her salon. She tidied up the bathroom counter (Matthew hated clutter) and set out some tea-light candles around the vase of daisies. The backdrop for a perfect evening was set.

Her taxi driver blared a Bollywood soundtrack on the car stereo as her thoughts drifted to this moment in her life. Clare was now at the top of her career, making decisions that impacted the entire publishing industry. Thanks to some contacts she had in Alberta, she was able to entice the reclusive Canadian fantasy author Thom McIlwaine to their publishing house for a three-book deal. His works were all the rage in moody college student and hipster circles. She imagined she could hear the enamel on enamel gnashing of her peers' teeth over her persuasion skills.

She rarely returned upstate to visit her family, though she kept in good contact with her mother. In each phone conversation she'd drop news of her latest achievement—a bestseller, a promotion, a humanitarian award—knowing that her mother would disseminate the information among her sisters. Clare imagined that they'd be in awe of her success, as they should be. It was hard earned!

Clare thoughts turned to Matthew. He was a brilliant, well-respected economist, asked often to join pundits on Sunday morning news shows. They traveled in fascinating circles together and were photographed often at red carpet fundraising events—the perfect power couple.

Her birthday celebration started off so pleasantly. As soon as she arrived Matthew ordered pre-dinner cocktails. Alessandro brought out a plate of thinly sliced rustico bread spread with soft Taleggio, then a chiffonade of prosciutto crudo and topped with balsamic-soaked cherries. It was the perfect marriage of earthy and sophisticated, salty and sweet, crunchy and soft. "Mmm," Clare purred as she ate it. She could have eaten the whole plate, but when the new, model-thin waitress appeared to take their dinner orders, Clare refrained from taking another bite, despite the gustatory pleasure it gave her.

Matthew placed the wine order for dinner. He always did that without asking Clare what she wanted with the meal. Actually she thought a pinot grigio would match her menu choice better.

"How has your day been?" she asked just as the waitress brought over the Montepulciano, opened it and handed the cork to Matthew to inspect. He swirled the small amount of red wine the waitress poured into his glass, let a sip roll slowly over his tongue and winked at her.

"Perfect," he said, with a slight raise of his eyebrow.

Did he just flirt with this woman, Clare wondered. She shrugged it off and awaited his answer.

"Fantastic! Tom and I did a great interview with the *Journal* this morning. I met Simon for lunch at Côte d'Azur to discuss the bubble in the Asian markets. The president's economic adviser called this afternoon. He needed some feedback on foreclosure rates in the Midwest. You know, it was just a typical Friday." He cracked his knuckles and puffed his chest slightly. Clare waited for him to in turn ask how her day went. Instead Matthew smiled at an elegant couple strolling down the sidewalk toward them. The man came over and shook Matthew's hand.

"Thanks for that suggestion, Matthew. We closed the deal on the plant in South Korea this afternoon."

"Pleasure to have helped, Jonathan."

Just as Matthew finished his glass of wine, the waitress grabbed the bottle and held it over his glass. Clare saw his eyes travel from her shoulder blades to the curve of her back and down her legs.

"More wine?" the waitress asked her, with an almost joking tone to her voice. Clare nodded as she thought, *is something going on here?*

"What's shaking in the publishing world?" he asked finally, watching the waitress return to the kitchen.

"The first McIlwaine book is in editing. Right on schedule, thank God. Saw some drafts of the cover art. All gorgeous! We're working with a photographer from Canada, a friend of the author's, and he...."

The waitress interrupted. "Who had the lobster fettuccine with sage butter sauce?" Clare nodded as the woman slid the plate in front of her. "And the veal chop with risotto Florentine must be yours," she said, placing the dish directly in front of Matthew. "Excellent taste, as always," the waitress said breathlessly.

"As always." Those two words dangled between the couple. *Isn't she new here*? Clare wondered to herself. *Was that just a rote phrase from a tired waitress, or does Matthew know her from someplace else*?

Matthew dived into his veal voraciously and dropped the conversation that had started before the interruption. Clare watched him devour his dinner and thought there were three things that mattered in his life: money, food and sex. Depending on the day, the order of importance shifted. On weekends, sex rose to the top of that list. Did it matter that sex involved her, or could any woman fit the bill? He had always been flirtatious and Clare thought it was just innocent fun to him, but something felt different tonight. She saw the waitress talking with some new customers and wondered, *has he already slept with her? Is this why he insists on keeping a separate apartment?*

His not-so-subtle dismissal of the importance of her work had been eating slowly at her ego over the years. She was every bit as important in her career circle as he was in his own. Yet, why did he always make her feel second best?

Clare reached into the breadbasket for a slice of bread to dip into the rich sauce of her pasta. Matthew raised an eyebrow.

"So, did you go to the gym this morning?"

She retracted her hand. "What's that supposed to mean? Of course, I did the whole circuit."

He frowned slightly. "Nothing. Don't be so sensitive. Just trying to make conversation."

"Since when have you needed to *try* to make conversation with me?"

The waitress reappeared with impeccably bad timing. "How are your meals?"

"Magnificent," Matthew said. "More wine, Clare?" Just then her cell phone rang. She shook her head and dug into her pocketbook to retrieve it. Noreen was calling. "Hey, Sis, what's up?"

"I'm worried about Mom. Gary and I stopped by the house last weekend on our way back from Skaneateles and she seemed off, distracted."

"That's nothing new. Had she been drinking?"

As Noreen rambled on to Clare, Matthew excused himself and went off to the men's room. Clare watched him walk away as she tried to focus on her sister's concerns. And there it was. Matthew touched the small of the waitress's back as he passed by her. She turned toward him and he whispered something. She nodded.

"Gary thinks it's dementia. I wonder if she's having mini-strokes. What do you think, Clare?" Noreen asked.

"I think my boyfriend is having an affair with the waitress in this restaurant," Clare said, her thoughts spilling out unexpectedly.

She was off the phone by the time Matthew returned, twirling a fork in the center of the fettuccine on her plate. Her food was as cold as her relationship felt at that moment. Clare's wineglass was empty, but Matthew neither offered to refill it again nor noticed her lack of appetite.

"So what crisis was your sister calling about this time?" Matthew asked as he sipped his drink. His tone annoyed her.

Clare dragged her fork across the plate and set it down, no longer interested in her meal. "Something's not right with my mother," she said as her mind replayed the exchange between her boyfriend and the waitress. Matthew looked away toward the humming Friday night traffic and two coeds approaching the café. He grinned at them. They looked at each other and giggled, then one blew a kiss at him. The gesture infuriated Clare. Here she was, vulnerable at the news about her mother and he's eyeing more skirts. It was disgusting. There was nothing worse than dating a man in his late forties who was obviously having a midlife crisis. He was so desperate for reaffirmation of his masculinity that at this point he could get off by being yelled at by a female traffic cop for jaywalking. She was supposed to be his girlfriend, so why wasn't he focusing on her words at the moment? Matthew never asked any follow-up questions about her mother. Instead he took advantage of the disconnected conversation to launch into a dull elucidation about the effect of warm weather on consumerism.

After dessert, Clare feigned that she was getting a cold and insisted that Matthew not escort her back to her apartment. He didn't seem to be disappointed and never mentioned any birthday gift—that stung her already wounded ego. As she got in the cab, she saw him walk back into the café and start talking with the waitress. She knew in her gut that now she'd crossed the threshold of fifty, he'd deemed her too old. This relationship was finished and not worth any effort to save. To be honest, it had been broken for years and she didn't want to admit it.

When she got home she checked her answering machine. Part of her hoped that Matthew called to apologize or express concern about her mother. Instead there was another anxious message from Noreen. She'd been calling all of the sisters updating them about their mother's condition. Clare was surprised to hear her say that she'd even attempted to call Maggie. No one had spoken with her in years.

How would she live without Matthew in her life? Clare thought about that moment years ago when Noreen and Gary's engagement was announced. Somewhere along the line of pursuing her fabulous career, she'd let romance slip out of her focus. At the time she was three years away from turning thirty with no serious relationship in sight and she had just nine months to find a date that would be so impressive so that guests would think, *oh it doesn't matter that she's not married. She has a fabulous life in Manhattan.* It wasn't that she wanted to divert attention from Noreen; it was just that Clare needed to be reminded that people still thought she was beautiful. If she was not married, it was not because there was anything wrong with her. She was living a life people envied and was single by choice. Her life was *that* successful.

Just as if she were marketing a book to be a bestseller, Clare crafted a plan for how she'd snag the perfect date. To impress the family most, he'd have to be not only handsome and successful, but free of any baggage such as an ex-wife or child. She made a list of her best friends who might know eligible bachelors. Over the next month she'd have to ask their assistance in finding someone who met her criteria.

The plan appeared to be working at first. Clare was invited to gallery openings, cozy dinners in her friends' apartments, hikes in the Catskills and holiday parties in the Hamptons. While she met some terrific men, none of them met her high standards and there was no discernible chemistry. She'd know when she met the right one. The process was starting to depress her. Nothing could lift her spirits more than shopping. She took a Friday afternoon off from work in February, bought some fabulous new chunk-heeled boots and an exquisite Hermes silk scarf. They worked with the outfit she had on so she changed shoes, tied the accent elegantly around her neck, touched up her makeup and then stopped for a drink at her favorite Upper East Side pub—Clontarf on Second Avenue.

The manager was a handsome Irish immigrant named Conor with whom she'd flirted off and on. "Och, you're breakin' me heart there, luv," he said. "You ought to be arrested for breaking the law of allowable beauty."

"Conor, what would I do without you to cheer me up? Thanks." She gave him a peck on the cheek. He grinned.

"For that I'll give you the best seat in the house." He started to grab a menu but she shook her head.

"No, I'm just going to park myself here at the bar. Thanks. Any fascinating men here tonight?"

"Besides meself? Hah. Hmm, well avoid that one there talkin' with the waitress. A bit of a 'Donal' Juan, I'd say. Now then, this one in the corner is just off the plane from Ireland. Seems like a nice lad. He's a professor of modern Irish literature at NYU, so you'd have that in common."

Slim pickin's, she thought as she sat midway between the ladies' man and the professor. Clare flagged Una the barmaid, a beautiful girl from Galway with thick black hair and striking celadon green eyes. The woman had been chatting with the ladies' man and kept talking to him as she approached Clare.

"I'll have a shot of your finest Irish whiskey." The two men looked up when they heard her order and turned their chairs slightly toward the young woman who seemed eager to get drunk. Clare threw back the peaty whiskey and its fire raced down her throat. She felt a blush rise in her cheeks and then warmth dispersing across her forehead and neck. The ladies' man snorted and the professor laughed.

"Another please," Clare said, flaring her nostrils as she gestured to the barmaid. The two men watched her throw back the second shot skillfully. The professor nodded in admiration as he noted that the alcohol didn't seem to affect her at all. The ladies' man noted what great legs she had.

When Clare started to order a third shot, the ladies' man cleared his throat to get the barmaid's attention.

"I can't stand to see a beautiful woman drinking alone. Make it three shots, one for each of us, including our friend in the corner there."

His name was Matthew Rich and he was an economist. The professor's name was Matt de Paor and he hailed from Dublin. Torn between two Matts, she was, and stifled her laughter at the thought she was somehow dropped into a scene written by James Joyce.

Outside the straw-pale winter daylight faded into cobalt-shadowed dusk. They were now sitting in a booth as they posited hazy theories on how to solve the world's situations. Their conversation touched on all manner of things, from politics to religion to sex. The men appreciated the fact that Clare had strong, educated opinions and she was not afraid to voice them. Both men were also Catholic, and they enjoyed discussing how differently each of them interpreted their chosen religion. Matthew was conservative and agreed wholeheartedly with papal opinions on modern issues. Clare said she couldn't understand why women couldn't become priests or why priests couldn't marry. Matt was far left of the church's teachings and thoroughly embraced liberation theology in Latin America. Their views on abortion were all over the place and surprisingly, Matthew was less strident on this issue.

As she listened, Clare noted their apparel. Matt wore clichéd professorial garb: a dark umber wool turtleneck with a leather jacket and wide-wale corduroys. His clothes were rumpled gently, which gave him an endearing demeanor. Matthew wore a navy, wide-lapel, three-piece suit with subtle pinstripes. His sky blue dress shirt was adorned with a wide, heavily starched white collar and monogrammed gold cuff links. A glint from his cuffs caught her eyes and Matt the professor became a distant memory.

She thought she'd landed a date for her sister's wedding. What she landed instead was an on-again off-again relationship that was unfortunately "off" when her sister's wedding occurred. Then again, it lasted longer than many marriages. Now that it was over, twenty-two years later, what did she have to show for it? Not even a crockpot!

A thought came to mind when she unstuck her train of thought from the quicksand of nostalgia: had she *ever* been in love with Matthew, or was she solely fascinated by the challenge of penning the only man she'd never been able to control?

Chapter 23

Noreen curled upon the overstuffed beige leather sofa in the airy sunroom of her home (that Clare called teasingly a McMansion). She'd just completed an endless round of phone calls leaving one final message on Clare's answering machine. Her mother's odd behavior during a recent visit weighed on Noreen's mind and she wondered why her sisters didn't share her immediate concerns. Sure her mother had always been distracted as a working mother, but how could she forget something as basic as how to work the coffee pot? Then there was the uncharacteristic mean crack she made about Noreen's weight gain. She also thought Molly was the name of Noreen's dog and had to be reminded that it was the name of her youngest daughter.

Her siblings' lack of worry over what she thought were vivid warning signs brought back some memories from her childhood of how different the girls were from each other, a fact that made her wonder sometimes if she was really related to them.

When Noreen was brought home from the hospital, Uncle Pat told her years later, he carried Clare over to say hello to her. Clare wailed and threw a kicking fit of hysteria. Everyone thought it was extreme behavior for a toddler. On another afternoon a couple of years later, Frances set Noreen asleep in her crib and asked Joe to watch her as well as Clare. Joe waited about fifteen minutes, then opened a beer and sat down in the kitchen to listen to the Yankees game on the radio. Clare walked into the kitchen to get a molasses cookie sent from her Grandma Mame and on the way back to the living room, passed her sister and twisted the soft skin on her arm. Noreen woke up screaming. Her father told Noreen later that he found Clare hiding in the other room, smiling as she ate the cookie slowly, savoring the crunch of sugar crystals atop the cake-like cookie. After that, a passive animosity wedged permanently between the two.

Noreen also recalled being told that the day she turned four, Clare broke the head off the pretty porcelain doll that their mother got from her Great-Aunt Bertha. The older sister had been jealous about the doll from the moment Frances let Noreen play with it. When Clare was confronted, she protested. "Why should she get a doll prettier than mine?"

Noreen spent most of her unmarried life trying to prove that she was just as fabulous as her older sister. It never quite worked. Clare led academically, no matter how hard Noreen studied. She knew that she'd never be Harvard material—there was no way could she compete with Clare on an intellectual level. Instead, Noreen opted to pursue early childhood education at SUNY Cortland. Her cumulative average was just as impressive as Clare's, however Harvard's reputation obviously carried more weight.

After she graduated and began teaching at a school in Batavia, Noreen realized there *was* a way she could one-up her successful sister. The answer came when she met the new varsity football coach at the high school in 1971. Gary

Pomeroy, a recent Princeton graduate, was the oldest son of a wealthy Skaneateles family. Noreen caught his eye when she threw a Frisbee astray during a fitness festival with the students. He ran across the athletics field to return the disc and introduced himself. She recalled that the first thing to enter her mind at the moment was that Clare had never dated a guy more handsome.

Noreen was infatuated with Gary like a teenager, to the point of writing his name over and over on scraps of paper, shopping lists and even in the margins of notes for her teaching lessons. She sure hoped that none of the other teachers would notice her interest in him because it would make grist for the faculty gossip mill. And if ever any student realized how she felt... well, forget about it.

She asked her coworkers discreetly about him and learned that his father was a respected obstetrician and his mother ran a chic interior design import firm. He graduated from a prep school in Connecticut and then majored in American military history at Princeton, where he was also a quarterback on the football team. His cousin was the superintendent of public schools in Noreen's district and when the football coach position opened, he thought immediately of Gary. The fact that he could also teach history was a plus. Although his grades at Princeton were solid, Gary never considered himself a scholar. Instead he sought a way to put his knowledge of military history to practical use in everyday life. This job in Batavia, offered soon after graduation, was less prestigious than his parents might have wanted. Gary knew that as a Princeton grad in a small town, he couldn't help but command attention. That idea appealed strongly to him.

Gary's stature was tall with a broad shelf of shoulders and the elongated legs that were a trademark of Pomeroys. He had strawberry blonde hair that swept long over his ears into long, fluffy layers. He was forever tan. The Pomeroys were an avid boating family, both motorboats and sailboats. Even in the dim light of a snowy February afternoon his skin was tanner than Noreen's in the summer. Of course it helped that the family escaped each winter to their seaside "cottage" in Aruba.

All the women on the faculty thought him gallant because of the way he'd hold the doors open for them. They were endeared with the slight broadness of his A's that he picked up during his Connecticut school days. He dressed impeccably in navy blazers, oxford shirts, silk ties and khaki pants. You didn't see his like often in Batavia. One look was all it took to know his family came from old money.

Noreen remembered the first day that they really conversed. She was sliding a tray along the cafeteria line toward the cashier when she discovered her wallet was home. The cashier muttered something about privileged teachers and how much they make and Noreen stammered that she could pay the woman tomorrow. A hand holding out a ten-dollar bill cut into their terse exchange.

"Let me pay for both of these lunches and keep the change, Marvella," Gary said. Noreen nearly died when she turned and saw Gary smiling behind her. She smelled the cologne he wore, Canoe—its *sillage* always announced his presence in the hallway. Noreen found something about the fragrance intoxicating yet also familiar, in a paternal way. She mumbled a wobbly "Thank you" and walked away with her head down to hide her red face.

"Care to join me?" he asked as he followed her into the faculty lounge. She hoped her fellow teachers did not notice how enthusiastically she said "Yes!" Over their lunch hour Gary enthralled Noreen with tales of exhilarating outdoor adventures across the country. He'd climbed Mount Shasta, paddled the Colorado River's white waters and explored caves deep underneath New Mexico. She knew he wasn't just bragging; his toned physique was a testament to his travelogue. Noreen wanted to hide the piece of cake on her tray as he discussed his idea of the optimal diet to create an Olympic-level athlete. He mentioned casually that before he came to school that morning he'd run five kilometers and lifted weights for a half hour. It exhausted her just thinking about it. Her regimen? She just remembered waking up, letting the dog out and drinking two cups of coffee while she read the paper. Although Noreen was reasonably toned for someone without a workout schedule, she felt like a complete sloth compared to him.

What she didn't realize was that as she was thinking about her faults, Gary was processing visual clues that they could produce a good-looking family together. Her chestnut hair was thick and shiny; she had good bone structure and an elegant smile. He'd have to create a good workout regimen for her so she could lose an extra fifteen pounds to strengthen her joints and hips. Twins ran in his family—even a set of triplets were on his uncle's side—and if they married, she'd have to be strong enough to carry multiple babies at once.

Noreen and Gary began having lunch together daily, and when he pressed her for details on her family background she was embarrassed to admit her "credentials" were not on par with his. He didn't seem too impressed that her father was in sales (she didn't tell him right away that her parents were separated). Her mother's job was equally unimpressive. He did smile when she said that Grandpa Jimmy had been a pharmacist and Grandma Mame had been an elementary school teacher.

"It's unusual for most people to have a grandmother who's a college graduate," Gary said. "She used pioneering education techniques, too. Good for her."

Noreen lived close enough to walk to work, so it was no surprise to her when Gary volunteered to escort her home that day. As soon as she opened the front door, her dog Paddy rushed out to greet her, but then barked agitatedly at Gary.

"No, boy. It's OK. This is my friend." Gary held out his hand so the three-year-old golden retriever could sniff it. Paddy drew near to him slowly, nosed his hand, and then looked into his eyes.

"Maybe Rex would like to go for a walk?" Gary asked.

As soon as Paddy heard the "W" word, he panted and circled them on the porch.

"That's a yes," Noreen said. "Let me get his leash. His name's Paddy, by the way." She dropped her briefcase inside the foyer by the door and returned with the leash. The dog sat calmly wagging its tail as Gary petted him.

"Here, allow me," he said connecting the leash to the dog's collar. Paddy smiled at him and panted with anticipation of running around the yard.

"He looks regal, like a king. I think I will call him Rex. That's a much better name." Gary's use of future tense captivated Noreen's attention. His cult leader-like decree punctuated by a dazzling, charismatic smile banished red-flag thoughts about altering Paddy's name. It had been an endearing appellation to her because of the McNamaras' Irish roots. But now there was something so upper crust about introducing her dog as Rex when people stopped to admire him.

Other changes happened, too. She was no longer waking up slowly in the morning. Gary would knock on her front door by six a.m. for a run through the neighborhood. He started her off at a mile and now she was running close to five kilometers a couple of times a week. By the time they'd arrive at work, she'd already done more outdoor exercise than she used to do in a week.

The effect of all of this activity was evident almost immediately. Her coworkers asked for details of the miracle diet she was on. Although they were keeping their relationship quiet, part of her wanted to scream "It's the falling in love diet." The faculty certainly wasn't stupid and soon even the students knew she was dating Gary. The principal had no problem with it as long as they kept their relationship discreet—which they had. In fact, the principal appreciated seeing the subtle transformation taking place in Noreen's appearance and thought she was a good example to her students about the power of physical fitness.

When Gary visited her house, he was always moving things around to places where they'd make more sense to him. He rearranged the plates and cups in the upper cupboards and made a rack for pot lids in the lower ones. One time when she was cooking their dinner he repositioned the furniture in the living room so the lounger was facing the television head on and the couch offered a side view. This meant that when they sat together on the couch to watch TV, she was always in his line of vision.

Her girlfriends suggested this meant that he was nesting, and preparing the house for the day they'd be married. Noreen wasn't even sure that'd he'd propose. Somehow she never felt like she lived up to his expectations. Any time he saw her eating junk food, he'd give her a look that she interpreted as "Keep that up and I'm out of here." It took a while, but soon she was eating apples regularly instead of chocolate chip cookies. She was by no means a slob, but Gary often commented on the lack of thoroughness of her housecleaning, too. This was a trait she also attributed to his health-conscious lifestyle. After she was invited to meet his parents at their sprawling Greek revival mansion on the west side of Skaneateles Lake, she understood where this obsession came from: his mother was a neat freak. The difference was, of course, that she had maids who assisted her. That seemed so silly to Noreen. The woman was younger than her own mother! She guessed that Gary just didn't take that into account, though, and held her up to Mrs. Pomeroy's unreasonable standards. This relationship wasn't relaxing; it was constant work, hard work.

Each time Gary's caustic comments deflated her ego, she thought of her sister down in Manhattan living alone among all those overcrowded alleys of steel. Gary was the entire package: drop-dead handsome, wealthy, in great health and a lot of fun—when he relaxed. She knew that the relationship miffed Clare. Of course it was petty on her part, but that was one of the reasons why she tolerated his rigidness.

One Saturday morning in October 1972, he surprised her with a spontaneous trip south of Batavia to Letchworth State Park. The skies were a vibrant turquoise and the crisp breeze twirled tangerine-colored leaves at their feet as they hiked trails by the waterfalls. He stopped at an overlook and before she knew it, he was down on one knee with a ring box open in his hand. It was a more romantic proposal that she'd imagined. Of course she said "Yes." (Or did she scream it?) She wanted to find a payphone so she could call her mother. Once they made it back to his car, though, Gary insisted on driving straight to his parents' house to tell them the news. When they arrived, she found out the reason for his urgency: Mrs. Pomeroy had invited about fifty of their closest friends over for a surprise engagement party. As they were toasting with champagne, all Noreen was thinking about was that she wished her own mother had learned the news before her future in-laws. It didn't seem right to be celebrating like this before Gary had asked her mother's permission.

Later that evening when most of the guests were gone, Noreen suggested to Gary that they could drive down to surprise her mother the next day.

"Nah, let's wait until next weekend. My mother's planned a big brunch for tomorrow. Making a detour to Binghamton after that will be trying to pack too much into one day. Relax, Norry. Your mom will find out soon enough."

Yes, it was a logical decision from his point of view. But to Noreen, making the trip to share the big news with her mother was equally as logical. She was bubbling over with excitement about the engagement. How could she possibly contain it all until next Saturday? What would she do if one of her sisters called? It would be hard to pretend nothing had happened, especially if she heard from Clare.

The next weekend Gary got a pair of fifty-yard line seats from his former coach for the Princeton-Colgate football game. He announced to Noreen that they were going, much to her protest. He said he couldn't refuse them but promised they would stop by Binghamton on their way home. She relented. As Noreen shivered in Palmer Stadium though, all she could think about was getting to Binghamton and telling her mother the news.

Princeton lost and that put Gary in a foul mood for the drive home Sunday. When they arrived in Binghamton that afternoon he remarked that they could just stay a half hour because he had to get back and grade some tests. It wasn't fair, she thought, but at least she was getting her wish of telling her mother in person.

Molly answered their knock on the door. "Noreen!"

she squealed. “What are you doing here?” She was overjoyed to see her sister and reached out to hug her. Molly noticed the tall guy standing behind her sister and wondered who he was. Noreen didn’t want to introduce him as her fiancé yet.

“You’re alone? Isn’t Mom home?”

“Nope. She’s at the mall with Terrie and Eileen.” Molly wondered why the guy had such a sour face.

“Will she be home soon?”

Molly shrugged her shoulders and Noreen bit her lip. *Oh boy, this will upset Gary further*, she thought. It was so important to her that he make a good impression on her mother. “Mind if we wait a little bit here, to see if we can catch her?” Noreen asked Gary. He sighed, but nodded as Molly opened the door wide and Noreen introduced him to her youngest sister.

“Do you guys want a sandwich?” Molly asked brightly. “Oh, and I made some cookies last night.” Noreen and Gary followed and sat down at the kitchen table while Molly prepared bologna sandwiches, being sure to use that spicy mustard her Grandma Mame liked and adding some sweet pickle slices and potato chips to the plates. She set them before her sister and her boyfriend. “Want some pop?”

Gary sneered at the paper plate laden with food. Noreen caught his eye and shook her head. She knew Molly was pretty sensitive to criticism and one flip comment might hurt her deeply. It was too late.

“Is something wrong with the sandwich?” Molly asked.

Gary ignored Noreen’s pleading eyes, turned toward

Molly and nodded. "Bologna isn't the healthiest type of sandwich meat. It's filled with nitrates and there's too much fat in it. A lean protein would be better."

"Nitrates," Molly repeated, making a mental note that whatever it was must be bad. "I could put some lettuce on the sandwich. Would that help?"

"What would be better is whole grain bread. This white bread's a killer."

"Killer?" Molly frowned. "I didn't know white bread was bad for you. Isn't it supposed to build strong bodies?"

"It's over processed, filled with carbohydrates and has too little fiber," Gary said. "You shouldn't be drinking that soda pop, either. Way too much sugar. Someone your age should stick to drinking milk. It's good for your bones."

Noreen was furious at his insensitivity toward her youngest sister. Why did Gary have to be so harsh? It was one thing to offer advice to an adult, another to berate a child who didn't know better and was just trying to be hospitable. What he just did was rude!

Molly was unfazed and processed his criticisms. How could she rectify the situation? She glanced around the kitchen. "Hey, would you like an apple instead?"

"Now you're talking, Molly." He smiled broadly with his handsome teeth and Molly couldn't wash and dry off the apple quick enough.

Molly's impromptu lunch allowed Noreen to stall and make small talk for more than an hour. Gary recognized and grew impatient with her tactic. "We better get heading back to Batavia, honey," he said throwing away their plates.

"Remember those tests I have to grade?"

"You have to go? But I know they'll be home soon." Molly went into the living room and peered through the front curtains, looking up the West Side street. Noreen didn't know what to do. She wanted to deliver their big news face to face. If she didn't tell her soon, it would be awkward.

"We have to go *now*, hon. C'mon!" Noreen didn't like the way Gary barked at her but what could she do?

"Thanks for the apple, Molly. See you at the wedding," he said as he patted her head.

"The wedding? Whose wedding?"

Noreen ushered Gary out the door. "Oh, we were planning to be here next summer for my friend's wedding," she said to her little sister, hoping to get the word wedding out of Molly's mind. She hugged her goodbye. "Tell Mom I'll call her when we get back to Batavia."

It was but ten minutes after they left when Frances and Terrie returned from the mall.

"Guess what," Molly said, "you just missed Noreen and Gary. I fed them lunch—a healthy one. Did you know that white bread is bad for you? Gary told me that. Anyway, they said they'll see you at the wedding."

"Whose wedding?" Terrie asked.

"I dunno. I like Gary, though. He's tall."

See you at the wedding? Frances spent a few moments trying to decipher what those words meant. She'd never met this Gary although she knew Noreen had been dating him for a while. Had their relationship become serious and they were here to tell her that they were engaged? Noreen seemed so young. Actually, when Frances thought about it, she was twenty six—eight years older than she was when she married Joe. That said, this was happening too fast. Was Noreen telling people they were engaged before Gary even asked her for her daughter's hand? It was not a good precedent.

When Noreen called that evening, she sensed immediately that her mother was upset.

"Is there anything you need to tell me, Noreen?"

"What do you mean, 'need'?"

"Oh, something a little bird named Molly said got me wondering."

Argh, Noreen thought, she was caught. If only Gary had kept his mouth shut.

"Well, Mom, there was an important reason why we stopped by to see you today."

"So when is the wedding date? You *were* going to let me know about that, right?"

"Hey, Mom, don't be angry. I'm sure Gary was going to ask your permission to marry me. He's got manners. His family is quite wealthy and they put on a party for us. You should see their mansion on Skaneateles Lake." She realized as soon as she spoke those words her mother would explode.

"You've met his parents and *they* know about the engagement already? Glad to know how much you value your own mother. Sorry I'm not wealthy like your fiancé's family. You know it hasn't been easy raising you six girls alone."

"Whoa, whoa, whoa, Mom! Let me explain."

"There's no need to explain. Now that you've moved away and have a life of your own, I'm not as important."

"Hey, I thought you were proud of me and my teaching job. Why are you over-reacting to this? Aren't you happy for me? I wanted to tell you the good news in person."

"That's right, but only after *his* family approved of you. Well, last time I checked I was still your mother. Don't you think *my* opinion should matter?" Her voice cut off and was replaced by a dial tone. Noreen held the receiver away from her and mouthed "What?" Had her mother really hung up on her?

***

Years later, memories of that phone conversation still made her cringe. Noreen was now forty nine, just four years older than her mother was when they had that awful row over the phone. What she didn't realize then was that her reaction was probably from the emotional ravages of perimenopause magnifying how long she'd been without a husband. The older Noreen got, the more empathetic she grew toward the challenges in her mother's life.

"Man, Mom really had it tough." Noreen hugged her knees on the soft couch.

Chapter 24

Noreen couldn't sleep and called her night-owl sister Terrie to discuss changes she'd noticed in their mother. She was surprised at Terrie's lack of insight on the matter. After all, she had lived with her mother until she was forty. She'd lived at home the longest of her siblings. If anyone knew Frances McNamara the best, it was Terrie.

That arrangement changed one day when she tired of her mother complaining about the stray cat she brought home from work at the no-kill shelter. It was time to move out. She'd been working then for about twenty-five years and had a decent amount of money in her savings account. There was enough to buy a cottage in Conklin near the banks of the Susquehanna River. The house came with a big back yard, which would allow her to expand from rescuing cats to dogs, as well.

There was a time when her family wondered if she'd ever have such independence. Terrie arrived in the world three weeks premature and Frances endured a complicated labor when she was born. Looking at her plus-sized figure, you'd never guess that she'd been a delicate preemie. While there was no evidence of damage to her brain during her difficult birth, Terrie's intellect moved blocks behind her quick-paced siblings.

She was the quintessential overlooked middle child. Three strong-willed, lively sisters preceded Terrie; two sensitive ones followed. It never seemed like there was enough time in the bathroom to curl her dull brown hair or to apply makeup just right. She eventually gave up trying to be like the others. The stylish clothes her trim older sisters wore could not be used for hand-me-downs because Terrie was at least three sizes larger.

With such lack of familial attention in her life, she sought refuge and comfort in the few things in life that gave her pleasure: caring for stray pets, eating sweets and reading science fiction. Terrie was a first generation Trekkie and her first crush was on Captain Kirk (a poster of him on the deck of the *Starship Enterprise* still hung over her bed). She never had a boyfriend in high school, though she had a couple of close male friends who were in the sci-fi club.

All of the stray cats that big-hearted Maggie dragged home, to her mother's chagrin, were cared for by Terrie. When her father brought them a collie as a gift during a rare visit with his daughters, she was beside herself. Terrie took great care of the dog that by default became more hers than the family's. His name was Tiberius, after Captain Kirk's middle name. Terrie walked the dog as soon as she got home from school. Saturday mornings she'd groom him.

Her grades in high school were so-so, and the guidance counselor suggested to her mother that Terrie be placed in the animal science program at the vocational school. Frances bristled at the thought, yet when she discussed the matter with her, Terrie was overjoyed.

Once she got her diploma, Terrie found a job right away at a pet store at the mall. She loved her job, arriving early most days. The problem was, she'd become too attached to the pets—even to the point of telling customers what names she'd given them. If she thought a customer and a specific animal were a bad combination, she'd tried subtle methods to dissuade a sale. Once her boss caught wind of this, he let Terrie go.

Frances's youngest daughter Molly was away at college now and she resigned herself to the fact that Terrie would probably never leave the nest. And when Terrie's depression deepened, Frances tried to come up with tasks that would encourage her daughter to at least develop a sense of self-worth. There were always problems that she'd ask Terrie to solve. The tasks did work and would distract Terrie for a few days, but then she'd go back to watching hours of inane court shows on TV after work or eating entire bags of sandwich cookies while reading comic books.

Despite the fact that she was a young woman who should be out with her peers enjoying the best years of her life, Terrie allowed her mother to become her social director instead. She accompanied her to her many Right to Life rallies and helped out at the Catholic relief center by serving meals at the soup kitchen or folding clothes on weekends at the thrift shop. One Saturday while working there, she heard two women talking about a no-kill animal shelter in Kirkwood. Terrie asked several questions and before long had an interview at the place. Frances was thrilled when her daughter got the job. There was a caveat, though: Terrie didn't know how to drive. Because the shelter was not on a bus route, Frances was Terrie's chauffeur for the first year of her job. Terrie's boss was kind enough to allow her hours to be arranged around the times when Frances could drop her off and pick her up. However, after a few evening scotches her mother reminded Terrie about how the arrangement wore her out and her no-good husband should be the one carting her back and forth. That was all the hint she needed. Terrie took an evening driver's ed class and eventually got her license and with money she saved up, bought a used car.

The knowledge Terrie picked up on the job about animal care was invaluable. Frances suggested that Terrie should consider going to college to learn more about veterinary science thinking it would lead to a higher paying job. Terrie shrugged it off. Why waste the money and time when she was learning what she needed to know already on the job? Frances acquiesced when she saw how happy Terrie was at the shelter. Theirs was a genial relationship now in a big house that once housed eight people and she wanted to keep that going.

It didn't last long.

In the spring of 1982, Eileen paid a surprise visit one evening, She was driving down from her home in Ithaca to New York City, but wanted to drop off some clothing donations for the thrift shop. After dinner, Frances, Terrie and Eileen sat around the dining room table, listening to the exciting tales of her time in El Salvador. The phone rang and Terrie answered it in the kitchen. After a few brief exchanges with the caller, she started crying and set the phone down. Eileen went to her sister to see why she was sobbing. Frances knew enough by the sound of her daughter's voice to brace herself for something awful.

"What is it?" Eileen asked.

"Dad's dead," were the only two words Terrie could utter between her hysterical sobs. Of all the daughters, she was the one who loved her father the most. It was somehow easier for her to forget the troubles he caused her mother. To her he was the most handsome man she knew and she never gave up the hope that he'd one day move back home and the family would be reunited.

When Frances ran into the kitchen and saw the looks on the girls' faces, she was afraid to ask what had happened.

"Your grandpa?" Frances said as she held her hand over her heart.

The girls shook their heads. Terrie ran to her mother and hugged her. "No Mommy, it's Daddy!" Frances noted that despite her age, Terrie spoke like a child at that moment and held her tight for a few minutes, looking away as a lone tear slid down her cheek. Suddenly her face shed its look of grief for anger. Instead of holding back the thoughts in her mind, she let them fly.

"I hope he died in the arms of his whore! That's what she deserved!" she hissed.

Terrie gasped and pulled away from her mother. She glanced at her mother's anger-tight face, probing her eyes to see if her mother really meant the dark words she'd just spoken. And when she realized that she did—that Frances hated Terrie's father that much—she pushed her away and ran out the front door, crying down the block.

"Damn you Joe McNamara!" Frances yelled. "You're

dead and still ruining this family."

Eileen was as equally stunned as her sister. She weighed which family member needed her most at the moment and grabbed her jacket as she headed for the door. "I have to go help my sister," Eileen said. "I know our father treated you abysmally, Mom, but you have to realize that Terrie needs your compassion when it comes to this issue. After all, he's the only father she knew." Eileen could see tears welling in her mother's eyes, but at the same time was concerned deeply about her sister. "Let's discuss this some more, later."

A permanent distance came between Terrie and her mother that night and although they were pleasant to one another afterward, it was too much for the daughter to hear cruel sentiments toward her departed father. She had no idealistic views about him; she knew he'd left her mother in a difficult position. Still, she was of his blood, and her mother needed to accept that.

With time, their distance narrowed. Frances' exasperation with Terrie's "zoo," as she called her six ever-shedding cats, would flare up from time to time creating an unsettling atmosphere. When she brought home a seventh stray, Frances dropped a not subtle hint that Terrie needed to find her own place.

Once Terrie bought the cottage in 1995 their strife eased. Before moving in she spent a wonderful day with her mother shopping for used furniture, curtains, linens and kitchen accessories. And with her mother's help the walls were painted in warm shades of peach, shaggy rugs were added to warm the distressed wood floors and perennials dug up from Frances's garden were planted in the fertile riverside loam. The day they spent working in the various flower beds around her home was one of the best mother-daughter memories the two shared.

Perhaps it was the fact that she saw her mother frequently that Terrie didn't notice any change in her behavior. Then again, it might have been because Terrie's attention had been diverted toward the neighbor next door.

***

Elvin Lord retreated to his riverside cottage twenty years ago, right after (as he often repeated the tale) he told his boss at the aerospace company to "take my job and shove it." Back then his office overlooked the Susquehanna River by Owego. Many were the days when his mind tried to wrap around the physics of a software design and he'd stare out the window at shifting river currents below, waiting for inspiration. Most often the creative roadblocks he faced were raised by budget-conscious managers urging the staff to do everything for less. He hated the headaches; he wished that he was fishing on the riverbank instead.

His first stop on his way home after quitting was the bait and tackle shop where he purchased smallmouth bass lures and a new rod and reel. He'd been fixing up the cottage for many years. Lucky for him, he'd just installed a new furnace and completed replacing the insulation before he left his job. With the money he got selling his modest home on the West Side of Binghamton (not far from the McNamaras' place), he could afford to stay in this idyllic riverside retreat through the end of his days.

Even though he was nearly eighty years old, Elvin couldn't sit still for long and was always puttering in his yard, maintaining the upkeep of his home or walking his dog. That's how he met his new neighbor, Terrie. She was picking wild purple asters by the river when Shep, Elvin's old beagle limped past her. Terrie couldn't help but smile at the old dog with droopy eyes and pepperoni-like halitosis.

"Hello little fella. What's troubling you?" she asked as she tried to examine from a distance what was wrong with his bad leg. The dog attempted to howl, but could only emit a weak gargled noise at her. After a few minutes it sighed and sat down on the riverbank. Now she had a better view. It looked as if the dog had a hot spot on its hind leg that had become infected. She had some ointment in the house for it—an herbal concoction that she made from a Native American recipe. When she returned with the ointment, Elvin was sitting next to the dog patting its head.

"This your dog? I have some medicine to help its leg heal."

"And I should trust you why?" Elvin asked.

"It's OK, I'm a veterinary assistant," Terrie said. "Here, hold the dog while I spread some of this ointment on the sore."

Elvin smiled as the kind woman tended to his dog.

"This is all natural, so even if the dog licks it, you don't have to worry about him getting sick. What's his name?"

"Shep. We match in dog years." That made Terrie

laugh. "I'm Elvin Lord. What's your name?"

"Terrie McNamara. I live in this cottage."

"Ah, yeah, I noticed someone moved in there. You have that orange tabby cat, right? You should know that he hides beneath my bird feeder and has caught more than a few mourning doves that were too dumb to notice his presence."

Terrie grimaced. "I'm sorry. I call the little terror Mad Max. Even though they're domesticated, you can't breed the feral out of felines."

That made Elvin laugh. "So what's brought you to this riverside paradise?"

Terrie sat for a few minutes before speaking and then, she couldn't help herself from blurting out the truth. "I was mad at my mother for not being sorry that my dad died."

Elvin's eyes widened at her frankness and he rubbed his forehead while trying to stifle the grin forming on his mouth. It sure was awkward, but he knew her comment deserved a sympathetic response. "I'm sorry to hear that. Did she have good reason?"

Terrie picked up a birch twig and began tracing a frowning face in the dirt. "I guess so. My dad left Mom after my youngest sister was born and moved down South with his girlfriend. They never got divorced."

"So he just up and left you, your mom and sister?"

"Oh there are six of us kids."

"Pffft! He's lucky she didn't cut off his...," Elvin looked at her innocent face and hesitated before using the word he was about to speak. "Well, that must have been humiliating to your mother. I can understand her anger. Same thing happened to me, only in reverse. My wife met this construction worker who was replacing the old windows in our house and she left me, taking our only son. They live down near Pensacola now. Haven't seen my son since he was eleven. I showed up unannounced a few months after they moved. My ex's boyfriend forbid me at gunpoint to stay on their property. Every time I called, they'd hang up or not even answer the phone. Tried getting the courts involved, but my ex brought up my fondness for whiskey at the time, and I was deemed a risk as a parent. Gave up the drink after that, but it didn't help. I learned through my sister-in-law that the boyfriend's still married to a woman who owns a home renovation business up here.

"Now despite what happened in your life, Terrie, that doesn't take away the fact that your father was responsible for you coming into the world though, right?"

She nodded and put her head down. If there was one thing Elvin couldn't handle it was seeing a woman cry. He patted her shoulder awkwardly. "There now, didn't mean to upset you. You must remember the good times you shared with your dad. Don't be too hard on your mother, though. Maybe you moved out just because it was time for you to embrace being an adult."

She looked up at his kind fatherly face and nodded. "I'm glad I did it. Mom and I are cool now. She helped me plant the gardens around the house. I have some other plans, too."

"What are they?" Elvin asked politely and then

listened for almost an hour as Terrie described how she wanted to open her own dog and cat shelter right there. The big challenge she faced was contracting with a licensed veterinarian who focused on homeopathic care. To complement that, she had created a line of natural remedies for pets that she bottled at home. She'd also developed her own recipes for cat and dog treats. Friends would buy them from her and that income had been adding nicely to her salary from the shelter. She also had a grooming business on the side, but she could just handle a couple of pets a week.

"Well, you need to do a couple of things," Elvin said after listening carefully. "You need to fence in your property so you could let a dog run safely in the back yard. Also, have you filed a DBA yet? Or, more important, do you have any sort of business plan?"

It was obvious from the blank expression on Terrie's face that she had just a vague idea what he was talking about. Elvin saw some of himself in Terrie's ambitious eyes. She, like him, just wanted to focus on doing the work that she loved and was meant to do, unencumbered by the government-enforced paperwork.

"I can help you build your fence, Terrie. You start thinking, in the meantime, about what you want to achieve with your business. Then we can sit down and plan it out."

Terrie called her sister Eileen a few weeks later after the first posts for the fence were set in the ground to tell her about the good fortune of having Elvin Lord for a neighbor. Eileen hoped this man's intentions were good. She feared her sister's lack of experience with men could make her vulnerable in such a situation. What did Elvin expect to get in return for his assistance? That would be the key to this situation.

She made plans to come down from Ithaca for a visit the next week. Eileen suspected there was a similarity between Elvin's tutelage of her sister and the priest who had changed her own life. In a sense, they'd both been drawn to these men because they fulfilled a paternal void. Later when Eileen met him and realized how old Elvin was, she discounted all thoughts that her sister was interested in him romantically. It was obvious that Elvin had essentially become Terrie's father.

Chapter 25

At an early age Eileen exhibited a contemplative and solemn demeanor. By the time she reached sixth grade she was obsessed with the life of Mahatma Gandhi and his nonviolent methods for effecting change. Whenever she heard news about race riots down South, she'd fast in solidarity with the oppressed. She never told anyone about this. That's because like her mother before her, she'd also become obsessed with the life of St. Thèrése of Lisieux. Frances had once given her a relic that her Great-Aunt Bertha brought back from a trip to Normandy. Like St. Thèrése, Eileen preferred to suffer in silence, because to point out her fasting to another would be less holy.

When she reached eighth grade Eileen stopped eating meat for a year. "It bothers my stomach," she told her mother. It was more that she thought eating an animal's flesh was wrong. Mame noted early on in her life that Eileen carried "the weight of the world's sorrows in her heart." A wan child, Eileen's rare laughter never registered as forceful as a guffaw. It was more a puff of glee that carried just enough heft to spin a lone dandelion seed aloft.

Her penchant for worry carved permanent lines on her face by the time she was in high school. Maybe it was because she had to supervise her younger sister Molly—her complete opposite, a bundle of energy—while their mother joined the struggle to overturn the 1970 New York State law allowing abortion. It was a movement that Eileen also embraced fervently, and when she could, she wrote letters to their local assemblyman and state senator urging the law be overturned. Eileen hand-lettered numerous posters for her mother's protest marches in Albany.

The summer between her freshman and sophomore years St. Malachy's Parish sponsored a weeklong retreat for teenagers in Windsor. Eileen met there a young and charismatic motorcycle-riding priest named Father Dan Coleman who had spent time with the Peace Corps in El Salvador. His descriptions of life in the impoverished country fascinated her. Father Dan told them how he showed farmers methods of rotating crops so as not to deplete the nutrients in the soil. He also taught them how to irrigate their fields more effectively and fight soil erosion.

One evening as they sat around a bonfire at the lakeside camp, he strummed a guitar and sang folk songs learned from the Salvadorans. Father Dan rose suddenly and all six foot four of him towered above the students as he danced the *El Xuc*, a native folk dance. He sang a song in Spanish and invited the students to spin like he was, dancing around the fire. Eileen was not prone to such exuberance, but when she relented and danced with the others—uninhibited and giddy—something inside her caught fire. Yes, *this* is what she needed to do, become a missionary for the Lord. Oh how she'd love to spend her life assisting the poor of the world! Her eyes met Father Dan's briefly, and he saw the bonfire flames reflecting in hers and grinned. Eileen felt her heart leap inside, filled with the fire of the Holy

Spirit's charism. *This must be how St. Thèrése felt*, she thought.

On the last day of the retreat, she questioned Father Dan intently about what the Peace Corps was like versus becoming a missionary. He touched her elbow briefly.

"The power of the Lord is working through you, Eileen. I can see it on your face. Give me your address and I'll send you some information on different orders abroad as well as contacts I know in the Peace Corps." He hugged her and her heart leapt again. This was it. No need for college. Instead, she'd learn life's lessons serving the poor in the Third World.

At the start of her sophomore year in high school, Eileen's father Joe reappeared briefly. He was passing through to attend his father's funeral in Rochester. No one, especially her mother, wanted to talk with him, but Eileen the peacemaker did and greeted him on the front porch.

"I forgive you, Daddy, for walking away. Don't worry about us at all. God will take care of our family. Go in peace and just take care of yourself. Please bring our condolences to our grandmother." There was no sarcasm tingeing her words about the relatives she'd never met—Joe knew that. She was speaking honestly and from the heart. Frances was obviously doing a wonderful job raising their girls.

Joe found Eileen spooky, because it almost felt as if she could peer right into his soul and feel the guilt he had for the bad things he did throughout life. Eileen's aura of religiosity created a barrier between them that Joe couldn't cross. He had amended many of his ways—his girlfriend

Brenda had successfully tamed the womanizer in him—but when it came to the responsibility of helping to raise his six daughters, it was still too constraining. He and Brenda ran a convenience store off of Route 17 on the outskirts of Savannah. They weren't rich, but they didn't lack for the basics, either. He liked being near the river, but deep inside part of him longed for those lazy afternoons spent on Keuka's shores with his buddy Eddie.

Every few months he'd send a check to Frances, but the amount was never quite enough for what the girls needed at the time. Joe and Frances never discussed what happened, why he left. She, of course, assumed that *she* had done something wrong. Truth be told, Joe actually still loved Frances. The moments they shared that she felt were special, he did, too. He just had this restlessness about being burdened by the exclusiveness of marriage, and his sexual appetite was something that he refused to control. In turn, Frances threw her sorrow at being rejected into anti-abortion efforts across the country. Maybe she couldn't save her own life from its troubles, but she had to try to save those without a fighting chance.

***

The time neared for Eileen to discuss plans for college with her mother. She was afraid to tell her mother about the vocation she yearned for. Yet, something had to be said.

Eileen visited Father Dan at the rectory and asked if he could meet with her mother Frances to help bolster her vocation argument. It was St. Valentine's Day when she visited the rectory, and Father reminded her that the saint was a priest who aided the persecuted martyrs of Rome under Claudius II. "You must do what you know is right in your heart," Father said.

He stopped by her house two days later, after the Ash Wednesday evening Mass was over. Eileen had been too afraid to tell her mother that he was coming over, so he was taken aback when Frances seemed startled by his appearance at the door. The other McNamara sisters still at home, Terrie and Molly, were in the kitchen, giggling over how cute Father Dan was.

"So, Mrs. McNamara, Eileen has told you why I'm here, right?"

"No." Frances glared at her daughter. If she'd known that a member of the clergy was coming, she'd have baked some cookies or put on a pot of coffee.

Father Dan took in a deep breath and started. "Last summer your daughter professed to me at the youth retreat that she was considering a vocation."

Frances turned toward Eileen with a look of shock that turned into a slight smile. "Is this true?"

Eileen twisted her arms together in front of her and nodded, not meeting her mother's eyes.

"We've discussed some options for her, and your daughter seems especially interested in missionary work. I suggested that she try out the Peace Corps for a couple of years to see if she is suited for such a life and then if she likes it, later she could explore missionary religious orders to see which one is the best match for her."

"Where would she go?" Frances asked, as she thought how naïve and fragile her daughter looked at this moment. Was this priest trying to boost his vocations bounty and she was an easy mark? Or was this really God's plan for Eileen?

"I spent time in El Salvador and loved it. She could go several places. South and Central America. Africa."

"*Africa*! No daughter of mine is going all the way to Africa."

"But Mom, what if God is calling me to do work there among the poor?"

"I'm sorry but that's just too far away. Central America sounds good enough to me."

"But, Mom...."

"I agree, Mrs. McNamara. Central America would be the perfect place for her to work. There was a terrific host family I stayed with in El Salvador and I could recommend that she be placed there."

Frances did not want to get in the way of her daughter's spirituality. After all, she had similar devotion at that age that was derailed later by Joe McNamara. But was Eileen strong enough to handle the challenges living in a foreign country would bring? Unfortunately she had studied French in high school, not Spanish (which would have made more sense), but there was time to get her into a class next year and maybe get some tutoring on the side.

If she deferred going to college now, that would also be one less expense for Frances. She knew from her own experience that life had plenty enough lessons to teach if you were open to learning new things, which Eileen definitely was. They all met again to discuss the logistics of applying and Frances finally gave her approval. And thank God, as Eileen said, the Peace Corps gave theirs too. She'd be leaving in September 1973 for twenty-seven months (a month of training followed by a little over two years of working with the poor in El Salvador).

Eileen learned just before her sister Noreen's wedding that Father Dan had plans to go back there next year, so their stays would overlap. She looked forward to that day when their lives would intersect again. What sort of adventures would she have had by then? How would she have changed? Would she be able to teach him a folk dance or two?

Chapter 26

The beginning of Eileen's Peace Corps work in El Salvador was pretty much what she'd expected. She arrived in the capital San Salvador toward the end of the rainy season in late September 1973, and when she passed through the airport gate the humidity frizzed her hair instantaneously. *Welcome to the tropics*, she thought, imaging the snide comments Clare would be saying about her hair now.

After initial assessment and a month of agricultural techniques training in San Vicente, she traveled by "chicken bus" to a *caserío*, a hamlet in the shadows of an old volcano where *campesinos* (country folks) lived. Bus patrons paid their fare and then paused to touch the feet of the statue of Our Lady of Guadalupe on the tiny dashboard shrine, a good luck gesture for safe travels.

Eileen moved in with the host family that Father Dan knew, Luis Rivas y Aguilar and his wife Esperanza plus their three children Joaquin, Victoria and Graciela. "*Mucho gusto* (Nice to meet you)," Eileen said as she shook hands with her hosts at the bus stop. Luis spoke English well and told her that he worked on a coffee plantation about an hour and a half away and Esperanza did piecemeal seamstress work at home besides her long day of regular chores. Their lives were more stable than most but Eileen could sense that they were one natural disaster away from abject poverty.

Her work with the campesinos would include teaching them safer methods of irrigation, pest control and crop rotation. They leased their property from a wealthy landowner on a sprawling estate overlooking the city of San Vicente. This land had been rainforest once, and the campesinos who leased it had to clear the trees first before they planted their own subsistence crops of corn, beans and sorghum.

For the first few days, Eileen shadowed Esperanza's daily chores. Her first challenge was waking before dawn to fetch water from the stream that was an hour's walk away. Afterward, they'd gather wood into the pit of a cement outdoor stove, light it afire and place a griddle on top. Her next task was to make enough corn tortillas for the day. Esperanza soaked corn kernels in water and white lime before grinding the dough it made with a *mano* (hand stone) on the *metate, a* curved larger stone. Eileen helped her knead the dough and then slap it back and forth between their hands into thin patties. The patties were fried on top of the griddle, called a *comal.* Once cooked, the tortillas were eaten hot with cups of coffee for *desayuno* (breakfast).

Eileen accompanied Esperanza to the market after that, where they'd buy fresh produce and some meat. There were chickens at home, also used for eggs and meat. She treated Eileen to her first *pupusas* (cornmeal disks filled with pork and spices accompanied by *curtido*, a marinated cabbage salad). It was at the market where she first encountered the legendary native machismo, with ensuing wolf whistles and calls of "*Gringa*!" At first she felt a little flattered, but when she encountered it at every turn of the street, Eileen panicked. She felt as if she were part of the market's offering that day.

The family's main meal was the *almuerzo*, a noontime dinner. Esperanza served soup, more tortillas, rice, corn, beans and some fresh squeezed pineapple or mango juice. Afterward all activities ceased for the siesta. Eileen never fought taking the forced nap; the heat was always beastly then. Chores started up again as early as two. Since there was no running water in the home, laundry had to be carted back to that stream, washed and carried back home to dry on an outside line.

Esperanza's mother Isabella and her Aunt Pilar also lived with them in the adobe home with a tiled roof and dirt floor. While Esperanza did chores, her mother and aunt tended to the children. Together they worked in the garden and fed the chickens and pigs. The roosters, Eileen came to realize, were on their own time schedule, crowing whenever it seemed to please them.

Life was hard for sure in the tropical setting, but there came an idyllic satisfaction with the everyday routine. When the mountain's mist parted she'd see the volcanic peak of San Vicente. At that moment Eileen would think of the ever-present dangers these people faced. And when the earth would tremble from the mountain's seismic yawning, those fears were reinforced.

It was discomfiting to go from a place where your worst concern was icy roads in winter to a place where each step you took must be weighed for its safety or wisdom. One morning during her second week there, she forgot to shake her shoes and thrust her feet inside one only to have a scorpion sting her big toe. Before she left America, she'd gotten shots for all sorts of threatening diseases and was glad for the malaria medicine because mosquitoes were ever present. Her arms were always covered with bites.

She was still learning Spanish, so it helped to be immersed in the Rivas's home where they knew just a handful of English phrases. Despite her lack of fluency, she understood that when people whispered it often had to do with the rumblings about unrest throughout the country.

El Salvador was predominantly Catholic, and when the Latin American Bishops had their post-Vatican II conference in 1968, the seeds of liberation theology were planted firmly there. This theology focused on meeting the needs of the oppressed using community as the vehicle to correct class wrongs. The country had the densest population of any in the world and a terribly skewed ratio of rich landowners to farmers who had no land to farm of their own. Luis told Eileen how some landowners who'd allowed campesinos to lease property from them—that first had to be cleared of its rainforests—would revoke the leases several years after the land had been made viable for planting thanks to the hard labor of its residents. The beauty of this "deal" to the landowners is that the labor to prepare their new farmland was virtually free.

Some of the priests who embraced the liberation theology would visit the caserío once a week to say Mass in the evening. The two-hour service would include not just gospel readings, but news of recent social injustices. After the final blessing there would be discussions and reflections about how all of this related to their own lives. Some of this sentiment inspired the campesinos to take the matters into their own hands and fight the corrupt government that favored the control of land in the hands of the wealthy few.

Back in the 1930s, Augustin Farabundo Martí Rodriguez (a co-founder of the Communist Party of Central America) led an unsuccessful guerilla revolution of indigenous farmers. Martí lost his life at the hands of government forces along with thirty thousand of the indigenous campesinos during the uprising, a death toll referred to as *La Matanza*—the slaughter. The United States feared communism would take hold in the country because campesinos later adopted guerilla tactics Che Guevara introduced to spread revolution throughout Latin America.

Catholic campesinos were viewed as potential subversives, and here was Eileen, a Catholic gringa helping improve the lives of the farmers. When the coffee bean harvest started in October, Luis left to live on the plantation for the next three months and warned Eileen to be careful, that he'd heard rumors of death squads roaming the fields and back roads. She tried not to show any fear on her face, but inside she was terrified. There was a *portón* (metal gate) on the door to protect the home from intruders, but how well would it work?

One night a couple months after Luis left, they were all sitting around a bonfire eating tamales as Isabella told the tale of *El Justo Juez de la Noche*—the just judge of the night.

He was a terrifying specter who roamed back roads in the dark and would not let strangers pass, threatening them with his machete. You could not see his face, Isabella said, only his glowing eyes through a column of smoke. She had a cousin who came home late from a party once where he had drunk too much Tíc Táck—moonshine-like liquor made from sugar cane. He crossed over a shallow stream and as soon as he reached the old road that led to home, he encountered a shadowy figure who asked, "Do you not know that the night has an owner? It is mine—the just judge of the night!" They found him the next morning asleep on the side of the road with a machete stabbed into the ground less than an inch away from his face.

Eileen didn't sleep that night, or much of the following nights. Most of the husbands and eldest sons in the homes surrounding theirs were off helping with the coffee harvest. That left behind the aging grandfathers or young boys who'd be no match for any death squads. She was always conscious of this fact when they went to market and the wolf whistling began. It really bothered her during the early morning water runs with Esperanza.

"Don't you ever worry that you'll encounter him, you know, that headless judge?"

Esperanza laughed at Eileen and pulled out a crucifix on a chain around her neck. "*El Señor* (Jesus) has more power than any devil in the night. As long as I have him, there is no fear."

Eileen was continually impressed by the courage of her hosts. She'd always felt her faith was strong, but now in this foreign country and culture, it felt tenuous. Sure there were dangers back home in America, but they weren't as palpable. News traveled through market conversations with people who had access to electricity and radios. But up here near the mountains, it was as if she lived on the moon. Who knew where friend or foe was? She did notice that when they left the Wednesday night Masses said by that priest from San Vicente, there were two men listening in the back of the church who never said a prayer or received communion. Were they spies for the government, she wondered? Had she already been marked as a possible Marxist?

Her fears grew when another visiting priest, Father Ruiz, asked them to pray for some Maryknoll nuns who'd been harassed by National Guardsmen one night while walking home from a community-building meeting. If they were harassing nuns outright, would anyone be safe?

***

Esperanza caught a bad stomach virus that was going around the caserío in late December, and since her mother and aunt were too old to fetch the water, that meant Eileen had to do the task alone. She was terrified to make the hour-long walk in the darkness, with only the sounds of awakening birds in the distance. Once she arrived at the stream, she encountered some of the women neighbors and conversed a bit. Then her eyes caught the glow of a cigarette coming from a man leaning against a tree nearby. Her breath whooshed out of her when she recognized the man as one of the people she suspected was spying on them for the government. Eileen filled the buckets as quickly as she could and then started walking back down the road. She kept looking over her shoulder, but all she could see behind her were their neighbors. When she neared home at dawn, a man passed her on bicycle—it was the man watching by the stream.

She ran into the house, nearly tripping over the chicken out front. "What's the matter?" Isabella asked.

"I think I was followed by a government soldier!"

"You have done no wrong," Pilar said. "You must be imagining things."

About two hours later a rooster crowed and the neighbor's dog barked an alert. They heard a woman's cry and the children ran to the back door. "Eileen! Eileen! *Venir aquí*!" Joaquin yelled to her. She ran to the doorway and saw a young pregnant woman obviously in labor leaning against the shed where they cooked. A guerilla stood guard with an AK-47, looking around to see if anyone was watching. Eileen gasped and her heart pounded a weird rhythm when she saw the rifle. Esperanza rose from her sick bed to see what was going on. As soon as she saw the couple, she recognized the girl as her friend Ana's daughter. The girl disappeared last winter and her mother suspected she'd been kidnapped by government soldiers. She was almost relieved to see her with the young guerrilla.

"Quick, bring her inside to my bed!" Esperanza said, gesturing to the terrified couple. Everyone stood back from the doorway as the pregnant girl entered and Esperanza led her to the bed.

Isabella and Pilar started boiling a pot of water on the fire. Eileen tried to not be thrown by the fact that she was about to witness her first birth and gathered clean rags for Isabella. The young man never relaxed his grip on the rifle's trigger, as if he imagined the National Guard would burst into the house at any moment. He was a first-time father, Eileen guessed, because he looked so helpless despite being fully armed.

Outside the neighbors' dogs started a cacophony—more strangers were around. Esperanza looked at her mother who handed her a rag which she tied around the woman's mouth so as to muffle her cries of childbirth. Esperanza gestured to Eileen to stand watch at the doorway.

Her hands trembled as she held onto the portón to peek outside. Down the street near the main road was a Jeep carrying a group of National Guard. They were going from house to house.

"Psst!" she said, gesturing to the young guerrilla. He came over to her and she pointed at a path between the houses that led to a mountainside route on which he could escape.

"Go! We'll take good care of her!" she said in Spanish. The young man went back to the girl, brushed her sweaty hair away from her face and kissed her goodbye. Then he made the sign of the cross and disappeared as quickly as he'd arrived.

Eileen bolted the door shut when the dogs' barks turned to snarls. A soldier swore at the dogs and there was an odd noise and then a dog's yelp. The soldiers' boots fell heavy on the compacted dirt outside of the door. Then a fist pounded on it.

"Open up, *now*!" a soldier commanded in Spanish.

Pilar gestured to Eileen to put a shawl over her head and kneel on the floor with a rosary before she unlocked the door.

"Let us inside! We are searching for a guerilla pig!" Before Pilar could respond, six armed guards barged past and poked around the small dwelling. They paid no attention to the woman giving birth in the bedroom (though they did look under the bed). One waved the tip of his rifle past Joaquin's nose as he sat on the floor. They all laughed when he wet his pants.

Two soldiers whispered as they pointed at the back of Eileen's head, who in her fear couldn't recall the words of the Hail Mary, although she'd recited the prayer thousands of times. All she kept saying to herself was "Save us, God! Save me, Jesus!" She tried to calm herself by imagining she was looking at Keuka Lake at dawn from the McGrath's screened porch, watching ribbons of pink fog rise from summer-warmed waters.

The leader ripped the shawl from her head with one hand as he spun her around with the other.

"Gringa! What are you doing here?" He smacked his lips as he leered at her.

"She is with the Peace Corps," Esperanza yelled, holding the hand of the young woman whose labor pains were agonizing.

"Where is he?" the soldier asked as he slapped Eileen's face. The impact pushed the inside wall of her cheek against her teeth, and her mouth filled with blood.

"*No entiendo*!" she replied.

"Where are you hiding him? Tell us or his whore and bastard will be shot!"

Eileen looked wide-eyed toward Esperanza, who gently shook her head as if to say, remain silent.

"Come here!" a soldier outside the house yelled. The guardsmen ran to the door as the other soldier explained that a neighbor saw a young man running down the hill toward the stream, heading toward the village. Eileen knew the neighbor lied; now two of them could be killed if the truth came out. The soldiers filed out except for their commander who'd slapped Eileen. Had he paused to apologize to her, she wondered. Instead he lit a cigarette slowly and leered back at her. The glare of his dark violent eyes branded onto her fears.

"I'm watching you, gringa!"

Pilar hugged trembling Eileen after the men left. "You must never let them see the fear in your eyes," she told Eileen. "That only fuels their hate."

Ana's daughter cried out again and now their attention was focused back on the birth of her baby. From the difficulty she was having pushing out the child, it was obviously this woman's first baby and she endured agonizing labor through the night.

Eileen spent the hours comforting the children as they tried to sleep, but each time the woman cried out, they'd awaken in terror. Around half past two in the morning they heard the baby's first cries from the other room, but then Isabella screamed out in concert with it. Eileen ran in to see

Esperanza holding the baby wrapped in a blanket, but his mother lifeless on the bed.

Eileen fell to her knees and cried out to God. "Why, Lord? *Why*? What did this young woman do to deserve this? And the poor baby?" The women wailed, and the children who were awakened by the haunting sound, clung wide-eyed to Eileen's side.

About half an hour later, there was a knock at the door. It was the young father, returned from the guerilla hideout in the mountains. Esperanza put his newborn son in his arms and hugged him. He was so happy, he wept.

"*¿Dónde está Rosita*?" he asked. The women looked at each other and he knew something was wrong. He brushed past them into the bedroom and then let out a cry of anguish that carried through the thick adobe walls, woke up the roosters outside and rolled up the mountainside toward his camp.

"¡*Dios mio*, no! ¡No, Rosita!" He knelt next to the bed and took her lifeless hand. Isabella walked over and knelt next to him.

"It is God's will, my son. There is nothing you can do. Raise your child with love. That is all."

The young man covered his face with his arm to wipe away the tears he could not hold back. Soon the tears were replaced by anger.

"No! NO! This is not God's will. Rosita's blood is on the government's hands. This is because of the injustices landowners force on us campesinos. God had *nothing* to do with her murder."

"You must leave with your son. It is not safe for either of you here," Pilar said.

"But that baby must be fed at a nursing woman's breast. It's not safe to take him up into the mountains," Esperanza cautioned.

The young man rubbed his forehead as he looked at his beautiful newborn son. "Eduardo's wife has also given birth recently. I know she will help me. My boy will be safe." He looked at Eileen. "Tell me the name of your father."

"Joseph," she said.

The young man smiled. "Like San José, patron saint of the worker. The child shall be called José because you saved my life."

The women packed up some tortillas, fruit and towels and sent the baby off with his father under cover of night.

Eileen had not seen much death in her life and the thought of trying to sleep in a house with a corpse in it terrified her. That's why despite her exhaustion, she was more than happy to accompany Esperanza into town to tell Ana's parents so they could come and get their daughter's body.

Poor Esperanza. She was barely recovered from her illness and this was such a traumatic thing for her to have to do. Eileen provided the moral support she needed and later returned to the stream to fetch their water for the day.

After she worked in the garden with the neighbors, helping them build an irrigation trench, Eileen came back home exhausted and collapsed in the hammock, the strings closed up around her body like a cocoon. She imagined it was the loving arms of her family back home. That was something she could really use right now. Oh how she missed the joy of young Molly, and Terrie's cat menagerie, and heck, even Clare's sniping. Every night she'd been praying for all of them. She hoped they were doing the same for her now.

She'd been in the country four months now and had yet to sense that it was a place where she belonged. Had this been a big mistake? Why did she choose this work on purpose?

She envied her family back home. Their biggest decisions that day would be what to eat for dinner or what to wear to school. If they wanted a drink of water, they simply crossed the room to the faucet. If they wanted to read a book in bed, they'd leave the light on in the bedroom. If they needed new shoes, they'd get in the car and drive to the mall. Here it seemed that sheer existence required far too much effort.

Oh how she'd love to listen to some Beatles or Beach Boys music on the stereo. How fun it would be to make a bowl of popcorn and watch the late night movie on the TV. With what she was experiencing in El Salvador though, she could be living on another planet.

She thought a lot about little José, the baby born under such terrifying circumstances, and wondered what would his life be like being raised among the guerillas on the mountain. Would he ever know a life of peace? Would he ever live a day without fear? Was her life back home something he'd only dream about?

Eileen wondered what her father would think of a Salvadoran baby being named after him. Truth was she could barely remember him in her own life. Eileen didn't want to tell anyone—they'd probably think she was crazy—but she swore she saw him standing in the back of the church at Noreen's wedding.

What if he'd been around more when she was growing up? Had she known Joe like other daughters knew their fathers, perhaps she wouldn't have felt the need to escape a Third World away on this Peace Corps adventure. And just like the young guerilla, she decided that her lot in life was not hers to blame, but a direct result of the actions of her father. The fear of what she experienced earlier in the day now morphed into uncharacteristic anger toward him for abandoning them and putting the onus of rearing his children on her mother's shoulders.

The hammock must have been picking up the vibe of her anger she felt, because it started swaying like the tick of an alarm clock. Then suddenly she felt dizzy. *Oh no*, she thought, *I've probably contracted what Esperanza had.* The swaying became suddenly more pronounced and it appeared as if the horizon was moving, too.

"*¡Dios mio!*" Pilar cried. "*¡Terremoto*!" The family gathered in a circle outside the house and started praying. It was a strong temblor, and though the shaking felt interminable to Eileen, it was over within seconds. Then another wave hit that made her feel like she was on a sailboat during a gale, but soon after the movement stopped. Minor quakes continued throughout the rest of the day. In all, pots rattled and a few adobe bricks cracked, but that was the extent of the earthquake's visible effects. When the roosters calmed down finally, Eileen thought it probably meant that the worst of the quakes had passed.

Tears flowed as she lay silently in her bed that night. Eileen felt like the past twenty-four hours broke her resolve. How could she continue like this? She needed to return home, yet she had twenty more months committed to working in El Salvador. Could she ask the director of the program in San Vicente if she could be sent somewhere else? Eileen figured if she explained the situation, she could convince them that it was too dangerous where she was. As she quieted down, she thought of other Peace Corps volunteers in situations far more desperate than hers. If they could do it, she must find the strength to stick to her commitment.

A few days later Luis returned from the coffee harvest though, and gradually the family's life regained normalcy. With the warm dry weather, the family did more recreational activities together.

Eileen organized a mini-*fútbol* league among the neighborhood children and they had games once a week in a small field she was allowed to use for the purpose. The team stats were registered on a sign she hand painted and nailed to a post by the field. The children looked forward to checking their scores and bragging about their victories and epic feats during the games. She teased the kids, giving each team a special nickname. The league leaders called themselves the *guanacos*, a Salvadoran nickname that means hard workers, and it amused Eileen to see evidence of machismo brewing at such a young age.

One morning around that time she awoke to help Esperanza, but felt odd. When she tried to stand up, the whole room began to spin. She laid herself back down, and when she re-awakened, a strong smell startled her and so did the sight of an old man leaning over her wearing a necklace of garlic. Eileen shrank away from him thinking he was a hallucination, but Esperanza was right there and held her shoulder.

"Do not be afraid. You had a bad fever and have been asleep since yesterday. I asked the *curandero* (healer) to come. He is good."

Eileen watched as the man took out a brown egg from a little pouch around his neck. The man held it tightly as he swept it over her body, making repeated signs of the cross with it as he prayed.

After a few minutes, he walked outside and then held the egg up to the sunlight, studied it, and then shook his head. Esperanza translated his diagnosis.

"You have been subjected to *mal de ojo*. A person with sight that is too strong has looked upon you. It is a child's illness, but since you are like a child in this place, you have been affected. He says that you must eat the meat of the iguana for the next three days to be cured."

Eileen thought immediately that he must be speaking of the National Guardsman who'd barged into Luiz's home. In this weakened state, it was not difficult for her to believe that brutal man possessed the evil eye's power.

The curandero took Eileen's hand and looked directly at her. He didn't speak, but somehow she heard his voice in her mind. It felt as if he were reaching into her soul! "*No se preocupe* (don't worry), *es la voluntad de Dios* (it is God's will)." And then something odd happened: the man's face changed into that of Grandma Mame. Eileen's heart leapt to see her again. Oh how she missed her! Grandma Mame reached her hand out to touch Eileen's cheek where she'd been hit by the evil soldier. When she made contact, there was a bright flash and suddenly both the vision of her grandmother and the curandero were gone.

Esperanza followed his suggestion and went back to the market to buy iguana meat for Eileen. She cooked a simple soup with it and fed it to her reluctant patient. The odd treatment worked and within three days Eileen had completely recovered (and was likewise cured of any desire to ever eat iguana again).

***

A year later Eileen was watching a fútbol game, when an iridescent blue morpho butterfly drifted out of the woods and landed by her feet. Its shimmering giant wings were spectacular—they couldn't be real. It was one of the magical things she adored about this country. She turned full circle slowly, trying to take in all of the natural beauty in this tiny caserío. To her left were the lush slopes of the volcano, which she had climbed one afternoon with Luis and Joaquin. There she saw orchids in every shape imaginable growing in the wild. To her right was the long stony path to the stream where they collected water and did laundry, on whose banks the wildflowers drew a colorful array of hummingbirds. She closed her eyes and imagined she could hear the marimba music in the courtyard near the market. Then she tried to recall what the market smelled like: tortillas cooking on griddles, fresh pineapples and mangoes being juiced, the samples of *queso blanco* held out by friendly cheese mongers, fresh-caught snapper and tilapia. All of this she must remember in detail when she left.

Her real home seemed so distant. She closed her eyes and envisioned sitting next to Grandpa Jimmy on the wraparound porch, telling him about her adventures. What would he think of this place? She wondered how her experiences here compared with Uncle Pat's time in the Philippines, too.

Now that she had finally adapted to El Salvador, Eileen was especially cognizant of how fast her day of departure was coming and she wished she could delay it. In its own way, this place by the mountains that was dedicated to San Lorenzo—patron saint of the poor—was a paradise. Her mind seemed to gloss over the everyday drudgery of chores. Had she imagined all of those scary events of the past, too?

The next day she was at the market with Esperanza and a woman approached her and invited her to come to their house for almuerzo after the noontime prayers. Eileen knew it was the custom to accept any invitation for a meal, lest one offend, but she'd never seen this woman before. She asked Esperanza what she should do and her answer was mysterious.

"I think God wills it." She averted her eyes and pretended to be interested in a display of mangoes.

"*Venga, por favor*," the woman said to Eileen, gesturing to follow. She hated to leave Esperanza and not help her carry the groceries back home. Yet, when she thought about it, Esperanza had done just fine for years without her help. Eileen nodded and followed the woman through a deep maze of alleys that led to the foothills of the mountain. She tried to notice landmarks that would help her find her way back home, but the woman walked so briskly, scattering chickens scratching for corn, that she had to focus on not losing sight of her.

The woman disappeared into what might have passed for the neighborhood kids' playhouse back home: pieces of odd-shaped corrugated metal nailed to a leaning wood frame with a matching pitched roof. It was dark inside, but the smell of food cooking on the makeshift stove was welcoming.

"*Siéntese aquí* (sit here)," the woman said, pointing at the bench.

"*Muchas gracias, señora*," Eileen said and sat down on a rustic bench by a long table against the wall. It was so bright outside and so dark inside that she experienced momentary blindness. All she could do at that moment was savor the appetizing smells of whatever this woman was preparing.

As her eyes adjusted to the play of light and dark, Eileen saw that the sleeping quarters had been given some privacy by an old bed sheet hung over rope strung across the ceiling. There was some movement behind the curtain. Just like that, her paranoia returned. Who was behind there? Was it that spy from the church? She held her breath as the sheet fluttered and three children ran toward her, giggling as they held out a bunch of *Flores de Izote* (yucca blossoms) for her.

"Muchas, muchas gracias!" Eileen said with a big smile. She sniffed the fragrant blossoms and sighed. Movement by the doorway startled her and her fear rose when she saw a military-looking figure blocking the light. The man approached her and held out something in his arms toward her. Her heartbeat rippled when she saw the thing squirm. When she heard the baby's cry she looked up at the man's face, now discernible in the dim light. It was the young guerilla soldier.

"José?" Eileen asked, expressing surprise at how big the baby was now. His cheeks and limbs were chubby and when he mirrored her smile, Eileen's heart melted. "¡*Cómo guapo eres* (How handsome you are)!" The woman who had invited her to dinner was evidently the young man's mother, who was delighted to see José smiling in Eileen's arms. Eileen realized that this was a meal of thanksgiving for saving both of their lives.

The woman ladled big bowls full of the soup and brought them to the table as the young man took back José into his arms. Although Eileen had never eaten it, she knew this woman had prepared them *sopa de pata*, a hearty soup ladled over a section of corn on the cob, cabbage, yucca, sliced plantain and tripe. The cow's feet and tripe used to make it were probably more than this woman could afford, so Eileen knew the importance of this gesture. Until this moment, she'd managed successfully to avoid eating tripe. The sight of its fatty webbed texture made her cringe. She knew she could not refuse it though, so she closed her eyes and took a bite of the gelatinous chunk. It was not as bad as she feared and carried the flavors of the wonderful spices stirred into the soup.

They did not converse as they ate. Instead they cooed at the baby as his father held him with one brawny arm while he sipped soup. When they finished, the older woman brought out bowls of *arroz con leche* (rice pudding) with freshly grated cinnamon on top. The youngest girl, Maria, broke a blossom branch off of Eileen's bouquet. She came over to Eileen and stuck it tightly in her hair, over her right ear, and then kissed Eileen's cheek. It was a tiny gesture, but one that she knew was a true Peace Corps moment. What unbridled joy she felt right then. There was no barrier of language or culture at this moment—just celebration of gratitude and hope.

And just as if on cue, like in the movies, a butterfly similar to the one she saw on the fútbol field fluttered into the home and then slipped out the back window. As Eileen's eyes followed its wings floating away, her senses picked up fluttering shadows in the doorway. There was a loud popping noise. The woman who'd welcomed her for dinner slumped against the wall, shot dead. Her shock was so deep that Eileen tried to scream but couldn't as she watched the woman's splattered blood drip down the wall behind her. She could not move; her heartbeat pounded like timpani in her ears from the fear of the sudden violence.

Everything over the next few minutes felt like it happened in slow motion. There was a scuffle and she saw little José fall from his father's arm onto the table. Coarse hands gripped Eileen's throat as she felt a body press hers from behind and pull her upright. She cried out as the man tied a blindfold tightly around her eyes and yanked her arms behind her, binding them roughly with a rag. The young man cursed their captors and then Eileen heard the sound of something heavy slammed against the side of the house. Someone groaned. The children screamed and little José wailed in response. "¡*Cállanse*! (Shut up!)," a man's voice snarled. Her knees trembled as she heard what sounded like three or four men discussing the fate of the children. Eileen hoped her mind could transport her thoughts into theirs: *Please be quiet, little ones.*

She'd heard legends about the *escuadrones de la muerte*—death squads hired by the government to wipe out any hint of opposition. Until this moment, she thought it was just the paranoia of oppressed campesinos. Now she knew differently. The children were abandoned as the men led her and the guerilla out of the house and down a stony dirt path. Every once in a while, the butt of a rifle poked her back, a reminder that she wasn't marching fast enough. How was she to know where to step next, though?

"¡*Apúranse*! (Hurry)!" a man said. Eileen recognized his voice—it was the National Guardsman who'd given her the mal de ojo.

Urracas fluttered in the trees above making staccato birdcalls, their odd vocalizations made her wonder *are they avian journalists typing up the crimes they're witnessing?* She felt filtered sunlight warm her face and wondered which direction they were heading, in case the opportunity to flee arose. Since the sounds around them were more of nature than village, she figured they were being led somewhere remote. Up ahead she could hear the sound of a rushing stream. *Do they plan to drown us*? With her arms tied, there would be little chance of rescuing herself, she thought.

The terrifying march toward the water reminded her of that night on the dock by the Keuka Lake Outlet, when her distraught mother acted like she was going to drown herself and Molly. Oh how she wished that Clare and Noreen, who'd both had such presence of mind that night, were there now to save her.

As they neared the water she recited some prayers in her mind and asked God to forgive her sins in preparation for death which was surely near. Was this *really* God's will? She stumbled on the slope to the stream and bumped into one of the soldiers. He slapped her face so hard that the sound echoed down the stream bank.

"¡*Vamonos*! (Let's go!)" the leader barked.

"¡*Bastardos*!" the young guerilla cried out defiantly.

She heard the soldiers rush toward where his voice came from and heard him groan as they punched him hard. There was a loud splash and struggling in the water, then the sound of someone being dragged out and tossed near her feet. Eileen felt like she was going to throw up, but tried to calm her gag reflex because she feared she'd be shot for doing so.

"¡*Dime! ¿Dónde están los otros guerrilleros*? (Tell me! Where are the rest of the guerillas?)

"¡*Nunca*!"

A soldier grabbed Eileen suddenly and pushed her toward the stream. She tripped and fell hard, face first into the water. Water rushed into her mouth and as she plunged surprisingly gently to the bottom, an image popped into her mind. In it, she was a four-year-old child, sitting in Grandpa Jimmy's lap as he rocked on the wraparound porch. She could smell the fresh air scent lingering on his shirt that Grandma Mame had just taken off the clothesline. He was singing that Irish folk song about the milkmaid that his grandfather taught him. The melodic tune and rise and fall of his breath as she laid her head on his chest had the effect of a lullaby on her and the last thing she recalled was the sound of cicadas buzzing from the elm tree.

***

She awakened in a fetal position, still bound. A rare cool breeze drifted across her cheek. Was it dusk? She smelled cigarette smoke and heard the soldiers talking about her, referring to her as the American whore. There was a clinking noise, like a small bottle of something, and the next thing she knew, someone approached her. His breath reeked of alcohol (probably that crazy Tíc Táck stuff, she thought).

"*Despiértate*! (Wake up!)," the leader said as he grabbed her by the hair and rolled her over. He laughed loudly as his hands started to rip her blouse. Suddenly one of the other soldiers jumped to his feet and shushed their leader.

"*Cállate*... jaguar."

The leader dropped Eileen as if her touch was burning his hand. He knew the sighting of a jaguar was rare. In this culture the animal symbolized the power of the gods. Not only did the animal's presence make the guardsman fear for his life, it made him feel that it would displease the gods to take another life on this spot.

"*Vamos para al campo*. (Let's go to the field.) ¡*Apurate*!"

Eileen was heartened to hear the groans of the young guerilla; it meant he was still alive. One of the captors pulled her to her feet and they began marching again, their steps slower now. The sound of the stream grew faint and she could tell they were climbing. There seemed to be less vegetation around them and she could smell burning garbage. Before long they were stepping through ankle deep refuse and the smell of the rotting food made her gag.

"¡*Alto*! *Vamos a matarlos aquí* (Stop! Let's kill them here)," the leader yelled.

Their captors released their blindfolds, and Eileen was horrified by what she saw in the flickering firelight. The young man's left eye was swollen closed and there was a gaping wound (that looked like it had been caused by a machete blade) across his cheek. She wondered what she looked like, too. At that moment she was conscious of dried blood at the corner of her mouth and what felt like a broken finger. Her whole body ached like she'd been beaten with a whip and she gave thanks that the jaguar had saved her from being raped.

The leader took out a pistol, cocked it and strode toward them. He pointed it teasingly, eliciting the fear response he wanted: she gasped and the young man threw up. When the leader saw that he bent over with mocking laughter.

"*¿Dondé está tu valor ahora*? (Where's your bravery now?)" His face dropped its look of mirth and donned an expression of evil that terrified Eileen. He raised his pistol next to the young man's head and caressed the trigger. That pause before imminent death was excruciating. The leader snorted, puffed his chest and....

She heard the sound of an approaching motorcycle from behind them and then its engine cut off. "¡*Mira*!" the others exclaimed. The leader glanced to the other side of the bonfire. A towering figure in black with glowing eyes stood with a raised hand clutching a machete.

"*Es...es*...El Justo Juez de la Noche!" one soldier cried out, pointing at the dark specter. The men looked at each other and although she couldn't turn around, Eileen knew by the terror on their faces that whatever was behind her was something to be feared. They stumbled backwards and then spun on their heels and scattered in all directions screaming. She saw the leader paralyzed by the phantom before him. Eileen prayed in her mind that the fear of what he was beholding would not cause him to pull the trigger accidentally. *Please, Lord, spare us*!

Then the specter spoke in a measured tone to the remaining soldier. "*Mátalos, y te voy a perseguir para siempre*. (Kill them, and I will haunt you forever.)"

The leader lowered the pistol, stepped backwards and released it to the ground. He cried out to the others and fled into the darkness. Eileen and the young man remained facing forward, afraid to turn and see whatever was behind them. They glanced wide-eyed at each other as they heard the footsteps approach them through the garbage. She gasped when she felt a tug on the rags binding her arms behind her. Whoever this was loosened them, though, and when she turned to see him do the same to the young guerilla's hands, Eileen saw the person was wearing black sunglasses with blinking lights over a black hood.

The young man fell to the ground and began kissing the boots of the man, who touched his shoulder gently and said, "*Usted es libre.* (You are free.)" The young guerilla looked around and then ran off toward the direction of the stream.

Eileen thought the voice sounded familiar and when the man removed his hood she nearly fainted. *Wait, it couldn't be...,* she thought.

"¡*Dios mio*! Eileen! Is that you?"

Her legs gave out and she dropped to the ground, but her rescuer fell to his knees and propped her up with his strong arms. Eileen felt faint as she looked into his eyes. She couldn't believe it! Her prayers had been answered by a *deus ex machina*—God had delivered her into the arms of Father Dan Coleman.

"My God, what have these savages done to you?"

He told her later that he'd been in the country for a few months helping protect priests and nuns from the death squads. Someone he knew had disappeared recently and he'd been prowling this spot because it had become known as a killing field. Father Dan knew the powerful symbolism of the Just Judge upon a superstitious people. At the same time, he knew he was being watched by the government, and he explained that was why he had yet to visit her at the Rivas's home.

They got on his motorcycle and rode out of the garbage dump toward a guerilla hiding place in the mountains. After a few days, an envoy was sent quietly to retrieve her belongings from Esperanza, and the two fled the country into Honduras where they caught a flight from the airport in Tegucigalpa back to the States.

***

Eileen had much difficulty readjusting to the First World. When she turned on the faucet for a drink of water, she couldn't help but think of Esperanza trudging to the stream to fill buckets—a two-hour task! Americans took too much for granted, they were so spoiled. She was also depressed by the rampant corruption in oppressive governments such as El Salvador's, where few savored privileges earned off the sweat and blood of the masses.

Frances was concerned by Eileen's dashed hopes for changing the world. This was not the same faith-filled daughter she'd sent off on a Peace Corps adventure. Something had changed dramatically and Frances tried to pry the reasons from Eileen. She asked her daughter repeatedly to share details of her Central American experience but Eileen remained close-mouthed. What direction would her daughter's life take now? Was college still an option?

Dan left the priesthood soon after his return from El Salvador. He'd witnessed too much horror and yearned to find inner serenity, yet still do God's work. His increasing desire to marry and have a family proved greater than his professed vows. He petitioned the Holy See to be returned to the lay state, and once it was granted, moved onto a new commune near Ithaca called Commonweal Acres. It was inspired by Dorothy Day's Catholic Worker movement with the purpose of creating an agrarian community that would sustain others as well as its members. Here was where Dan could use the skills he'd developed in El Salvador as well as continue spreading the message of Jesus Christ.

The first task Dan volunteered for was tilling the field where their community garden would be sown. The hours spent laboring as he turned the hard clay fields freed his mind for reflection. He found he couldn't stop thinking about Eileen. Dan composed a seven-page letter to her, expressing his longing to see her and sharing his dreams for the commune. His eloquent prose made Eileen's heart sing at a time when all her hope had vanished. One Saturday morning she bought a one-way Greyhound ticket to Ithaca leaving a note for her mother on the counter. "I'll be OK. This is God's will."

Within months, Frances got a phone call from Dan requesting Eileen's hand in marriage. She was stunned, but his words felt sincere and when Eileen got on the phone and she heard joy once more returned to her daughter's voice,

Frances acquiesced. They were married soon after on a warm October afternoon in front of a foliage-framed waterfall. A priest well-known for civil disobedience during the Vietnam War said the outdoor Mass on a makeshift altar. The couple were surrounded by family—his parents and younger brother (the best man), her mother, grandparents, uncle and four of her five sisters. Terrie was her maid of honor. The gesture forged a special bond between the two sisters.

Clare made a pronouncement to the others as they watched the couple contra dance during the reception back at the commune. "That is the type of husband you meet once in a blue moon."

Chapter 27

Noreen remembered Clare's blue moon comment when she called Eileen to discuss her mother again. It took a few sessions of phone tag because she and Dan had no phone on the commune, and often her sister was out working in their organic fields or downtown feeding the homeless. Noreen thought it interesting that her sister rattled on about her work with the needy of their community, yet she missed warning signs coming from her own mother.

Of course Eileen thought they all needed to keep an eye on Frances, but just like Noreen, she felt that it would be easier for Terrie and Molly to keep a closer eye on their mother because they were both single.

Molly wasn't much help when Noreen called, either. Oh, she loved her mother and was close with her, but it wasn't the same special bond she'd shared with Grandma Mame. Perhaps it was that by the time she was born, Mame was retired from teaching and had more free time to spend with her granddaughter during their visits, teaching her how to cook. Frances was overtired and too concerned about keeping their house and putting food on the table to bother teaching her daughter those skills. Molly was a happy-go-lucky child who, since she barely knew her father, didn't feel his absence either, the way her sisters did.

The sharing of culinary knowledge came to an abrupt end the day Mame died. When they came back home from the funeral in Penn Yan, the first thing Molly wanted to do was make fried cakes in her grandmother's honor. Frances didn't know the recipe, though, and had never deep fried anything on her own before. That loss of tradition was the aspect of her grandmother's death that hurt Molly the most.

Besides cooking, Molly had a flair for language and after high school she studied linguistics at SUNY Binghamton. She won a fellowship to spend a semester abroad studying Italian in Florence. Although she was also fluent in Spanish and French, Italian was her favorite language. She was fascinated by the different dialects present near Binghamton, where a high influx of immigrants came from Italy to work in the shoe factories, seeking owner George F. Johnson's promise of a square deal. She decided to make this the focus of her thesis.

In her field work with local residents though, conversations often turned to food, and Molly found herself asking as many detailed questions about meal preparations as she did dialects. After the interviews she'd jot down in detail each recipe shared and would later try to replicate them in her mother's kitchen. If she liked a recipe, she added it to her collection in a loose-leaf binder. A true scholar, Molly would add details such as special cooking utensils used and provenance of the recipes.

Once out of graduate school in 1984, she tried to find work as a translator in Manhattan (always ambitious, Molly completed her BA degree in three-and-a-half years). The job market was tight, though. Clare put her up for a month, but did not relish the effect her sister's stay had on her private life—making Matthew scarce—and started dropping hints that maybe it was time to look for work back upstate. That's when she heard about the opening for a Spanish language teacher next fall at the high school in Penn Yan. Her Uncle Pat was still living with Grandfather Jimmy in the house with the wraparound porch. There was plenty of room in the old house if she wanted to stay there.

It was an arrangement that suited all: Molly cooked for them; Uncle Pat was free to take care of his aging father who was eighty-two now. It lifted Grandpa Jimmy's spirits to spend time with his granddaughter every day, too. Once she moved in, it was obvious that a woman's touch had been absent from the house for several years. Not wanting to step on either her uncle or grandfather's toes, Molly asked if she could rearrange the kitchen to her liking. Uncle Pat raised his hands as if backing off and grinned. "It's all yours, Molly."

While rearranging Mame's cookbooks one day, a lard-stained index card fell onto the linoleum floor. When Molly picked it up she gasped—it was the fried cake recipe Great-Grandma Virginia gave Grandma Mame, written in her own hand. She held it to her heart and waltzed around the kitchen with joy. Molly took that as a sign that Grandma Mame was watching over her. She fried a batch that weekend and surprised Grandpa Jimmy on the front porch.

"This is...."

"The best taste on earth," Molly said, finishing his sentence. He touched her hand as tears formed in his eyes. Through a little bit of culinary magic, Molly conjured up fond memories of his wife. *Mame taught Molly well*, he thought.

At work Molly soon became friends with Alice Reasoner, the French teacher. They ate lunch together and were always trading recipes. Alice's family was in the hospitality business and ran a beautiful (and pricey) inn on Bluff Point overlooking Keuka Lake. She would often tell Molly about her parents' escapades with tourists and the occasional celebrity or two that would stay at their inn.

"You should come work for us during the summer vacation," Alice said.

Molly was delighted by the invitation. "I'd love to! I can always use extra cash. Would I be able to work in the kitchen?"

Alice raised an eyebrow then smiled. "Perhaps. I'll talk with my parents and see what's available."

By the end of the school year in 1985 a summer job was lined up for Molly at The Wild Rose Inn. It wasn't what she was hoping for, though. While Alice helped her parents with bookkeeping, Molly changed linens with the maid staff. She didn't object to the work though because the pay wasn't bad. At least she was able to chat with Chef Leo on occasion and discuss how he planned daily menus for three meals plus high tea. He'd planted a rambling herb garden outside the kitchen's back door and Molly took breaks there. She'd walk the flagstone path memorizing each labeled herb in the tidy beds—Dalmatian sage, Italian flat-leaf parsley, Greek oregano, sweet basil, tarragon, garlic chives, rosemary, dill, lemon balm, fennel, cilantro, lemon thyme and various mints. Molly always sat on the Lutyens-style bench under the cherry tree and read as she ate an apple or a sandwich creation Leo wanted her to test. She'd often have trouble focusing on the foreign language novels that she hoped to finish by summer's end. Breezes stirring scents off the herbs provoked culinary ideas of her own and she'd stare at swallowtail butterflies dancing around shrub roses while her mind figured details of the recipes. This sheltered patio became her sensory paradise.

Molly's thoughts also drifted to her sisters and mother. She wondered what they were doing now. Did her mother feel lonely with just Terrie in that big house or was she glad that five of her six daughters had left town? What was it like to lead an exciting life in Manhattan like Clare? She figured that whatever Maggie was doing at the moment, it would upset her mother. Sometimes she wished her spirit was as free as Maggie's. When she thought of Noreen's perfect life, it made her sad. Would she ever marry a soul mate of her own? Her sadness turned to worry when she wondered what Terrie and Eileen were up to. Terrie's world was stuck like a tire in back-roads mud. How could she not have *any* of the drive her sisters had? Would she ever leave home? Her passive existence seemed so foreign to energized Molly. Eileen was scary thin, beginning to look like she lived in the Third World, not America. Molly feared she'd developed malnutrition of her own while putting the starving people of the world first.

Molly often wondered what was ahead in her own life. She enjoyed teaching, but already felt restless about it as a career. Maybe it was because her grandfather and uncle both seemed to be aging rapidly and she knew that her time living in the house was limited. There was no way that she could afford to live there on her own. An old house like that would require constant upkeep, as she already knew.

Alice invited her to a meditation class in Hammondsport and Molly tried practicing the techniques of mindfulness and gratitude she'd been taught. Just when she'd find a sense of calm and contentment with herself, she'd see a happy couple staying at the inn on their honeymoon and feel the empty pangs of her relationship-less life.

The problem was she rarely met anyone she'd consider going out with. It wasn't that she was judgmental or had unreasonable standards; it was that she truly knew with whom she felt comfortable and just couldn't fake it, like some women obviously did. Oh how she ached for fascinating conversation that never once drifted into discussion of the current weather. She knew plenty of farmers' sons here, some Finger Lakes old-money families and randy college boys back in Binghamton. Whom she didn't know were any guys who shared her adventurous culinary tastes. She was a magnet for the meat-and-potatoes type! Forget meeting anyone who was into the bossa nova music of Antonio Carlos Jobim and Vinicius de Moraes, or her love of taking spontaneous back-roads trips.

Molly made the mistake of mentioning her yearning for marriage to Alice, who took it upon herself to become her *yenta*. It didn't take long for her to go through the list of available men around town who'd possibly be a match with Molly's requirements. On one occasion Alice and her boyfriend Gunter invited Molly to a double date on a Friday night at the West Side restaurant, Steaks on the Lake. (The name cracked up Molly, who envisioned seared sirloins adrift on Keuka's waters.)

"This guy is *perfect* for you," Alice said. "Your senses of humor are soooo alike!" Molly was hesitant, but relented to Alice's constant badgering about how she had to "be the change" in her life. "His name is Sumner," Alice said, "and his family made their money in Finger Lakes real estate, especially the priciest parcels of available land on Skaneateles and Canandaigua lakes." Her description of him sounded wonderful. He called himself a gourmand, a world traveler (including Brazil, she noted) and was five years older yet never married.

"This one's ripe for the kill," Alice teased.

Molly tried to keep her romantic imagination in check, but by the morning of the date, she'd already envisioned what her wedding dress would look like, where they'd travel on their month-long honeymoon and what they'd name their three children (two boys and a girl). She knew she had to make an extra effort for this date so she scheduled a French tip manicure and hair appointment. What to wear, what to wear? She wanted to make an impact and decided she needed something with a hint of sexiness and a lot of elegance. It had been a while since she wore high heels, but she felt they completed the ensemble perfectly. After Grandma Mame died, Frances gave Molly some of her rhinestone brooches. She decided to wear one shaped like a little bow, just to give a hint of sparkle to her carnelian red dress. By the time she was ready to be picked up that Friday night, a purse to match the heels was added.

Jimmy watched her pace in the foyer from his seat at the dining room table where he read the sports page.

"You look beautiful tonight, Mame," he said with a face of sheer adoration.

"You mean Molly, Grandpa." She'd noticed his mind wasn't as sharp as it used to be.

"Are we going dancing tonight, dear? Oh, I love a good foxtrot." Jimmy held his arms out as if he were leading a dance partner around a ballroom. *Uh-oh, hope he doesn't frighten this guy away talking like that,* Molly thought.

"Nope. We're having steaks on the water, at least what the restaurant seems to imply. Oh, they're here already. Uncle Pat, would you please open the door. I don't want to appear too eager."

Uncle Pat set down the *Life* magazine he was reading and walked toward his niece, adjusting her rhinestone pin. "You look stunning, Molly. I hope you knock this young man dead!" She scurried into the den to wait so she could make a grand entrance. Uncle Pat answered the front door and welcomed Alice and Gunter inside, shaking their hands. Then he paused and looked at her date who was waiting out on the porch.

"Sumner, is that you?"

Sumner ran his fingers through his hair and squinted. "Well this is awkward," he whispered. "You're related to my date?" He made air quotes when he referred to Molly.

Uncle Pat grimaced. He'd known Sumner for a few years. They had mutual friends and met at a housewarming party in Naples, a pretty town nestled in the hills outside Canandaigua Lake. There'd be no future for Molly with this guy. He was a notorious cad.

"Molly, your friends are here."

She walked out of the den wearing the inner sophistication of Audrey Hepburn. Uncle Pat had never seen his niece radiate such beauty. He sighed as she made first eye contact with her date, and wondered what she was thinking.

The first thing Molly noted was that this guy was wearing a pink angora Ralph Lauren Polo sweater. She ignored the way their fashions mis-jibed, chalking it up to the fact that her date was a preppy. As they left the house after a painful introduction to Grandpa Jimmy (in which he insisted that they take him dancing in Hammondsport), Sumner was the first to walk out the door, leaving Molly to close it behind them.

Throughout the rest of the evening, Molly feigned a smile as she listened to him prattle on about this old money family or that interior designer who'd been featured in the latest *Architectural Digest*. He knew Gary's mother—small world! Sumner was dropping so many names of "important people" that Molly imagined she was reading scrolling film credits. Yawn.

His palate was surprisingly conservative for a supposed gourmand, and while Molly explored nouvelle cuisine options on the menu, Sumner ordered a classic T-bone with mashed potatoes, gravy and several double single malts. Molly tried to have an open mind and not be judgmental, but listening to this guy speak she wondered how her friend could think they'd ever get along. Any chance he got he slammed his mother, referring to her by the diminutive "Corkie."

"And then Corkie ordered the oysters...in a month that *didn't* end in -er. *Quelle horreur*!" His smug laugh annoyed her. And as he kept running his fingers through his gray-blond longish locks, she fixated on the color of his sweater. *So what if it's Ralph Lauren? The men I'm attracted to don't wear pink*, she thought. She imagined introducing Sumner to her buddies from Wednesday night trivia at the tavern. They'd never stop laughing over that hideous sweater with the pompous polo player, and they'd especially guffaw at Sumner's name. Ugh, she couldn't wait for this date to end.

It wasn't lost on her that her date, the wealthiest man at the table, made no effort to reach for the check when the waitress brought it to the table. The hell with this, she thought, and grabbed her purse to pay for her own meal. Gunter shook his head, and then whispered to Alice as she discreetly slipped him some twenty-dollar bills under the table.

Again, when they went to leave, Sumner did not try to assist with her chair and instead walked briskly away from them. When he asked where they were all going next, Molly couldn't get "Home!" out of her mouth fast enough.

Alice apologized the next day while they worked at the inn. It was an awkward conversation.

"I've never seen that side of him," she said.

You mustn't have looked at him hard enough, Molly thought. What made things worse that day was that they were prepping the inn for a wedding. It was nauseatingly perfect with a gorgeous couple besotted endearingly with each other, an exquisite wedding gown, an azure cloudless sky and the fragrance of roses everywhere. After the ceremony, Molly was part of the waitstaff for the reception. She felt like she'd been scratched by a room full of feral cats and then shoved into a salt mine. To be reminded so vividly of what she didn't have was agony.

When she got home in the late afternoon, Uncle Pat greeted her with a frightened expression.

"I don't want to alarm you, but Grandpa is missing."

"*Missing*? What happened?"

"He was napping, so I drove into town to pick up the New York papers and a cup of coffee. When I returned, he was gone."

"Did you ask the neighbors if they'd seen him?" She let her purse drop to the floor as she slid into a dining room chair, the weight of her uncle's words crowding her thoughts.

"Yes," Uncle Pat said as he paced the room. "Everyone's been alerted. The neighbors. Cousins. Police."

"OK, let's try to figure out where he'd want to walk. You checked the cellar and the backyard and garage?" Pat nodded. "Did he have plans with any of his friends to meet down at the Elks Club or the country club?"

"Nope. Called them all. No one's heard a thing."

"What time did you leave the house?"

"You had already gone to work, so it had to be after noon. It was probably closer to one. I was home within an hour."

"Any chance he might have walked to the McGraths' cottage?"

"Geez, you know he could have. That's quite a hike, especially on a warm day. Let's get in the car and drive out there."

Uncle Pat followed the route through the village Jimmy would have likely taken if he was walking to the East Side cottage. There were plenty of "summer people" speeding up Route 54, which made Molly nervous. What if an inebriated winery tourist hit her grandfather as he meandered up the shoulder? There was still no sign of him, and when Uncle Pat turned onto the quiet lake road, they asked everyone they encountered if he'd been seen.

The cottage was locked, and Molly ran down to the front porch facing the lake, but no one was there. She even ran to the end of the dock and scanned the clear lake bottom in case he fell in. Heat from the reflection of the setting sun was intense. She shaded her eyes as she panned the horizon around them. Grandpa Jimmy was nowhere in sight.

Uncle Pat crossed the shale stone beach to join her on the dock.

"I was afraid to check the water, you know, with his history of it, but couldn't help myself," Molly said. "Thank God, he's not here."

"Even with his growing dementia, I think he recalls how much he fears the lake," Uncle Pat said. "Where could he be?" They stood silently as they ran all possible scenarios through their minds. Molly remembered how he'd thought she was her grandmother last night. It made her so sad to think he'd never dance with her again.

"You don't suppose he's up at the cemetery by Grandma's grave?" she asked.

Uncle Pat's eyes widened. "Yes! I bet you're right. He was talking about visiting Mother this morning and I paid no attention to what he was saying. That's it!"

They didn't find him by Mame's grave, although there was a loose bouquet of flowers dropped by it, pulled obviously from a flower urn nearby.

"Looks like he's been here," Uncle Pat said.

Plum shadows of creeping dusk inched across the sloping lawn. Uncle Pat expressed concern that they needed to find Grandpa Jimmy soon before the cemetery became shrouded in darkness, and suggested they split up. Uncle Pat climbed the hill as Molly wended her way through the lower section. The property was surrounded by woods and a vineyard. Both of them feared having to extend their search in those directions.

Molly was halfway to the bottom when she noticed a big limb dangling off an old beech tree to the right. Lightning from the recent severe thunderstorm must have hit it. Something about the tree drew her near and when she reached it, she noticed in its shadow was a lone grave for an infant whose grass-covered tombstone read "Our beloved infant son, Michael." How sad, she thought as she bent down to pull away the grass so the stone would be more visible. It was from her squatting vantage point that she noticed someone lying in the grass below.

"I FOUND HIM!" she yelled up the hill and as soon as she heard her uncle shout back, she sprinted toward the graves down the slope. Her steps froze when she got a better look and she thought, *Is he dead*?

"Oh no, oh please God, no!" she whimpered.

Uncle Pat wheezed from exertion when he reached her, still a bit away from Jimmy's body.

"Oh, Lord. Is he...?"

"Can't tell. I'm too afraid to check."

Uncle Pat put his arm around his niece's shoulder as they approached. They saw blood on Grandpa Jimmy's forehead; he must have hit a gravestone when he fell. Molly covered her gasp with her hand. It upset her terribly to see his lifeless body, arms lying by his sides, palms facing up.

"What should we do?" Molly asked.

"Better check if he's still breathing." Uncle Pat knelt down next to his father, and the sight was too much for Molly. She started crying. He touched his father's neck but recoiled in shock as his father mumbled into the grass.

"Where am I?"

"Grandpa! Are you OK?" Molly dropped to her knees and took his hand.

"Mame? What are you doing here? We better get back before the kids get home from school." They grimaced at his question.

"I don't think we should try to move him, Molly. Let me run over to the produce stand and see if they can call an ambulance. I'll be right back, Dad. Don't try to move, OK?"

Molly stroked her grandfather's hair as he lay on his stomach.

"That's a beautiful dress you're wearing, dear. Are we going dancing?" She blinked away tears. "Anything you want, Jimmy," she said, pretending she was Grandma Mame.

"I see Skip and Ralphie are over there. Don't dance with them if they ask, Mame. They'll try to get you to drink some of that bootleg gin of theirs."

Molly laughed. "Thanks for the warning, dear." She happened to glance at the names on the tombstones and was chilled—they *were* the graves of the young men who drowned that night on the lake back in 1920.

Jimmy's face went sad suddenly and he began to cry. Molly feared that he was in pain, or maybe he realized that his wife was dead.

"I'm sorry, you two. I never kept my promise." His body heaved up and down as he took a deep breath.

"What promise was that?"

"I never swam across the lake in your honor when I turned thirty. It's always bothered me. But boys, you gotta understand, the water by the Bluff is so deep and...." His tears fell faster now. Molly leaned in and wiped them away with her hands.

"Dear," she whispered, "after we get home and get you better, I'll take you out in the boat and the two of us will dive in and swim across the lake in their honor."

Jimmy squeezed his granddaughter's hand, took another deep sigh and said "Thank you, my love."

***

The most difficult decision Pat ever made was putting his father in a nursing home. After that escapade though, and the fall that gave Jimmy both a broken hip and concussion, he knew it was not safe for him to stay at home anymore. Jimmy did not seem to be aware that he was living in a new place, partially because when he became so agitated that he couldn't go out on the porch, Molly and Uncle Pat brought his rocking chair to his new home. When he crossed the room from his bed to that chair, in his mind he *was* sitting on the wraparound porch.

"We'll have to tell your brother Mike that the old homestead needs a new roof," he'd say to Molly, still playing the role of Grandma Mame.

"I'll give him a call later," she said, knowing that Mike and Mame were already reunited with their parents in heaven.

A few months later on a frosty October morning, while dreaming he was with Mame at that jitney dance back in '35, Jimmy's soul slipped from this world.

Chapter 28

By 1998, Molly had been living with Uncle Pat for fourteen years. It felt as though she owned the house; she'd made many of the maintenance, repair, and decorating decisions. The mortgage had been long taken care of, though, and all Uncle Pat had to worry about the house he inherited was paying its bills. Molly even paid a good deal of those. The notion that she had invested so much into something yet didn't own it wasn't lost on her. It was another reminder of how unsettled her life still felt compared to her sisters. Each one, except maybe Maggie (whom they had not heard from after she missed Grandpa Jimmy's funeral also), was doing what they wanted to do with their lives. Clare was named editor of the year by *The Trade*, a publishing industry magazine. Both Noreen and Gary had won several teaching awards; their twin sons Phillip and Gerard were star soccer players at Colgate University. Eileen and Dan were committed wholly to the Ithaca peace workers movement and busy raising their son Francis and four daughters, Esperanza, Thérèse, Kateri and Dorothy. Terrie had been preoccupied with tending to her neighbor Elvin's medical needs. She was his primary caregiver after he had a stroke two years ago at the age of 84. When he died in the spring, he willed Terrie his riverside property and new dog, Shane. Elvin also left her a modest sum of money that she used to convert his house into a pet shelter.

Several years passed with little word from Maggie. She'd told Molly on her rare visits back East that she'd never felt like she was truly a family member. Of course Molly laughed at the suggestion. Perhaps she had that feeling because she'd spent so many years apart from her sisters. (It didn't help that she'd missed Eileen's wedding.) When Molly thought about it though, Maggie *was* different on many levels. She was overtly sexual, which made Molly uncomfortable in their discussions about men. Her language was coarse, she drank heavily and she was the only sister who was a smoker. They assumed that Maggie used drugs regularly and was probably high when they spoke with her on the phone.

The reality was that Maggie *wished* her life was as exotic as her sisters imagined. She'd been working at least two jobs most of her life. Even though she'd be fifty soon, she still wrote for the alternative newspaper that Ronnie founded, *The Rap Session*. The offices had relocated from The Haight to The Tenderloin. It was hardly an alternative newspaper anymore; the paper was actually producing some good breaking news stories and investigative pieces.

Up to this point in her life she'd eluded the bonds of matrimony, though she'd had five live-in boyfriends over the years. The last one, Carlos—a third generation classical guitar maker from Paracho, Mexico, moved out in January. Great, she thought, now she'd probably have to face turning fifty alone.

That milestone weighed on Maggie's psyche. She'd spent so much of her life feeling adrift from her family and the rest of the mainstream. She didn't have a car or a house of her own, and her rent was crazy high. When would this thing called adulthood show up? When would she no longer feel like a perpetual college student? She'd love to put down some real roots like Noreen had. That said, she did not envy her older sister at all. Maggie thought Gary was a churlish bully.

She earned a meager income from the paper and the Vietnamese strip club where she bartended. It was becoming obvious that she had to do something else; she had little savings to buffer the effect of a new rent increase.

Maggie dabbled in creative writing over the years and had a binder full of short stories set in San Francisco. She even got up the courage years ago to show them to a professor from the New College of California at a party in the Mission District. They left the party and discussed her work for a few hours over some bottles of Tecate at a nearby taquería. The conversation continued in his bedroom up the street and she ended up living with him for a few months before she realized he didn't give a damn about anything she'd written. *Sigh*, she thought, *chalk that up to another lesson in sexual stupidity.*

Last year she began jotting notes for a novel brewing in her imagination. Maggie had never attempted to write anything that long, yet ideas for the plot kept begging for her attention. She knew if she did not jot them down, they'd be lost forever. Her story was about women of different ages and how they viewed their sexuality depending on the era in which they were raised. As she researched decades of societal trends for the story line, Maggie found it fascinating that promiscuity trended in alternating generations.

With her fiftieth birthday two years away, Maggie set herself a goal: get this novel written and published before she turned that milestone. She carved out sacred hours in her day designated as her writing time. Turns out she did her best work right after she rose from sleep, assisted by a tall mug of coffee and a few cigarettes. It was tough not having the extra income that a third job would have provided, but through the bar she got banquet waitressing gigs a couple of times a month. The money was always under the table and helped immensely with her rent.

The main characters in the novel were a mother and daughter who argued over the issue of her sexual exploits. She wrote the mother as a frigid and straight-laced character, while the daughter explored unabashedly the Sixties era of free love. What added tension to the story was the intrusion into their arguments by the young woman's outspoken grandmother, who'd written her own racy chapters during the Roaring Twenties. Of course the novel wasn't intentionally biographical in Maggie's mind, but in a twist of plot, readers learned that the mother had to get married and was considering an abortion. It was never revealed whether it was the truth, but characters in the novel insinuated that the daughter was the product of brief fling between the mother and her first love.

Maggie completed the novel on her mother's birthday in September. The irony was not lost on her. Had things been different in their relationship, she would have called her mother at that moment (it would have been about five a.m. back East). Somehow she knew her mother would never approve of *this* story, though.

Ronnie had a friend who ran a small press that focused women's issues and suggested that Maggie contact her. He gave her the editor's phone number and they met for lunch so Maggie could make her "elevator pitch." The editor liked the plot, especially knowing how controversial the novel would be. She gladly took a copy of the manuscript that Maggie brought in a manila envelope just in case. Maggie was so excited when she returned to work she could barely focus on the news story on immigration trends that had to be completed by five o'clock.

She'd hoped to hear something within a week, then a month and then by the end of the year. Was this normal? Of course she could have asked Clare about this, or even sent her the manuscript first. No, that wouldn't work for her. If she was going to make it in this business, she didn't want it to be through nepotism. So what if her sister was a senior editor at one of the Big Six publishers?

Her emotions soared when she completed the novel; by the end of the following March she was utterly depressed. Maggie started taking liquid lunches at the bar around the corner from the newspaper. Ronnie noted the smell of beer on her breath but ignored it. She was his best investigative reporter. Her knowledge of the city was invaluable to the paper. He'd have to live with her drinking indiscretions.

"Hey, McNamara, the phone's for you," he called out when she returned from her pub lunch one afternoon.

"Take a message," she said, tossing her coat on the chair by her desk. She was the only employee who could get away with saying that to the boss. Or so she thought. As she stashed her purse in the desk drawer, she sensed a shadow over her and looked up to see Ronnie with arms folded, looking un-amused.

"Pick up the damn phone, Maggie. You'll want to take this call. Trust me."

Maggie shrugged as he walked back into his office and then she picked up the receiver. "McNamara here. Whaddya want?" Within seconds she felt the air rush out of her chest and a hot flash bloom across her face.

"You what? In June? Are you *kidding* me?"

Sacred Feminine Press released a paperback version of Maggie's book, *Sex War Three*, on the twenty-sixth of June 1999. Although Maggie had never heard of the press before Ronnie introduced her to the editor, it was quite well connected to feminist communities across the country. The editor, Amy McGill, did a thorough job of pre-publication press releases and sent a review copy to a friend—a college roommate from Brown—who also happened to review books for the *Los Angeles Times*. The critic praised the debut novel in a review that ran the Sunday after the publication date. Word began to filter out slowly about the book. Unfortunately it was released close to the Fourth of July holiday; many readers missed the review when it was published.

In July, Ronnie joked to Maggie that she needed an agent. By early August, he was asking all of his friends for recommendations for her. The agent Maggie eventually selected booked her on a morning news program in San Francisco. Their network affiliate loved it and arranged an interview with her on their morning news program.

Clare never watched that morning TV show *Sunrise America*, but for some random reason she turned on the broadcast one day as she sipped a mug of coffee in her kitchen. The show was heading for a commercial break when the TV cameras panned to Maggie sitting in an L.A. studio.

"When we come back, author Maggie McNamara discusses her insightful new novel that discusses how generations of women view sex." The coffee mug slipped out of Clare's hands and shattered on the floor. Instead of running for paper towels, she ran for the phone.

"Noreen? Sorry to call so early, but you must turn on *Sunrise America* right now. I have to call the others." Clare speed dialed her way through her sisters' phone numbers. When the show returned from the commercial break, there was Maggie sitting with a reporter, dressed in funky San Francisco clothes with newly highlighted and feathered hair.

"Damn she looks good," Clare said as she used a paper towel under her slipper to mop up the spilled coffee. Terrie smiled gleefully as she watched on her fur-covered couch with several cats milling about. Noreen watched from the TV in the basement so she could focus on the interview. She was afraid that Gary might interrupt and make snide comments about Maggie. Eileen didn't own a television set, so she went next door to her neighbor's house. Molly had just gotten out of the shower when Clare called and she sat wrapped in towels on the recliner, hair dripping onto the leather seat. (Uncle Pat was at the hospital getting blood work done that morning and missed Maggie's network television debut.)

Sunrise America's anchor Jill Kilmer conducted the interview. "Critics are praising your novel, Maggie, and I have to add that though I enjoyed it, the story is sometimes a bit rough to read. The family's anger is so palpable. Is this novel autobiographical?"

Maggie looked away as she shifted in her seat. "This is *strictly* fiction. That said, however, I know some women who have had to make tough decisions like these characters have."

"Do you mean some women such as your own mother? Did she ever consider an abortion?" Jill asked as the camera zoomed in on Maggie's darting eyes."

"Of course not—nothing could be further from the truth," Maggie said with a nervousness that made her interviewer wonder if she was being honest.

Four of the sisters watching across New York State, uttered two words at exactly the same moment: "*Oh shit*!"

Clare called Noreen first, while Eileen called Molly. Terrie called their mother.

"Mom, did you see Maggie on *Sunrise America* just now?"

"Maggie was on TV? Just now? What was she doing?"

"She's written a novel and it's about sex. And guess what? You were the inspiration for the mother in the book. Isn't that cool?"

"She *WHAT*?"

Frances nearly fainted. *Oh, what has that daughter of Joe's done now?* After their estrangement, she'd assigned Maggie the status of being Joe's daughter despite the fact that she raised her from birth. *Good heavens, what if the monsignor hears about this? Could I be fired if my daughter has written a filthy novel?* Frances felt sick to her stomach, and then came the first of a daylong series of phone calls from her friends asking if she saw the interview. By dinnertime she was completely exhausted and went to bed forgetting to eat. She couldn't sleep, though, she was so agitated.

Meanwhile, the sisters were debating whether they should call their mother to discuss it that night. They agreed that Clare should call Terrie to see how their mother was, and then depending on what she said, Clare would call Frances and give her the news.

"Hi, Terrie. What did you think of seeing Maggie on TV today? Cool, huh?"

"Oh yeah, Clare. I'm so proud of her. I called Mom right away but she missed her. Too bad."

"You *what*?"

"I called her. Right after the show."

Oh dear God I'm too late, Clare thought. "What did she say? How did she respond to the news? What did you tell her about the book?"

"I told her that the mother in the book is based on her. She sounded shocked. I hope this means we'll get to see Maggie again now that she's famous."

Probably not until hell freezes over, Clare thought. Ugh, they'd have to get a copy of this book right away to see if they can run interference with their mother. At that moment, Clare was furious with Maggie. All the pent-up anger erupted in a tirade against Maggie that blistered Noreen's ears during their subsequent phone conversation.

"First of all, why didn't she approach *me* about getting published? I have so many connections. Of course I would have helped her. Second, how could she be so insensitive to write a novel about sex and hinting that it involves Mom having an abortion? Oh. My. *God*!"

"I want to be happy for my sister, yet I'm ashamed by what she's done," Noreen said. "The news must have really upset Mom."

"I'll call Mom tomorrow from work. Let her have a good night's sleep. Wonder if her friends found out?"

***

Maggie's agent arranged a book tour starting in September on the East Coast and working back across the country to San Francisco. The New York City dates were near her mother's birthday, so Maggie arranged some time to be added in so that she could surprise her mother. Maybe now that she was on the road to literary success, Maggie could heal the tenuous relationship with her mother and she'd finally be proud of her. Frances was turning seventy-two on September eighth. Who knew how much longer she'd be with them?

It was a good thing Maggie didn't know how angry her mother was about the book. She'd ordered it from a chain bookstore out of town and drove there to pay for it with cash, too ashamed to use a credit card with her identification. When Frances sat down to read it, she immediately linked the characters to herself, her mother and Maggie. After all, like the main character in the book, her daughter had aborted her only child. When she read the passages about the grandmother's retelling of her promiscuity in the Twenties, Frances was furious. How could a daughter of hers write such filth? Oh, but she remembered, this daughter shared no blood with her. She was all Joe's, and it figured that no-good carouser and his mistress would have a daughter obsessed with sex.

When Frances read the mother in the story got pregnant after an affair with her first love, she was livid. Had Maggie heard the persistent rumors that her father was really Tim Lennon? Did she know the truth about Frances's only son Michael who died in childbirth, whom she never got to mourn, and that he was "replaced" by her? Did she twist that reality somehow into thinking that Frances aborted her son?

The story was so upsetting. Though her daughter was a continent away, she felt like Maggie was kicking the womb that never carried her. What if everyone who read the book assumed Maggie wrote a story based on reality? She was so ashamed when she went to Mass, wondering if parishioners or the priest were imagining her private sins. Any time the monsignor stopped by the office on business, she held her breath until he left, wondering if he'd ask her point blank if there was anything she needed to confess.

Maggie's sisters were stunned by the book. Its frank sexuality and graphic descriptions of the abortion clinic made them wince. What truly made them uncomfortable was wondering if Maggie pictured the characters as being herself, their mother and grandmother. Noreen went so far as to deny she was Maggie's sister once when she was in a bookstore in Batavia. Terrie hated any mention of abortion (or deliberate killing of any living being) so she never finished the book.

Clare was more ticked that her sister wrote a bestseller and she had no part of it. One day she had to take a subway uptown, and the lone seat open on the crowded car was covered with dust. She grabbed a discarded newspaper to brush it clean, and when she sat down, she realized the headline on the book review page facing her was about Maggie's novel. It was outpacing sales of the latest Thom McIlwaine book. Oh how that irritated her.

It was different with Eileen and Dan. They discussed the book analytically at great length with members of their peace activist community. Dan brought Eileen around to the mindset that Maggie succeeded in portraying women who've had abortions as normal people who've struggled with difficult choices, and she wrote it without demonizing them. After all, had not their greatest inspiration Dorothy Day gone through the same life trial? Molly found the book riveting, though a bit graphic for her taste. She actually was quite proud of her sister, and when she saw the book on the *New York Times* Bestseller List, she called her. There was no answer, of course, because Maggie was on tour. She left a message: “Congratulations, Sis! I’ll be first in line to get my autographed copy.”

Frances didn’t have to volunteer at the Right to Life office on her birthday, but somehow she thought doing work for others on that day might atone for her daughter’s sins. Her usual task was filing and assembling information packets on alternatives to abortion, and how you could get assistance if you needed to raise a child alone or give it up for adoption. Although the office was on a main street, it was typically quiet. The staff knew it was her birthday and they were going to surprise her with a sheet cake. They’d left Frances alone to watch the phones as they went to pick it up from a bakery a few blocks away.

Minutes after her coworkers left, the phone rang. It was a young man quite agitated that his girlfriend was planning to have an abortion. He said what made her decide to go through with it was a book called *Sex War Three*. As soon as he mentioned the title of the book, Frances felt a blinding headache. Would the evil unleashed by Maggie’s book never cease? *Oh dear Lord*, she thought, *what can I do to stop this*?

“Has your girlfriend made an appointment yet?” She asked, steadying herself with one arm on the front desk.

“Yes. Tomorrow morning.” His words gave Frances some hope.

“Oh, son, then it’s not too late. We have plenty of literature here that might help persuade her to save that baby’s life. Come down to our office and I’ll prepare a whole package for you.”

Frances got a plastic bag from the cupboard and filled it with persuasive materials she thought would help this young man's girlfriend. And then she remembered the Miraculous Medal around her neck that she received as a little girl from her mother. Her daughters weren't the medal-wearing types. She slipped the medal and its chain off of her neck and stuck it in the bag saying a quiet prayer that it would protect the life of that unborn child.

As she waited for the young man to arrive, she smiled, remembering talking with her father about Jesus's mother, the Blessed Virgin Mary. He used to tell her that when the sky was bright blue it was because Mary was using her cloak to protect the Earth from harm. And here it was, a beautiful sunny September day with not a cloud tainting the turquoise sky.

The front door opened and a young man in his twenties walked in. He glanced all around the office and noted that Frances was alone so he approached her.

"Are you the young man that called?" He nodded and Frances smiled at him. "You're courageous for coming here. God thanks you for what you're doing. Here are some pamphlets for your girlfriend and a Miraculous Medal for her to wear."

The young man took the bag. "Thank you." Sweat glistened on his brow.

"I have one more question, ma'am. What's your name?"

She assumed that he wanted it to write a thank-you note later and smiled.

"I'm Frances McNamara. Anything else I can do?"

The young man nodded and he looked outside the front door and all around the office again. Frances wondered if his odd expression meant he was high. Then the horrible thought occurred to her that he was going to rob her. *Oh Blessed Mother protect me*, she thought, as she tried to figure out what was the best way to protect herself if he did try to rob her. Her hand reached instinctively to touch the medal around her neck, but she realized she'd given it to him. She felt vulnerable and her heart pounded in her ears.

"So then, are you that author Maggie McNamara's mother? You know, the lady that wrote the book my girlfriend read? I heard she was local."

Frances's vision blurred suddenly, and before she could open her mouth to answer him, she collapsed on the floor. The man was spooked, he'd had brushes with the law in his past, and dropped the bag on the floor. Her coworkers arrived just as he was racing out the front door, and when they saw Frances, called 911.

***

Earlier that morning, Maggie had interviews at a radio station and a sister alternative newspaper in Brooklyn. Her next stop was Buffalo, so she caught a Greyhound at Port Authority and headed to Binghamton for a surprise overnight stay. She was hoping her mother would see her, yet she didn't want to spoil her birthday by upsetting her. It was worth taking a chance.

She noticed a florist down the street from the bus station, so Maggie stopped there to buy a birthday bouquet and then took a taxi to her mother's house. When she saw all of the cars out front, she figured her sisters and friends surprised her with a party. *Great timing*, she thought.

Maggie wondered if it would be best to walk right in or ring the doorbell. After all, her mother was 72 and it might startle her if she just waltzed through the door after all these years. She could see people milling about inside as she rang the bell. Maggie was delighted when Eileen answered.

"Oh! Maggie! You're here. Thank God! We didn't know how to reach you."

She thought that was a bit of a dramatic welcome to their mother's apparent birthday party.

"Well I was passing through and I remembered it was Mom's birthday, and...."

"Oh my God! I'd forgotten it was her birthday!" Eileen gasped and covered her mouth.

"This isn't a party for her? What are all these people doing...?" Maggie's mind was trying to process what was occurring before her. *Why was Eileen's face so serious? Why is she calling Clare out on the porch? Why are they acting like bouncers, keeping me from Mom's party? Is she still that angry at me?* Just as she was about to hurl a barb at her sisters, Eileen whispered to Clare.

"Maggie doesn't know yet."

"What don't I know?"

Clare took Maggie's hand while she told her that their mother had a sudden, massive stroke and died earlier that day. When the office workers saw the young man run away, they suspected foul play. He was caught by the police although after questioning, they realized that he was just terrified when she collapsed in front of him. He feared that people would think he killed her. Which of course, they did.

"No! No! This can't be possible!" Maggie shrieked as her sisters hugged her tightly, sobbing together on the porch. Clare fetched Irish whiskey for her sister whose hands trembled as she took the glass. The other sisters had followed Clare back onto the porch and they waited in silence as she took a few sips to calm down.

It was Terrie who first noticed. "Hey, five of us are wearing our Keuka Lake necklaces today." The sisters looked down and fingered the silver pendants around their necks. "What a coincidence. Sisters of the Lake, right, you guys?" They nodded wistfully as Maggie placed her hand at the base of her throat, where the necklace would have fallen on her. Eileen took Maggie's arm and escorted her inside. She introduced her sister to France's coworkers. Uncle Pat waved from the kitchen. He was drinking alone. Maggie thought he looked quite tired.

"Maggie, dear! Come give your old uncle a hug." She embraced him and burst into sobs. "I know this is so hard on you because of your book. But listen to me; you're not responsible for what happened. The doctor said her arteries were clogged terribly and it was just a matter of time. You know how your mother avoided going to the doctor to save money. You've done nothing wrong." She whimpered and he backed away. He pointed his finger at her when she looked back at his face. "And I want you to know something. I read your book and I think you're a fine writer. You delved into some touchy subject matter—not my usual cup of tea—but it held my interest to the end."

Why the hell did I ever want to write, Maggie thought. *Look what my stupid book did. Many lives changed for the worse because of the words I was compelled to publish.* Her uncle continued talking to her but his words got softer and softer in her mind as she tried to drink away the pain.

***

The book tour had been canceled of course at her request. That gave her time with her sisters and she didn't realize how much she'd truly needed to reconnect with them. After the funeral, they made Maggie vow to stay in better touch and come back to visit. But when they drove her to the airport to catch her flight home, Maggie looked back at the purple hills and suspected it would be the last time she'd ever visit her birthplace.

The other sisters waited outside the fence and waved as her plane taxied down the runway. As soon as it was airborne, Noreen turned to the others and said, "You know, I wonder if Mom would still be alive if Maggie hadn't written about her abortion."

Eileen, Terrie and Molly offered their theories right away, but the usually over-opinionated Clare remained silent, arms crossed as she watched the plane vanish into the clouds. Once they were back at their mother's house to decide what to do with her belongings, Clare went directly into the kitchen to pour a full glass of wine. Noreen asked the other sisters if they'd noticed.

"Definitely. What was up with her?" Molly asked.

"You don't suppose our oldest sister had an abortion, too?" Noreen folded her arms as she raised her eyebrow.

Chapter 29

Five years had passed after her mother's death. Molly was *still* single, living with her uncle and teaching at the high school. Her social life had dwindled to almost nothing. All of her friends were married and, well, it was just awkward having a single woman in a crowd of married couples. In two years she'd be forty-five and the chance of ever having children of her own was a fading dream.

Uncle Pat contracted pneumonia in the spring of 2004 followed by a monthly series of difficult respiratory ailments. One day in early March of the following year he had a violent coughing spell; Molly noticed blood on his handkerchief. That couldn't be good. She made an appointment with his physician and asked that he be given a chest X-ray. Her absolute worst fears were confirmed—he had advanced lung cancer.

There wasn't even a chance for surgery or treatment such as chemotherapy because his health deteriorated swiftly after his diagnosis. Within a couple of weeks he was in hospice care at home. All of the sisters except Maggie barely made it home before he died on a day in April that felt oddly like the first blush of summer. (After Sept 11, 2001, Maggie refused to fly anywhere, much to the disdain of her agent who was trying to book events for her latest novel.) There was no way she could drive to Penn Yan in time for the funeral. The sisters decided to have a private celebration of his life that summer, allowing her the opportunity to plan a drive back home.

Uncle Pat's wake drew many mourners they'd never met who offered uplifting anecdotes that comforted the grieving sisters. One man said he'd allowed him extra time to pay the family's overdue credit bill after his wife had emergency surgery. The man then received a statement from the department store saying it was paid in full. Uncle Pat never admitted that he did it, but the man was pretty sure he had. An Army veteran he served with in the Philippines shared several tales of his quiet heroism in addition to the act of bravery that earned him medals. Many of the older generation remarked how he'd inherited his father's gentle temperament and they'd rarely seen him angry. Molly was shocked to see Sumner, her insufferable blind date, in the receiving line, and he seemed genuinely upset over her uncle's death.

"This was an exceptionally good man," he said as he shook Molly's hand.

The church was crowded for his funeral Mass and it was a beautiful tribute. Once all her relatives left the following day and there was nothing else to do, Molly wandered onto the porch and sat in her grandfather's rocker. It was a bleak afternoon colored with the slate hues of late winter. The mood added to her sense of loss, as did the murmuring of starlings huddled noisily in the budding trees.

She flipped up her pea coat lapels to ward off the chill. Molly rubbed her arms and sighed as she realized that for the first time in her life, she was completely alone. Her grandparents and uncle were now gone, so were her parents. Eileen, who lived the closest distance, was an hour away.

Molly closed her eyes and tried to imagine the whole family was still there surrounding her. It was summertime and she saw herself carrying out a tray of fried cakes as her grandmother held the door open for her.

"That's the best taste on earth," Grandpa Jimmy said, as if it were the first time he'd ever used the phrase.

"Sure is," Uncle Pat said with a nod.

A crow cawed from the top of her great-grandparents' house across the street where the widow Flannery now resided. Molly opened her eyes and noticed two other crows had joined its rooftop perch. *Why do crows always congregate in groups of threes,* she wondered. They reminded her of the three muses of Greek mythology.

She thought about Uncle Pat's gracious gesture to sign the house over to her last year and how it had made her life this week so much easier. He felt that she'd contributed enough to the rent and repairs over the years that she'd earned the right to remain in the house. Besides, the thought of looking for a new place to live now that she was middle-aged seemed too traumatic. This is where she felt comfortable. This was where she truly felt she was home because of all the family memories linked to this house—and this porch.

As she rocked she imagined her grandfather looking across the street on the day when Grandma Mame's family moved in. *Did he know in his heart, upon first glance at her, that she would be the love of his life? What did that feel like,* she wondered. Theirs was the sort of love that young girls dream of. Grandpa Jimmy never displayed a need to put down his wife as a way to puff up his own ego. In fact, he acted like he had no ego. They had total equality in their marriage—a partnership in the truest sense of the word. On top of that he was so handsome, so kind, so fun.

She considered her own dead-end love life and felt a sour pang in her stomach. Why was love always associated with heartbreak in her life? Had God deemed that she should never have a real chance at love and that was it? Oh, how it hurt, and the thought triggered tears that she wiped away with her chapped hand. She saw happy couples her age all the time with perfect families—some even with grandchildren now. It didn't seem fair. She was a good, kind woman and she knew she'd be a wonderful life partner for the right man. Why had romance evaded her? What was she doing wrong? How could she find a right man at *this* age, though? That was the problem.

Molly's way of dealing with the lack of romance in her life was by escaping into books. It wasn't what you might expect; she was not a fan of bodice-ripping romance novels. Instead she preferred to curl up with cookbooks. She loved reading about foreign cuisines and then using their themes in experiments within her own cooking style. Unfortunately, her focus on food was also manifesting itself on her figure. It was amazing how quickly the pounds added up now that she had reached the age of forty-three.

The last semi-relationship she had was with Tim Lennon's youngest son Kerry, who taught music at the high school now. They had a couple of platonic dates, but Molly was afraid to let the relationship progress fearing the rumors about his father being her sister's father might be true. What if he was Maggie's half-brother? It was a line of weirdness she couldn't cross. He was fun, though, and they'd often visit new restaurants in the area, then go to a nearby bar and review it between themselves.

As she rocked on the porch, Molly recalled Kerry saying that her cooking was so much better than what they'd find in local restaurants and that *she* should open a place. That thought crossed her mind often, but seriously, was it something she could do? Would it be enjoyable or would cooking for money destroy her creativity? Her income from teaching and working at the inn was decent—more than enough to meet basic needs—but there was always something needed in this house. How much longer could she afford to live there alone?

The state offered grants for female entrepreneurs, but would they invest in a woman her age with little professional experience in the culinary field? Added to that deterrent was the cost of renting a decent location. From her experiences in gardening, she knew it was better to start out with a "small pot" location and then transplant the business when the "roots" got too crowded.

If she truly wanted to pursue this dream, she'd need a lot more money than was in her savings account now. Would it all be worth the risk? What if she lost this house as part of her mid-life career gamble? That would be unbearable. She'd feel as if she let her family down somehow.

If only there was some easy way to transform her home into a café without the real-world worries of health regulations or rent or staffing payroll. She mused about this conundrum in silence until the temperature dropped another five degrees rapidly, and she could no longer brave the cold and went inside the empty house. Her footsteps made a hollow sound as she crossed the threshold. It was the echo of loneliness. Molly draped herself across the couch and fell into a deep sleep, still wearing her coat.

The next morning, she opened the refrigerator crammed with food cooked by her well-meaning neighbors and a plastic container of lasagna fell out. She stuffed it back in and looked at all the food, but realized she had little appetite for eating.

It was so odd to be in this big house all alone. Some people might be afraid to stay in a house where someone had died, yet it didn't bother her at all. In fact, it brought her comfort to think that maybe Uncle Pat's spirit lingered to watch over her (as well as the shades of her mother and grandparents too).

The summer-like outdoor temperature belied the fact it was still April, another example of the vagaries of upstate New York weather. Molly poured a mug of coffee and carried it out to the porch with a thick slice of apple cake baked by her next door neighbor Mrs. Salisbury. The joyous birdsong and warm sunshine reminded her of the morning after Noreen's wedding. Molly laughed as she recalled turning the front porch into a restaurant that day. She closed her eyes for a minute to relive the laughter and conversations.

Huh, she thought, *now that I think of it, that was the day I first met Kerry.* Even back then he liked her cooking. It made her smile to think how she'd dressed up each table with a centerpiece and linens. Everyone played along as if it was the real thing, too.

Molly sighed deeply and looked around the empty porch. She actually could envision it transformed into a real café with damask tablecloths and tiny white lights entwined around the porch bannister. Four tables would fit comfortably, she thought, and each could be decorated with a seasonal flower arrangement—peonies and roses in June, tiger lilies in July, brown-eyed Susans in August. She thought the music of Django Reinhardt strumming snappy gypsy jazz chords would set the perfect café mood.

What would she have to do to make a dream like that happen? Were there zoning laws she'd have to consider? There'd have to be plenty of state regulations mandating whether or not she could do it. And then the thought occurred to her, what if it was something she did just on a monthly basis? What if it was more like a loosely structured culinary club among friends where people paid her for supplies and she put on the meal for them? That way she could circumvent the hassles of regulations.

Those daydreams persisted and she casually mentioned the idea to Alice one day at school. She thought it was a great concept. "You're such a great cook. Who knows, maybe this is how you'll meet the man of your dreams."

Molly decided she'd give it a try and her first porch restaurant meal would be held on a Saturday in May. She pored over her collection of cookbooks and created a menu with roast lamb in a tarragon mint butter sauce, a potato and leek terrine, grilled balsamic asparagus and spring greens mix with a honey champagne dressing. She decided to offer a choice of desserts: a panna cotta drizzled with a port berry sauce and a bourbon pecan pie. She priced what it would cost to prepare enough for sixteen people only—an exclusive supper club. Alice helped her circulate the menu among their friends and acquaintances, and within a couple of days they'd placed their reservations (paying $20 each) and she was booked.

Molly bought French cotton tablecloths at a gourmet store in nearby Geneva. At a local home goods store she found beaded lampshade covered candlestick holders and votives to fit inside them. She ordered the lamb at the butcher shop (sourced from a local farm where the sheep were grass fed) and bought as many of the other ingredients that she could from local produce vendors. The final touch would be flowers, so she stopped at a new florist in town to place an order. She was startled when the owner came out wearing a buckskin vest over a calico shirt, jeans and cowboy boots. He looked like he'd just ridden in from the sagebrush.

"May I help you, ma'am?"

Normally that word made her cringe, but there was something so lovely about the slight, almost Canadian accent in his voice that she didn't mind. His feathered hair was the color and texture of ripened wheat.

"Yes. I'm looking for seasonal flowers that would be good for a café, something arranged in low dishes."

The man looked at her and grinned. "You a chef?"

Molly smiled. "How'd you guess? I'm a freelancer, kind of. I'm putting on a dinner this Saturday and turning my front porch into a restaurant for the night."

"That must be some porch," he said, laughing.

"Oh, yes, it's one of those wraparound porches. I can seat sixteen people on it."

"Do you have a license to do that?"

Molly blanched. *Uh-oh,* she thought, *I've said too much. What if he has connections with the health department?*

"Oh, this isn't a *real* restaurant. It's kind of a play restaurant. I've invited friends to join me. We're going to have live music, too. Do you know Mr. Lennon from the music department at the high school? He will be playing jazz guitar."

"That so? Sounds like a nice evening. I like all jazz, but especially bossa nova. Let's go see what I've got in the cooler that would be perfect for your play restaurant." He winked as he turned to walk away.

Molly's jaw dropped. Did this "cowboy" just say that he liked bossa nova? What were the odds of that? He returned with a sample bouquet of cornflowers (that matched his eyes, she noted), Shasta daisies and pink roses.

"We could do something like this," he said as he grouped the flowers with some fern fronds and baby's breath in his left hand. Molly noted the thick silver band carved with a stylized elk on his ring finger. The design matched the slide of his bolo tie. "I have some shallow bowls I could sell you. Do you have four tables seating four?" Molly nodded. "These are celadon, real antiques. I can cut you a deal since this is the debut of your restaurant." He flashed a genuine, heartwarming smile.

"Sounds perfect. May I swing by Saturday around noon to pick them up?"

He scratched his chin and shook his head. "We have free delivery for new entrepreneurs. How 'bout I drop these off a little before your dinner so they'll be nice and fresh?"

Molly tilted her chin and grinned slightly. Was this guy flirting or was he just exuding cowboy charm? Whatever it was, it worked. "OK, deal!"

Luckily she got her grocery shopping done on Friday after school so she could make the desserts and assemble the potato leek and goat cheese terrine. Saturday morning she was called into work unexpectedly to cover for a sick coworker. "I can work until two, that's it," she told her boss. He was willing to bargain with her; what else could he do? She flew down the highway hugging the West Side of the lake after work and got home with enough time to prep and season the lamb for roasting. She'd made the tarragon mint butter last night to be added to the drippings for a sauce. The grill was all set for charring the balsamic marinated asparagus. All she had left to do was set the tables.

Sparkling sunshine and clear skies made for a perfect afternoon temperature in the mid-seventies. Alice arrived after her work shift and together they set up the four card tables and chairs, covered them with the French fabric tablecloths and folded cloth napkins.

"Oh, I forgot the lights!" Molly raced down cellar to fetch the ladder and white Christmas lights which she strung on hooks she and Uncle Pat had installed a few years ago. Alice plugged them into the extension cord that was connected to an outlet in front of the porch.

"Oh wow, that makes the porch resplendent!" Alice said. She helped Molly set out the lampshade candle holders.

"Great, now all we need are the...." Molly couldn't finish the sentence before the florist pulled up in his van to complete it.

"Wow, now *this* is what I call a porch restaurant," he said as he carried the box of bouquets up the steps. "It looks like the real deal, Miss McNamara. Hi," he said to Alice as he took off his cowboy hat and extended his hand, "I'm Austin Bordwell, owner of Florabundance down on Maiden Lane."

Alice smiled as she noticed Molly's face redden slightly. "Pleased to meet you, Austin. I'm Alice Reasoner. Are you new in these parts?" Molly rolled her eyes as her friend's speech shifted subliminally to cowboy lingo.

"Nope. Grew up on a dairy farm in Pulteney on the other side of the lake. Married a girl from Wyoming and spent the past twenty years out there."

Drat, Molly sighed as she noted his comment. *He's married. Ah well.* She lifted the arrangements out of the box and was delighted to see the short celadon vases matched the color of the window sashes on the house. The flowers' colors were a vibrant contrast to the vase, and the tea roses were especially fragrant.

"Perfect, Austin!"

He nodded his head. "Thank you. Glad you approve. I tell you what's perfect, the smells coming out of your kitchen. Is that lamb roasting?" Molly proceeded to describe in great detail every aspect of the menu and he asked where she found her inspiration.

"I read cookbooks like people read novels. It's fun for me to experiment with flavors and textures."

"So what you're telling me is that you're not just cooking food, you're creating art?"

"Yes! I love creating menus with varying textures and flavors to see how people react to them."

"The man who marries you will be one lucky guy," Austin said. "Have a good evening, ladies. Thanks much for the business, Molly."

Kerry Lennon arrived early wearing a dress shirt, black vest and tie that looked quite elegant. He handed her a chilled bottle of sparkling wine. "It's a blanc de noirs from Loughmare, that new Irish-owned winery on the East Lake Road. Hope it brings you luck," he said kissing her cheek sweetly. "Molly, this looks like a *real* restaurant!"

"Thanks. I think so, too." Molly hugged the bottle. "I'm so excited to see this coming true. Thanks for your encouragement, Kerry. This is partly your fault. I'm going to chill this for later."

Kerry strummed Django Reinhardt's "Minor Swing" as the first diners stepped onto the porch. Alice took their drink orders and lit the candle lamps. Molly was out back grilling the asparagus. You'd think her mind would be focused on the evening ahead, but she was replaying the scene of when Austin arrived with the flowers. Was it her imagination or was he dressed up a little bit? He had on a turquoise thunderbird bolo tie and beautifully stitched black leather boots. She definitely was attracted to him. Damn, why did he have to be married? It wasn't fair.

"All the seats are filled. Drinks have been served," Alice said.

"OK, bring out the cheese and fruit plates while I carve up the lamb."

Alice returned and helped Molly plate the dinners. When they carried the first dishes onto the porch, the guests applauded.

"You might want to hold that until you taste the food," Molly said. Her neighbor, Mrs. Salisbury, laughed.

"Hey, I already know what a good cook you are."

By the time the desserts were served, the rest of the diners concurred.

"That, my dear, was a superb meal!" the guidance counselor at the high school said. "What's the date and menu for the next one?"

"Really? You think I should do another?" All the guests nodded. "Well, since it will be June, I was thinking of traditional picnic fare such as Southern fried chicken, biscuits and gravy, a Penn Yan pea salad, and some take on strawberry shortcake. How does that sound?"

Ed Taylor stood up. "Here's my $20. Consider it your first reservation."

Molly and Alice were just finishing up clearing the tables when Austin drove down the hill slowly and waved. He turned around, rolled down the passenger window and called out to them.

"How'd it go, ladies?" Molly and Alice gave him a thumbs up.

"Want to try some leftovers?" Molly yelled to him. She was so giddy from her success that she didn't care if she sounded forward. He backed up and drove his van up the driveway. He burst into a big smile when he stepped onto the porch.

"Man it's been a long day. I just got back from delivering some arrangements to that new winery just over the hill on Seneca Lake. Of course I had to chat with the owner and sample some of their wines. I kept thinking how good his cabernet sauvignon would be with your roast lamb."

"You're in luck. We just happen to have some cab sauv inside."

The three sat around the dining room table picking at the lamb roast and potato terrine. Molly told Austin that she'd already gotten a reservation for her June dinner.

"Not surprised. This might be the tastiest lamb I've ever eaten."

They shared stories of the most memorable meals they'd ever had. Alice recounted a vineyard picnic in the Graves wine region of France. Austin shared his memory of a midnight dinner under the stars in Jackson Hole, Wyoming. Molly spoke reverently of Easter Sunday dinners around this same table at which her grandmother served roast pork with gravy (she found ham to be too salty) and the most heavenly dish of square-cut potatoes in a béchamel sauce. The conversation drifted to their favorite guilty pleasure foods. Alice loved a New York strip steak, pan fried for dinner. Molly talked about the cabbage pirohi luncheons during Lent in Binghamton's First Ward. Austin reminisced about the breakfasts his grandmother made on the farm and how the best part of the meal was her homemade fried cakes.

"Did you say fried cakes?"

"Yes, ma'am. The best!"

"I *love* them! My Grandma Mame taught me how to make them."

"Maybe I need to taste her recipe, you know, to compare whose were the best?"

"You've got it. Next time I make them, I'll bring some by your shop. Speaking of sweets, anyone care for dessert? I hear men like pie," she said with a wink toward Austin. "You a fan of pecan?"

After the last of the coffee was poured, Austin left and Alice stayed to help clean the rest of the dishes. They were finally done close to midnight.

"Let's go have a glass of wine on the porch," Molly said. She opened the refrigerator to get the sparkling wine Kerry gave her, but then saw the already opened bottle of cabernet sauvignon. *Hmm, maybe I should save this "lucky bottle" of wine for a special occasion,* she thought. She poured two glasses and handed one to Alice. They dragged out the rocking chairs that had been moved inside to make room for the dining tables. Molly sat down with a sigh. "Aww, now this is heaven."

"We did it, or I should say, you did it."

"Couldn't have done it without your help, Alice." Molly clinked her wineglass with Alice's. "Thank you."

"That Austin's quite a dish. I think he's taken a fancy to you."

"Really?" Molly sat up. "You think?" Alice nodded. "Argh, too bad he's married."

"Well he mentioned getting married, but if you noticed he's not wearing a wedding ring."

"He wasn't?" She stopped and smiled as she remembered he was wearing that elk ring but not a wedding band.

"Where the heck's your radar, Molly? You'll never get married if you don't keep that tuned."

"Hmm, you're right. I saw his silver ring with an elk on it, but it wasn't a wedding ring. He seems to like turquoise jewelry. Did you see that cuff bracelet he was wearing, too?"

"Yep. That must be worth a few dozen long-stem roses. Don't see many men in Penn Yan wearing bracelets."

Alice's words made a thought come into Molly's mind: *Is Austin gay and his marriage broke up because of it and that's why he was now in Penn Yan?* Hmm...after musing on that possibility for a while she thought, no, he definitely seemed to be flirting with her.

The following Monday, Molly rose early to make a batch of fried cakes. She boxed a half dozen, still warm, and stopped by Florabundance on her way to school. When she opened the door, she was startled to see a woman behind the counter. *Uh-oh*, she worried, *is this the wife*?

"Hi, is Austin in?"

"Sorry. He's off on Mondays. May I help you?"

Darn it, she thought, *now what should I do*?

"Hmm, I guess I'll come back tomorrow."

"Do you have something there for him?" She was pointing at the bakery box tied with a neat bow.

"Oh, yes. Here. Tell him Molly stopped by to thank him for the great job he did on the centerpieces for my restaurant."

The woman gave her a studied look.

"Of course, I'll see that he gets them tonight."

As Molly walked away, she thought *what an idiot I am*. She tried to erase all the images created previously by a runaway imagination of her lakeside wedding to Austin, the amazing reception in a hall filled with a floral wonderland and their subsequent honeymoon spent in a cabin near the Grand Tetons.

"Well, what did he think of the fried cakes?" Alice asked her at school.

Molly shook her head. "It was his day off. Ended up handing them over to his wife I think."

Alice grimaced. "Oh dear, maybe that *was* a wedding band. Ah well, plenty more fish out there. Don't give up hope. The right one will come along. Someday."

Chapter 30

Word spread about Molly's café and so many new people wanted to join in the fun that she'd added two full tables on the porch by the time of her final dinner in early October. Molly was careful to couch the terms of what she was doing as cooking a meal *for friends*. They gave her *donations* to help pay for the cost of supplies. This was *not* a restaurant. She had to make sure this was well understood so that she'd not be in any violation of health department or other laws.

The more she got to know Austin, the more comfortable she became around him. Since he was married and there was no future in a romance, she began to view him like a brother that she never had. They teased each other a lot and he listened to her dreams for next year's season of meals from May to October. Austin was a great sounding board and he kept encouraging her to pursue opening a real restaurant, although she insisted that it wasn't what she wanted from life.

***

On the first Saturday of December, Molly awoke to a rattling noise that sounded like a woodpecker attacking the front porch. It was snowing out and she put on her bathrobe to peek out the front door. She was startled to see Austin there holding a wreath in his hands.

"Darn! I wanted to surprise you."

"What are you doing?"

Austin took her hand and led her down the front steps so she could get the full effect of the balsam wreaths with garnet-colored bows and gold ornaments he'd hung from the sashes of windows on the first floor.

"Oh! They're beautiful! Austin, that's so kind of you."

He leaned in and kissed her cheek. "Merry Christmas, darlin'. Thanks for being such a good customer and sending all those new clients my way. Ho ho ho!" And off he jogged down the steps, waving back at her. Stunned by his unexpected gesture, Molly made a half smile as she waved back and as soon as his van was down the street, she ran into the house and thought, *my God, did he just kiss me*? His gesture thrilled her, yet at the same time her feelings were confused by the thoughts that, *no, you can't let yourself get carried away. He's married.*

She went back to bed and fell asleep. Austin found his way into her dreams, and he just started to kiss her again when she heard knocking once more. Molly sat up in her bed and thought, *is he back*? She giggled as she threw on her bathrobe, dragged a brush through her hair and rushed downstairs. When she opened the door she was startled anew by what she saw. It wasn't Austin.

"Man, do you always sleep this late?"

Molly gasped and blinked. Was she still dreaming? "Maggie? *Maggie!* What the hell are you doing here?"

"Hah, that's a fine hello. Well Sis, it's a long story. Mind if I come in?" Molly shook her head and opened the door wide so Maggie could carry in two large suitcases.

"You staying for a while?" Molly joked.

"Well, to be honest, I was wondering if there was room here at the inn."

"Room?"

"I've left California for good. After being here this summer for Uncle Pat's memorial, I've realized that all I want to do is write about *this* place—this house, that porch, Penn Yan, Keuka Lake. It's really hard to do that a continent away. Funny, but this *feels* like my hometown."

Molly rubbed her eyes. She was awake though she wished she was still dreaming of kissing Austin. "So, let me get this straight. You're moving back to town and you want to stay here until you find a place of your own?"

"Well, to be honest, I'd love to live here with you. But if that's a problem, you know if there's not enough room...."

Hah, Molly thought. Boy did her sister know how to toss the guilt around. Of course there was plenty of room in this big house. But to be honest, she hadn't lived with her sister since she was seven years old. They were almost strangers in a way. How would they get along? What if this became a nightmare?

"Well, we'll take it day by day I guess. So, let's start again. Welcome home, Maggie."

Phew, Maggie thought as she hugged her youngest sister. It worked. She was glad she hadn't sent an email (like she originally planned to do) because it would have been easier for her sister to refuse. There was no way she'd say 'no' to her sister in person. *Ah, yes, you can always count on good old Catholic guilt*, she thought.

Molly rustled up a quick breakfast for her sister as they discussed myriad family topics, including their mother's stroke and Uncle Pat's death.

"Weren't you lucky to inherit this house?" Maggie said, a bit wistfully.

"To be honest, instead of inheriting it I feel like I paid a virtual mortgage for all the repairs and improvements I've made to the place since I moved in." Molly updated her on her job and then filled her older sister in about the "play restaurant" and how successful it had been.

"That's so cool! What a creative concept, Molly. You know I like to cook, too. I've learned some great Pan-Asian recipes living in California. You'll have to let me cook sometime for you."

And in an instant, Molly was no longer living alone. Maggie settled in the household easily for the first week there, probably because she and Molly had so much catching up to do. Soon Molly had to insist that Maggie smoke outside on the porch because she was "allergic" to cigarettes and Maggie insisted that Molly use headphones to listen to music when she was writing. There were a few rough spots of adjustment, but they adapted quickly.

The master bedroom had been Molly's room since Grandpa Jimmy died, so she gave Maggie the second largest one—her mother's former bedroom. Of course it was Frances's room decades ago, but Maggie felt her presence was still there and it unnerved her. She had not shed her guilt for the way the novel affected her mother. Maybe that's why she was afraid to sleep in the bedroom initially.

Maggie didn't tell Molly this because she didn't want her to think that she was ungrateful or weird. So to hide her fear, she'd stop by Molly's room for heart to heart chats until she was thoroughly drowsy, and then she'd return to her room primed for sleep.

It was nice for each of them to have a sister to confide in. During their late night chats, they learned a lot about each other, too. Maggie was impressed by Molly's academic achievements that got little attention under the shadow of Clare's bright star. She envied her little sister's travels in Europe, too. That was something she yearned to do but she never had enough cash.

Conversely Molly envied her sister's trips across the West. There was so much in America that Molly hadn't seen yet. Her older sister was skillful storyteller and she loved it when Maggie talked about the psychedelic scene in Haight-Ashbury and all the famous people she'd interviewed or partied with there. Her descriptions were so vivid that they made Molly feel as if Maggie's stories were shared memories.

The sisters discovered they had markedly different impressions of their father. Molly's connection with him was tenuous, since he abandoned the family shortly after she was born. Over the years her mother's anger toward him clouded any remaining bits of fond memories. Maggie filled in the gaps about their father. She told Molly that he always smelled like Aqua Velva aftershave, drank coffee black with two sugars and enjoyed the music of Johnny Mathis. They'd had an amicable father-daughter relationship from an early age, Maggie told her. While growing up, she noted the way he used words as tools of persuasion and adopted some of his techniques for survival skills in her own life, and now, her writing.

"He gave me my first cigarette, you know."

Molly's eyes widened. "Are you kidding me? How old were you?"

"Twelve."

Molly didn't know what to say. She wished her sister could kick the habit, especially after she saw what Uncle Pat endured with lung cancer.

That conversation brought them to the subject of men in general, and both girls shared war stories of hellacious past dates.

"Don't you wish there were more men out there like Grandpa Jimmy?" Molly sighed as she hugged her pillow.

"Remember the night of the blue moon, when he danced with us? That was the nicest thing I've ever seen a man do." Maggie sighed and leaned against the headboard looking at the ceiling as if a scratchy film of that memory was playing on it.

"That night was pure magic. Remember the lightning bugs escaped from the jar and blinked through all our bedrooms that night? Grandma was so lucky. I wish I could meet a man as romantic as he was." Molly debated whether to open up to Maggie about her jumbled feelings for Austin. Just as she started to speak, Maggie interrupted.

"Indeed," she said with a big yawn. "Well, see ya in the morning, Sis."

Chapter 31

Molly hadn't told her other sisters about the new living arrangement and she wasn't sure why. Noreen still harbored palpable anger toward Maggie for writing the book that inadvertently led to her mother's death. Clare remained mute about Maggie's success, though she took quiet delight in the fact that her sophomore novel was published to less than stellar reviews. Terrie and Eileen were too busy taking care of children and pets to think much about their sister on the West Coast, who, to be honest, had made little effort to keep in touch with them all.

It was now two weeks before Christmas and Terrie called to see what Molly's plans were. There'd been a holiday visiting pattern to the past couple of years: Molly spent Christmas Eve with her sister in Binghamton and Christmas Day with Eileen's family in Ithaca.

"Why don't you come up here this year, Terrie," Molly suggested, never letting on about Maggie.

"But what about the animals?"

"Can't you just ask your assistant Cheryl to stop in and check on them?"

"Well, I guess she could do that. It sure would be nice to stay in Grandma and Grandpa's house again. OK, I'll try to make it up Christmas Eve."

"Wonderful!"

***

Clare was extremely stressed at her job as a senior editor with the publishing company. With all of the recent downsizing she was being asked to take on extra work now that assistants used to do for her, in addition to her regular duties. She had a couple of vacation days left and decided to use them before they were lost at year's end.

On top of that, it had been ten years since she broke up with Matthew. Clare had occasional dates, mainly with men she'd met in the trade, but was shy of getting involved in an exclusive relationship again. She felt like the years with Matthew had been a huge waste of her emotional energy. If it were ever to happen again, she'd prefer that her beau expend equal or more emotional energy on her this time. Clare needed to be the priority in her life, not some midlife-crisis male.

Her life had such a rigid structure these days that its sameness wearied her. She thought it would be fun to do something spontaneous for a change. Maybe she'd drop in on Molly and spend the Christmas holiday at the old family homestead. Perhaps if she sent flowers it would soften the shock of a surprise visit.

***

Molly and Maggie made a pact to sleep in Christmas Eve morning and rise when they felt like it for a late brunch. Molly hadn't told Maggie that Terrie was coming that day—she thought it would be fun to surprise them both. As Maggie snored in her room, Molly snuck downstairs early to start prepping their brunch. She blended a batch of fried cake dough and as soon as it hit the bubbling hot grease, the house was filled with its signature scent.

"What? Are you kidding me?" Maggie yelled down to her sister. "This is so cruel! I can't sleep anymore now. I need fried cakes, now! Ohmigod I haven't had one of those in years."

Maggie wrapped on her bathrobe and pushed the crazy bed-head hairstyle off her face. The dining room table was set when she walked in and there was coffee, scrambled eggs, bacon, and of course, hot fried cakes.

"You're spoiling me Sis," Maggie said as she crunched a slice of crisp bacon.

They heard a van pull in the driveway and a knock on the door. Molly answered it.

"Austin! What are you doing here?"

"Special delivery for the lady of the house," he said leaning in for a quick peck on the cheek. Molly prayed that Maggie wasn't watching. "What's that heavenly smell, darlin'? Are you making your famous fried cakes?" He walked right into the house, startling Maggie as she sat in the dining room.

"Oops! Sorry, didn't know you had company, Molly."

"Austin, this is my older sister Maggie. Sis, this is Austin, the best florist in town. Now tell me, who the heck sent me this beautiful poinsettia?"

"Read the card. I believe it's in English," he teased.

"Clare! How nice. She's never done that before."

"So, about those fried cakes."

"Be my guest, Austin." He picked one up and it was still warm to the touch. He took a bite and savored the crunch of the crust and the hint of nutmeg in the cakey middle. "Can I buy a cup of coffee, too?"

Maggie laughed and got a coffee mug for him. "I suppose you'll want some sugar," she said with a flirty tone as she noted how well his jeans defined his rear end.

What the hell was that about? Molly thought as she watched the display and felt an unexpected surge of territorial jealousy. *But wait, relax,* she thought. *Maggie isn't aware of my feelings for him. Cut her some slack.*

"Oh, one *never* refuses sugar," Austin quipped in a randy tone that Molly had never heard from him.

"Well, I've got plenty of cream if you want it," Molly said. Then both she and Austin laughed, surprised by *her* tone.

"I think I've died and gone to heaven, ladies."

He didn't stay long and as they were cleaning up the kitchen, Maggie asked casually if Austin was married.

"Yes!" Molly replied, harsher than she should have.

There was another knock at the door.

"Ah, maybe he's come back for my phone number," Maggie said, beating Molly to the door. She swung it open and the two sisters stood together gape mouthed.

"Clare?" they gasped in tandem.

"*Maggie*? What the hell are you doing here?"

"What the hell are *you* doing here?" Maggie snapped back good humoredly.

"Clare, are you here for Christmas?" Molly asked.

"If you'll have me. Oh my God how I needed to get out of the city. I thought it would be far more relaxing to spend a traditional Christmas with you at the old homestead. Celebrating the holidays here always reminds me of that film *It's A Wonderful Life*. There's such a Forties vibe to the place. So what brought you here, Maggie? Passing through on a book tour?"

Was it just her, or was there just the slightest needling of sarcasm in her voice, Maggie wondered.

"Actually, I'm living here now."

"Living *here*? With Molly? *Really*? Since when?"

"Since a couple of weeks ago."

Clare glared at Molly, as if to say, you should have told me about this. Molly ignored it and said, "You can put your things Uncle Pat's old room and I'll get out some clean sheets for the bed. OK?"

"Perfect. You're a dear sister for letting me crash your Christmas. Hey, what's that I smell? Have you been making fried cakes?"

And just like that, through the power of familiar food, the awkwardness of the multiple surprises melted away. The three sisters lingered over coffee in the dining room until Molly happened to gaze at the clock and noticed it was half past two and she was still wearing pajamas.

"I better get dressed!"

"Why? Going somewhere with your boyfriend the florist?

"He's not my boyfriend." Molly gave Maggie an evil look.

"You're seeing someone?" Clare asked with a slight tone of surprise in her voice.

Molly raced to her room hoping she could get changed before Terrie arrived at any moment. She was brushing her teeth when she heard the front door open.

"Hello?" Terrie sang out.

"*Terrie!* What are you doing here?" Clare asked.

"Clare? Wow, what a cool surprise!" They hugged and then Terrie noticed Maggie over her sister's shoulder. "Oh man, Maggie's here, too? Double wow! How are *you*, Sis?" Terrie's embrace hit Maggie like a linebacker and they stumbled backwards. Their high-pitched glee sounded as if they were children at play.

When Molly came downstairs, they all stopped talking. Clare folded her arms and squinted.

"So, when are Eileen and Noreen expected?"

"Trust me, if they show up I'll be as surprised as the rest of you."

Molly bought a hefty standing rib roast for Christmas Eve dinner (hoping there'd be leftovers if Austin stopped by) and she had to prepare it for roasting while the other sisters caught up in the dining room. After a while they heard footsteps on the porch followed by a firm knock on the door.

"I bet it's Eileen," Clare said.

"Nah, it's gotta be Noreen," Terrie countered.

"Would someone please answer that?" Molly called out. "My hands are covered in beef rub."

"Hah! No comment," Maggie sniggered as she went to open the door. Outside stood a young blonde dressed in a faux fur coat over a T-shirt and jeans. She looked vaguely familiar but Clare couldn't place her.

"May I help you?"

"I don't know if you can. I was looking for a woman who lived at this address at one time. Her name is Frances McNamara."

Maggie stepped backward slightly, startled by hearing her mother's name spoken. It was a rare occasion when she was caught off guard and she stared blankly for a moment wondering what the young woman wanted. She sized her up as a saleswoman of some sort and replied curtly. "Listen, let me cut to the chase. Whatever you're hawking hon, we're not interested. It's Christmas! Please leave us alone!" She slammed the door in her face.

"Who was that? Why were you so rude?" Clare asked.

"Dunno. She was looking for Mom. It freaked me out."

"Mom?" Clare touched her fingers to her chin as she raised her eyebrows. She went over and peeked out the dining room window. Her sisters followed to look at the stranger who had paused on the porch steps when she noticed them watching her. Clare walked over and reopened the door.

"I'm sorry, but we were wondering, *who* are you?"

"Hi. My name is Mara Levin, and I'm doing some genealogical research on my...."

"Stop!" Clare interrupted. "Tell me, where did you grow up?"

"Manhattan. My parents were friends with a Clare McNamara and I've been having difficulty locating her. Thought I'd connect with her mother who grew up here."

Clare covered her mouth with her hand as she glanced over her shoulder to see if her sisters were nearby and closed the front door behind her. Now that Clare had gotten rid of her landline because she used a cell phone exclusively, her name was no longer in the phone book. She'd lost contact with the Levins several years ago. "Are you... wow, you must be... Sarah and Sol's daughter, is it?"

"Why yes. Do you know Clare? I think she might be my birth mother."

Clare blanched as if she'd seen a ghost. Actually it was more like she was looking at a family photo from her youth. She smiled slightly. "Yes. As a matter of fact, I'm Clare. I'm sorry, but I'm not your mother." She opened wide the front door and gestured for the woman to step inside. "Won't you come in, Mara? Let me get my sister," Clare said as she pointed at Maggie. "I think she can help you."

Mara glanced around the cozy living room seeking clues to what her birth mother's family was like. Clare asked Molly and Terrie to go into the kitchen for a few minutes. They shrugged and did as they were told. "Maggie, I need you to come to the front door."

Maggie wondered what all the mystery was about as she stood up and tightened her bathrobe to follow her sister back to the door.

Clare draped her arm around Maggie to steady her. "OK, take a deep breath. Maggie, I'd like you to meet your daughter, Mara."

Maggie opened her mouth but no sound came out. Her heart fluttered and she felt as if she might pass out. She looked at Clare and her sister nodded. It was true. Finally she gathered her wits. "But are you sure? They weren't supposed to ever tell... how did she find...?" Her eyes examined the girl standing before her for visual clues that she was indeed her flesh and blood.

"It doesn't matter now, does it, Maggie?"

"*You're* my mother? Oh, hey, it's nice to meet you...Mom."

Maggie now understood why the young woman looked familiar. It was like gazing into a mirror about thirty years ago—same build, hair color, eyes and the same funky taste in apparel. That made her smile. This young woman was the daughter she'd given up when she was just twenty-three to Clare's childless friends. When it came down to it, she just couldn't have an abortion. Guess she *was* like her mother. Maggie and Mara's adoptive parents had fallen out of touch many years ago, although she did wonder what became of her daughter.

At the time Maggie sought a complete break from the child after she was adopted and never requested so much as a photo of her, preferring the occasional update. That would give her a better chance of dealing with her choice, Maggie thought. It wasn't that easy. Over the years she wondered often about her daughter. *Does she look like me or Kevin? Has she married now, am I a grandmother?* Maggie blamed her struggles with depression on her chosen separation from her unplanned daughter. It inspired that first novel.

Maggie pushed back her hair as she pulled the collar of her bathrobe together. "Oh man, I'm such a mess. I don't usually spend the day in my pajamas." Her hand fumbled in the right pocket of her robe and pulled out her cigarettes and lighter. "Let's go on the porch to talk, OK? I need a smoke."

The young woman was taking as many mental notes of her birth mother as Maggie was of her daughter.

"So it's Mara, you said? That's a pretty name."

"Sarah said it was a Celtic name meaning the sea. They told me it was because they liked Celtic mythology. I found out recently by mistake that I was adopted. My mother needed a kidney transplant and I wanted to donate one of mine, so I quietly had some blood work done to see if I'd be a good candidate. That's when I found out our genetics didn't match up. When I confronted Sarah and Sol, they told me they'd given me the name because it matched my true heritage, actually part of my mother's surname. It was so weird to find out I'd been living with this lie for so many years. But you know, kind as they were to me, inside I never felt like I belonged to them."

Maggie nodded, feeling shame that she also lived such a lie.

"I'm just wondering, Maggie, why Sol and Sarah? Were you friends with them, too?"

"No, just Clare was. I never met them in person. Not without any extra effort on your mother's part, though. She wanted me to move East until you were born. I refused. Too many bridges burned back here. You needed to be carried in sunshine, and there was no better place than California." Maggie took a long drag on her cigarette, and waved the smoke away from her daughter. "After I gave birth to you, I contacted them again, we signed the agreement and their lawyers picked you up and flew you to your adoptive parents." Rising emotion caught her words at the back of her throat. She felt so awful about the way the truth was revealed to her daughter. This was not how she'd imagined their first encounter. "So, you just had a birthday. What are you, thirty-two now?" Mara nodded with a slight smile. Her birth mother hadn't forgotten.

"Man, I'm finally meeting my daughter three decades after I gave birth to her. What a strange trip *this* is. Tell me, Mara, what do you do for a living?"

"I'm a journalist. I work for a newspaper in Cleveland."

Maggie laughed so hard it triggered a coughing fit. "Hah-hah! You've got to be kidding me. How did you get involved in that crazy field?" She flicked her cigarette into the snow and finally did something she'd wanted to do for thirty years—Maggie reached out and hugged her daughter. It was more magical than she'd imagined. Despite their distance all these years, at this moment she felt the instinctive natal bond between mother and child. And it was *so* wonderful!

Maggie couldn't keep her tears in check, and from the muffled sobs, obviously her daughter was having the same problem. They parted and Maggie stroked Mara's silken curly hair. Her daughter had green eyes that matched her own. Even the perfume she was wearing smelled like her favorite aromatherapy blend she bought at that head shop in San Francisco. Her heart ached as she thought how happy this reunion would have made her own mother. This moment was an unexpected gift and there was no way Maggie was going to refuse it. She welcomed Mara inside. Introductions were made to her stunned, but delighted, aunts (who'd of course thought Mara was aborted).

"Here, let me take your coat," Molly said. When Mara slipped it off, Terrie noticed a glint of something familiar hanging around her neck.

"Where'd you get that necklace?" she asked.

Mara fingered a silver Y-shaped pendant. "My parents gave it to me when I turned twenty-one. Mom said she thought it was a rune signifying my name. I thought it was odd, but I've grown to like it."

"That's not a rune," Clare said. "It's what our sister Noreen gave us as a bridesmaids gift. That's the shape of Keuka Lake, which is just down the hill about mile from here. Maggie, is this your necklace?"

She bit her lip and nodded. "I was angry at Mom for not delaying grandma's funeral so I could make it. Until that moment I hadn't taken it off. But it represented her history, her hometown and it just made me angry. I yanked it off and stuffed it in an envelope. When I was preparing Mara to be flown to her parents, I found it in my dresser drawer. It symbolized her heritage and I thought it would be nice for her to have a token of that. So I slipped the necklace into the envelope with her birth certificate. Glad your parents didn't throw it out."

"I am too," Mara said as she held the pendant over her heart.

"Did you know that if you're wearing one, it also means you're a sister of the lake," Terrie added.

"What's that?"

The sisters explained the pendant's significance and after a few hours of dinner and conversation, Molly invited her niece to stay overnight on the bed in the den. It took her but minutes to accept the offer and cancel her reservation at the hotel in town.

When Molly awoke Christmas morning, the first thing that crossed her mind as she got dressed was what should she tell Eileen and Noreen when they'd call later that day? Would they be mad at her for not being invited to the impromptu sisters' reunion? What should she say about Mara? Was it better to let Maggie explain?

The spontaneous gathering made Molly miss her mother terribly. She wished she'd known the truth, that despite the tough façade Maggie projected to the world, the two of them were more alike than you'd suspect. Molly wished they were all gathered together now, Eileen and Noreen, and more importantly, her mother. Oh how she ached to see her again. What she'd give for a sign to know her mother's spirit was with them.

The coffee sputtered as it finished brewing, and Molly wiped the tears away with the back of her hand and then poured a tall mug. She heard light footsteps coming toward the kitchen. It reminded her of tip-toeing downstairs in footed pajamas to see what Santa Claus left under the tree.

"Good morning," Mara said, squinting as her eyes adjusted to the kitchen fluorescent light. "Must. Have.

Coffee." She giggled as she pretended to walk like a zombie. Molly raised her eyebrow when she saw Mara's sleepwear.

"Here you go," she said handing her the mug she'd poured for herself as she stared at the oversized T-shirt's graphic. Mara wondered if she was mad at her, because of the serious expression on her face. "Where did you get that shirt you're wearing?"

"Oh, this? Maggie, uh, Mom, bought it in Mexico. She gave it to me last night and said it's Our Lady of Guadalupe and that she will protect me from harm. Pretty cool, huh?"

Molly caught her breath as she recalled that on every December twelfth—the feast of Our Lady of Guadalupe—her mother would drag her and whatever sister was around to Mass. She always wondered why, and recently she'd read that Pope John Paul II deemed her the patroness of the unborn. Had they been praying all these years for Mara's soul? If so, it *worked.* Chills tickled the back of her neck. *There's my sign*, she thought, *you* are *here, Mom.*

She heard a quiet knock. *Now who's here,* she thought as she went to answer the door. Her heart leapt. Austin grinned as he held out a wrapped box with holes punched in its side.

"Now before you say a word, I want you to know that you can refuse this, but I found this in my back yard and thought you'd like it."

Molly smiled with puzzled amusement as she took the box from his hands wondering what this mysterious gift could be. The first thing that crossed her mind was *why didn't I buy him something for Christmas*? The second thing she thought was *what's moving inside the box*? He lifted the lid and a calico kitten with a red bow on its collar mewed at her.

"Ohh! It's darling!" she said bringing a hand to her mouth. "Where did you find it?"

"Hiding in the barn under the hay. Now I know it's Christmas and stores are closed, so if you *do* want her I also have food and kitty litter in the car," he said, raising his eyebrows, unsure what her reaction would be.

"Of course I'll keep her, Austin, she's beautiful. Thank you. This makes me feel like a little kid on Christmas morn."

He leaned over the cat to kiss Molly's cheek sweetly. "That's just what I hoped. Now, what shall we call your calico café cat?"

She caught her breath again, grinning as she thought of a name. It was a struggle because she distracted by his use of the word *we*.

"Since she's multicolored like a bouquet, how about Flora? That was the name of the Roman goddess of flowers and spring."

"Perfect." He went back to his van and brought her the food and kitty litter. "Here you go, little Flora. Well gotta run now."

"So soon?" Molly asked. "Won't you at least come in for a cup of coffee?"

"Can't," he said as he jogged down the steps. "I've got breakfast waiting with the family at the farm today. Merry Christmas!"

Her heart sank. She was so confused. This gift and his

kiss had the air of a romantic gesture, yet he made of point of saying he was spending Christmas with his family. She didn't want to show him how disappointed she was, so she forced a runner-up beauty queen smile as she waved goodbye.

"Please wish your wife and family a Merry Christmas from me!"

Austin couldn't hear her words as he pulled away, but he wondered why Molly's smile appeared tinged with sadness. He hoped that she wasn't pretending to like his gift.

Terrie stepped off the staircase just as Molly walked inside with the kitten.

"Where did you get that pretty little calico?" she exclaimed as she held out her hands to pick up the kitten. Flora purred instantly when Terrie cuddled her in her arms. *Funny how animals know who likes them*, Molly thought.

"This is Flora. She's a Christmas gift from my friend Austin."

"Austin's giving you Christmas gifts?" Maggie asked as she followed downstairs. She scratched the kitten's head. "Hmm, this looks serious," she said winking to Molly. "What a beauty she is."

"Who's Austin and how serious is this relationship?" Clare asked as she appeared suddenly and wedged between Molly and Terrie, like an alpha dog pushing its nose ahead of the pack to the food dish. While Terrie played with the kitten, Clare herded the others to the dining room table where she stared at Molly as she waited for her to explain. Molly was trapped, and so she told them how confused she was by their relationship because it felt like he was interested in her although he was married.

"So what if he's married? Have yourself some *fun*, girl. You deserve it, Molly!"

Mara snickered at her mother and Clare rolled her eyes. "Nice, Maggie, I'm sure that sentiment won't surprise your daughter," she said with a sneer.

"Oh, I would never date a married man." Molly's tone was firm. "After all, if he cheated with me, what would stop him from cheating with another woman?" Maggie wished she'd kept her stupid mouth shut.

"Ah yes, the cheating male. Wonder if we'll ever be able to breed that trait out of the species?" Clare's comment made all the women laugh, though deep down, each one had buried the pain of being hurt by a man's indiscretion.

The five women dressed and went into town for Christmas Mass. Clare sighed when she settled into the hard-backed oak pew of St. Urban's and looked up at those milky stained glass windows she'd gazed at for decades. Here was where all of her older relatives gathered daily for spiritual strength. *Look at what it got them through*, she thought. *Drownings. Floods. World Wars. Infidelity.* She wished she'd stayed closer to her faith instead of being a cliché Christmas-Easter Catholic. It wasn't too late to change that, though.

It was the first time Mara had been inside a Catholic church—she'd been raised in the Jewish faith. She had many questions afterward about the rituals of the Mass and they suggested she speak with Eileen about them. After all, she was the family's religion expert.

Molly called Noreen and Eileen to invite them over for a spur-of-the-moment reunion. Both agreed to stop by in the early afternoon. Dan volunteered to stay home with their children and encouraged Eileen to take advantage of the rare get-together. Gary insisted on driving Noreen there because he didn't trust her with their new SUV on country roads, especially on a foggy, drizzly day like today. They arrived within minutes of each other, and Maggie was thankful because it meant she only had to introduce them all and explain her daughter Mara's existence once. As introductions were made, Mara suspected that there was something else to the deepness of their shock of meeting her.

Eileen came forward and hugged her niece like she'd always been part of their lives, then turned to hug Maggie with equal fervor.

"I knew you couldn't have done it," she whispered so Mara couldn't hear. "Thank you for your courage. I'm so proud to call you my sister." Her words brought a slight tremble to Maggie's lip and her eyes glistened with tears held in place.

Noreen wanted to hug Mara in the same manner, but with the judgmental eyes of Gary watching, she restrained herself and tried to transfer the warmth she felt through her smile and a quick handshake. When Gary shook her hand, he said, "Nice to meet you," but never met Mara's eyes. Clare noticed the slight, and of course so did Maggie.

Gary took advantage of the moment when Noreen excused herself upstairs to use the bathroom to tell the sisters he was planning an early sixtieth birthday party for her next June. It was a surprise event and would be catered at his parents' home on Skaneateles Lake. The sisters were surprised, all right; he rarely celebrated anything about Noreen's life. She'd spent a good deal of their marriage trying to achieve the always out-of-reach standards he set for her. Once menopause hit, she stopped trying to be a Pomeroy and was just happy to be herself. One good outcome from that was the rivalry she once had with Clare subsided. Lately they'd taken to emailing weekly updates to each other and with her command of the English language, plus her inner psychologist, Clare suspected as she read the emails that things were not rosy in the Pomeroy household.

Noreen was embarrassed to have Clare and Maggie both see that she'd gained about thirty pounds since the summer. She joked that it was from the French cooking classes she was taking. Eileen feared that she had some deadly disease. Maggie took one look at her face and knew the answer: she was obviously in a loveless marriage. That's why Gary's plans for a sixtieth celebration were so curious to her.

For the first time in many years, the house with the wraparound porch bubbled over with laughter. Molly had poured them glasses of the sparkling Loughmare wine Kerry gave her and the sisters shared funny tales of Christmases past with Mara. Gary was bored out of his gourd, as he liked to say, and told his wife he was going out to the car to listen to the audiobook on Nixon that she gave him for Christmas. Noreen rolled her eyes as he closed the door behind him.

"Men! It's so good to be here with all of my sisters. I

say we dump them all and move back to the house with the wraparound porch for the rest of our lives."

"Yeah! Cheers!" the other sisters said as they clinked champagne glasses. Eileen looked a bit sheepish joining in on the toast. She *did* have a good marriage.

"Would we be able to keep Dan, though?"

Maggie winked and draped her arm over her sister's shoulder. "You're right, Eileen. Dan is a good man. You know, he reminds me of Grandpa Jimmy with that quiet strength. If ever there was a man who should have been cloned it was Jimmy O'Donoghue." Crystal clinked again. "And as for Dan, I say we keep him. What do you guys think?"

"Keep him!" they cheered. "Clone him, too," Molly added. Eileen touched the crucifix around her neck and smiled. How she loved these sisters of hers.

Molly noticed the naked Christmas tree in the living room and then realized to her embarrassment that its decorations were still sitting in boxes below it. She was hoping that Terrie and Maggie would help her with it yesterday but then the Mara chaos ensued.

"Hey, anyone want to help me decorate the tree?"

The sisters rose eagerly to assist her with unpacking the lights, ornaments and metallic "icicles." Maggie held up an old papier-mâché orange and the girls paused with reverence.

"This always goes on first," Maggie told her daughter. "It was hung on the first Christmas tree Grandpa Jimmy and Grandma Mame had."

"Let me string the lights on the tree first," Clare ordered. She unwound the strand of primary color bulbs and tested it first before weaving it through the branches. "OK, now we can hang the orange."

"Mara, I'd like you to have the honor," Maggie said, holding out the frail-looking ornament. She hung it on the where it was visible as soon as you walked in the house.

"Perfect!" Clare said. The others smiled. It was not a compliment that their eldest sister dispensed carelessly.

Mara picked up little Flora, stroking her soft fur as she watched her aunts enjoy reliving their past through the symbolism of each ornament. She loved what she was feeling in this room, having never experienced the bond that only siblings shared. There was endearing warmth among them and she had a feeling that it was a genetic trait handed down from the great-grandparents Mara wished she'd met.

Molly put on a Motown Christmas CD and the sisters soul strutted around the tree as they trimmed it with all manner of sparkling ornament. While they were distracted, Mara glanced out the window and saw Gary parked in the driveway, laughing as he talked on his cell phone in the SUV. *What could be better there than what was going on here? There's so much joy in this room now. Stupid men,* she thought.

Mara left for Cleveland the next day with generations of family stories to sift through on the five-hour drive home and a promise to return for a week-long visit the next summer.

Chapter 32

In May, Molly resumed her porch café. There were now so many people demanding that she add them to the seatings that she had to move her car up the driveway so she could set tables under the porte-cochère. Maggie enjoyed taking a break from her writing to lend a hand along with Alice. Molly needed two assistants by now, and Maggie was equally good with prep work in the kitchen. Austin made a habit of showing up for leftovers after the café, and the three women enjoyed their tradition of sitting on the porch with him, shooting the breeze with a celebratory glass of local wine.

Maggie could tell Molly's feelings for him were deep, so she backed off from her initial attraction to him. It was such a pity that he was married because Maggie felt the pair would make a cool couple. They had so much in common. She wondered what Austin's wife must think about his late return home on these nights (and that brought up uncomfortable memories of her father). On the other hand, he gave the sincere impression that he was a decent man. Perhaps his wife was cheating on him and because he was too honorable (or stupid) to divorce her, this was where he could find solace. *Life is too short for such tiptoeing around private matters*, Maggie thought. It was time to get things out in the open. Molly would probably hate her for this, but she had to speak her mind.

"Next month you'll have to bring your wife along for the leftovers, Austin. She must wonder where you are on these nights."

The sting of her words drew Austin's mouth downward. *I must be right about her cheating,* Maggie thought. Molly was furious and embarrassed that Maggie spoiled the happy vibe. He put his head down and sighed.

"What's the matter? Some trouble at home?" Maggie asked. Molly kicked her sister's foot and made a *stop it* face.

"It's just that, well, guess I thought I'd told you, but my Emily passed on four years ago from breast cancer. That's why I returned home. Too much sadness back there in Wyoming."

Molly gasped. Maggie couldn't decipher if it was from empathy or opportunity.

"Oh, Austin, I'm so sorry," Molly said, touching his arm. "No, you hadn't told us. I didn't realize. All this time I thought the woman working in your shop on Mondays was...."

"Huh? Do you mean Gwendolyn?" He chuckled and then smiled softly as if he was thinking deeply about something. "No, we're not married. I must say she's been a godsend with her office skills and flower arranging talent." He paused and his face shifted back to a solemn demeanor. "Emily was much different."

Molly nodded. "Well, you're so kind and to be honest, Gwendolyn didn't seem as...." She stopped speaking when Maggie gave her a cautionary look, as if to say just let him talk.

"You both would have loved Emily. She was a free spirit, much like a McNamara." That made them smile. "We met one spring day in Jackson Hole. I'd moved out to Wyoming with my buddy Ned from college to escape my impending doom as a dairy farmer in Pulteney. The farm had been in the family for two generations and my father expected me to take the reins after graduating from ag school. Not so fast, I thought, not before I see the world. I made it as far as Wyoming, hah!

"Ned and I met her at the annual elk antler auction in Jackson Hole. Just outside town is a refuge where thousands of elk gather in the winter. They shed their antlers before returning to graze on the mountains in the spring. Every March the Boy Scouts gather them up for an auction downtown. It's a great project because it raises thousands of dollars to sustain the refuge and also supports Scouting.

"I kept seeing this little slip of a woman bidding on antlers that were almost as tall as she was. As she hoisted the antlers into the bed of her pickup I went over and asked if she needed any help. Emily said she didn't need it, but she wouldn't refuse it. Ned and I pitched in and the truck was practically spilling over with antlers by the time she was done bidding.

"Emily asked if we'd like to follow her to her studio to help take them out of the truck. She said she could pay us in beer and bison burgers. Sounded like a good deal. Turns out she was a renowned artist in those parts, designing and selling chandeliers and furniture made with antlers under the name Wapiti Works. You should have seen her art. They could be used like regular furniture yet they were shaped in these fantastic designs. Her creativity was boundless.

"Those burgers we had that night around the campfire were the tastiest I ever had in my life. And the sky, wow, you've never seen the Milky Way that vibrant in the Finger Lakes. Talk about romantic. I thanked my lucky stars that we were married by the time the next auction came around."

He started twisting the elk ring on his left hand and Molly realized it probably *was* his wedding band and he hadn't removed it yet. His wistfulness made Molly uncomfortable. If they were to have a relationship, would he be settling in his mind for second best? Would he ever get over his late wife Emily, or would she always be there in the background? She wanted to say something that would comfort Austin and also show that she appreciated him opening up about her.

"Sounds like Emily was an inventive artist. I know I would have liked her." *Ugh*, she thought. *That was clunky.*

Austin sighed and took a deep sip of his wine. "You would have become good friends, kindred spirits. Sometimes you remind me of her, Molly. More than you know." He smiled as he reached out to pat Molly's hand.

While the gesture toward her was heartfelt, it felt odd, especially noting the way Maggie raised her eyebrow when he did it. It was slightly patronizing, as if he was saying although they were similar, Molly could never replace Emily in his mind. As soon as Austin left, the two sisters discussed what had occurred.

"He's a great guy and nothing would make me happier than to see you two together," Maggie said, "but proceed carefully, Molly. He's obviously not over Emily yet."

Molly couldn't hold back her tears. "Dammit! I finally meet a guy I feel is *the one*, yet he's still in love with his dead wife. Why can't I have love like everyone else? Look at Alice and Gunter! Look at Eileen and Dan! How come they're allowed happiness and not me? Tell me, Maggie! What did I ever do wrong to deserve pain like this?"

Maggie stared across the street at her great-grandparents' former home, noting the sagging roof needed new shingles desperately. It was a good diversion as she gathered her thoughts. She knew there were no words she could speak that would comfort her sister. It wasn't fair. Molly deserved happiness and the love of a good man such as Austin. Then again, she deserved it too.

She stood up from the rocker and stretched as Molly sat there looking broken and helpless. "Be patient. I believe it *will* work for you guys. You just have to give him time."

Molly pondered her sister's advice and frowned. *Yeah, what does he need, like forty more years? We'll probably be in a nursing home by then!*

While she'd been embarrassed by her sister's method of directness for getting the information out of Austin, she was certainly grateful that she had done it. Now she finally knew where she stood with him. Now she knew that there was a sliver of hope where none seemed to exist. What she didn't know was if she had the patience to wait and see if their relationship would grow.

***

Over Memorial Day weekend, all of the sisters got the official invitation in the mail from their brother-in-law Gary to Noreen's surprise sixtieth birthday party on the thirtieth of June. They all responded promptly to his email account and were looking forward to a fun time at the Pomeroys' swanky digs in Skaneateles.

Around that time Molly was busy planning her menu for the June 23rd porch café and came up with a Greek-themed meal. She pictured an appetizer plate with stuffed grape leaves, grilled haloumi cheese and small spanakopita triangles. For the main course she'd grill tenderloins marinated in a ton of garlic and oregano accompanied by kalamata olive couscous and fruit salad with almonds and a honey yogurt dressing. Dessert would include baklava, of course, and an assortment of cookies like those she'd get at the Greek festival back home.

While browsing an antiques market in Branchport, she came across a large set of hand painted dinner plates from Greece with leaping blue dolphins on them. They'd be perfect and she bought them just for the dinner. Rifling through the used CD bin, Molly discovered the soundtrack to *Zorba the Greek*. Perfect! At the checkout she noticed cobalt glass vases in a display behind the cashier and bought them for the tables. Her concept was coming together nicely.

She stopped at Florabundance on her way home to deliver the vases to Austin and make the final flower order for the dinner. Molly felt awkward waiting in his shop for him to finish arranging a late party order with Gwendolyn.

He fussed over the bouquets trying to make them as similar as possible. Gwendolyn struggled with the ribbon bow on the main arrangement as Austin watched over her shoulder.

"Here, darlin', let me...," he said as he reached around her waist to hold down the center of the bow while she looped wire ribbon around it. Gwendolyn tossed her head back laughing and Austin's face was covered by her long hair. It didn't seem to annoy him. And then she touched his wrist when the bow was finished.

Uh-oh, that gesture...she's definitely into him, Molly thought. She wished she could rewind time and go back to when she thought Austin was unavailable. That was easier to stomach than knowing every woman who walked into this flower shop was a potential rival for his affection. Florabundance was doing a lot of business thanks in part to Molly's café. She'd have to make her move on Austin soon, but it would be so much easier if he did it instead.

Unfortunately, the weather that Saturday night of her dinner was awful. A series of torrential downpours—almost biblical in their intensity—passed through the Finger Lakes that evening, making grilling the steaks quite an adventure. (Alice had to hold an umbrella over her as she cooked them.) Of course the guests were dry under the wraparound porch's roof, but the seatings under the porte-cochère had to be moved inside to the dining room table due to the stream of water racing down the driveway. Despite the lousy weather, they handled the dinner with aplomb.

The guests had been gone at least an hour by the time Austin arrived for the post-dinner party.

"I don't like rain the way it falls lately," he said as he filled his plate with leftovers. "It's too intense and the ground is saturated. I think it could affect the crops."

"We're going to start building an ark out back," Maggie laughed. "Speaking of out back: Alice, would you lend me a hand with something in the kitchen?"

When the two women left, Molly finally found the courage to ask Austin something that had been on her mind.

"A week from today my brother-in-law is throwing a surprise party for my sister's sixtieth birthday. It's at his parents' mansion on Skaneateles Lake. Should be quite the spread. Say, would you like to join me, Austin?"

Austin grimaced. Molly's stomach fluttered.

"Damn, wish I'd known sooner. Already have plans for the evening. Thanks for asking though, Molly. Sounds like fun." He patted her hand again. Ugh, the gesture made her feel like a little girl.

Molly and Maggie analyzed Austin's response to her question after he and Alice left.

"Do you think he's seeing someone?" Molly asked, afraid that her observant older sister would say "Yes."

"Hmm, I can't get a solid read on that. It's obvious that you mean a lot to him. Without previously observing his relationships, though, I can't say if he thinks of you romantically or platonically."

Molly put her elbows on the table and tugged at her hair as if she was trying to pull a solution out of her mind.

"This is driving me crazy. I can't stand this not knowing where I stand with him. It puts my life on hold."

"*You're* putting your life on hold. Remember, *you* control the direction of your life, *not* other people. Why don't you look around for someone new?"

"Where, Maggie? Where! Show me where all the men you're talking about are."

"What about Kerry the guitarist. He's kind of sexy, you know, in a dorky way."

Molly shook her head as she thought, that's a fine way to talk about your possible half-brother.

"Not good enough? Hmm, I wouldn't write him off so cavalierly. Listen, sis, I think if you want a relationship so badly maybe you shouldn't keep your standards so high."

Molly shook her head and glared at Maggie as if she were crazy. "It's not that my standards are high, it's that I can't lie. Why should I fake that I'm into a guy just so I can say I'm dating someone? I wouldn't do that to a guy."

Maggie snorted. "Why not? Guys do that *all* the time to women. You know what you need, Molly? You need to get laid. That would cure this situation."

Molly's jaw dropped, then her brows knit together as she pounded her palms on the dining room table, stood up and stomped upstairs without speaking a word to her sister. When she slammed her bedroom door, Maggie nodded. "Uh-hmm, I think that's a 'yes'."

Stormy weather simmered over the next few days. Inside the house an icy chill settled between the two sisters while eighty miles away, a steamy deluge of rain beset Binghamton. Had she not been so mad at Maggie, Molly would have paid more attention to the news about flooding down in the Southern Tier. She first heard about it when Eileen called Thursday night, her voice rising with fear.

"Have you seen the videos from Conklin? I've been trying to get through to Terrie, but she's not answering."

"What videos?"

"Oh, Molly, they're saying it's the worst flooding around Binghamton in a hundred years! Part of Interstate 88 collapsed and two tractor trailers plummeted into the creek."

When they hung up Molly went online to check the flooding reports from the media in her hometown and was horrified. She knocked on Maggie's door, which was closed because she was writing.

"Hey, I'm worried about Terrie. Did you know it's flooding real bad in Conklin? I just saw some news photos on the Web. Eileen called and said she hasn't been able to get in touch with her. Hope she's OK."

Maggie pushed her reading glasses back against her hair like a headband as she looked into her sister's eyes for the first time in days. They shelved the silly malice between them quickly as their focus shifted to the immediate danger confronting Terrie.

"My God, her place *must* be underwater. She's right on the riverbank." The two sisters nodded, thinking of Terrie's home and how it might never recover. "Are the roads passable to Binghamton? Should we try to get down there?"

"I don't think we could reach her place if we wanted to, yet. Do you suppose she's been evacuated?"

"Did you check the newspaper's website? Maybe they have a list of the shelters."

"Good idea. We have plenty of room for her to stay here if she needs to. She'd have her choice of Uncle Pat's old room or the back bedroom."

Maggie nodded. "Do you suppose Noreen's surprise party is still a go? Should we call Gary and let him know?"

"I don't want to talk with him. Why don't we have Eileen ask him?" Molly grinned. Maggie was happy to see her sister smile again.

"Hah-hah! We're such cowards. Great idea."

The phone rang. It was Noreen. Terrie called and told her she'd been evacuated from her home and did not yet know how badly it was damaged. She and Cheryl were able to get all of the pets they were boarding into a rescue boat. Problem was the shelters were not taking any pets. Terrie called her former employer and they were able to take in the rescued animals. She didn't know what to do about her own six cats and dog and she refused to be parted from them. For now they were staying together in her car in the parking lot of a church that was ministering to flood victims. The home was surely damaged, so she needed to figure out where she could stay for a while.

Molly said she had room to take in Terrie, but wasn't too keen on adding all of her cats and the dog. Taking care of Flora was enough for her.

"Oh, Gary would never let me take in all of those pets," Noreen said. *Of course not*, Molly thought, *because he cares more about his freaking furniture than Terrie.*

"I wonder if Eileen and Dan could take in some of the pets," Noreen suggested.

"I bet they could. Surely there's room in the commune. Let me call her, Noreen, and I'll get back to you. If Terrie calls again, tell her she can definitely stay here and we'll see about finding a home for her pets."

As soon as they hung up Clare called. "Did you see the news? I can't get an answer at Terrie's number."

"Noreen spoke with her. She's OK but she doesn't know about her home. We're trying to figure out temporary housing for her."

"Well, it's obvious she'll stay with you. You know Gary won't take her in. By the way, is the party still a go?"

Molly laughed. "We think so. Maggie and I are too afraid to call him though. We were hoping Eileen would do the deed for us."

That made Clare laugh. "Why are we all so intimidated by that jerk?"

Eileen and Dan were happy to welcome not just Terrie but also her pet entourage. There was plenty of room at the commune for them and Terrie could stay on their couch, she told Molly. It was no bother for her to call Gary and ask about the party, too. If her sister answered, she'd pretend she was calling to let Noreen know that she'd help Terrie. The commune had a fenced yard where the dog could stay during the day. Eileen had no qualms about cats running through her house. It brought back fond memories from El Salvador of waking up to see the neighbor's chicken in her room. With five kids, her house was always in a state of chaos, too.

Circles of phone calls were made and on Friday, when

Terrie was finally able to get out of the flood zone, she drove to Eileen's, made the pets comfortable and then showered and changed into clean clothes for Noreen's surprise party (she'd been able to fill two suitcases before the evacuation). "I feel so bad that I have nothing to give her," Terrie said in the back of the van sandwiched between Eileen and Dan's two teenage daughters, Thèrése and Esperanza. Their oldest daughter Dorothy and son Francis couldn't come because they were working at a youth peace camp near Rochester that day. Kateri, their youngest daughter, was at a fiddler's school in the Berkshires.

"Terrie, don't be silly. Your presence is a gift enough after what you've been through. I'm so glad you're here with us," Eileen said as she turned and smiled at her sister, though worry about her future shone through it.

When they arrived and Terrie saw the Pomeroys' mansion, her eyes filled with tears. Its imposing pillars and rolling lawns of perfectly trimmed fescue was a stark contrast to how little she had back in Conklin. What would she find when the river receded? Did she even still have a home?

The Pomeroys erected large tents near the lake's shore, and although Gary told them casual dress was fine for the party, it was apparent that he meant country club casual. Eileen drew many stares for her sleeveless Indian gauze dress and sensibly clunky vegan clogs, her silver crucifix on a chain serving as her lone adornment. Terrie wore flip flops, distressed jean shorts and a rhinestone studded tiger T-shirt, drawing even more stares. The sisters had not seen Gary's parents since the wedding and Mrs. Pomeroy smiled rigidly as she scanned their attire disapprovingly. Clare, however, earned Mrs. Pomeroy's approval for her beige espadrilles, elegantly paired white slacks and a periwinkle boat-neck top, receiving an air kiss as endorsement.

For the surprise setup Gary told Noreen they were going to a graduation party for his nephew, Brent, so she wasn't startled to see the big tent when they arrived. Her in-laws had refined the art of over-the-top parties. Everyone watched for her reaction when Gary led her into the tent and a hundred people yelled "Happy Birthday!" It wasn't the gape-mouthed, hands-on-cheeks look of shock they were expecting. Noreen looked mad as a batted wasp and she confirmed her expression by slapping Gary across the face and marching up the lawn back to their SUV in the circular driveway. Eileen drew Thèrése and Esperanza close to her as the argument unfolded.

Gary's face reddened. He held one finger up to the guests. "Hold on, people. My wife just hates surprises and she's not crazy about the fact that she's turning sixty. We'll be right back." He jogged up the hill to retrieve her as the McNamara sisters raised their eyebrows at each other. Mrs. Pomeroy whispered to her husband and pointed at them.

"What the hell was that all about, Norry? My parents went to a lot of trouble putting this party on for you. That's some thanks you just showed them."

"Outside of your parents and my family, I don't know anyone here. Is this really to celebrate my birthday, or is this a public display to prove what a thoughtful husband you are?

Well, wouldn't they all be surprised to know you've been sleeping with the principal's secretary!"

"I apologized. What *more* do you want, Norry? It was one lousy time! Can't we move on? Is this because of your menopause? Maybe you need to go back to your doctor and get some anti-anxiety meds and more hormones."

"Why do you really want me to get them? Are you more concerned about my never-ending hot flashes or the fact that you haven't gotten sex from me in six months?"

Clare unfortunately reached the quarrelling couple just as Noreen let slip her embarrassing personal truth. She'd wanted to make sure her sister was OK, but from the look on Noreen's face she knew she'd inadvertently made things much worse.

"Boy, this must make you happy, Clare! Guess you've *finally* won."

"*Won?* Won what? What on earth are you talking about, Noreen?"

"You've always been better at everything. Now the one thing I held over you has been ruined! How fortunate you are, Clare, always taking home the prize."

Clare couldn't believe what she was hearing. She glanced at Gary who stood there awkwardly like he didn't know what to do. Was this more about her sisters than him?

"Get the hell away from her, you jerk!" Clare barked.

He was stunned by her swipe at him, yet she appeared angrier than his crazy wife at the moment. Gary wisely heeded Clare's snarl and hurried back to the tent. Noreen guffawed at the sight of him fleeing down the hill.

"What?" Clare had no idea what her sister was thinking.

"How'd you do that?" Noreen said as she wiped a tear from her left cheek.

"Do what?"

"Get my husband to obey you like a dog? I do believe his tail was between his legs when he skittered off." Now both sisters were laughing, so hard in fact they stumbled where they were standing. The guests down below suspected they were drunk.

Clare's face regained seriousness first. "Noreen, what was all that nonsense about me just now?"

Her sister sighed deeply to the soles of her feet. "I always wanted to be like you, Clare. You have it all: brains, beauty, success, men fighting over you."

Clare snorted and put her hands on her hips. "Who sold you that boatload of crap?"

"C'mon, everything you've done has been a fabulous success. I've always been second best."

Clare snorted. "That's utterly ridiculous! For your information, Noreen, I always wanted to be more like you! To me you had it all: beauty, a job you loved, the perfect family with two handsome sons to carry on the family name. Your life has so much security. Mine always feels like it's going to break apart at any second."

"Yeah but you have the excitement of Manhattan with all those great restaurants and museums and Broadway...."

"And bedbugs and noise all night long and impatient people and crowded sidewalks. What I'd give to be able to have a nice quiet sleep and not wake up in a cold sweat worried that I'd missed a major plot flaw in a book already rolling off the presses."

Noreen clasped her hands and gave her sister a bemused look. "Hmph! So all the time that I was jealous of you, you wanted to be me?" Clare scrunched her mouth, raised an eyebrow and nodded.

"By the way, you can have my job if you want it because it's not mine anymore."

"You've retired?"

"I wish. Nope. The publishing company just laid me off. They wanted to end the fiscal year in the black. Most of us long-timers got the severance plan."

"*What?* Oh, Clare, I'm so sorry. Do the others know?"

"Not yet. I figured Terrie's loss was greater. And now to hear what's going on with you...."

"That bastard cheated on me. Christmastime, can you believe it? Remember when he went out to the car while we were chatting with Mara? They were setting up their tryst."

"Oh, you've got to be kidding," Clare said as she shaded her grimacing face with her hands. "I'm so sorry, Noreen. Look at you! You're gorgeous! You don't look sixty at all!" As she hugged her sister Noreen started to cry again. She knew she'd gained weight and had lost some of her beauty. She also knew that Clare never made false compliments.

"And by the way little Sis, you don't own the record for cheating bastards. I do believe I beat you to that. His name was Matthew."

Noreen laughed as she pulled away from her sister's embrace. "See what I mean. I'm always second to you. Hah!" They stood in silence for a few minutes looking at the puzzled guests down below. "What do I do now? I can't face those people. Frankly, I don't want to spend any time with them at all."

"Why should you? Let's grab the others and go somewhere for a bite."

"Oh, yeah, I could *so* rip into a cheeseburger now. I'd rather be helping Terrie fix up her house anyway than wasting hours in halting conversation with these boors."

"Great! Let's figure out a plan for Terrie over burgers and beers." Clare hugged her sister once more, then they crossed the lawn arm in arm to fetch their sisters.

"So you've come to your senses, Norry?" Gary said smugly.

"As a matter of fact, I have. And by the way, the name's *Noreen*. Don't wear it out, you cheating BASTARD!"

Gary cursed at them as they deserted the party. At least they had an actual excuse to turn it into a graduation party for his nephew now. Dan took his stunned daughters back home to Ithaca while the sisters headed to Noreen's favorite sports bar in Cortland.

When they walked inside they were assaulted by the din from competing big screen TVs, blathering baseball announcers vs. grunting tennis stars. All six sisters squished together at a circular table near the bar and scanned menus the waitress tossed at them. The air smelled like deep-frying Buffalo chicken wings.

Despite what had occurred, the tone of their conversation was pleasant. Everyone caught up since they'd last been together. Molly gave Terrie some photos of Flora who'd grown quite a bit since Christmas. Eileen asked Clare for publishing advice about a book of meditative essays she planned describing her experiences in El Salvador. Maggie asked Noreen about her twin sons who owned a software design company in Dallas. Neither of the eldest sisters let on to the others about the sadness weighing on their minds.

Their beer and food arrived quickly, which made them happy. Terrie grabbed an onion ring and was just about to bite it, when her eyes glanced at the headline news network on the screen above the cash register. The other sisters noticed her freeze suddenly like a pointer dog and followed her eyes to the screen.

It was a newscast about the flooding near Binghamton and the reporter exclaimed "You won't believe this!" as video footage showed a house swept up by the swift current of the Susquehanna impale itself on a bridge in downtown Binghamton.

Terrie dropped the onion ring like a tiny lifesaver onto her plate as her hand pointed to the TV. The sisters saw the impact of the roof ripping off the house and lumber smashing into smithereens with a terrifying noise that sounded like scaffolding collapsing.

"That was Elvin's house!" Terrie's lower lip jutted out like a storm drain to catch the tears rushing down her face.

"Are you sure?" Clare asked. Terrie nodded with closed eyes.

"His roof had half green and half red shingles on it like that. He needed to repair a leak where some flashing rotted underneath the shingles on the backside of the house. The red ones were on sale and he said, 'No one's gonna see the difference except the trees and they won't talk.'" She laughed slightly through her tears. "I was thinking about having the roof redone this year."

The sisters kept one eye on the terrifying footage as they reached out to touch Terrie's hands that were knit together on the tabletop as if she was praying.

"That home was his lifesaver. He used to tell me that when I took care of him after the stroke. He was pretty bad, couldn't do any basic self-care anymore. It wasn't easy, but I'd been used to equally messy work taking care of cats and dogs all of these years. Elvin used to call me his guardian angel, because I promised that I'd do my best to keep him there instead of stuffing him into a nursing home to die. And I did. I set his wheelchair on the back screened porch most days so he could watch the river while I worked next door. He could use his right hand a little and so if he needed help he'd call me on the walkie-talkie I put on the table next to him. Elvin wanted to pay me, but I refused it. I wouldn't charge any of you either if I was taking care of you—or even your pets. The doctor didn't want him to drink, but I knew that giving him one beer with his dinner wasn't going to matter much. Heck, he was already in his eighties. Let the man live a little."

Terrie clutched her napkin. "The thing that makes me so sad was that I wasn't there when he died. He was so kind to me. I shoulda been there." Maggie rubbed her back as Terrie sobbed. "I thought it was odd that he didn't call me on the walkie-talkie that morning, because he pretty much was on a schedule of when he'd need help. I was grooming a collie that had a mess of burrs caught in her fur, and was so distracted that I didn't notice he hadn't called until past his lunchtime. When he didn't answer my call on the walkie-talkie, I ran over there. But he'd already passed." Her sisters' hearts were breaking to hear this story for the first time. Terrie acted as a background character in their busy lives and never spoke much about her world. How could they have been so insensitive to not realize that though she was different, she experienced the same emotions they all did?

"But what really, really got me when I found him slumped in the wheelchair, was remembering that after I made him breakfast that morning, he squeezed my hand and said, 'You're the daughter I never had, Terrie.' What kind of daughter isn't there when her father dies?" Her body shook as she let her tears flow freely.

Maggie knew Terrie's words meant no ill toward her, yet she felt like they kicked her in the gut. Eileen sensed that, and draped her arm around Maggie, pulling her near. The others all thought about the loss of their father and how much they missed their mother.

"And you know what," Terrie continued, "If his house floated away, that probably means my business and home are gone, too."

Chapter 33

They waited for the five-foot deep floodwaters to recede the following Monday so they could drive from Binghamton down Route 7 to see what had happened to Terrie's home in Conklin. At Eileen's insistence, the sisters got tetanus booster shots at a flood relief center and while there, Clare picked up a couple of the free cleanup kits and respirator masks. Noreen also grabbed them bottled water; the sun was blistering hot and with all the standing water around, it would be easy to get overheated doing a simple task.

As they made their way down the main road slowly, the sisters were stunned by the science fiction-like scenes of destruction. Car oil twirled in rainbow streaks across puddles in front of homes with dirty waterline marks halfway up the first floor windows. Volunteers in muddied boots tugged rolls of filthy soaked carpet to the curb. Buckled bookcases, kitchen chairs, pole lamps and picnic tables teetered in haphazard stacks like surreal jungle gyms. Young men wielding snow shovels pushed foot-deep sludge out of garages. Pink fiberglass insulation and wallboard piles rose higher than the workers, creating mini-Himalayas of debris. Soggy clothes that had been hung on tree branches to dry fluttered like Buddhist prayer flags.

All sorts of random belongings lay tossed across the landscape as they turned down Terrie's road. A soccer ball was wedged high up in the crook of a willow tree branch. A recliner tilted back with its leg rest fully extended as it faced the chocolate-brown river. A full-sized plastic Santa leaned against a refrigerator lying on its side, looking like he was tipsy on eggnog. Beyond the evergreens up ahead was Terrie's property, and Molly held her hand as the car approached slowly, swerving around a child-sized mattress in the road.

She shrieked when they passed the line of trees.

"It's still there! It's still there! Oh my God!"

Clare parked the car in the road and they went to examine the damage Terrie's house sustained. At the foot of the driveway was a single glitter-covered red ballet flat with mucky rhinestone baubles.

"Look!" Terrie said pointing at the forlorn slipper. "It's a sign. There's no place like home!" She grinned widely, but her sisters looked grimly at the twisted wire fence, a felled tree blocking access to the back yard (wondering if it had damaged the back of the house) and the debris-strewn lawn. The smell of dank mud was almost suffocating and Clare reached for the masks.

Eileen noticed a neon orange spray-painted symbol on the front of the house. There was a large X with letters or numbers in each of its quadrants. Next to that was a square with a slash in it. "What's that graffiti?" she asked.

As Terrie slid her key in the front door lock, a National Guardsman called out to her.

"Hey there! Ma'am, I can't let you go inside. Your house is not safe."

"But...why not?"

"See these markings? We left them when we checked the neighborhood for victims. On the left is the code for our division, the 6-29 on top is the date we checked your house, this empty space means no hazards like a gas leak, and down below, the Ø shows no bodies were found. What's most important to you is this square with a slash in it. That means this structure is unsafe for entry."

"But I just want my business records and they're inside the living room."

Her pleading look touched him, but he had to be firm. "Don't risk it, ma'am. If I recall, we marked your house because that tree smashed the back wall off leaving it exposed. I cannot verify that it would be safe to enter just the front room. You're going to have to wait until that back part is stabilized. OK?"

He tipped the visor of his cap and continued on up the street. All six sisters linked arms as they stood in silence on the lawn for a few minutes staring at the house that represented all of Terrie's dreams. The hot sun burned against their backs.

A loud boom thundered a few blocks away.

"What the hell was that?" Maggie said as she turned to look behind them.

"Was that a gas explosion? Yikes! We better get out of here." Clare looked frightened; that didn't happen often.

"But all my belongings are in there!" Terrie pouted. It pained her sisters to see her so distraught.

"Just tell us what you want most inside there and

where it's located," Clare ordered.

Terrie closed her eyes and reviewed the interior of her house.

"My comic book collection is upstairs in my bedroom. And my Star Trek DVDs are by the TV and...."

"Terrie, *focus*!" Maggie interrupted. "If your house was on fire and you had three minutes to grab something, what would it be?"

Her words upset Terrie even more and she jammed her hands into her jean pockets as she kicked the mud. "My business records are in the file cabinet just around the corner from the front door. I have some family photos on the top shelf of the bookcase in the living room. And I'd get the painting of Tiberius over the TV. There's also a teacup and saucer from Great-Grandma Virginia on a shelf in the entryway."

"I'll get them," Maggie said, stepping forward as she put on a respirator mask and pair of latex gloves. Someone stand by the door in case I call for help. The others should watch out for that guard and let me know if he comes back this way."

Silt deposited by the wayward Susquehanna limited how far she could push open the front door. Maggie used all her body weight to shove it back farther and created a space barely wide enough for her to slip through. She was stunned by what she saw inside. When the floodwaters surged they churned the home's furnishings like a blender. Chairs and tables tumbled into upended stacks. The clothes dryer was parked where the couch used to be and the file cabinet with her business records was unreachable in the far corner of the room. Maggie was upset to see the bookcase had fallen face first, so all of those photos Terrie wanted were trapped underneath. The painting of Tiberius the dog was still hanging on the wall, as were the teacup and saucer. She stepped on the bookcase, sliding a little from the greasy mud, and unhooked the framed canvas, then slid it out the door to Eileen. Maggie peeked inside the closet and saw some of Terrie's short coats had not been touched by the water (though they were permeated with a mildew smell). She handed them out the door to Molly. Maggie would have explored more, but she heard the house frame creaking from the heat outside and it made her nervous. She took down the cup and saucer, holding them next to her heart as she scanned the room for anything of value that could be recovered easily.

Foreboding black mold crept past the watermark on the kitchen wall and the sour odor of rotting food made her gag. This house would never recover, Maggie thought. *Poor Terrie, she's never done a mean thing in her life. Karma, why are you treating her so badly*, she thought. Maggie stepped back slowly toward the door and her eye caught a small porcelain sculpture of a beagle in a curio cabinet within reach. The little dog had not been touched by the floodwaters, and she stuck it in her pocket. Terrie burst into tears when Maggie dropped it into her hands. It had been a gift from Elvin. Terrie took that as a sign that her life would be OK, just not today.

Her neighbor Thresa came over to commiserate

about their damage. Terrie introduced her sisters and as they were talking about the incomprehensible destruction, another loud bang shook the neighborhood. When Thresa saw the fear on the sisters' faces she laughed.

"Don't worry, hons. That's just another refrigerator filled with rotting food bursting in the sun."

"Get out!" Maggie said. "That's what that noise was?"

"Yep. Seen it with my own two eyes. My fiancé Tom and his buddy drug our 'fridge out of the kitchen and set it on the lawn over there yonder. He forgot to empty it. It was so hot, gases built up inside and it just went *kablam!* Hah-hah! Door flew clear across our yard. Still there, in fact."

The sisters were eager to get out of the "war zone" and dropped Terrie back in Ithaca to spend the night with her pets at Eileen's home. Over the next couple of months Clare hired a contractor to shore up the back of the house so a professional flood cleanup crew could get in, gut the contaminated walls and floors and put them at the curb for pickup. Volunteers from a Christian organization in North Carolina helped Terrie go through what was left of her belongings—it wasn't much.

With the high cost of construction, Clare knew that rebuilding would be far more expensive than its current worth and what little flood insurance Terrie had for free from the government would not be able to touch that cost. Hopefully she'd receive relief funding to cover basic needs for salvaging what she could from her home and eventually get a buyout for her property. Terrie had to face the truth: her riverside paradise was gone forever. Luckily Molly welcomed her permanently into her home into the spare room next to Maggie's. The pets were quite happy to stay on the commune in Ithaca where they got a lot of attention and her dog had plenty of buddies to roam with. At least they weren't far away from Terrie if she needed to visit them. In the meantime, Flora became *her* cat.

Chapter 34

Clare spent the summer with Molly, Maggie and Terrie since it was closer to Binghamton for helping with the flood recovery effort and paperwork. Molly continued her monthly porch café and her sisters enjoyed being part of them. Terrie set up, bussed and cleaned the tables, Maggie assisted with the cooking and Clare got involved with reservations and menu planning, offering exotic ideas from her world travels. Molly embraced each suggestion enthusiastically because they broadened her cooking skills.

When she went to order the flowers for the café in late July, Clare accompanied Molly to Florabundance. Both Austin and Gwendolyn were working, and as Molly discussed design options with Austin, Clare observed carefully his body language toward her sister, then Gwendolyn's reaction to their interactions and then the way he touched Gwendolyn when checking the centerpieces she was making for a winery dinner.

There was a marked contrast in his behavior toward each woman, and from the way her face flushed when he neared Gwendolyn, Clare suspected the two were having an intimate relationship. She didn't have the heart to tell Molly; she figured the truth would be made known soon enough.

"OK, Molly, I'll see you Saturday," he said walking them out. "By the way, I have a special surprise for the after party to celebrate your success."

Molly beamed and winked at Austin as she turned to leave. "I look forward to it."

He arrived after the café just as Terrie and Clare were wiping down the tables before folding them up to put in the old garage out back. Austin carried the tables away, two at a time and Clare ran ahead to open the garage for him. Molly and Maggie were washing dishes as they saw him pass by the kitchen window.

"Oh, he's here," Molly said. "How do I look?"

Maggie fluffed her sister's hair and stood back. "Gorgeous as usual."

"What do you suppose he's brought me as a surprise?"

"If you're lucky, himself on a platter."

The sisters giggled as they heard porch chairs being dragged back outside.

"Where's the best chef in the world?" Austin asked as he came into the kitchen holding a gift-wrapped bottle that he handed Molly as he kissed her cheek. "This is for later, darlin'. Hmm, Something smells intoxicating and I'm not talking about the platter o' meat on the dining room table."

Molly blushed. "Alice brought me back some perfume from her anniversary trip to Paris. Isn't it pretty?" Austin leaned in for a better whiff.

"There's definitely jasmine, maybe some orris root and a hint of rose, am I right?" Molly shrugged, she was just happy to have him invade her personal space.

The sisters and Austin filled up their plates and headed out to the porch to sit down. It took Molly a few seconds to realize that there were rocking chairs for all of them including one to spare.

"Wait a minute," she said, "where did the other rockers come from?"

"Surprise! Gwendolyn told me about them. She found them at an antiques barn on the West Lake Road."

"Wow, they're a perfect match!"

"I know! Just a little token of appreciation for all the great meals you've fed me and the new business contacts. These dinners have really helped to get my name out there. I'm deeply grateful, Molly. Here's to much more culinary success." They raised their wineglasses to clink with his.

It was a lovely summer evening with faint light on the western horizon. The air was pleasant and not humid. Even the crickets seemed content; their chatter took on a purring quality.

Molly sighed. It had been a tough year in many ways, but tonight seemed impervious to the bad luck the family had been experiencing. As she watched her sisters and Austin dining happily on her art, it brought such joy to her heart.

"What a perfect night," she said softly, almost to herself. Austin heard her though.

"It's about to get better," he said as a car pulled in the driveway. Molly was surprised to see Gwendolyn get out of it and climb the porch steps.

"Oh damn, there goes the bliss," Clare mumbled to Maggie. She nodded. They held their breath waiting to learn what this arrival would portend.

"Gwendolyn? What are you doing here?" Molly asked.

"Hope you don't mind," Austin said as he slipped his right arm around Gwendolyn's waist and lifted his wineglass in his left hand. When Molly saw the gesture she noticed his elk wedding band was missing just as Austin said, "Friends, we have an announcement." She felt her stomach rise to her throat and braced herself to force a smile when the words she knew would be coming did indeed follow. What she wasn't expecting was his added bit of information that once they got married they'd be moving to Asheville, North Carolina, where Gwendolyn was from. They'd bought a successful florist business there and also hoped to get involved with the state's budding wine industry.

Molly was the first to congratulate Gwendolyn and she had a feeling that when she hugged Austin he knew how difficult a gesture it was for her. She fixed a plate of food for his fiancé and gave her the seat she had next to him.

"Anyone need more wine?" she asked, then headed for the kitchen where she cried quietly, washed her face with cold water and returned with filled glasses and a smile. Molly held it together until they left and the sisters gathered in the kitchen to put away the last of the food and dishes.

"Are you OK?" Clare asked. That's all Molly needed to hear, and before her first sob Clare had folded her tightly in her arms.

"I'm so sorry," Terrie said, patting Molly's shoulder. "He's such a nice guy."

"There's got to be another guy out there even better that you're about to meet, Sis," Maggie whispered. "I can feel it." She excused herself and went out to the front porch for a cigarette. Clare followed.

"I expected that was coming," she said to Maggie.

"Why do men have to be such assholes?" Maggie shook her head. "Damn, it breaks my heart to see Molly so hurt."

Terrie went up to her bedroom to read the latest graphic novel she'd bought leaving Molly alone in the kitchen. She leaned against the cupboards in the unforgiving fluorescent light, the hum of a bad ballast mildly annoying her. She folded her arms like she was in a straitjacket and made the angriest face she could muster. This routine was so tiring. *Oh great, I enabled him to buy that new business, to get married to Gwendolyn and to eventually move away from me. Always the bridesmaid, never the bride*, she thought. That made her angrier. The gift-wrapped bottle Austin gave her sat atop the refrigerator unopened. Not tonight. She couldn't bear to expend one ounce more of energy on that man.

***

The McGraths invited their McNamara cousins to the family cottage on Keuka Lake for a reunion that August. Maggie contacted Mara and asked if she could plan her visit then. She'd get to meet more of her family. Cousin Gerry and his wife Joan, plus their kids Martin, Michael, James and Kate—all married now with children—would be there, so it would be an epic gathering.

Mara took the whole week off from work and stayed with her mother and aunts. Maggie's heart leapt when she was reunited with her daughter. She realized how much she'd missed Mara, even though they kept in frequent contact via email. One of the first things they did was pour glasses of wine and sit on the porch together. Mara sat in her great-grandfather's favorite rocker.

"You don't know how long I've been waiting to rock in this chair, Mom. Oh, this is such an awesome porch! I can imagine how pretty it looks during Aunt Molly's dinners."

"You know, something magical occurs when you sit here—especially in that chair, Mara. Maybe it's the sound of bent wood creaking on these old floorboards. Or maybe it's the evening breeze rustling the maple leaves while katydids start rubbing their wings together as if winding up an old Victrola...," she paused. "Did you know this street used to be lined with majestic elm trees? The view was enthralling as you walked up the hill from town. It looked like an alley of tall fountains. One by one they were felled by Dutch elm disease, though. Ah, the transitoriness of life!"

Mother and daughter sat together in pleasant silence for several minutes until it was broken by the sound of an approaching car that turned into the driveway of McGrath's former house across the street. A man from the realty in town carried a sign that said "SOLD" which he pounded into the front lawn. He waved at the two women, got in his car and left.

A couple of days later, Maggie and Mara went into town to buy groceries. The reunion at the cottage was a covered dish supper and they were going to make Vietnamese pork *bánh tráng* rolls, a recipe Maggie perfected when she lived in San Francisco. They were in the produce department when they overheard a conversation by two elderly women standing behind them by the watermelon bin.

"Did you hear someone bought the old McGrath place?"

"I heard he's an architect from Rochester. Not married."

"Those single McNamara sisters across the street will be fighting over him."

Mara winked at her mother. "You get first dibs, Mom," she whispered. Maggie pinched her playfully as they giggled.

"Well you know what Kitty told me many years ago? One of those girls is a half-sister to the others." Maggie's eyes grew wide at the smoking gossip grenade lobbed unexpectedly at their feet. She held her breath as she waited for the ensuing explosion.

"Which one? And which spouse cheated?" The two old women guffawed.

"Well, with that family, you never know." Maggie was fuming and she wanted to grabbed the ripest tomatoes from the bin and splatter them across the old women's faces.

"Kitty said it was...." She strained to hear the name but it was drowned out by the shopping cart wrangler rolling a clattering metal train into the store entrance.

Dammit, Maggie thought. She lingered in the produce section until she was sure the women had moved on. Later as they set the grocery bags in the car trunk she asked Mara if she heard the name.

"No, and I was trying to hear her, too."

Maggie turned down Keuka Street to show Mara where her parents once lived. Up the street the old woman who knew their family secret pushed a filled grocery cart up the sidewalk. Maggie half wanted to slam on the brakes, jump out and demand the truth from the busybody. She'd probably give the woman a heart attack, though, and then the family would *really* have a family secret.

The writer in her, and also the surprising, steadily growing spiritual side of her, knew that nothing happens by chance. Each action, no matter how small, must advance the plot of the story. She was meant to hear that gossip and the noise of the shopping carts was meant to prevent her from hearing the truth. Why? How would this propel the family story forward?

Maggie considered the possibility for each sister as they drove home. "You know, my mother and father had to get married. Clare was the reason," she said.

"Hmm, then that rules her out, don't you think? If they weren't both involved, why bother forcing them to get hitched. Right?"

Mara's logic was correct, Maggie thought. *So which one of the other five sisters is it?*

"Promise me you won't mention this to anyone, OK?"

"Of course, Mom. I can help you dig up details through research. Remember, I had to do all that work on my own adoption."

Maggie nodded. *Yes,* she thought, *the story shall be written by two investigative reporters that discover the news by accident. Who better to unearth the family truth?*

"I've got news, ladies," Maggie said as she carried groceries into the kitchen. "The house across the street was bought by an architect from Rochester. A single architect that is." Each sister smiled as she wondered who it would be and was the man available, was he in their age group and was he handsome?

"We'll have to ask the McGraths today," Clare said. "I'm so glad he's an architect. Bet the first thing he does is repair that sagging roof."

"Maybe he could give me some advice about putting an addition on here," Molly said with a grin.

"Someone's here," Terrie called from the living room. "Hey! It's Noreen!" She ran onto the porch to greet her sister and noticed she seemed upset as she took her suitcase out of the car trunk. As soon as her sisters began hugging her, Noreen dissolved into a torrent of tears.

In between the sobs, the sisters were able to discern that Gary left her. Things just got worse at home after her disastrous birthday party. He moved in with the secretary and surprise—*not*—had never ended their affair as he'd said. Gary blamed it all on the fact that Noreen was no longer taking care of herself like she did when they met. She had gained weight, close to fifty pounds Clare guessed, and she knew that each pound was measured in misery and a sense of abandonment.

"Bastard!" Maggie said, wondering as she hugged Noreen if she was the half-sister.

"Please don't tell any of the McGraths about this. I'm

not ready to make it public."

"Don't worry, Noreen. We'll stay by your side and if the topic of Gary comes up we'll create a diversion," Clare said. "Keuka swear?"

Just when the five sisters raised their hands together in Y shapes, Eileen walked through the front door.

"Wait, you're Keuka swearing without me?" she said with a laugh as she dropped her suitcase and ran toward the others with open arms. She'd come alone; Dan was taking Esperanza to summer college orientation in Purchase. He, Francis and Thèrése were going to hike in the Catskills afterward.

Later that day Terrie counted how many relatives were present at the McGrath family reunion: twenty-six! It was sweaty and noisy and fun. Thankfully, no one asked for an update on Noreen's husband Gary. The high point of the day was the massing of the family on the lawn by the lake for a photo portrait. Mara watched her cousin Martin line them up under the shade of a massive willow tree.

"Hey, daughter!" Maggie yelled, "Get your ass over here. Now!" Mara blushed as she squished between her aunts. *How wonderful to belong to such a cool family like this*, she thought. Martin set the timer, pressed the button and ran into the crowd to pose.

The cousins with young children left shortly after dinner. Next the college-age generation headed into town for a pub crawl. That left the adults who lingered for hours to reminisce about the previous generations who'd watched countless beautiful sunsets from this very porch. And tonight was no exception. Mara soaked in as much of the atmosphere as she could, planning to write about it in her journal later that night.

"Do you know anything about the guy who bought the old McGrath homestead across from us?" Maggie asked Martin as she poured herself another glass of wine. Eileen had been keeping track and it looked like Maggie was up to her fifth by then.

"Yeah, I do. Get this, his grandfather built your house. I think his name was Albert Rotils."

"Fascinating!" Clare said holding out her empty wineglass toward the bottle in Maggie's hand. "You don't suppose he wants to buy our place?"

"Watch out, Molly," Maggie teased as she filled her sister's glass sloppily. "It's all part of his plan to marry you for your property."

"Yeah, right," she snorted. "You'll all end up living across the street. Ahem, my wineglass is also empty."

"Guess I'm the designated driver," Eileen said, not in a judgmental tone but one that the non-sober sisters took as a warning that she was tracking their beverage intake.

"So cousins, got any family tree dirt to dish? Anything you've been holding in all these years?" Maggie said, watching all four of her cousins' faces to see if there was the slightest hint of nervousness.

James leaned back in his chair. "I guess Aunt Bertha was quite a wild one. Too bad she left most of her wealth to Corning."

"Who was she?" Mara asked.

The sisters counted generations in their heads. Eileen totaled them the quickest. "She was your great-great-great-aunt, Mara."

"She *was* great," Maggie said, her words slurring slightly. "Bertha ran a friggin' railroad empire. She traveled the world. Bet she had a lover on every continent, too."

"Maggie! She wasn't like that at all," Eileen corrected. "Bertha was a savvy businesswoman in an age where most women were confined to lives of servitude, not unlike what I saw in El Salvador."

"Someday I want to hear all about your Peace Corps adventure," Mara said to her aunt.

"I witnessed some unspeakable things there, Mara. I'm afraid I haven't even divulged most of what happened to my own sisters."

"What sort of things?" Terrie asked.

Eileen closed her eyes and her face shifted into a deeply pained expression. "Now is not the time. This is a joyful occasion. Right?"

"What the hell, we're sharing family secrets, Eileen. Don't hold anything back. Man, by the look on your face, did something awful happen there? Were you raped?"

Everyone in the room gasped.

"Maggie!" Clare said, trying to hush her sister.

As if on cue, the McGrath brothers got up to get more beer in the kitchen and then lingered on the back porch. Their sister Kate joined them shortly.

"Wow, those McNamara sisters have serious baggage. Glad we didn't get any of their father's blood," she said.

Maggie poured her sixth glass of wine. "Where did all those McGraths go? Chicken shits, they're all afraid of sharing a little family secret."

"I don't think you need more wine," Eileen said with a roll of her eyes.

"Don't tell me what to do, Sis, that is, if you really *are* my sister."

"Mom, don't...," Mara said as she touched her mother's arm.

"Don't what, tell them what we found out today?"

Clare set down her wineglass. "What the hell are you talking about, Maggie?"

Maggie laughed to herself as she sat back in her chair. Clare and the other sisters looked at Mara, as if pleading with their eyes for her to explain what was going on.

"We were at the grocery and overheard these old ladies talking and...."

"Some old bag said that one of us is a half-sister!" Maggie blurted.

Molly tilted her head. "What?"

"One of us is just halfway related to the rest."

The sisters looked at each other in the awkward silence, wondering if they were full- or half-blooded sisters.

"So Mara and I think it's not Clare. Remember when Mom said at Noreen's wedding that she *had* to get married. What would be the logic of having to get married if the child wasn't yours?"

Clare nodded.

Molly covered her mouth with her hand. "I bet I'm

the one, because Daddy left right after I was born. Maybe Mom had an affair and he found out and...."

"Mom having an affair? Puleeze!" Maggie laughed and finished her glass of wine. She stared off at the screen windows, noticing that they were not coming into focus well.

"Wait, wasn't there a rumor that she and Tim Lennon had a thing going on?" Noreen asked.

"Yeah, and they danced at your wedding reception after you and Gary left," Terrie added.

A flash of memory made Eileen gasp. When she cleaned out her mother's dresser after she died, she'd found an old embroidered handkerchief tucked under a false drawer in her jewelry chest. She realized now that it carried Tim Lennon's monogram.

"If I remember it right," Clare said, "the rumor started because of your blonde hair, Maggie. You have the same coloring as Tim Lennon did."

"Oh God, I hope I'm not related to that dull man."

"Hey, I dated his son Kerry. He's a really nice guy."

"So wait, if Tim *was* my father then that means you were dating my half-brother, right? Hah-hah!"

"Oh God, I hope not!"

"Daddy had green eyes just like yours," Terrie said. "I'm pretty sure he was your father."

"So where does my blonde hair come from then?"

It hit the sisters all at the same time. Of course, who did their mother have the most trouble with growing up?

Maggie recalled their heated exchange at Noreen's wedding. "You're so much like *him!*" Frances had said.

"Oh my God, it *is* me. But who did Daddy cheat with and how did I end up in the family if I wasn't Mom's daughter? *Shit*, I need some fresh air." She staggered to her feet and opened the screen door to go down the steps to the lake. Mara was right behind her, fearful that her mother would stumble on the staircase. Somehow Maggie was able to hold herself together and crossed the lawn to the beach where she walked the narrow plank onto the dock. She plopped down on the end and Mara joined her, dangling their bare feet in the dark water still warmed from hot afternoon. Maggie started crying and Mara hugged her.

"Let it all out, Mom. I'm here for you."

Her sisters could hear Maggie sobbing from the dock below. They were stunned by the revelation.

"Wow, this puts so much of our childhood in perspective," Noreen said.

"Guess Mom and Dad must have adopted her," Eileen said. "Any clue to who was her mother?"

"I'm trying to think of every blonde woman we knew back then," Clare said. "Remember that kid Joey who lived around the corner from us at home? He died when his house caught fire, remember?"

"Vaguely," Noreen nodded, "but didn't he have dark hair?"

"His mother was a blonde though. I recall her walking him to kindergarten. She was pregnant...."

A big splash interrupted her train of thought and then a few seconds later Mara screamed.

"Help! I think Mom's drowning!"

Terrie pushed back her chair and flew down the steps two at a time. She dived off the dock to where her sister was flailing in the water and tried to lift her head above the water. James and Michael heard the commotion and raced down the hill to the dock. They jumped in also to help the two sisters get to shore.

Terrie was fine, a bit out of breath though, but something was wrong with Maggie.

"What's going on?" Clare asked as she pushed through the crowd on the beach. Maggie lay unconscious as James tried to resuscitate her. Molly and Noreen whimpered as they watched the drama unfolding. Mara knelt on the beach next to her mother.

"BREATHE, MAGGIE MCNAMARA! *BREATHE*!"

Maggie coughed, turned her head and threw up lake water on the shale stones next to her head.

Eileen made the sign of the cross. "Oh dear Lord, thank you!"

"Should we call an ambulance?" Kate asked.

"Let's give her a few moments and see if she's OK," James said. "Maggie, can you hear us?"

She nodded and lifted herself slightly, then braced the palms of both hands on the stony beach as she coughed. Eileen knelt beside Maggie and rubbed her back as her fear of the trauma of the near-drowning subsided. After several minutes they raised her slowly into a sitting position.

"What the hell just happened?" Maggie asked.

"Well, you said something about being sick and tired of hot flashes, Mom, and next thing I knew...." Mara tried to keep a straight face but began giggling, and then so did her mother. Clare snorted, and that set off the rest of the sisters. The McGrath brothers rolled their eyes as they shook their heads. *Crazy McNamaras*, they thought.

Once Maggie was stable enough to walk, the McNamara sisters bade farewell to their cousins. When they got home she went right to bed and Mara stayed in her bedroom to make sure she was OK. The other sisters gathered on the front porch to talk about what happened.

"Well, that was a tad exciting tonight," Molly said as she sat down on the steps instead of a porch rocker.

"Man, Terrie, I didn't know you were so brave." Clare patted her sister's shoulder.

"Neither did I, hah!"

"What are we going to do about Maggie's drinking?" Eileen said, not really expecting an answer.

Molly got up from the steps and sat down next to her sister. "Don't you think it happened because after she heard those ladies, she suspected that *she* was the half-sister? Can you imagine what that must have felt like to her? I know I'd be freaking out."

Eileen nodded. Molly was right. "We have to assure her that the news changes nothing. She's still one of us."

"Psst, look across the street," Noreen whispered. "There's a light is on in the living room. The new neighbor must have moved in today."

The sisters strained to see the face of the man walking around the house. He started for the window and they tried to pretend they were talking with each other, though watching out of the corners of their eyes. He pulled the drapes shut and they laughed.

"Ah, another mystery to solve," Clare said. "Guess it will wait until tomorrow."

Chapter 35

The next night was Mara's last day of her vacation. It was decided that they'd all stay another night for a farewell family dinner in her honor. Had last night been different, Molly would have swung into full culinary mode for the occasion. But both she and her sisters were emotionally drained after yesterday. It was time for an easy meal and so she headed to the grocery early to get the fixings for burgers, Penn Yan pea salad, potato salad and a summer berry cobbler. She swung by the ice cream place on the West Side to get some fresh-made peach ice cream, too.

In the meantime, Eileen, Terrie and Maggie took Mara to the cemetery so she could see where her relatives had been buried. Mara brought a camera and notebook to record locations of the graves if she needed further reference. At each grave, Eileen shared an anecdote about the relative. When they got to their mother Frances's grave, Maggie's emotions got the best of her and she began to sob.

"I spent most of my life arguing with you, Mom. Now I realize what you did and I am in awe, just complete awe. The shame you must have endured...your humility to take me in, the child of another...." Eileen hugged her sister tightly. Maggie wiped her wet face with the back of her hand then reached out to pull Mara close. "Oh, how I wish she could have met you, Mara. She'd be so proud of you, a big city journalist. Mara, meet your grandmother Frances

O'Donoghue McNamara, a remarkable woman."

Maggie put her hand on her heart as she cleared her throat. "You know, because of the example she always set, I had the courage to give birth to you. I'm going to reveal something, Mara, and I hope you'll forgive me. I'm so ashamed, but at one point, and mind you it was just a short time, I had planned to abort you. There was no way I could afford to raise you—so I thought. Then Clare introduced me by phone to your parents and they'd offered to adopt you. Your mother insisted, though, that I move back East to give birth to you, so they could assure I had proper health care. That was the last thing I wanted to do. I thought at the time that I needed a continent of space between me and this woman lying beneath our feet. In my mind she was the worst woman on earth, but now I realize that I was terribly wrong—she was the best mother on earth.

"The appointment to abort you had been made. I was walking to the clinic when I passed a candle burning inside a windowsill. It was one of those glass votive candles with the image of Our Lady of Guadalupe on it. Something about seeing that candlelight at that moment gave me hope in my personal darkness, made me turn around and go back home. I waited until you'd been born before I contacted your parents."

Eileen covered her mouth with her hand and began to smile.

"It was God's will that you be born, Mara," Maggie said.

The revelation was not too surprising to Mara, given

her birth mother's wild past, yet the profoundness of the moment stirred her soul deeply. It was all out now, not a secret remained between mother and daughter. At that moment she felt reborn.

***

Terrie spent the day at home reading graphic novels and playing with Flora—she just adored her calico cat. She missed her dog and other cats, but at least they were living an idyllic life on the commune with plenty of children to play with them each day. Clare spent the day "reading" the *New York Times* on the front porch—she was actually watching Mr. Rotils move the rest of his belongings into the old McGrath house. Her interest was quite piqued: he appeared to be of a similar age, had greying brown hair and a tidy goatee, owned several bookcases and paintings. From the size of the pet carrier he brought in, Mr. Rotils owned either a small dog or a cat. She hoped it wasn't one of those yappy dogs. That could send her straight back to Manhattan, and to be honest, she was getting quite used to the rural charm of this neighborhood.

The sisters' last supper together was joyous. It was Mara's turn to discuss her life and she spoke fondly of her brilliant and kindhearted adoptive parents, gave details about her live-in boyfriend whom she'd met at Ohio State, and then shared hilarious anecdotes about various corrupt politicians she'd interviewed. Nothing was rushed at the meal, and they sat a good hour talking before they cleared the table after the main course to bring out dessert.

It was when Molly was spooning peach ice cream

onto dishes of cobbler that her eyes drifted upward toward the top of the refrigerator to that still-wrapped bottle Austin had brought her. *Hmm, maybe it would be fun to open that later and see what it is,* she thought.

Clare shared her updates on the mysterious Mr. Rotils as they ate dessert. All they knew was that he was from Rochester, an architect and related to the man who built this house. "I think he's single, ladies. Didn't see any clues of a female presence."

"All right then," Maggie laughed. "Yippee! I declare open season on Mr. Rotils!"

"What do you think his first name is, Clare?" Eileen asked.

"Elbert. Theodore. Allen. He's definitely not a Jason or a Todd."

"Maybe he's an Albert, named after his grandfather," Molly said.

"I still think he just wants to marry Molly for this home," Maggie said with a wink.

"Oh, speaking of my miserable love life...." Molly got up and went into the kitchen to retrieve Austin's gift. "OK, here's the next mystery: what do you think Austin gave me as a surprise?" She passed the wrapped bottle around the table and each woman felt the shape of it before handing it back to her.

"Hmm, wrong shape for a wine bottle," Maggie said.

"She's right," Clare nodded, "perhaps it's some sort of liqueur."

"Baileys?" Terrie asked brightly.

Noreen felt the package. "It's not quite a Bailey's shape. Maybe it's a genie bottle."

"Remember, the first thing you ask for is more wishes," Mara said. They all laughed.

"OK, time for the big reveal!" Molly opened the envelope attached to it. It was a glossy photo of an elk antler carved with the profile of the goddess Athena with her owl Bubo. "Hmm, this must be one of Emily's artworks." She flipped over the card and saw the logo for Wapiti Works in Jackson Hole, Wyoming. "Yep. Wow, this is beautiful work. Look at the details."

Molly sighed as she opened the card to read it, fearing it had some message from Austin inside that would make her cry. Instead there was only a hand drawn peace symbol and Austin's signature. "Huh? Is this supposed to be some sort of peace offering?" She slipped off the wrapping paper as her sisters read the card. Underneath was a corked, label-less brown bottle. A tag was draped around the neck with a length of twine.

"What the hell?" Maggie frowned. "Is it well water from Wyoming?"

Molly flipped over the tag and read aloud the label written in an exquisite script with a blue fountain pen: 'This is a bottle of FLOOD BRANDY tapped from a keg that floated down Keuka Lake after The Great Flood of '35.' Wow! I wonder where he got this?"

"Wonder how much he paid for it, under the table, I'm sure." Clare inspected the tag. "Do you realize this is at least seventy-year-old brandy?"

"I bet you could get a lot of money for that," Noreen said. "Sell it to my in-laws for a pretty penny."

Molly grinned as she held the bottle to her heart. "Mara, did you ever hear the story of how Grandpa Jimmy and Grandma Mame survived the Flood of '35?" She shook her head. "Ladies, let's adjourn to the porch. Someone please get the liqueur glasses out of the china cabinet and I'll meet you out there with the brandy."

"Oh, Sis, I love your style!" Maggie said.

"And how I love you all!"

A Canadian chill settled into the evening as was often the case on late August nights, making the katydids less conversant. Eileen sat on the baluster with her head resting on a pillar as her sisters and niece settled into the porch rockers. Clare passed a tray with liqueur glasses around and then she sat down in her grandfather's rocker. Molly stopped at each glass like a hummingbird in reverse, pouring decades-old nectar into the narrow stems.

"I propose a toast to Jimmy and Mame," she said, lifting her glass high. "*Sláinte*!" They clinked glasses and Molly retold the frightening tale of that night more than seventy years ago, in exactly the same manner that her grandfather would, including the walk into Hammondsport that was "a good stretch of the legs" and dinner at the Rotils.

"Wait, you mean he was the grandfather of the guy across the street?" Mara asked.

"Yep!" After that tale, Molly felt it was necessary to explain Grandpa Jimmy's fear of the lake and she told about the awful drowning of his friends.

Maggie set her glass down on the table next to her chair and leaned forward. The others thought she might be ill.

"Oh my God, now that you tell that story...yesterday when I was drowning, I heard this voice. It said 'Breathe, Maggie McNamara.'"

"I was that voice, they'd dragged you onto the beach," Mara said. Maggie turned toward her daughter and shook her head.

"No! It wasn't you. I think it was Grandma Mame. It's all kind of foggy, but I'm sure it was her. She saved me."

Eileen nodded knowingly, but the other sisters didn't know exactly how to respond. Was she hallucinating, or did she really hear her?

Terrie grinned and leaned back in her chair. "Do-do-do-do, do-do-do-do," she sang, mimicking the opening notes to *The Twilight Zone*. The sisters cracked up, especially Maggie.

"Look, a car is pulling into Mr. Rotils' driveway. Hope it's not your competition, Molly," Noreen teased. A man got out carrying a suitcase and a bonsai plant with a bow on it.

"He's got good manners, I see he has a housewarming gift," Mara said as they watched him ring the doorbell. Mr. Rotils welcomed him inside and closed the door. Through the undraped front window they watched the men enter the living room and then Mr. Rotils kissed the man on the mouth with fervor. The jaws of the sisters and niece dropped in tandem followed by gales of laughter.

"That's some housewarming gift!" Maggie cracked.

"See, I knew it was too good to be true!" Molly said with a deep sigh as she stood up from the rocker. "Who needs more brandy?" They all raised their hands.

"Hey Molly, all's not lost," Maggie called out after her. "I guess you can date Kerry freely now, you know, since we know he's not my brother."

Molly grinned when she returned with the bottle. She refilled their glasses and they sat there for a good hour in silence staring off at nothing in particular. Each woman was thinking deeply about her life, about her family and about her loves won and lost. Each thought about the sisters and when it all came down to it, how their relationships with each other were the most important things in life. Each realized that whatever future memories were to be made, they would always return to the house with the wraparound porch.

THE END

Made in the USA
Monee, IL
20 July 2021

74004628R00298